SHARDS OF DESTINY

Scott P. Vaughn

Also by Scott P. Vaughn:

Tales of the Hero-Lore

Eronica Unbound (writing as Scarlett Vaughn)

The Binding Realm (writing as Scarlett Vaughn)

Crimson Cutlass & Chameleon & the Cabinet of Dr. Faustus

Also by Scott P. 'Doc' Vaughn and Kane Gilmour:

Warbirds of Mars webcomic (www.warbirdsofmars.com)

Warbirds of Mars printed comic, issue #1

Warbirds of Mars printed comic, issue #2

Warbirds of Mars: Stories of the Fight! Anthology

Warbirds of Mars: The Golden Age printed comic

SCOTT P. VAUGHN

SHARDS OF DESTINY

BOOK I OF THE **HERO LORE**

BY SCOTT P. VAUGHN

Dedication

This one is for Kane Gilmour, my longtime friend and fellow weary traveler who has taken the time over the past quarter century or so to help nurture HERO-LORE along, politely inform me of what sucked while suggesting a different spin, and complimenting me when I got it right. He also edited this, so I guess no good deed goes unpunished after all. Thanks, man; it's a better series for your efforts and now it's finally seeing the light of day.

Acknowledgments

This book is one of those 'labors of love' that has gone through many versions, ideas, and attempts at publishing over the course of my life. It's nice to see this project finally get legs.

-Special thanks to Regan Schroeder who has been there since the first horrible sketch I ever did of Hero. Thanks also for the coolest Hero novelette anyone could have written for the anthology and for the help formatting my publishing ventures.

-Thanks to the *M&V*ers for their past enthusiasm that helped get me this far.

-To the Phoenix Art crowd and all the Writers, Artists and Friends I have met at the Phoenix comic cons and events over the past two decades.

-To my sister Max, and my Parents, for believing in both of us; I look forward to the day the Vaughns all have a shelf to themselves in at least one bookstore somewhere.

-Thanks should also go to: My childhood aspirations and friendships, where this saga began and where some of its creators got left behind.

-To Faber (RIP) for Kezeron.

-To Daryl Mallett for fervor and the co-scripting of issue #1.

-To Brian Flynn for being just as keen a conversationalist and fanboy as he is a writer.

-To Jesse, Ang, and Erica for posing with me for art references over the years.

-And to Java (RIP), for preening happily on my shoulder for hours while I wrote the first stories and chapters.

And to Absent Friends. I miss you all (well, most of you).

-Scott P 'Doc' Vaughn
Glendale AZ, 2020
vaughn-media.com

SHARDS OF DESTINY

Prologue

*And the Traveler brought forth twelve elements to the
Triialon People, from which to forge the Twelve Artifacts
of Power. And the Triialon artisans, scientists, and smiths
worked for twelve years until the Artifacts were completed;
until at last they were brought together as one.
And across the gulfs of the Cosmos, the being known as*
Zone awoke…

Desert winds blew over rough terrain with the force to cut
mountains. A Warrior stood with an army at his back, their capes and
banners billowing in time with the harsh gusts.

The Warrior was positioned atop the dune overlooking the
fragmented crystal city below. It had taken a day to traverse the wasteland
between the city of the Triialon and that of their enemy. Every sight that
had greeted him from the transport's view port and every look in every eye
of the five hundred men and women who went forth with him told him
that this was at last the end. The war against the Shard and his Death
Warriors had lasted three lifetimes, until finally the sandstorm gathered
and had never stopped. The Warrior had not expected the city below to
also be so affected by the yearlong storm. But he had expected the three
thousand shimmering Death Warriors that even now marched forth to
meet the last army of the Triialon.

There was a flash of light, its haze refracting off of the billowing
dust. The Warrior held aloft *Strength*, the Sword of Kings, and for a
moment the surge of its power played along his armored body, teasing the
ancient inlay, briefly illuminating the golden edges and revealing the tiny
imperfections and battle scars in its blue-white light. He stood there,
sword raised high, with his face hidden beneath the black helm as he
challenged his foe to come out and face him one last time. The sword fell,
and without looking back he knew his army followed him against
terrifying odds to end a war that had decided the fate of the galaxy. For a
moment he wondered if anyone would ever know of the battle that would

be fought that day; if even his armor would survive to be found by future generations. He at least knew with conviction that his enemy's remains would be scattered to the wind, the crystallized structure of their silicon-based life lost to the dust they had made of this world.

The Warrior rushed down the sandy hill as his gunships took to the air and his artillery flanked the charging soldiers. Each held a cannon in one hand and a blade in the other, but only the Warrior held a weapon like *Strength* in hand. An Artifact of the Triialon, it held the might of an army within, as did its companion piece, the *Prizm*, a gold and silver bracer on the Warrior's right arm. The bracer was bejeweled by three stones, the largest being its centerpiece; a crystal which glowed with inner power, a light subtle and yet magnificent. He transferred the sword to his left hand and aimed the *Prizm* at the onrushing Death Warriors. The crystal centerpiece erupted with light and hummed with intensity. He howled, and that light became energy, a beam the width and breadth of a soldier. The shot strafed across the frontlines that rushed to meet him, mowing them down by the hundreds. At last the energy stopped, and another two thousand Death Warriors raced across their burned-down comrades and the sands that had turned into smoldering glass. They rushed forward to meet the remnants of the Triialon army.

Groups of gunships fell upon the bulk of the Shard's army. Those that weren't quickly shot down flew on, past the defenders to begin the burning of their city. The second cheer since the Warrior's initial *Prizm* volley went up from the Triialon soldiers as the first crystal spire shattered, shrieked and fell under the weight of a Triialon gunship's firepower.

Bolts of cannon energy flew between the onrushing groups until finally the two armies clashed with a horrible impact. Golden-black armor buckled and limbs were cut. Crystal figures cracked and flesh burned. But the Triialon army battled on, fighting with a vigor not felt in years, striking forth despite the smiles on their faces, the tears in their eyes, or the limbs they left bleeding on the desert floor beneath them. Leading them, spurring them to victory was the Warrior, hacking a path through the thousands of crystalline Death Warriors before him. Lightning flashed off of *Strength*, tracing its arc back and forth, up and down, over and over as it sliced, parried, hacked and cleaved dozens of the Death Warriors.

Finally, he alone broke through the lines and rushed on into the melting city, his blade leaving hundreds of his foes dead behind him. The Warrior never looked back, but raised his sword in salute to the cheer that carried him into the very den of evil.

He entered the central dome and was greeted by a vast chamber. The dome was completely hollow, as tall within as the Triialon pyramids, and stretched out on all sides. It had little or no equipment to fill it, save the central structure under the top of the dome. There a being waited, strangely illuminated by a shaft of light from the very top of the dome. The Warrior knew it was Shard, the symbiotic leader of the Death Warriors. The Warrior also knew what he must do.

The crystalline hulk stood, standing easily a foot taller than the Warrior, and held aloft his own curved scimitar in challenge. Strange, singsong shrieks reverberated from beneath the Death Warrior's helm, the alien noise they called speech. "Three generations of war," it said, "measured in Triialon lifetimes. And how do you measure this war? Your planet turned to dust - your culture lost in war. Your son, the only child born to a now barren species in nearly fifty years. The last of your people lie dying in my city as we speak, and the Artifacts of the Triialon here in the temple of Shard." The taunt was followed by a sound that could have cracked teeth, and the Warrior knew it to be Shard's laughter. "By my measure, the victory of the Death Warriors; The failure of the Triialon."

The Warrior, his sword held in both gauntleted hands, took a challenging stance before the figure atop the lighted dais. "No. I know the secret of the Death Warriors' symbiosis to you, Shard, and the Artifacts are not all in your possession." There was a spark of blue energy, flitting out as though it were choreographed by the Triialon fighter himself. It briefly ran from the Prizm on his arm to the sword he brandished at his enemy. "You could never wield the Artifacts. My son is now off world, and even should we all die to the last this day, the Triialon shall live on in Lance." He took a step forward, prepared for the final battle. At last, it had come.

Shard held out his hand. "Destroy me and destroy his future. My death may shatter my warriors, but my temple is programmed to cast forth the ten Artifacts I have stolen into the cosmos, lost forever in the

4

continuum of time and space." He pointed to the shaft of light, its illumination reflecting on the surfaces of ten Triialon weapons that lay there. "It will have all been for nothing."

The Warrior stopped for only a moment, then replied with ice in his voice and steel in his heart. "Then that is how it shall be."

Their swords met with a clash that threw out a wave of energy that was echoed back from the temple walls and out across the face of the planet. Shard leapt from the dais in time to avoid a blow that would have cut him in two, landing behind the Warrior only to defend against a second attack of raining slashes. Sparks from the dueling turned into bolts of light, and with each collision of the strange metal blades the power increased. Soon streaks of light were leaping forth from each barrage, the energy striking walls and cracking the temple's hallowed structure.

At last Shard gained an advantage, striking the Triialon's sword hard enough to create a brief opening in his defenses. But when next the blade fell, it was met by the Warrior's Prizm, stopping it dead with a thunderous crash. He barely had the time to defend against the following sword stroke, and by that time *Strength* had removed the Death Warrior's hand from its arm. There was a terrible shriek, the Shard rearing back in pain and rage. The Triialon Warrior did not even hesitate to strike down his nemesis; the next flashing cut decapitated Shard's crystalline head from his torso.

There was a sound akin to a million glass buildings smashed at once, and the chamber was suddenly bathed in light. The Warrior watched as his foe crumbled before him, the slabs of now dulled crystal sliding off of one another and shattering as they hit the ground. He turned as the lit dais exploded in a wash of color. A shockwave burst from the dais outward, knocking the Warrior from his feet and then quickly rippling out through the whole city. Then darkness.

The world of the Triialon was silent for the first time in over two hundred years. Only the howling of the dust storm outside of the dead temple met the Warrior's ears. He rose, walking to where the dais stood smoking beneath the minimal light offered by the dome's open ceiling. The dais was empty, the stolen Artifacts of his people gone.

He stepped forth from the gray structure into the storm's remaining bitter whispers. The battlefield around him was littered with the dead, the fallen buildings, and crashed ships. Where there had stood two armies locked in vicious conflict, now only lay the bloodied armor of his fighters and the melted chunks of crystal lattice that had once been the most evil race ever known. The war to end all wars was over, and the bittersweet victory was his. *Worth it*, the Warrior thought, *to end all of this.*

He never knew if every one of the Triialon had been cut down in the final attack, or if some had escaped into the dessert, or somehow lifted by their deities to another place - safe, away from all of this death. In any case, nothing answered his call except the wind.

At last the man his people had come to call their Hero found an undamaged desert flyer gunship that had somehow soft-landed during the battle. He sheathed the victorious *Strength* and took one last look at the world that had been his home before lifting the ship into the air and away from the planet forever.

Chapter One

We can discern the end of the Triialon/Shard War almost down to the day just by the activity at the Court of Worlds, because there wasn't any activity. As soon as the Gods got word that the Triialon Home World had been deserted, Memfis disbanded the Court, and the Gods began to truly rule from the shadows. There was really no one left to stop them. And thirty years later, the only ones who might have even had the military or political power to do so were the Coalition... and they had their own problems.
History of the so-called 'Gods'
- Dr. W. H. Redfield

Lise ran her fingertips down the material of her uniform. She was loath to wear it. For such an occasion she was certain something more endearing was needed. But formality was formality, and while she may have been brought up under more aesthetic pretenses, she was still proud to be a member of the Galactic Coalition, even if it meant wearing a uniform to a diplomatic function. She decided on the skirt and officer's jacket and got them out of her tiny closet.

She found herself oddly nervous about the coming delegation. It was always nice to be asked to do something that wasn't so 'militant', but Lise didn't consider herself an expert on relations either. She had been raised an aristocrat, simply another daughter from one of Sparta's ancient, rich families and the blood-ties that position entailed. All of that had been a long time ago. Entire worlds had died since that time. Her whole world had died since that time. Five years had passed since her seventeenth birthday; the day the Lordillians had first attacked Sparta. Now she was no more than another soldier and officer in a war so much bigger than anything she could have imagined before that day.

Lise forced aside such terrible thoughts and turned to the mirror in her small quarters. Stepping into the black skirt she watched her shapely legs, making certain there were no runs in the dark stockings, and finally secured it around her curvaceous hips. She slipped the tight, high-necked jacket on over the lace-patterned bra, her ample cleavage threatening to spill over its scandalously cut form. The rationing of war being what it was, she had taken to wearing sports underwear during strike missions or even bridge duty, so she welcomed the chance to feel rich and womanly again in the sexy garments she would have otherwise already frayed holes in, if worn as often as she preferred. Lise finished buttoning the jacket's gold buttons all the way up to her neck and then, sweeping the long cascade of her raven curls back over her shoulder, she smoothed down its front as she inspected her image in the mirror. Smiling with meager satisfaction, she picked up her bag and turned to shut off the cabin lights.

Stepping into the cramped corridor, Lise almost collided with admiral Jo'seph. She quickly came to attention, almost outwardly cringing at her luck. The Admiral regained his composure from nearly having been slammed into the corridor plating.

"Sir," she said at last.

The admiral had the good grace to smile after his initial expression of disgust. "Commander Lise." He signaled her to ease and held his arm out for her to continue on her way. "After you. I assume you are on your way to the Shuttle deck?"

Lise fell into step beside the man, who, in tandem with admiral Jay'salan, essentially controlled every move of one of the greatest fleets ever assembled. "Yes, sir," she said, taking a chance to look more closely at the figure she saw so often on a cruiser or base-bridge from afar. The fatigue clearly showed on what were otherwise boyish features. She was certain, were it not for the neatly-trimmed beard, that his flowing blonde locks of hair and his round, smiling cheeks would have combined to make him look much too young and much too charming to be the man he truly was. Every survivor of Sparta followed the Admirals into the unknown after some of the worst destruction anyone should ever have to see, and admiral Jo'seph more than any other man was so often their guiding light. But the tides had turned once again, and even Jo'seph's temper was beginning to show during the aftermath of each battle. Some of the higher-ups had noted his sarcasm becoming more biting and his mood more somber as each day wore on. But Lise could hardly blame the man; he simply had the fate of the Galaxy in his hands, pitted against the very force that had laid waste to his own world.

The admiral caught her looking at him, and Lise turned her eyes to the looming elevator door ahead. "You, ah, studied the reports concerning today's activities, commander?"

Lise looked at him with a mustered seriousness and nodded. "Yes, admiral. I've read the reports several times."

Jo'seph smiled. "Good," he said. "I'm glad that makes one of us." Lise shot him a nervous look before she'd even realized it, and then blushed. "Gotcha," he said.

She was almost nervous, being this close to him and what had become his notorious sense of humor, but there were bigger diplomatic concerns this day, and she wasn't about to be put off by her own admiral.

The couple made their way into the diminutive elevator. They descended to the flight deck of the Spartan cruiser in an uncomfortable silence. Finally, the admiral looked at Lise, his face a mask of mock contemplation. Clearing his throat, he almost stammered as he tried to sound as nonchalant as possible. "You look very nice, commander."

Lise simply stared forward, still standing at attention. "Thank you, sir." She tried to sound as bland as possible.

Admiral Jo'seph grinned as he shook his head. "At ease, commander. I'm only the bloody admiral."

Suddenly feeling sheepish, Lise again tried to relax and made an attempt at a smile that she was certain came out looking as foolish as she felt. "Sorry, sir."

The Shuttle deck smelled of ozone and fighter fuel. Just as commander Lise and the admiral stepped out of the elevator platform, the hanger door opened and flooded the deck with fresh air and light. Lise's ears popped as the deck's pressure stabilized. She cleared moisture from her dark eyes and peered across the hold as the sun's light illuminated it. Several of the new so-called *Bat* fighters rested next to the smaller, older style wedge-shaped *Interceptors*. Lise looked at them with delight but couldn't help but wonder if even the *Bats'* new design and armaments would be enough to fend off total destruction at the hands of the Lordillians. The cruiser she was about to disembark, the '*Return*', was one of the newer, sleeker ships in the fleet. Like the *Bat*s, they were still few in

10

number. Constant combat had meant little time to supply the demand needed to even the playing field against their bitter foes.

Lise saw the larger transport *Bat* with its boarding platform down and smiled. Admiral Jo'seph was making a show of their recent technological advances by showing up with so much new hardware, and Lise for one was glad to be riding to the planet below in style. She looked to the skyline beyond the launch portal, marveling at the pink clouds against the purple atmosphere. "Join the Coalition, see the Universe," she said to herself. She broke her momentary reverie and headed past the ancient shuttles and equipment to the waiting *Bat* fighter beyond.

She set her bag down next to the other equipment and took her place with the soldiers and diplomats set to accompany the admiral. Letting out a breath, she smiled and nodded to the others about to board, hoping that she was more prepared for whatever might happen on the surface below than she really felt inside.

The admiral was giving a momentary briefing to each member of the team going below. When he finally got to Lise he again smiled. "I suppose you're wondering how you got lucky enough to come along on this mission, commander?"

Lise tried again to loosen up a little, so she returned the smile wryly. "I was lead to believe it had something to do with my aristocratic upbringing," she replied. "That or my charm." *Namely my ass, which everyone comments on*, she thought, but decided not to voice aloud; she didn't think that she was quite at that frank of a level with the admiral's sense of humor just yet.

"Partially, commander" he said quite simply. "In just two years you've proven yourself a competent officer and soldier, quickly attaining your current rank. A formal upbringing combined with your guerilla and military training makes you a perfect support member of this team." He leaned in a little. "In other words, I not only intend for you to help advise me on matters of state, but as you can never quite be sure what might happen during political negotiations, I intend for you to watch my back as well." Admiral Jo'seph inclined his head to the soldier on Lise's right. "You'll be issued a small weapon upon arrival within the city that you are to keep secreted. Understood?"

"Sir!"

"Very good. Carry on, commander." And with that, the admiral boarded the craft.

The ship flew to the surface below with speed and ease. Lise could see the capitol city of the planet Moonshau on the horizon. The initial landing point was on the outskirts of the city, among endless fields of tall grass and rolling clouds. She watched the sunrise colors dim to the morning hues from the small view slit in the transport's side until the sky was at last a startling blue. Then the green hillsides loomed into view for their landing approach. Lise smiled to private Zhade, the soldier sitting next to her, all of her preconceptions and nervousness forgotten. Zhade smiled back evenly, probably seeing less novelty or interest in yet another planet fall. He had been in Lise's strike team a month now, and while she was impressed with his skill with the rifle, Zhade's lack of enthusiasm made it hard for her to like him sometimes. She turned back to the view of the surface, the landing nearly complete.

As soon as the gear touched ground, the cargo hatch opened and the armed soldiers rushed down the ramp to secure the landing zone. They stood at attention to either side of the ramp as the admiral, Lise, and the other delegates walked down to step foot at last on Moonshau soil.

Lise quickly took stock of her surroundings; a table sat not ten yards away, several men standing before it, waiting for their guests. On either side of the transport *Bat* landed two of the new fighters flying escort, their tail-mounted canons curling up under the fuselage of the ships for the long landing gear to reach the ground and then lower exit hatches. As the escort pilots climbed down to also stand at attention, Lise briefly looked up, finding the '*Return*' floating some forty thousand feet above them. Even from that height she could discern the sheer size of the near half-mile long battle cruiser.

As the engine noise and winds finally died down, the Moonshau delegates came forward. "I am Daysuan, Prime Minister of the providing Government of Moonshau. I am honored by your presence, Admiral Jo'seph of the Galactic Coalition." He held out his hand and smiled. Lise watched as the admiral took the hand of friendship, studying the humanoid faces that greeted them. Their skin was blotched with subtle color, but seemed fairly common otherwise. Moonshaun hair, while apparently the same texture as a Spartan's, was brilliantly more highlighted, with three or four ranges of color mixed in.

There was a brief moment of awkward silence before the Admiral at last spoke. "Sir, the honor is mine. Allow me to introduce commander Lise." Jo'seph released Daysuan's hand to motion to Lise. She stepped forward, smiling pleasantly. The alien delegate's hand had six fingers, and was colder than a Spartan's skin, shaking hers lightly.

The admiral finished introducing the representatives he had brought from the Coalition and soon they were shown to the table where more Moonshaun men waited. Papers and computer consoles were set on the table, and it was soon apparent that there were a number of official documents to be ratified before the proceedings could continue. Lise waited patiently with the others, knowing from her briefings that the Moonshau were a fastidious race and that their politics, procedures, and lives alike were often an endless debate. But their technology was great, and their armies battle-hardened by those debates over the centuries that had gone awry. Even if it took months, Admiral Jo'seph was determined that today would be the groundwork for accepting the peoples of the Moonshau into the Coalition.

Finally the paperwork seemed complete, and soon they were escorted to waiting transports that took the Coalition members into the city. Outlying simple buildings lead into a central metropolis of towering skyscrapers of a very modern design. Transparent exteriors housed communities, commercial districts, and offices. Each section was woven by sleek transport rail tubes that curled around between the exterior shielding and the levels within. Distribution nodes began and ended at either end of catwalks that connected the structures over the clean streets below. Glass and steel surrounded her, and everywhere there was technology with both form and function. Each hard line of the city was glossed over by appealing colors or commercial signs, but nowhere was there anything but the highest level of craftsmanship. Hanging above it all were the airships, slowly moving between the massive structures, watching.

Within the hour they were at last in the council chambers where the debates could begin. Lise found herself both relieved and feeling slight trepidation at this fact, but she kept her posture and her smile from fading, shaking each new hand and remembering each new name as best she could, and when all backs were turned to her for just a moment, already past any detectors, Zhade slipped her a small sidearm.

Servants walked into the room in single file, each one bearing a tray of fruit or drinks. Lise watched the delegates from both parties smile and pick up refreshments to nurse while they made small talk before the more serious matters at hand could begin discussion. She looked around the room at the politicians and soldiers, the senators and servants, and she was reminded of home. The moment was as close to anything she could call 'normal' in her memory since before she had even heard the word 'Lordillian'. Lise's smile faded, and a brief moment of melancholy replaced an even shorter time of anger. Sparta's fate now laid at the very doorstep of Moonshau, and yet they were blind to it, just as Sparta had been. Replacing the frown that had crept onto her features with a forced pleasantness, she smoothed down her uniform and tried to keep her emotions from making her fidgety.

At last everyone was seated, and the talks had begun.

"The governments of my world have watched the events of the last decade unfold with deep concern, and its peoples have watched in fear." Daysuan addressed the small throng of people that had fit in the chambers, speaking loudly so that all could hear but with a voice full of assuredness. "The Lordillian menace has spread like a plague, a great horde of destruction that has arisen like a barbarous force to crush all before it. Once we feared for our neighboring star systems, but ultimately chose to keep our forces at home for our own ends. Now the battle lines threaten to spill into our star system, and many now ask if we have already waited too long to become involved. They say that it may already be too late to keep that horde from battering down our door and destroying all that we have built and loved. That if we had already helped an honorable cause to defeat the Lordillians, that we would not see this menace so close to our home."

"And there are those who believe that we still have no business getting involved in a fight that is not our own." Another Moonshau senator had stood, speaking evenly but with an obvious hidden anger. "Indeed, that this war would most probably never be ours, the Lordillians having no reason or real reach to attack Moonshau."

"Then I would tell such persons," answered admiral Jo'seph as he stood, "that they should pay closer attention to the events that led to the previous attacks and subjugations of the other worlds the Lordillians have already conquered." He turned to the men and women who now were forced to listen to him, waiting for the rumble of conversation to die down. "I know you all wish to protect your own interests, be they those of your governments, or peoples, or gains." The throng again began to mutter at this, but the admiral continued unabated. "And it so happens that unless your world allies itself with the Coalition now those interests will mean nothing the moment the Lordillian heel sets its mark on any world or moon in this system.

"Daysuan does not exaggerate when he describes the Lordillian horde as a plague. They spread just as quickly and suddenly, and with just as little regard for those it can use as those it can simply destroy. They multiply their forces with the speed of an infection, destroying from within." The admiral's fist slammed into his own hand to help drive home his point, his spirit evident on his features with each word he now uttered. "This is not simply the fears of a paranoid nation or man, this is the proven truth; that Chebonka's machine nation, the Lordillian horde, does not discriminate as it works its way across the galaxy to make each system its own, whether that system has strategic significance or not. A policy of anchorite neutrality can no longer be exercised or seriously considered by a world that is literately within the path of a plague that travels ever forward."

"What admiral Jo'seph suggests," helped Daysuan, "is that we join the Coalition now and commit what help we can before the Lordillians have the chance to land their forces on our colonies or, disastrously worse, on our home planet."

"Help the Coalition may soon be in desperate need of, as I understand it," said another senator, this one old and angry sounding.

15

"Your war goes badly, admiral. Shall we commit out men to simply die beside your own?"

"There is strength in numbers, sir," supplied Lise at last. She felt her own anger over this ignorant debate rise along with the constriction in her chest as she stood to address the court. Taking a deep breath, and finding that all eyes had turned on her, she continued. "Ladies and gentlemen, I have seen firsthand what it is to be invaded by the Lordillians. They know no mercy and have no conscience. They are simply programmed to crush all resistance in their path and take what they know is now theirs. For each one that you may have the firepower to knock down, another rises in its place."

Lise took another breath, turning so that each delegate and senator within the chamber could hear her voice and see her face. "But I have also seen what it means when the few who remain rise to the challenge of facing those things and work towards kicking them off of their world. I've seen it in the faces of my friends as they died destroying hundreds of those metal monsters. Men and women who were simply people defending what was left of their home. Not soldiers, just defiant people. But I've seen that same look in the face of every single one of my fellow soldiers and officers alike within the Coalition." She paused, coming to stare at the old senator. "All it takes is strength and the heart of nations defending what they believe in. Do you believe in your way of life, sir?"

"I do," said the old senator. "And I still have no reason to believe that our current comfort and security will not continue." He turned once more to the throng in their seats. "Why should we enter a war with these alien races and their Coalition that may fail when the Lordillians may never even enter our star system? Why commit our resources and soldiers to battle and bring their wrath upon us when we could be negotiating a treaty with Chebonka at this very moment, ensuring our current way of life *does* continue into the years to come? Instead we sit here and debate spending billions in currency and possibly in lives."

There was a rumble of agreement among many of those seated, and Lise watched, tears kept barely in check, threatening to run onto her blushing cheeks as history again prepared to repeat itself.

"Enough!" Lise had almost screamed it, slamming a palm onto the table and causing every face to turn to her in surprise. Her rage was unabated, passions surging as she stared back into each set of eyes locked with hers. She swept her arm wide. "All of this will be gone. No deals, no treaties, no mercy will be shown! When the Lordillians want this corner of space, either for what you possess, what you know, or simply because you're in the way of the next parsec they want, then they will come and they will take it." At last the emotions flowed without shame, yet Lise showed them with pride, her chest swelling with the words as they came. "My father and the politicians of my race once thought as you do. But that power out there is not simply someone else's problem, nor is it an issue to be bargained with. When they came, the Lordillians killed not only my father, but also my mother, my friends, their children.

"Were it not for the foresight of this man," she said, pointing to the admiral, "then all would have been lost. He and admiral Jay'salan had already mobilized and begun planning a defense against what they knew was coming. Yet still it was too late, for if there is anything that so featureless and spiteful a race as the Lordillians possess in spades, then it is speed and surprise. The small portions of our fleet that had been allocated to Jo'seph's cause returned to a world under siege, a race being wiped out, and a planet in flames. They became the Admirals of the Fleet by default, for everyone else was dead." She stood there, pleading with them for their own lives, her eyes brimming with moisture, arms out, and hands that balled into fists or opened in gestures of hope or despair. At last the feelings flooded out of her, and she sighed, relaxing a little, placing her hands on the table before her to lean on them. She shook her head at the waiting delegates. "Why don't you see it? Why didn't *they* see it? Why don't you realize that some things that are right must be fought for, that some things out there truly are the evil in the dark that will devour your children just as surely as your neighbor's?"

Her face lowered, long tresses of black curls obscuring her visage, shoulders slumping as she sat down. Lise leaned back in the chair, shrugging to her audience in resignation. "Do as you will, but know this; if you do not prepare for what is truly coming, you will be swept aside along with the rest of us."

The room was still, and no one spoke for long moments. Lise looked up, and found Daysuan smiling to her, and Jo'seph nodded.

"One moment my home planet of Sparta was preparing for what it thought might be a possible invasion by Lordillian forces," continued Admiral Jo'seph, "the next we were fleeing for our lives and finding the stragglers from other civilizations that had suffered the same quick fate in order to strike back as one. We all perish if we let them simply take us down one by one, but together, with each new army, each new piece of knowledge or technology or weapon we can prevail." He formed a fist in front of him, glaring up at the seated figures around him. "But we must act now, or bear out the sum of all our fears within this chamber."

Suddenly there was a flash, like a light bulb overloading.

Just as Lise caught the movement from the corner of her eye, so private Zhade was already moving to his admiral's side. By then the blasts had already sailed between them both, catching an even faster-to-react Coalition bodyguard full in the chest. The man slumped against admiral Jo'seph, and they both crumpled to the council floor. The whole of the council erupted in a collective gasp of surprise, and suddenly the room was a flurry of confused motion. Lise and Zhade tracked the shots' origins, and Lise had the small blaster in her hand just as her counterpart brought his rifle to bear on a figure near the chamber doors. The man, whom Lise had not noticed before, was robed just as the other delegates. He turned to meet the gaze of the admiral's guards, firing another shot that sent a plasma blast just over the shoulder of Zhade's left arm. As he ducked aside, Lise got off her own round, the bolt striking the robed man in the neck, forcing him down. Zhade ran forward, shouting for anyone near to move away as he reached the fallen man's gun to kick it aside and cover the prone figure.

"He's dead," Lise said, coming to stand next to her fellow soldier.

"Nice shot," replied the private. "He hadn't expected you to be armed."

Lise raised an eyebrow in disgust. "He was misinformed." She holstered the weapon and, leaving Zhade to watch over the assassin, turned to find admiral Jo'seph. She hurried back across the room. "Admiral!"

"I'm all right, Commander." The man stood, brushing off his officer's jacket. Lise's eyes returned to the gallery around her, ignoring the startled delegates to watch for any further attempts on the admiral's life. "Private Culnari is down. His armor took the brunt of the attack, but he'll need immediate attention."

"I need a medic over here, please. Now!" She turned to a Moonshau guard. "Is there a hospital center close by?"

"No, commander," replied Jo'seph. "We're taking him with us. We're leaving."

"But the delegation," objected Lise.

"Can wait. It's adjourned, in case you haven't noticed." He smiled at her wearily. "Don't worry, I haven't given up."

"Commander," came Zhade's voice from the chamber entrance. Lise and the admiral's group moved to where the soldier knelt. A Coalition delegate gasped, and Lise looked to where Zhade had pulled some of the burnt flesh of the assassin's neck aside to reveal charred metal and wires.

"Lordillians," hissed Lise.

"But this man is partially organic." Daysuan had come to stand beside Lise, his face drawn and pale from the surprising incident and its violence. "I thought Lordillians were completely robotic, not cybernetic."

Lise never took her eyes from the smoking corpse. "Those who want power are promised it by Chebonka in the form of partial conversion. Prove your worthiness to the Lordillian cause, and the Lordillians then make you immortal, downloading your mind into the final form of the Lordillian shock trooper." She looked briefly to Zhade. "Private!"

"Ma'am."

"We're leaving. Have a stretcher party set up, and double-time it. I'll contact the escort and the 'Return'. You're now the first line of defense between the universe and the Admiral."

"Understood, Commander."

Admiral Jo'seph came to stand next to Daysuan as the room continued to empty of its senate. "No pressure, private Zhade." The soldier just looked at him, almost registering surprise. "Delegate Daysuan, I believe today's proceedings have ended. I don't think anything further can be gained by putting both our lives in jeopardy."

Daysuan was almost visibly shaking now, staring down at the dead figure bleeding on the council carpeting. "I see," was all he said.

"However, I hope that today's events will not be the end of our endeavors. Indeed, perhaps this attack might sway opinions, or at least the time consumption of debate, in our favor."

The Moonshau delegate turned, gripping the admiral's hand in his. "Sir, I can only offer my apologies and sincerest hopes. I... I don't know what to say, except that I too hope to continue this as soon as possible." He looked again at the fallen assassin, a look of disgust passing over his features... "They're already here. I must redouble my efforts."

"I will be in touch with you within the week, then, senator." And just as suddenly the Coalition group had moved into the waiting transport just outside the chambers and began making their way back out to the field where their transport waited.

A shock ran through the metal helm, causing circuits to respond and signal hydraulics to react and momentarily spasm. If Chebonka, the 'android born of man', still had eyelids they would have fluttered open at that moment, but instead the shock of waking from the dream only automatically switched on his viewing circuits with that much quicker a response.

Chebonka sat on his charging console, a huge power outlet that resembled a chair. The room was black and filled with smoke, a byproduct of the power that had just flowed through his huge metal body. He stood, commanding the door leading to his throne room to open, again finding himself contemplating the strange fact that he had never been able to purge the dream state of the subconscious from his system, finding that to be strangely unsettling.

The throne room was enormous and spacious as it was dark and foreboding. No mortal being had entered its hallowed recesses in the years since the base's completion, yet Chebonka found the moody lighting served to further his contemplations even if no man now entered in fear. Large metal supports criss-crossed the chamber and steps led to the dais upon which his ruling throne rested. He sat down within its steel supports. There were no mirrors within this chamber of horrors on the

20

Lordillian's lightning world, but if there had been then Chebonka's sight would have been met by his own hulking visage; an armored and masked apparition of robotic power, complete with wide, metal-padded shoulders and a cowl of equal temper that flared about his helmed head. The face was devoid of common human features save the slated eyes, the mouth being simply vents cut horizontally through the creased mask. Despite the cold alien nature of his design, those edged metal eyes couldn't hide the hate they glowered from within.

A robotic servitor rolled forward, holding Chebonka's symbol of power, a large sword of ancient design, and stood at its master's side. The ruler and inventor of the Lordillians sat upon his throne and called for his generals. "Report."

From the darkness two large silhouettes with burning eyes emerged, and from metallic voices came their pledge to Chebonka. The first bowed before beginning his report and a file within Chebonka's electric brain approved, having created the Lordillian race in his own image even though the machines resembled him little physically. "Two Lordillian battle cruisers en route to planet Moonshau. Estimated time to arrival is now five minutes, proceeding then to atmospheric entry followed by a low-level attack formation. ETA to target is twenty minutes. We calculate minor resistance from surface batteries and destruction of any Coalition forces within an additional fifteen minutes."

The figure stepped back, and its counterpart stepped forward and bowed. "Lordillian ground forces on planet Sparta report slave labor uprising. Opposition crushed after a two percent loss of garrison forces. Mining operations continue, but natural resource output has fallen by another forty percent. Planet Goleida garrison reports operations up five percent. Planet…"

"Enough," commanded Chebonka. He rose from the throne and took the sword from the servitor. "Download complete report to memory core and contact Kordula to arrange further materials transfer." He stepped back through the portal to his personal meditation and energy transference chamber, saying as the hatch closed behind him, "Inform me when we have confirmation of the destruction of all Coalition forces on Moonshau." He knew without looking back that his Lordillian generals again bowed to him, for that was what they were programmed to do without fail.

Within the blackened chamber Chebonka listened, the network of transmissions, information, memory, and every other fiber of activity within the enormous Lordillian base sifting through his mind. His connection with the station's memory core optimized with a single thought, and he again began to sift through the files on ancient weaponry, its origins, uses, and artistic forms. For the five hundred and fifty-third time since the blade had come into his possession and symbolized his power, Chebonka tried to access any source information on that particular sword's origins. Again he hit a collective wall, and again he felt the frustration and anger rise, believing despite evidence or logic that those of Kordula withheld that knowledge from him. For if there were any beings within the vermin infested universe that he reluctantly counted as allied to his cause that knew what he wanted to learn, it was the race that called themselves the Gods of Kordula. He knew somehow that they were hiding the history of the very artifact within his metal hand.

Chebonka fought the strangely mortal desire to howl in rage. As the strength of anger poured through his systems the sword in his hands began to react, blue tinted power flowing like acidic smoke from the now-glowing blade, illuminating the metallic helm of Chebonka. He stared down in calculation as the energy ran like lightning around the sword, tracing the triangular symbols of the Triialon on its ancient hilt before dissipating.

Lise watched the capitol city of Moonshau recede onto the horizon behind their transport as her team made its way back to the landing zone. The young woman found herself trying to fight down a terrible sense of dread. Despite her training and all of the battles she had already encountered in her life, she had never been so close to any sort of assassination attempt on anyone who meant so much to the Coalition as admiral Jo'seph did. During these desperate times they needed more allies than ever before, and the events of the delegation may have served against the Moonshau entering the Coalition. All this and more flooded through Lise's mind, and she glanced at Jo'seph. Seeing him simply staring forward and waiting to board his craft after a day's work as if the events were everyday made her smile to herself. The door of the transport opened to let the Coalition members disembark and she brushed aside a strand of her hair blown across her face by the winds across the plain. Lise stood, looking at the sky and then back to her admiral. She saw a moment of concern pass over his features. The foreboding returned. "There's a storm coming," she said to no one in particular.

"Be ever on your guard, commander." Jo'seph said to her. "Saving my life once today doesn't let you off the hook."

Lise smiled. "Sir."

The wind picked up again, and for the briefest moment Lise found herself adjusting her stance so the gusts did not knock her over.

"Sir, I can't raise the *'Return.'*" Zhade had a com-set in his hand, a look of concern in his eyes. "I think the signal's being jammed."

"A spy among the Moonshau?" asked Lise.

"Could be, but I doubt the Lordillians would have needed an insider to get that hit man into the council chamber. I think it's something else." Jo'seph called over the wind to the escort pilots waiting by their fighters. "Get airborne, and be on alert!"

The Coalition team and their admiral were making their way over to the transport when the air suddenly changed. There was an echoing explosion, as if from a long distance off, yet loud and terrifying, rumbling around the grassy hills. Lise ducked slightly, startled, and looking up she saw dust and fire raining down from the cruiser above. It had been hit moments before by unseen fire, which caused an explosion they were just now able to hear. There was a gasp from the massed troops watching the sky as a second volley was briefly visible, striking the ship and tearing through its hull. Lise quickly tracked the origin of the shot.

"There!" Lise pointed over the city. Hovering above the Moonshau spirals and towers were a pair of ships of equal size to their own cruiser. The Lordillian ships were ovoid in shape, laying on their sides, with fins, lances, batteries and other details mounted all over the hulls, projected sections in the front bearing each ship's bridge. An arch curved over the main body from one fin to the other, a main canon mounted in the center of the arch. One ship fired at the hovering Coalition cruiser again while

23

the second rained battery fire down onto the city below it, causing a deep rumble to reach their ears. "They must have entered the atmosphere on the dark side of the planet! The Moonshau airships didn't even see them come over the horizon they were so fast!"

The lead cruiser advanced quickly, heading straight for their damaged mother ship. Lise looked up, gripped by a fear she had not felt since the day Sparta was attacked. The Lordillian Cruiser loomed over them, casting a shadow down onto the exposed crowd, its guns trained on them. She glanced up one last time, watching one *Bat* fighter move to cover the Admiral's group. Another ship exploded, destroyed by a bolt from above that incinerated the craft before it could even lift off. Above the smoke and death the *'Return's* altitude dropped as it struggled to remain flying. Lise clenched her teeth, buffeted by the wind and explosions, waiting for death.

Chapter Two

*'Take what grievances the Evils give you and visit it upon
them tenfold.'*
-Excerpt from the book of Triialon

Lise gazed up at her looming black doom.

Something caught her eye, and Lise followed the movement. Streaking along in front of the Lordillian's hull was a large fighter craft, beaten and weathered, its desert colorings standing out in stark contrast to the black hull. The fighter defied all attempts from the cruiser's batteries at being shot down, and it easily sped past the ship, heading straight for the grounded Coalition team.

The *Bat* fighter covering the Admiral's group took a hit, and Lise realized with trepidation that their enemies were almost on top of them. The sky above was nearly obscured by the hovering Lordillian mass, and she could no longer see the *'Return'*, the single remaining escort fighter sinking to the ground amongst its own billowing smoke. All hope fled as the prepping transport was also hit, knocking the admiral to the ground. Lise gasped, the explosion sucking the air from her lungs.

The desert ship was instantly above them, and through the fear that gripped her heart and the tears flooding her eyes, she watched the fighter come to hover almost directly over her. The craft was tiny compared to the Lordillian cruiser above it, yet somehow it seemed to stay their execution, the only thing between them and certain death. A hatch opened in the bottom of the ship. Lise could hardly believe her eyes when she saw a man emerge, leaping the impossible distance. He fell, feet first, arms outstretched, a large sword in his right hand. She choked back a sob, finding the sound that escaped her lips at the strange sight more akin to a laugh.

The man hit the ground like a cat, gracefully landing, rolling, and coming to stand defiantly before the battle that raged around him. Lise watched the odd scene from her cratered vantage point some thirty yards away. He was tall and well built, with long, flowing dark hair and a chiseled face of indiscernible years. He wore a short, battered black jacket, with wide lapels and strange markings. He wasn't immediately handsome, but striking, with a look of determination that seemed to call down the thunder around him. He moved with speed and simple agility, as if each turn or spin was part of an ancient dance, yet it was stoic: the dance of the warrior.

The man transferred the strange sword to his left hand and pointed his right up to the sky, aiming what appeared to be a metallic bracelet, or bracer, at the Lordillian cruiser above. The huge ship seemed poised for its own killing blow, and for an instant Lise wondered if the 'Return' had already been destroyed, if anyone would be able to return to the Coalition's shipyards to tell of the death of admiral Jo'seph and those he commanded. There was a shift in the atmosphere accompanied by a low hum, the very air changing as a glow began from what seemed to be a crystal imbedded in the gold and silver bracer, and she felt the hair at the nape of her neck stand on end. The glow quickly became a searing blue-white light, too bright to look directly in to. Lise had to pull her wind blown hair back from wet cheeks to better watch the eerie spectacle.

Suddenly the light became energy, and a large, crackling ball of lightning-charged power leapt from the warrior's arm, arcing up into the sky and striking the underside of the Lordillian cruiser. The engines of the giant ship exploded, and a chain reaction soon engulfed the rest of the vessel, fire and smoke leaking into the air around it, its metal skin incinerated. The Lordillian cruiser lost its grip on the atmosphere around it and nose-dived, crashing deafeningly to the plains. As the smoke and dust rolled out to envelope her from the catastrophe mere yards away, Lise sank to her knees, mouth agape, not daring to believe that what she had just seen to be true.

Darkness swirled around her, and in the distance Lise could hear explosions that shook the ground beneath her. She wondered if the Coalition ship had crashed, or if it was secondary explosions from the Lordillian cruiser, or if it might be the destruction of Moonshau itself. A hand grasped her arm, but it was not the metallic gauntlet of a Lordillian trooper; it was the large palm of the man in the black jacket. The touch brought a shock through the material of her coat, one that reached into Lise's mind like the intimate contact of a lover, and she found herself short of breath. The dust began to settle, but a cloud hung in the air around them. She could make out his face now; lines of age around the eyes of an otherwise young looking person with long, brown hair swirling about his face.

"Are you injured?" The voice was deep, pleasant.

"No," she managed. She coughed and tried to smile, and then remembered. "But the admiral…"

"Where was he last," he asked, concern etched in his face.

"I'm not sure. I'm turned around in this fallout." Lise tried to wipe dust from her eyes. "He was nearing the landed transport when it was hit."

Still holding her hand, the man led her through the gray mist. She tried to study him and the sword he still held, but her vision swam through her watering eyes. She began to make out two figures standing close by, and before Lise could call out she was being led towards them. Within a few yards of them at last, she could see it was a dusty, if otherwise unharmed, admiral Jo'seph and private Zhade. Around them sat the injured or lay the fallen.

The man released Lise's hand and came to stand before her admiral. "Admiral Jo'seph of the Coalition?"

"I am. Who's asking?" Lise couldn't tell Jo'seph's mood towards the stranger, but then they had all been through a lot in the last afternoon.

The man relaxed a little and, swinging the sword around so that the tip of the blade touched the crystal embedded in the strange bracer, said something in an alien language. Lise watched in amazement as a shaft of light escaped the stone set there, then stared in silent wonder as the sword disappeared into the crystal and out of his hand, slipping away until it was gone from their sight. The strange light again ceased, and the warrior held out his hand in greeting. "I am called Hero."

Jo'seph shook the outstretched hand but looked dubious. "I thought Hero of the Triialon was a legend. I would be even more skeptical if I had not just seen you single-handedly down a Lordillian cruiser. In any case, I am in your debt."

Lise almost laughed aloud when she noticed Zhade, a look of open awe on his face. It was the first time she had ever seen him express anything but simple indifference. "A living legend," he said quietly, seemingly entranced. Then she heard another distant explosion.

"Admiral," Lise indicated, "the other cruiser."

"Our friend here provided enough distraction that the 'Return' was able to regain control and shoot down the other Lordillian vessel." Jo'seph looked up through the haze, still unable to make out the blue sky beyond. "It fell just beyond the edge of the city, I think. We'll find out the extent of the damage as soon as we're secure aboard our own ship." He looked again at the stranger before him that had saved their lives. "Well, it would seem events are moving quickly. For security reasons I must ask you to join us aboard the 'Return', but I would hope you might come aboard of your own accord so we might thank you more appropriately." He looked over their strange savior again, his face an unreadable expression. "As well as glean something of the truth of you."

Lise was about to interject at what seemed over-distrust concerning a man that had just rescued them. She too had heard of the ancient Triialon race, learning little of them in history courses and less in the rumblings of myth and murky lore. But even if he was not what he claimed to be, he obviously possessed abilities beyond any ordinary being's, and she felt they owed him their lives.

Hero caught her look and seemed to sense what she was about to say, and before she could voice her objection he smiled slightly and inclined his head. Again she felt a strange connection to this man, a magnetism she could not decipher. "I understand, admiral," he said with what she sensed as practiced cordiality. "Perhaps if I were to offer you safe passage to your cruiser via my own ship, we could ascend under an equal understanding?"

Jo'seph smiled wryly in return. After a moment he replied, "What can I say? Very well, we accept."

Without further word the man called Hero touched the bracer again. Within moments the fighter Lise had spotted earlier came to land within yards of the surviving delegates. The ship was large for a fighter, and she amended that description to gunboat, peering at its strange wing-like shape through the murky field of destruction around them. The tips of the flyer's wings had large thrusters at the backs and cannon mounts at the fronts. Towards the fuselage the wings widened to occupy huge Vertical-Take-Off fans and then meet the body of the craft. The sleek head of the ship stretched along the front of the main body, from wing to wing, and when the entry hatch opened she could see into the center of the craft between the two wings, noting its interior size for housing of personnel and the large weapons it carried. She briefly made out the outline of the ship's pilot greeting Hero. The five remaining Coalition crewmembers and the stranger himself easily fit inside, as they followed the stranger in. As she entered, Lise again looked up at the man calling himself a Triialon warrior. He met her gaze unwaveringly, his expression unreadable, before he made for the main cabin, leaving the dazed delegate members to find seats amongst the hold. Lise and the others sat in what seemed crew seats for paratroops, noting the craft had once served as a transport.

The flyer lifted off and soon they were speeding up to the damaged Coalition battle cruiser, the *Return.'*

The desert gunboat docked via the starboard hanger bay, a large hatch just below the main bridge tower. The tower projected up from the tail end of the lengthy, swan-like cruiser. Lise had watched their approach silently from a small viewing window until they had reached their ship, seeing the charred damage along the neck of the vessel. Further markings cut deep into the hull just behind the enormous Main Cannon port that resided under the extended neck. She didn't move until the flyer had safely landed in the bay and she could feel the vibration of the closing hanger door. So lost in thought was she that she didn't get up until a grimly smiling admiral Jo'seph tapped her on the shoulder, standing above her as the others disembarked.

"C'mon, Commander."

Lise exited the ship, feeling suddenly exhausted to her very soul. She watched the activity of the bay, thankful for the normalcy of her surroundings now that she was aboard the *'Return'*.

Admiral Jo'seph was calling for her again. She turned to face him. "Commander? Lise, are you alright?" He had never used her first name before. "Do I need to send you to sickbay before the debriefing?"

Lise shook her head. "No, sir. I just need a shower." She looked down, covered head to foot in dust and ash, and smelling of smoke. She fingered the frayed edge of her officer's jacket sadly. "Sick bay would be unnecessary."

"I insist…"

"No, sir, please. I'm fine. I want to be there for the debriefing." Lise glanced at Hero, waiting near the hatch of his ship for further word from Jo'seph. She realized she was staring at the large man, and when he caught her gaze she could only smile weakly at him and turn away. "I just need to get cleaned up."

Jo'seph looked at her a moment, then nodded. "Understood. Report to the bridge in one hour. All events from today are classified until I say otherwise." Lise turned for the elevator. "And Commander," he called.

"Sir?"

"Excellent job today. All of it. I'm glad you were there."

Lise soon found herself in her assigned quarters, uncertain as to how she had got there. She removed the destroyed jacket and skirt, tossing them in the disposal shoot. Then she peered down at her battered body and made certain there was no permanent damage. "Shit," she said when her eyes finally made it to her legs. The dirt-encrusted stockings were torn and shredded, holes ripped on each leg and caked in mud. She almost tittered, promising herself she wouldn't break down twice in one day. "I lose more lingerie that way." She laughed, wiping away the moisture in her eyes. "That's what I get for thinking it's just a diplomatic mission."

In the shower she washed the day's events out of her long hair. Lise leaned against the confined stall's interior for support and listened to the water splash onto the floor, felt it run down her body. When she closed her eyes she saw Sparta, her home town and the boy she had fallen in love with. She saw the youth grow into a man, fighting at her side for a home they had both already lost. When the sight of him lying there, dead from a Lordillian blast, finally flashed behind her eyes she opened them to let the water wash that last terrible sight away.

She wrapped her arms around her body, trying to just lose herself, to just forget everything and stop the strange feelings of loss that threatened to drag her down. But she couldn't let herself lose track of time. It wasn't her usual responsible nature that forced her out of the shower and into a clean uniform; she just didn't want to miss another chance to see the strange man that had come to her out of the storm and destruction.

Again Chebonka found himself woken by unwanted influence. Alarms were sounding all along the Lordillian information net, setting afire electronic synapses in his mind. He quickly left his private room, finding the barrage of signals and 'noise' to be distracting after so short a charging session.

The throne room was a buzz of activity. Lordillians moved back and forth across the floor from control center to control center, each one briefly illuminated under the console lights before moving on. Two generals saw their master enter and mounted the steps to kneel before him. "Report," he commanded them.

"A barrage of reports are just coming in. We were attempting to ascertain facts before waking you, as some of the reports are fractured."

"Fractured?" Chebonka asked the Lordillian general.

"Affirmative. By all data thus received, it would seem the two battle cruisers dispatched to Moonshau have been destroyed."

Chebonka felt rage and frustration welling up, two very base and despicable emotions he thought he had long since purged from his makeup. "Destroyed! How can that be? Show me the VID files from the ships."

"Lord Chebonka, those files are only now reaching base systems from the listening posts."

"Show me them, immediately."

"Immediately, My Lord," the general repeated. He turned to address the drones within the huge chamber. "Display all files immediately."

An enormous three-dimensional hologram viewer filled the center of the room before the dais, text and fragmented pictures scrolling down its glowing, unreal surface. The images changed to a static filled screen, interspersed with aerial views of a bombarded field being blasted by the perspective ship's cannons. At last the picture solidified enough to make out details; a destroyed Coalition fighter, scattered bodies and wreckage, craters and cross fire, and one man standing in the middle of the firestorm, unharmed.

"Viewer, enhance figure," Chebonka commanded, taking what his brain's subsystems instantly classified as an 'anxious' step forward. "Identify."

"Identity unknown," came the computer's reply.

The man turned to look directly up at the oncoming battleship, moving a sword from one hand to the other – a sword! He seemed to stare directly into the camera with unwavering attention, and Chebonka memorized that face, marking the man. The figure pointed some sort of wrist-mounted weapon up at the Lordillian cruiser. Chebonka watched in fascination as there was a flash from the weapon, then the picture snapped to static.

"The second ship was destroyed by the Coalition battle cruiser after the events we just witnessed," a soldier announced.

Chebonka was uninterested in the second cruiser. "Replay VID file and enhance unidentified figure." The order was obeyed, and again he observed the man turn to look into the watching cruiser's sights. "Pause and enhance. Show me the object in his left hand." The screen jumped forward, showing a slightly grainy and static filled image of the detail requested: the large, engraved sword in the stranger's grip. "Enhance." There, in the center of the hilt just above his hand was a triangular symbol, gold of hue and glowing slightly. Chebonka looked down at the blade in his own giant fist. The symbol was the same – Triialon. "So, it is true."

He studied the pictures for some time, trying to get a better view of the sword and any view he could of the strange bracer-like weapon the man, the one called Hero by all accounts, used to apparently shoot down a Lordillian battleship with ease. Few angles of that item were available, and Chebonka's curiosity peeked. "Computer," he ordered, "Create file. Designate figure 'Hero', life form, 'Triialon'. This man must be captured for his knowledge or destroyed at all costs, his Artifacts confiscated." The creator of the Lordillians turned to his generals. "Assemble the second and third fleets. While that task is being completed, I want a full-scale attack on the Coalition outpost on Nevartza 4, high-ranking prisoners are to be taken. This is a number one priority, general."

"Understood, My Lord."

"Priority on Moonshau intelligence; I want confirmation on the death of admiral Jo'seph."

"Statistics indicate termination of target probable before destruction of cruiser…"

"Until you are one hundred percent confirmed do not speak to me again!"

Lise sat in her position aboard the cruiser *'Sparta-one'*, a sister ship of the *'Return'*, which had rendezvoused with the vessel only minutes before. Lise had been ordered to report to the bridge as communications officer and await further orders. Sitting at her familiar post, she watched admiral Jay'salan overseeing the damage control of the *'Return'*. She was twirling a lock of her hair nervously.

Jay'salan was also from her home planet of Sparta, but he was from the continent of Monteak. His race was easily recognizable by his large, barrel-chested size, angular facial features and gray skin. He had cropped blonde hair and slit-iris eyes. She wasn't as used to being in his company, but she was no less inspired by him. Where Jo'seph may be the heart and soul of the Coalition, Jay'salan was the tactical brains. It was rare to see the man walking the corridors without a historical war reference book in his hand.

A message came through her Com-set. "Admiral, I've just received word that admiral Jo'seph is aboard and will be joining us in a moment. The *'Return'* is breaking for home."

"Very good, Commander," Jay'salan replied.

Lise glanced out the bridge view port, watching the damaged ship move from along side and prepare for its jump. She never tired of the magnificent site of a Dimensionalizer jump, be it from far away or within a vessel making the hyperspacial boost that propelled the craft on its course at speeds excelling even 'Star-leap' speed. Such recent technological advances had kept the Coalition one step ahead of the Lordillian horde for several years.

Until that afternoon.

The *'Return'* floated past the bridge of the *'Sparta'*, its engines flaring in brilliant contrast to the blackness of space around it. From the front projector of the craft a beam flashed out, mapping out a giant window of energy that hung in space before the craft. The engines powered up and the ship literally crashed through the window it had created, disappearing into the hall of raging energy and the path it had designed through hyperspace. The fragments of Dimensionalizer window burned out and vanished as they fell away into space, and the ship was gone, on course for it's secret destination.

The bridge level's hatch opened. Lise swiveled her chair to see who might step through its portal and froze, unprepared for how she reacted when she saw him again. The man calling himself Hero stepped onto *'Sparta-one's'* bridge, wearing the same dusty coat with a cloak over it, broached at the right shoulder. The long hair was now tied back, the coat open revealing a large, muscular chest covered by a thin white shirt. Lise's breath caught in her throat and she immediately amended her previous thoughts about his not being overly handsome. He was gorgeous, radiating a magnetism that everyone around her obviously felt in one way or another as well. Each officer in turn stopped to watch the newcomers stride into their midst.

Another man, in many ways equal yet opposite of the warrior, followed Hero in. He entered the bridge walking like a brawler, watching all around him with shifty eyes. This man was also muscular, but where Hero was vigorous and somehow carrying an air of dignity, his companion was an obvious mercenary, with a shaved head, old, squinty eyes, and an almost comical bushy mustache. He was dressed in a long duster jacket, with even more belts and weapons strapped onto his body than Hero. Indeed, they positively weighed the man down.

Jo'seph followed them in, and as the two admirals began their greetings, Lise watched Hero's eyes, slowly studying the large bridge. Those eyes finally met hers and locked down like a steel trap. Lise's chest constricted again, but before she could even find the strength to pull her gaze away, he had already turned to shake the hand of admiral Jay'salan.

She turned back to her station, hoping to find some distracting duty rather than force herself not to stare at his back. "Commander Lise?" The voice was Jo'seph's. "Would you join us, please?" The four men turned to exit the room, presumably for the conference room just behind the bridge. Lise quickly hid her surprise and calmly swiveled her seat to leave her post. Straightening down the short skirt, she followed her commanding officers and the two newcomers through the hatch, ignoring the murmur of activity from the other bridge personnel.

Once within the conference room, Lise was surprised to find private Zhade standing at attention near a chair, and Jay'salan ordered the guards to wait outside.

"If everyone would please be seated," Jo'seph said. Once they were all sitting, he cleared his throat, as if uncertain what to say next. "Well," he started at last, "I suppose I could start with formal introductions." He looked at Lise and motioned to Hero, sitting across the table from her. "Admiral Jay'salan, commander Lise, private Zhade, this is Hero of the Triialon. His companion is Osmar." A muttering of greetings was exchanged among the group.

Jay'salan looked at the two newcomers piercingly. "I have to admit, gentlemen," he began, "we are slightly dubious of your claimed background. You must simply understand our position for our reasons as to that matter." He leaned forward a little, placing his hands upon the table. "However, your apparent abilities offer a rare opportunity, and admiral Jo'seph seems to think that asking you to join our cause on some level is not an altogether strange idea. In any case, we owe you a debt for your timely intervention this afternoon."

"Yes," Lise said, "thank you. You saved our lives." She glanced at Zhade, who nodded slightly.

Hero inclined his head to her. "I understand your misgivings, admiral," he said, looking back at the admirals.

Jo'seph raised an eyebrow. "No, I don't think you do. Not if you are what you say you are."

The mercenary, Osmar, obviously couldn't handle incredulity any longer. Looking about as angry as any man Lise had ever seen, he burst out, "You dare doubt my Lord?"

Hero's hand rose to cut him off. "Osmar."

Osmar's rage was stunted. Looking surprised and somehow amused he sat back. "Aye, sir."

"Please, continue."

"Thank you," said Jo'seph. "Hero, you claim to come from a race long since thought extinct, and even then a legend. The ideals of the Triialon and their station as guardians within this galaxy have long held a place among the basis of the Coalition's aspirations. The race of Triialon is long since disappeared, and the name of the one called 'Hero' has remained in the last few decades as the mythic ramblings of space travelers, at least on this side of the galaxy. All this, not to mention the security protocols we must enforce due to the war, leads us to simply question your background, as well as motives, before we can further offer the hospitality and privileges of the Coalition."

"I understand." The warrior pondered his next words for a moment, and then leaned forward, placing his cards upon the table. "My motives are simple. I wish to help you, at least for the time being, both for my own reasons and to legitimately aid your cause. As to the question of my background, I am afraid my actions will have to speak for themselves. I am the last of my people. I have no credentials, save the Artifacts of the Twelve."

Jay'salan waved his hand. "Yes of course your sword is interesting and the bracer…"

"Prizm," Hero corrected.

"Prizm," Jay'salan continued, "is powerful, as demonstrated. But Chebonka claims to have a sword of the Triialon as well."

"Yes," Hero said, "and that is part of the reason I am here. If legitimate, that blade is stolen."

"You seem to know a lot of things," quipped Jay'salan. "Such as when a Coalition delegation headed by one of its leading admirals is going to be attacked."

Jo'seph's face darkened. "Jay'."

"I get my information from a long list of people," said Hero evenly, "all the more reason for you to be so careful with me."

Osmar said, "A Coalition admiral in so open an arena as the capitol of Moonshau is big news." He was sitting back in his chair, arms crossed, smiling evilly. "If we could hear of it, then so could Chebonka's Lordillians. Or others."

Lise suddenly chimed in with an unasked question. "You are not Triialon as well?"

Osmar turned to look at her, his voice calming a little to address her. Lazily, he pointed a gloved hand at his traveling companion. "No, lass. I'm afraid only His Lordship here has that honor." His demeanor became even more indignant when he crossed his booted heels over one another on the tabletop. "I'm simply an old fighter and gun-runner, ma'am, neither of which is worth mentioning in proper circles, I'm sure."

Lise realized then that Hero was studying her, watching her openly. "May I ask your background, commander?"

Lise, surprised, glanced at Jo'seph, who nodded. She turned back to Hero, lifting her chin and speaking with pride. "I am from the planet Sparta, like many of the Coalition. My parents were aristocrats, with a lineage that could be traced back to royal bloodlines when the monarchy was still a part of the politics of our world, generations ago. In short, they were rich, and I was raised well. Since the Lordillians attacked, I have been a guerilla freedom fighter, and finally a member of the Coalition."

Jay'salan sighed aloud. "I honestly don't know what to do." He looked Hero in the eyes. "I want to believe this man," then, turning to his fellow officer, "I want people to believe *in* this man."

"The last of the Triialon would be a hell of a morale boost to the home team, I agree," smiled Jo'seph.

"I would like to help." Hero's face and voice never wavered. Lise could not remove that stoic figure from her sight if she wanted to. "The Lordillians are a scourge, but more than that, Chebonka's Artifact, if it is indeed Triialon in origin, must be seized."

Jay'salan's eyes peered at him. "Why? How did he get it?"

"The Artifacts of Power, ten of the Twelve, were lost at the end of a war that destroyed the Triialon. My race died to protect the future, admiral." As seriously as anything he had said so far, Hero looked both men in the face and continued. "I made the choice to end the war that day and lose the stolen artifacts to the whims of chance rather than let an evil being, the Shard, go on to conquer the universe.

"The Artifacts are all weapons of great power, designed by my ancestors thousands of years ago. It was that power that put our race in the position it held as guardians for millennia. But the war with Shard lasted so long and entrenched our armies so deeply, that by the time of my birth we had lost most of our past." He sat back, visibly trying to relax and exhaled. "I must find what has been lost, to ensure the future."

Jo'seph shook his head. "The Lordillians are the future, unless we can survive this."

"Do you have visual files on Chebonka?" Hero asked.

The admirals exchanged looks. "Some," answered Jo'seph. "I assume you'd like to see that 'symbol' of his power?"

"If the sword is one of the Triialon blades, then it is the key. However he obtained that Artifact will lead us to knowing how the Lordillians rose to power so quickly. If I can get close enough to destroy him and take that sword, the Lordillians will fall."

"Well, that's the trick, isn't it," said Jo'seph.

"Nothing can get to him," said Jay'salan. "It's now impossible to even get within the Lordillian star system."

Private Zhade was the next to speak up. "What about that archive footage from Chebonka's home world, just after he'd risen to power but before he'd completely augmented himself..."

"Or slaughtered his own race," Jo'seph completed dryly.

"What of it?" Lise asked. "I've never seen it."

Jay'salan reached across to the terminal in the center of the table. "I know the one." He switched on the computer and began sifting through files on the screen. "It was big news, at the time, and some of the commentators criticized the barbaric symbol a sword was in the hands of a being that had just usurped political and military power." A picture came up of a crowd gathering around the steps of an official looking building. The camera view was from far above, perhaps that of a news robot observing from a distance. A man stepped before the crowd, large and imposing, with metallic arms glinting in the sunlight as he held aloft a sword, its blade thick and the hilt jagged and commanding. The crowd roared, whether in rage or celebration, Lise could not discern. "There," Jay'salan said, and he paused it, zooming in on the polished weapon.

Hero stood up slowly and leaned over the table, bringing his eyes close to the screen, staring at the image so piercingly Lise thought his gaze alone might break the monitor glass.

"Well, Lord?" Osmar asked, pulling his feet off of the table to Jo'seph's apparent relief.

Hero finally stepped back from the image. "That's it," he said quietly. For a moment he seemed lost in reverie, then, "In your tongue, admirals, the weapon is named *Justice* or 'The Sword of Warriors', once carried by the bodyguard to the King of Triialon. A device of power that I have been missing for… many years."

"At last," Osmar said, echoing Hero's obvious interest.

"Can he use it?" asked Jo'seph.

Hero finally took his eyes from the screen. "He should not even be allowed to touch its eminence." There was a flash of anger across his features, but the expression was quickly gone, controlled beneath the surface. "Beyond that, I can only say that no being that is not of Triialon blood should be able to wield its power. But the properties of the Artifacts may have been changed by whatever means transported them from Triialon, so I can not be certain." He nearly slumped back into the chair.

There was a chime from the Com panel next to the computer terminal. Jay'salan switched it on. "Yes?"

"We've lost contact with the outpost on Nevartza 4," came an officer's voice.

"I'll be right there." Jay'salan stood. "Admiral, I'll trust you to close this meeting. Gentlemen, if you'll excuse me. Commander." The large admiral exited the room hurriedly.

"When it rains, it pours," said Jo'seph, shaking his head disdainfully. He stood up and offered his hand out to Hero. "I offer you a temporary position and rank yet to be determined within the Coalition, Hero of the Triialon. Your quest is your own but our destinies would appear to be the same."

Hero took the hand. "Our journeys do seem to take the same path, at least for now."

"Understood," said Jo'seph, grinning. They shook hands. "Glad to have you aboard."

Lise watched, smiling. Jo'seph turned to her and Zhade. "You two; you're both under classified order. The events spoken of in this room today are not to leave it. Hero and Osmar's ranks will be officially announced later, and the other delegates have also already been briefed about this afternoon's original meeting. However, I hope you might both be so good as to recall the actual events of Hero's arrival and victory to your shipmates with gusto as soon as the opportunity arises. A Triialon fights for the Coalition now, so let it be written." He smiled mischievously. "No need to over-embellish the details of how he saved us by too much, though. His abilities are already hard to believe as it is, and I saw it all."

"I saw it all, sir," said Zhade, a note of passion Lise had never heard in the man's voice now clearly evident.

"And I," she said.

Jo'seph looked at them. "Very good. To your posts." Lise got out of her seat, smiling at Hero and instantly regretting her schoolgirl act. She calmed her expression, holding out her hand to shake that of her new shipmates'. "Gentlemen, will you accompany me to the bridge," Jo'seph asked them.

As Lise followed the three men back to the bridge, she suppressed a giddy laugh that threatened to find voice. Terrible things were happening in the universe all around them, yet she suddenly felt more hopeful than she had in a long time. The day she had found and joined the Coalition had been the happiest in years, and even that paled to the simple faith she had somehow been infused with since the moment Hero had leapt from his craft and into her life.

Chapter Three

"Tumultuous wasn't the word."
Personal journal
-Admiral Jo'seph Bel'ov

Memfis sat on a marble pedestal, nude save for his jewelry as six equally naked slave girls dried him and prepared his clothing. The women were some of the finest examples of beauty the humanoid race could conceive, but this day he ignored their ample assets. He waited in contemplation for them to finish, soon to join his fellow Gods in the Court of Kordula. One of the girls held a mirror before him as another finished working the braid into his mane. He regarded his features only briefly, thinking of how the long muzzle and black eyes on the sides of his stallion-like head were infinitely more refined than the slaves' round faces and hairless bodies. While he stood bipedal, with a large, muscled torso and arms like that of a humanoid, his size and power, and the workings of his mind, were so obviously more evolutionarily advanced than that of those around him.

He stood, careful not to crush a servant's toes under his hoof, allowing one of the girls to fasten the toga garment around him and apply the plate jewelry around his right eye. "Enough," he commanded, waving them away. "Be gone." He walked between the pillared archway leading from his chambers to the Court adjacent to his own building. He passed windows that looked out over the ancient yet advanced city of Kordula, its technological spirals reaching up into the sky from their cathedral stone bases.

The others were already seated around a large, rectangular table. The room was a clash of classic design and decoration mixed with holographic displays and terminals. Memfis had come to call this room and its trappings 'Home' so many centuries before that he no longer remembered his life to be any other way. Twenty of his fellow 'Gods', the remaining self-proclaimed immortals who had ascended beyond the bonds of their original, extinct species, all held their places at the table. Their appearance was much the same as his own, with variations in hair colors and patterns. Some, like Memfis, wore the rarest of jewels from across the galaxy. Other had become bored with such formalities and trinkets over time, and resided in simple robes only.

Memfis took his own seat at the head of the long room. Each one stared at their own screened hologram, displays of stocks, newscasts, and incoming information from sources both legitimate and nefarious scrolling past their eyes at speeds that would be amazing to most species.

"Memfis, how good of you to join us at your leisure," said Toapo, glaring from his end of the table.

"Perhaps you should spend more time monitoring your holosphere, Toapo, and less worrying about my concerns," replied Memfis.

"You *are* five minutes late, Memfis," said Galatis. "Is it not Toapo's duty to point such things out if he feels we have worked diligently in your absence yet again?"

"Not when my duties outside of this chamber are just as important," said Memfis, a threatening edge to his voice. "You forget, gentlemen, I control this Court. My whims are my own. As they are all ultimately in the interest of Kordula and our goals, I suggest you remember your place."

There was a murmur of agreement from the seated Gods, and Toapo snorted in frustration, turning back to his display. Galatis shrugged and did the same.

"The future will be ours so long as we retain vigilance, my brethren," said Memfis with a lighter tone, switching on his own holospheres and option screens. "When Zone comes we will greet him as the only heirs to his kingdom of the Universe. Millennia have come and gone and millennia may yet still pass before he arrives. Until then, we wait and pave the way for his coming. Now, on to business." His face was thrown into contrasting colors and shadow as the hologram sprang to life before him and he quickly assessed its output. "Interesting. I see Chebonka's mission to Moonshau was a failure."

Galatis nodded. "Yes, both of the ships he sent were destroyed before they could either wreak any real havoc on the capitol or destroy the Coalition vessel there. Our concern is that the Coalition cruiser is the source of only one of those Lordillian ship's destruction."

Memfis' brow furrowed. "I was not aware the Moonshau had anti-spacecraft firepower of that magnitude based around any of its civilian instillations."

"They don't," replied Galatis.

Toapo grinned. "There was a third player. *Hero* has arrived within the Lordillian expansion zones and controlled space." He spit the words with distaste. "He destroyed the other Lordillian cruiser and left with the Coalition, and all of this after your little assassin cyborg failed to kill the Admiral, and you saw none of this coming!"

Memfis merely glanced at him with displeasure. "Neither did you." He scrolled down the reports. "So Hero has entered the war at last. I had wondered when we might have to suffer his interference. It is little surprise, though, as his quest would have led him to Chebonka at some point."

"What of the Moonshau?" asked Tannek. "While our hand was not seen in the assassination attempt, the rift between Coalition and Moonshau technology was not widened either, it would seem. They could quite possibly join the Coalition, bolstering their strength even further."

"Let them," droned Memfis. "If they do join, we will aid Chebonka's cause further and eventually all parties will be wiped out. If they do not, it will simply mean the destruction of the Coalition in a more expedient manner, and the end of all possible nuisances such as Moonshau will follow shortly thereafter."

"Chebonka is in fact requesting further raw materials from systems under our control for a new fleet."

Memfis smiled. "Grant him three quarters of what he requests for the same price. Best to keep him on a short leash. Besides, we don't want him to believe he can just have anything he asks from Kordula."

"Or gain the truth of how much of his destiny we control," replied Galatis.

"Indeed."

"Perhaps we should not be so hasty," interjected Beletto. "Chebonka could become a loose element should he gain too much power too quickly. His army grows ever larger and will soon be able to stomp out the Coalition. What if he were to turn that army on those planets and interests of Kordula? He hates all sentient life that is not in his image." He shrugged. "It is among the possibilities."

"A possibility we have discussed before," said Memfis. "But if it so worries you, only grant Chebonka one half of his current request. Temperament might be a wise course anyway, as he does also have mining operations on many of the planets the Lordillians have already claimed. It would only take him longer to create the new fleet his hunger for immediate power would inevitably have."

"There is still then the matter of his Triialon sword," said Tannek. "What if he were to learn to control its abilities?"

"It is but one of the Twelve, and we will wrest it from him when the time is right in either case." Memfis sighed in frustration. "You forget this conflict's origins, my brethren. When Sparta and similar worlds were gaining in strength we were the ones to infuse Chebonka with the needs to combat them. We alone know the Lordillians' true weaknesses, and once the forces of the Coalition have been subjugated we shall exploit that flaw and wrest the Triialon Artifact from Chebonka's dead hands, leaving the Lordillian fleets to float, lifeless, like so much space junk. Until then, let the conflict rage, dragging more and more intergalactic powers into the fray and to their doom. They shall fall before the might," at this Memfis gave a biting laugh of sarcasm, " of Chebonka, and then he too shall learn his true fate."

"And what of Hero?" asked Galatis.

"He we shall watch, now that we again know his whereabouts. He has long been a thorn in our side but he has yet to truly stand in our way. We can decide what to do about him later. If he becomes too useful to the Coalition's cause we can always," Memfis paused, smiling wryly, "send him to meet his Forefather."

The others laughed quietly at this. Memfis looked across the table and into the eyes of Toapo, who stared back and then finally turned away, getting back to his duties.

Galatis held up a piece of parchment, scanning its official documentation and contents with his eyes before raising it to the table's attention. "I have here a request from Svea Magdalene of the Seethlings to join our court at Kordula."

"Seethlings," replied Memfis thoughtfully. "Why does that name sound familiar?"

Galatis laughed. "The Court of Worlds ordered their home planet to be destroyed by the Triialon some forty years ago. It was one of the last and most 'depraved' acts committed by the Court before you disbanded it five years later. The Seethlings were sentenced to genocide for acts of 'evil on an incalculable scale' committed by the entire race. At least, that was the official reason given, as I recall."

Memfis sat back thoughtfully. "The last of her race, eh?"

"One of two, yes. Her brother, Dahvis, also survives."

"Interesting. Very well, grant her audience and reply with our sincere desire to see her at court as soon as possible."

"As you wish." Galatis signed the paper and called for an agent to deliver the message.

Two figures covered from head to foot in tight black clothing moved stealthily through the darkness. Masks covered their faces but it was obvious that one was a physically toned male and the other a lithe female. They evaded the lights that searched the grounds, skirting around them and heading straight for the fort's walls. They were noiseless, formless, the abilities they were born with making them invisible to the compound's sensors. Inching around the corner, they spotted the front door. The female held up two fingers to her counterpart to communicate the number of guards posted.

A searchlight passed by, skimming the wall, moving over the guards, and out into the darkness. The two black clad figures slid around the corner, walking slowly in the dark as they hugged the wall. Within paces of the guards they sprang into action, pulling the twitching sentries inside the open door of the base, each one clamped tight within the electrifying grip of their assailants. Blue sparks shot from between the arms of the assassins and the smoldering uniforms and flesh of the dying men. The female dropped her prey at her feet, the powerful charge she had delivered to him just by touch having been enough to kill. The male duplicated the action, his hands releasing the dead figure as though the carcass were some lesser thing no longer worthy of his attentions.

The intersecting hallways were dimly lit with much of the small fort's compliment asleep. The female now followed the carefully advancing male down the corridors, past a busy control room. She watched him peek inside briefly to make certain their target was not there. He pulled back again into the shadows, shaking his head at her before they moved on.

The fool's bedroom was mere meters away, unguarded. He had made himself a target to his enemies politically and yet left himself so open to attack. He deserved his fate, the woman decided, and with that she was glad she was going to profit from the General's death.

The black-clad man watched for sentries while she briefly inspected the door for booby traps and alarms. She gave the 'all-clear' to her counterpart and silently opened the door, vanishing within the darkened room. Waiting in the blackness, her eyes soon acclimated to behold an obese figure in a single bed. The room was lit for a brief moment once more as the male slipped in. When the gloom returned, she felt him brush her with the signal to advance to the target. She did so, sensing she moved forward alone, and smiled to herself. The other was almost certainly finding the light switch, determined their prey should see his doom at the moment of truth. With one hand she let her fingertips skim the low ceiling, easily finding the edges of the trapdoor their client had informed them the mark used for any escape he may ever need. In moments she and her accomplice would slip up through it and be out before the charges they would lay to destroy the control room could consume them as well.

She sensed more than heard the charge mag-lock to the cell wall. She pulled the large, curved knife from its concealed sheath within her uniform, her body poised, blade ready, holding for the kill. Seconds passed before the lights switched on. Her free hand flashed forward the moment the General's eyes began to flutter open, smashing his jaw, leaving him to moan in pain and confusion for a moment before she seized the fat fool by the hair, forcing him to look at her. He stared at his attacker in surprise and fear, blood gushing from between his swollen lips.

"General Tollock," she said, sternly yet quietly, "President Robaxel sends his regards." The knife flashed, arcing out to slice his throat open, the sharp blade slipping through the tissue easily. A crimson fountain sprayed across the bare bedroom wall, his major arteries severed. The General choked and gurgled, thrashing in the soaked sheets as his lifeblood flowed freely from the gushing wound. The woman smiled to herself before jumping up through the secret hatch to freedom. She didn't even look back to make sure the other followed, knowing he would have climbed up the instant she was clear.

The duct led to an underground passage through a hill behind the fort. Halfway through that she heard the explosive charge ignite the General's room, the control center, and all of the files and personnel therein. The man behind her gave her a satisfied slap on the calf, his elation echoed by her grin beneath the black mask.

They exited the secret tunnel somewhere on the far side of the fort. It took them the better part of the night to carefully make their way back around to their waiting ship, evading any patrols that might be still looking for the assassins. The fort was undermanned in the first place, and the couple simply bided their time to make certain they weren't traced as they doubled back. Dawn approached when they finally found the ship. They boarded, removing the masks to reveal darkly attractive, hard features. Dahvis kissed her briefly. She smiled but pulled away, unwilling to give in to his celebrations just yet, when she found the waiting message from Kordula on the main computer. Svea grinned, genuinely thrilled, all thoughts of President Robaxel's money gone. She pointed the hoped-for words of the message out to Dahvis almost offhandedly before she made her way to the cockpit of the small spacecraft. She set course for home, a secret palace on a small moon a few light years away called Magdala. She couldn't suppress the pervasive, wry smile that twisted her lips while she warmed up the ship. Even as Dahvis entered the cabin she grinned, feeling his hands come to rest softly on her shoulders. "At last," she said.

Svea pulled the straps of her dress back onto her shoulders. "Look at this," she mock complained. "Now I'll have to do my hair all over again." They had returned from their mission to Tollock's fort two hours before, again finding the message from Kordula waiting for them at home, which renewed their celebrations.

Dahvis rolled over and reached for where she had just been in the large bed. She deftly stood from its edge and moved away before he could pinch her flesh again. "I couldn't help it," he said. "You've done so well. Accepted at the Court of Kordula." He studied the silver rings on his fingers. "Your references must have impressed them."

Svea made her way to the antique vanity of her bedroom, sitting with practiced charm on the pillows of its matching divan. "They impressed somebody," she said back, pulling her hair out of its pinning to try and remold it before the image in the mirror. The long, straight brown hair fell past the middle of her back. She gathered the bulk of it back up into an arrangement, leaving tendrils that cascaded down and wisps that she had to push back behind her pointed ears. Her dress was daringly cut to show off her ample curves, and she smiled to herself, admiring the beauty mark above her red lips, the grin causing her eyes to twinkle cruelly. She finished redoing her hair and then smiled back at her brother, turning seductively to look at him over her shoulder. "There. How do I look?"

"Gorgeous," replied Dahvis dryly, "as always." He rose from the bed naked, raking his hands through his slicked back hair before pulling on a pair of leathery black pants. His youthfully handsome yet unkind features turned on her and she watched him from the corner of her eye as he approached. He placed hard hands on her shoulders, his mood having suffered one of its habitual swings since crossing the room. Rough fingers seized her chin, so different from the same hands' soft touches only an hour before. He forced her to look up at him, now a hovering shadow hulking over her. She glared back at the eyes that burned into hers. "You'd better not screw this up, Svea. You wouldn't want me to repeat my last lesson."

She pulled her face from his grasp angrily, but then smiled as pleasantly as ever. "You forget, brother, just how proud you should be of your schooled sister, as she has not given you cause for anger since."

"Our benefactor schooled you," Dahvis said coldly. "I have since trained you." The last he said with menace.

She turned back to the mirror, busying herself with makeup and jewels. Her emotions briefly betrayed her as memories of the man she had come to think of as a father, Baron Magdala - their benefactor, filled her mind. Svea would never forget finding him there in a pool of his own blood; It was the last time she had seen his face. She pushed the past aside and returned her mind to the conversation at hand. "Perhaps you want me to fail, just so you can *train* me again." She said it with just a hint of the anger she felt, but the mood was not to be further spoiled, so she sighed and turned the corners of her mouth up once more. She stood and put her arms around his rigid shoulders. "We've worked all our lives towards the goals Kordula promises," she said to him. "Why should I fail?"

Dahvis' arms reached up to grab hers, and an electric shock passed to her with the touch. He delivered just enough to cause pain, and she stepped back, gasping. "Because sometimes you disgust me." He walked to an opulent dark wood wardrobe and picked himself out a black shirt, pretending to ignore her.

She absently rubbed her arms where he had shocked her, then smiled wickedly. "Don't look so worried," Svea said, stretching out on the bed like a kitten. "You know how well you've instructed me, what we're both destined for." She rolled onto her back, curling her legs around one another. Pointing her heeled feet towards the ceiling. she let her dress fall down around her waist revealing what she wasn't wearing underneath. "Just you watch. I'll have them all eating out of my hands within days, and have you moved in there with me within a month."

Dahvis just looked at her. He finished fastening the shirt up the front, carefully closed the wardrobe, and left the room without another word.

Svea let her legs fall to the bed and laughed slightly to herself. She spread her hair and arms out around her on the crimson sheets and grinned. "Kordula," she said, arching her back and running her hands down her body. The chamber doors closed behind her brother and she laughed aloud again.

The stars twinkled back mockingly, countless and bright in contrast to the endless, inky waste they floated in.

Hero stood at the front of the *'Sparta'*s bridge, arms crossed, staring out into the void. The noise of the anxious crew behind him fell on deaf ears, his contemplations of fate and the decisions he tried to make despite destiny consumed his senses. Osmar stood nearby, trying to respect his privacy while not getting in the way of the bustling bridge crew.

"Like a nest of hornets all worked up," said the watching Osmar. He shook his head, scratching his unshaven chin.

Hero ignored his companion. He knew what was happening to these people, and the conclusions still led him back to the commitment he knew he was making with the Coalition, though he felt loath to stay any real length of time with them after so many years of his relative loneliness. But this was where he needed to be for now, whether that sentence was decreed by chance or by design. Once more he resigned himself to the future. The quest would, in some regards at least, have to wait for a time.

The Triialon warrior turned from the giant view port and strode towards the two Coalition admirals on the control platform. He walked by officers who stared at him as he passed, some with open awe. The girl, Lise, was the only one that managed to grab his attention briefly on his path, yet even she failed to gain any real acknowledgment. He took the steps two at a time, quickly ascending to the command platform and coming to stand next to the two admirals, bending to read the display the men were hovering over and studying.

"Have you determined whether or not the outpost has been attacked?"

Neither man's eyes left the scrolling readout. "No," replied Jay'salan. Information from the scattered Coalition cruiser squads and installations poured in from their varied positions, but the data lines designated as the outpost on Nevartza 4 remained blank. "No one's reached it yet, and we're waiting here for the fifth squad to rendezvous before we move out to investigate it ourselves."

"It doesn't look good, though," said Jo'seph. "Not even the outlying fighters from that outpost are getting their messages relayed to any of the closer installations or listening posts. Still, we'll know soon enough. That gives us all here at least a few hours of rest." The admiral stretched and inhaled, inclining his head to Hero. "Gentlemen, I again thank you. Can I have someone show you to your quarters before I myself turn in?"

Hero took in a great breath, nodding in agreement. "Please. Further talks can wait for tomorrow." He removed his jacket and slung it over one arm, trying to put aside the feeling of immediacy that had gotten him worked up since hearing of the communications loss. "Is my ship safely stowed for the night?"

"Yes, of course," Jo'seph motioned to the control deck. "Commander Lise. You're off-duty in a few more minutes, I believe. Would you see our guests to their quarters?" The woman nodded, standing as another officer took her position at communications. She looked tired. "And would you join us in the conference room tomorrow at the beginning of your shift?" he asked her.

Lise smiled, her already beautiful face lit up further by the expression. "Yes, sir." She turned to Hero and Osmar, her eyes almost timid as they met the warrior's. "This way, gentlemen."

The door opened, and Osmar could see inside the cramped quarters he and Hero would be sharing. A pair of bunk beds was set into the wall, with one desk and computer interface terminal, a tiny bathroom and shower, and a few places to hang clothes. Some of their bags from the Triialon ship were waiting for them next to the bunk.

"I hope the quarters are adequate," said Lise, standing at the door in that tight, black uniform. "Mine are only slightly larger." Osmar had to tear his eyes from her ample chest in an attempt to remain cordial, realizing that she had been talking about the living space.

"They shall do fine, Commander. Thank you." Hero hung up his jacket, and Osmar found that the girl was still waiting outside the door, watching his master with keen interest. The mercenary was about to ask her if she was waiting for a tip when Hero turned to her again. "Is there anything else?"

Lise seemed to suddenly find great amount of detail in her feet, forcing herself to look back up at the man she was obviously fascinated with. Osmar screwed up his face and tried to ignore them, taking the lower bunk. He groaned audibly as he crawled onto the bed, though

54

whether it was from old bones or simply having to listen to the girl fawn over Hero, he wasn't certain. In either case, Osmar just hoped they had not heard him. Still, a show was a show, and he tried to remain inconspicuous as he watched.

"I was raised to learn the customs of my guests or hosts," she said with practiced conviction, her eyes framed by long lashes.

"The Triialon had very few customs left by the time the Great War was done with us," Hero answered. "Perhaps you would care to teach me yours?"

Osmar could take it no longer. "Should I leave you two alone?" he asked incredulously. It was worth it just to see the look on the girl's face, her eyes widening slightly and her cheeks flushing to a lovely shade of pink. She certainly was infatuated.

Lise cleared her throat quietly, attempting to regain her composure. "Um, well, perhaps another time. Good night, gentlemen." She held out her hand to shake his. "I-It was good to meet you, sir, and thank you." The shake was brief, and she hurried away as soon as she could, the door closing behind her retreat.

"I believe you embarrassed her," Hero said, one eyebrow raised.

"Saved you the pain," Osmar answered.

Hero made himself busy taking items from his bag. "Are you bored?" It was a scolding in the form of a question. Already he was on to just how frustrated Osmar was feeling aboard the Coalition ship.

"Something like that." The mercenary got up from the bunk, making his way to the door. "How long do you plan on being with these people?"

"Perhaps for some time. Don't worry, there will be plenty of heads to bash."

"They don't trust you," Osmar snapped. "They should. You deserve respect if nothing else."

"Their policies are wise enough, under the circumstances."

Frustrated, Osmar rolled out of the bed and opened the hatch. "I'm going for a walk, Your Grace. Don't wait up."

He could feel Hero's eyes on his back as he made is way out and down the hall of the Coalition cruiser. He didn't mean to be as rude as he sounded, but he'd had enough of the military mentality for one day, and he needed a drink. Figuring the galley would be closed for the night, he decided to head for the flight deck. Osmar avoided eye contact with the few personnel he passed, moving with a purpose, a stiff beverage now his only thought.

When he reached a hatch leading to the fighter bay, he could see a guard near the door. Not wanting to have to explain his lacking of a pass, he began searching for an alternate route. He found an unguarded door after another ten minutes of skulking about the ship. He picked the electronic lock easily and entered the dark, steam-filled hanger bay. Crouching slightly, to avoid any unnecessary detection, he slipped between fighters and shuttles, finding his way in the dark towards the Triialon gunship. He nearly walked into the ship's wing when he finally found it, sneaking around an *interceptor* through the shadows.

He was just working the hatch controls to enter Hero's ship when something alerted his senses. He turned, looking for the cause of his trepidation, and found a blaster muzzle pointed right at his head. Another two soldiers appeared and duplicated the motion. "Freeze!" the first soldier commanded.

Osmar was surrounded.

Hero entered the hanger bay and strode over to his ship. Waiting beside it was three armed guards, Osmar, and a very tired and unhappy looking admiral Jo'seph, his officer's jacket open over an un-tucked shirt. Hero crossed his arms and cocked an eyebrow. "Admiral?"

"Seems my guards caught your friend here in a restricted zone. As you two are such a... special case, I thought I'd come down here personally."

Osmar was waiting for Hero's bidding, so the Triialon nodded at the mercenary to commence with his explanation. "My Lord, as I have been trying to tell His Admiralty here, I was just coming down to get a few things out of your ship."

"Such as?" asked Jo'seph over his shoulder.

Osmar had the good grace to look sheepish. "This and that." Nobody seemed to buy the lame explanation if you judged by the silence.

"A drink, if you must know," he said, defeated and angry. He then put on a fairly unfriendly smile, showing teeth yellowed by age. "Care to join me?"

Jo'seph just looked to Hero. "The guards didn't see him enter through any of the main hatches, and spotted him in here sneaking between ships. I was hoping you might be able to shed some light on this behavior."

Hero relaxed his stance some, looking at his companion. "Osmar, as we are guests here, we are subject to the admiral's rules, whether you like it or not. We will follow proper procedures from this point on."

"Yes, Lord," Osmar answered, head bowed.

Hero looked back to Jo'seph. "As long as we've caused you the trouble of coming down, may he bring the desired items to our quarters?"

Jo'seph stood there contemplating. Finally he shook his head, frustrated and tired. "Very well. Thank you for coming down so promptly. Lieutenant, you're in charge." He gave Osmar a stern look. "No contraband," he said pointedly.

Osmar glared back. With that, the admiral left the hanger bay.

A few minutes passed as Osmar and a guard were in the ship, leaving the lieutenant and a soldier standing next to Hero. The men glanced at him uncertainly.

"Is it true you're a Triialon," the lieutenant stammered at last.

Hero looked the man in the eyes. "It is true."

The man contemplated that for a time, then asked, "Why now? Why didn't your people come to help us before it all became so... desperate?"

Hero thought about that. He had told himself for the last few years, as rumors of Lordillian power had grown, that he had stayed away because of the quest. That the Twelve was a more immediate concern. But that wasn't what this man was really asking. "Because I am the last."

"I thought I told you to keep out of trouble?" Hero asked the question of Osmar without meeting his gaze, the pair making their way back to their quarters after being escorted out of the hanger bay.

Osmar shrugged. "I didn't kill any of them."

Hero laughed only slightly under his breath at that, and Osmar looked at him in surprise before erupting in laughter himself, slapping Hero on the back.

Memfis stood on a balcony, overlooking Kordula. The city bustled beneath his gaze, its denizens blissfully unaware of the games played within the halls above. They were simply a civilized mob. The Gods protected them but left them to their ways in exchange for the worship they gave. They were, to some within the Court, a means to an end, to others a distraction. Memfis knew they were truly worthless, their bodies so fragile, their lifetimes so short. He kept them ignorant and content, swelling upon the fat of the land. They served their purpose in the interim, but the day would come when all who were not of the Power would be washed away.

A serving girl stepped up behind and awaited his leave to come forward. "Yes?" he asked.

"The Council sends word," she replied, holding out the note in her hand.

Memfis took the message and motioned the girl away. He opened it, reading the ancient characters that none save those of the Gods' original race could read.

Coalition Outpost on Nevartza 4 attacked by Lordillian fleet.

Prisoners taken.

Svea of the Seethlings accepts our invitation to court.

He smiled to himself when he was finished, letting the note drift from his fingers on the winds of the city spires.

Chapter Four

*Was there anything the man couldn't do? For all we
know he'd had centuries of warfare experience before
he even came to the Coalition. This man was warrior,
pilot, captain, and general all in one, to say nothing
of his knowledge in other fields.*
Books of War
- General Abtarth

Lise stepped into the mess hall groggily. The room was fairly empty,
but she knew that within an hour it would fill to capacity as officers and
soldiers prepped for the shift change. She was early, wanting to get a head
start on her day as well as insure her place at a COM table to send a coded
transmission through the listening posts to the Norpan asteroid belt. She
got a tray full of what passed on the ship for a morning meal and
navigated a path between tables and chairs before reaching a corner spot.
She then switched on the communications terminal while taking a bite
out of a purple fruit, ignoring the taste.

Lise put the listening piece into her right ear. It took the scrambler
several minutes to set up the connection, but at last her friend Tykeisha's
face showed up on the screen. Her darker complexion was usually
complimented by her exotic eyes, but today she looked tired. "Lise," she
exclaimed, smiling a little. "What's going on?"

Lise let her breath out, blowing up her cheeks. "Yesterday was one
hell of a day, let me tell you." She leaned in conspiratorially to the screen.
"I'm not certain exactly what all I *can* tell you, but I can say I was nearly
killed twice, saved the admiral's life, and got rescued from being blasted
by a Lordillian cruiser by the most gorgeous man I've seen this side of
Anozira."

The other woman's eyes lit up. "Wow." Then she smiled, leaning in
as well. "He must be if he's grabbed your interest. So who's the mystery
man?"

Lise smiled to herself, trying to keep her fingers from twirling her
hair or anything that might be equally juvenile. But she couldn't help

thinking about him, and the smile widened. "Oh, Tykeisha, the guy shouldn't even exist."

"What do you mean?"

She ran a hand down her face before admitting the truth. "He claims he's Triialon."

Tykeisha's mouth dropped open. "You're joking."

"I'm not. And after what I saw him do, I can't say I don't believe him."

There was silence a moment, then, "If that's true, can you think of the implications?" She looked Lise in the eyes again, turning her own musings aside. "Do the admirals believe him?"

"I don't know," Lise answered. "I think Jo'seph does. Jay'salan says he wants to, but I don't think he's been sold yet. Still, he wasn't there. I mean, the man single-handedly shot down a Lordillian battle cruiser. It was incredible!"

"With what?"

"I don't know, some sort of ancient artifact he calls a Prizm. What I do know is that if he hadn't shown up when he did, the *'Return'*, admiral Jo'seph and I would all have been scrapped." A group of people entered the mess hall, making their way to the cook behind the counter. Among them was a young soldier. He had short, light brown hair and dark circles under his eyes, and moved slowly as though from extreme exhaustion. "Gods," Lise said.

"What?" Tykeisha asked as she leaned forward, trying to see what the terminal's camera wasn't showing her.

"Private Gidiek just walked in."

"Who's that?"

"I went to school with him on Sparta before he joined up. He's been pretty quiet every time I've seen him. Lost his whole family back home. I'd heard he was finally cheering up lately because he was seeing this girl in B Company." Lise frowned. "Then I saw the girl's name on the casualty list last week. He looks horrible."

Tykeisha leaned her head on one hand, looking depressed. "How terrible."

Lise felt a sudden sorrow creep over her, unbidden. "Why even get involved during a war like this?" she asked. "All that happens is you lose them."

Tykeisha sat up, her soft features becoming stern. "Oh come on, you already answered that one yourself. For a time, Gidiek was happy. What are we fighting for if we can't even love?" She smiled slyly. "Besides, you're asking me a question like that when your dream man just dropped into your life yesterday. And you haven't even told me about the event with the Lordillians."

The door to the mess opened and Lise looked up to see Hero walk in. "Oh, Gods," she whispered, her eyes becoming saucers. "He's here."

"Who? The Triialon?" Again Tykeisha tried to lean around the edge of the camera's vision. "Ooh, let me see."

The man came into the room like a breath of fresh air, still wearing that black jacket, a white shirt underneath stretched across a muscular chest. His eyes briefly locked with hers, as if he had somehow sensed she was in the room. He also glanced at Gidiek before he picked up a tray and grabbed some food, sitting in a far corner.

Lise couldn't decide if she felt like hiding behind the terminal or sauntering over to his table just to be near him. "The camera doesn't turn that far, Tyk."

"So? Ask him over. I want to see."

"No!"

Three ground soldiers in full armor got up from their seats and made straight for Hero, the lead one looking irritated and arrogant. Lise's mood instantly changed. "Uh oh."

"What is it?"

"I'm not sure yet. Tyk..." The transmission screen went blank, cutting Lise off mid-sentence. "Tykeisha?" She stared at it, confused by the sudden loss of the conversation, until finally a screen popped up saying that the transmission had ended when the signal was lost. Keeping one eye on the three hotheads hovering over Hero's table and one on her screen, she tried to instruct the terminal to re-open the connection to her friend. Lise's first and still occasional post was as a bridge officer, working communications and computer interface, so she knew most of the tricks of the trades. She typed command after command, but still nothing worked.

Meanwhile the lead soldier had leaned over the tall Triialon man's chair. Hero ignored him, eating his fruit while reading a printed report. "Hey. I don't think you belong in here." He leaned directly over Hero, palms on the table, his fingers curling in anger. "I'm talkin' to you, stranger," he seethed. "This room is for infantry only. I don't see a military uniform on you, merc."

Lise got up from her seat, angered by the uncivilized display of bravado. She could see by the man's insignia he was just a second lieutenant, though obviously the leader of the group of soldiers, if only by bullying. She was prepared to take charge before the moment escalated. As it was, all eyes had turned on the confrontation as more people had entered the mess hall.

"I said I'm talkin' to YOU," the soldier yelled, slapping the food from Hero's hand, sending it spinning across the room.

"Lieutenant!" Lise barked the word in rage, sprinting forward.

Before she could even take three steps closer to the table, Hero was up out of his chair. Lise froze in her tracks. The look on the second lieutenant's face was even more surprised. Hero had grabbed the soldier's arm while sweeping his feet out from under him. His chin crashed onto the tabletop, and he would have been spitting teeth if he weren't still being held firmly up by his captured hand. A second man moved to help his friend, swinging an elbow at Hero's face. Without releasing the fallen lieutenant, the Triialon deflected the attacking arm with his free hand and easily kicked the man square in the chest, sending him sprawling.

The lieutenant's hand was being crushed, causing his teeth to grind and his eyes to squeeze shut, but his anger was only doubled by the humiliating stance of being held there on his knees. He lashed out with his free arm, trying to catch Hero off guard while he was facing down the Coalition soldiers. The move didn't even surprise the Triialon, and he caught it easily, then kicked the soldier to the floor. He had one knee on the lieutenant's chest, leaning over him like a stalking animal over prey; all the while he leveled the soldier's own captured sidearm at the other two men, having pulled it from its holster and aiming it before the others could even go for theirs.

"You could use a lesson in manners," Hero growled to them, "as well as honor." The Prizm bracer was pointed right at the face of the stunned second lieutenant, sizzling with sparks of colored energy menacingly. "This is no way to treat a guest in an army built by the Coalition of cultures and races, much less a man who could easily kill you." The light suddenly disappeared from the Prizm crystal, and Hero relaxed the knee from the man's chest, tossing the stolen and now disarmed blaster to his surprised friends before rising. He never took his eyes from them, though, and stared a challenge every moment. They didn't dare move on him again.

"Soldier," Lise said, scolding. "Meet Hero of the Triialon." She smiled slightly, an evil upturn of one side of her lips. "I trust you will tell your superior officer of this altercation and save me the trouble of telling them what an ass you've made of yourself this morning, dishonoring that uniform?" Her smile vanished. "If I should have to tell your CO myself then I'll make certain the consequences are doubled."

She stepped up to Hero's still-guarded form, placing a calming hand on his arm. Looking up into his eyes, she tried to hide her smile. "I believe we're due for a briefing this morning, sir." She inclined her head to the door. "The morning meal's already been ruined, we might as well go." She flashed him a sarcastic grin of white teeth. "Shall we?"

The admirals entered the conference room, sitting down at the table already

occupied by Lise, Zhade, Hero, Osmar and a couple of the ship's commanding officers. Lise tried to push aside conflicting emotions. She had been admitted into a very important circle of people through both skill and chance and she knew from now on her life would never be the same with Hero in it. But there was a sense of foreboding that had begun a half hour before when she had lost contact with Tykeisha, and it now threatened to become overwhelming dread, as she could not raise the Coalition council on any of the COM channels.

Jo'seph seemed to sense her worry. "Still no luck, commander?"

Lise worked diligently at the terminal before her to no avail. "No, sir. No signal whatsoever. It could be any number of anomalies."

"Or Chebonka could have found some of our listening posts," Jay'salan said grimly.

"Very well," Jo'seph ordered. "We should commence this meeting immediately. There's plenty of work to be done today."

The door opened again and a woman of late years walked in. The admirals were the first to stand, but the others in the room quickly followed suit, equally surprised. Lise recognized her as Councilor Bevanne, one of the more respected bureaucrats on the Coalition council. She had white hair that flowed past her shoulders and strong, alert blue eyes. She was in the twilight of her life, but her appearance and demeanor spoke of someone with strong convictions, along with perhaps, years before, style and beauty in her youth.

"Councilor," Jo'seph said with uncertainty. "I was not told you were coming aboard. If I had known you were on the *'Palleal'* when it docked I would have certainly asked you to join us here in person today."

"Your apologies are unnecessary, admiral," she said with a slight accent. Lise realized that the woman wasn't from Sparta but most likely Goleidan or one of its far-flung colony worlds. She smiled at someone in the room, and years melted off of her face. "I came aboard *'Sparta-one'* somewhat incognito. I wanted to see if the rumors were true." She walked around the table in silence, her eyes twinkling, until finally she stood before the towering form of Hero. "And I see now that they are." She gave the tall warrior a close hug, as if he were a friend she had not seen in years. Hero returned the embrace without question.

"You know this man?" Jay'salan asked, somewhat shocked.

Bevanne let go, but did not take her hand from Hero's arm. "I do, admiral Jay'salan. He is Hero, last of the Triialon, and once, long ago, he helped my people." She looked up at him again, shaking her head. "You've barely aged." She laughed a little then. "And look at me, thirty years later."

"You look elegant, as always, Bevanne," Hero answered, and Lise noticed the way he looked at her, almost feeling jealous.

The room was seated again. Jo'seph continued to appear surprised, so Jay'salan was the first to pick the meeting back up. "Well, this changes a few things. But we'll still need to convince the rest of the council of Hero's lineage."

Bevanne's brow rose, and she turned to Hero. "You are staying with us for a time, then?" Hero nodded. "I think, admiral, that it is at least safe to give him some honorary or military rank without yet having the council's blessing. I'll vouch for him until then." She studied Jay'salan's dubious look. "Is that not enough to put at least some of your fears to rest until the council can convene on this matter?"

The senior staff members mumbled in agreement, nodding to each other. Jay'salan had to smile slightly at that. Perhaps he too, Lise thought, wanted to give in to hope. "Very well," he said. "Admiral?"

Jo'seph scratched his chin in contemplation. "A two-bar commander would give him enough clearance for most of what we seem to immediately need Hero's help in. Is that acceptable, if temporary?"

"I accept," Hero said.

"We'll draw up papers later. As it is, I still have several other issues I'd like to address over the next day or so." He ran a hand through the waves of blonde hair on the top of his head. "A lot of this will be revealed to the entire fleet then. Ok, what's the next order of the day?"

An officer had just begun an opening statement regarding ship activities when a priority intercom message lit up Lise's panel. "Admiral," she called, interrupting the proceedings. "The bridge is signaling you."

"Patch it through," Jay'salan said.

"Admiral," came an officer's voice from the terminal before him, "we're getting an intelligence report regarding Nevartza 4."

"We'll be right up."

"I'm afraid this meeting will have to be temporarily adjourned," Jo'seph told the group, standing. He and his fellow Admiral of the Fleet exited the room, and the officers soon followed.

"See you in the mess hall," Zhade told Lise as he left. She had almost forgotten he had been in the meeting and, like her, he was probably wondering why he'd been privileged to be there in the first place. She turned her attention back to Hero, who stood talking to councilor

Bevanne, the woman who had seemingly vindicated him of any doubt as to his background with the admirals in one fell swoop. Lise tried to make it look as though she were busy on her terminal, feeling only slightly guilty about the eavesdropping she was attempting.

"I am surprised to see you here, Bevanne." Hero's hand was again taken by the old woman's. "You look well."

"I too am surprised, though pleased. I should have known you wouldn't change. Damnable Triialon genetics." She leaned in conspiratorially. "Care to share some secrets?"

He smiled at her sadly. "Not really. Your people; they are a part of the Coalition as well?"

"I was an ambassador to Sparta when the Lordillians came. I then decided my place was here. They have since seen fit to place me on their council." She patted his arm like a concerned mother. "And you? How goes the quest?"

Hero looked a little upset at that question. "Chebonka's Artifact will be the first that I have found. It has not gone as well or quickly as I had hoped."

"But not as badly as you feared," she answered.

"No," he shook his head and sighed a little. "No, not as bad as I might have feared." He balled one hand into a fist, looking out into a place neither woman could see. "To finally have found an Artifact of the Twelve, missing for so long, and to soon have it within my grasp." The fist fell. "It is an uplifting, if even more frustrating, feeling."

"Soon you will right the wrongs of the past, my friend." Bevanne took Hero's arm and steered him towards the door. "Come, you can escort me to the bridge. I believe we may be needed there."

Lise waited a moment, lost in thought, before she too left the conference chamber and made her way to her post.

Hero entered the bridge and made his way through the bustle of activity to the command platform. He quickly ascended to the admirals' level, noting the dire expressions on their faces. "I presume the outpost on Nevartza 4 has been destroyed," He said simply. "Do you have any tactically important personnel assigned there?"

The two admirals looked grimly at each other a moment before Jo'seph moved to his computer display, nodding. "Yes, our ships found the installation leveled just a few hours ago. A colonel and his command staff stationed there were on some of our coded intelligence rosters."

"Do the Lordillians take prisoners?"

"Not very often," replied Jo'seph. "But then they rarely know of our outposts. Usually our battles are fought as skirmishes. We hit them to either prevent an invasion or attempt to destroy their garrisons. More often than not it's ship to ship."

"They're looking for something," mused Jay'salan, still watching the monitor read-out. "That, or they're changing tactics concerning us."

"They're already moving aggressively against you," Hero put in. "They failed to drive an inseparable wedge between the Coalition and Moonshau, but still hope to catch you off guard and cripple your forces."

"Oh, you're just full of good news." Jo'seph turned back to his fellow admiral. "If they interrogate the command crew from the outpost they could eventually find the location of the Ship Yards."

The other admiral made his way down to the deck. "Commander Lise, prepare to encode a message to headquarters."

"Set course for the Ship Yards," ordered Jo'seph. "Corporal, ETA of the fifth fleet?"

"Ten more minutes, sir," came the reply.

"The Ship Yards are your secret headquarters," Hero said.

"Yes." Jo'seph looked at him, realization that his new ally had figured out the importance of the matter evident on his face. "The Norpan Ship Yards, a hidden base and our primary ship-building installation hidden within the vast Norpan asteroid belt. The Goleidans had set it up just before they were invaded. Since the union of the Sparta and Goleida refugee fleets, that's where we've been trying to build enough of these new-style battle cruisers to keep up with the Lordillian war machine." He turned back to the display, trying to hide his concern. "If Chebonka finds that we'll be back to square one. If he finds it before we've had a chance to evacuate it, we're as good as dead."

Hero crossed his arms thoughtfully, then shook his head. "Nevertheless, you should consider your security compromised."

"And evacuate our only real asset?"

"Yes."

"At least temporarily," said Jay'salan, stepping back up onto the platform. The hulking man leaned on the railing and looked out across the deck of officers. "Hero's right. If they're on to us we can at least get away with what ships we have before they move in. If they're not, we'll return and set up shop again."

Hero shook his head. "No, you need a more secure position."

Jo'seph looked unconvinced. "And just where would you suggest?"

"You know of a place?" Bevanne had been standing below the command platform, watching displays and officers at work during the scramble of activity. She looked up at Hero with hope in her blue eyes.

"I might."

"Sir, the fifth fleet just emerged from Dimensionalizer jump," an officer called. Hero watched six battered cruisers, their lengthy, boxlike designs marking them as the old-style Sparta ships, come into view off the port side of the bridge. As they floated closer he could see how they were somewhat smaller but only slightly less heavily armed than their more graceful big sisters.

"Good." Jay'salan made his way back down to the deck. "Commander Lise, have you sent that warning to headquarters?"

"Yes, sir," Lise said from her seat at the COM station. "But I'm not certain it has reached them."

"Keep broadcasting, and get me the Captain of the 'Ranger'. The fifth fleet leaves with us in two minutes."

Admiral Jo'seph began sending commands and working controls at various panels around the command station. "It will take about twenty minutes at Dimensionalizer speed to reach Norpan."

"And how long has it been since you lost contact with the outpost closest?" asked Hero.

He checked his intelligence. "Another thirty-five minutes since the last report, but that's not unusual."

"More than enough time, Admiral."

Jo'seph looked up at the man, unsure just what to make of him. "Are you trying to sound as negative as possible?"

"No," Hero met his gaze evenly. "Just trying to prepare you for what might happen."

Jo'seph turned back to his displays, his brow furrowed. "Yeah, I know. It never rains but it pours."

The seven ships crashed through their Dimensionalizer 'windows' and into normal space. An endless stream of bulky asteroids against the star field backlit by an enormous blue nebula greeted them.

"Impressive," stated Hero.

"Yeah, it's a decent vacation spot," Jo'seph said. "Contact HQ," he ordered.

Jay'salan watched the displays come back online, the computers having to realign after the jump. "Scan for activ…"

"Sir!" came the alarmed voice of Lise. "The Shipyards are under attack!"

"Confirmed," came another officer's voice. "Scan indicates heavy weapons fire within the belt."

"Best speed to HQ!" Jay'salan jumped from the command platform's staircase, frantically heading for an officers display. "I don't care whether the Fifth can keep up or not." Looking to the helmsman he asked, "Lieutenant, you feeling lucky?"

"I'll have us there in no time, sir," said the helm. "Asteroids or no."

"Battle stations," Jo'seph ordered. "Scramble fighters. Lise, can you raise the base?"

"Negative. They're being jammed."

'Sparta-one' darted away from the older ships, diving below the first looming rock that hovered in space and curving its flight path around the next batch of debris, making its way deeper into the asteroid field. The graceful craft accelerated further, leaving the other ships behind even as they reached top speed.

The cruiser's battery ports opened, preparing for battle. Hatches slid aside revealing dual lance-like projectors mounted on large generators that swiveled and searched, waiting for targets. Missile bays opened, each one double-lined with rows of twelve reloadable launchers. On the upper

70

sloping hulls that met at the top ridge and bridge decks of the ship, hanger bays on either side began to open. Inside, the fighters prepared for launch, each new *bat* squadron swiveling into position.

Hero watched the tactical portion of the main screen, searching between the giant asteroids for the first sign or signature of the Coalition ships or station. "I could take my fighter out and assist your squadrons," he said to whichever admiral might be listening.

Jo'seph was the one to answer his request, now commanding from the captain's chair. "Negative. I want you here. Besides, we all leave in a hurry and you're out there you won't know where to find us."

"Communications still jammed," said Lise.

"Keep on it, Commander." Jay'salan looked up at those on the command platform, and his voice lowered. "You think they're already there?"

"Probably. If worse comes to worse we'll have to scrap the whole yard and bug out." When Jay'salan looked ready to argue, Jo'seph continued. "The Lordillians can NOT get their hands on Dimensionalizer technology, much less one of our main canons. We're lucky we can outrun them now, considering they always have us outnumbered."

Jay'salan's massive shoulders almost sagged. "How could they have reached the ship yards so fast? I can understand some form of torture to get the location of our base out of the Nevartza commanders, even within minutes of their assumed capture, but still..."

"Then that's exactly *why* they attacked Nevartza," answered Hero. "They would already have had a force massed and ready to attack as soon as their agents on Nevartza had gained coordinates for the Yards. They failed to cut out the heart of the Coalition today," and he nodded towards Jo'seph, "so they went right for the head."

Jo'seph didn't hesitate. "Alright, once the battle is joined, we'll get in close enough to the base to get through the COM jam and order the retreat. From there, it's a scorch policy; anything that can't fly out with us gets destroyed. We burn down as many of those Lordillian bastards as we can, and we get the hell out."

The cruiser soared through a dense patch of asteroids and entered a relative clearing. There a massive installation built into a large, central rocky satellite floated with giant metal arms outstretched where ships both complete and skeletal were docked. Around it's immediate perimeter blazed streaks of light and explosions or fiery red gas and smoldering alloy. Lordillian fighters, small sled-like craft with long gun turrets mounted off of cylindrical main bodies, streaked in by the hundreds, firing on every target within their sites. Main canons from the base and from orbiting Coalition cruisers alike fired outwards, striking the Lordillian fighters' mother ships. Two or three hits from Coalition main-cannon fire would send Lordillian battle cruisers spiraling away into the asteroid field as twisted lumps of metal. Other blasts from Coalition batteries would disintegrate whole squads of the enemy fighters. Interceptors raced out to beat away the oncoming Lordillian fighters that broke through. Yet still they came, their sheer numbers always outweighing Coalition firepower in the end.

"Launch all *bat* fighters!" Jo'seph's commanding voice broke the momentary shock of the bridge crew. Many of them had been staring, stunned to see their secret base under such a heavy ambush. At the admiral's word they all quickly got back to work, relaying commands and manning their stations. "Helm, take us straight in to the command docking ring, maximum speed. Get me a strike team set up, on the double."

"Tactical display," boomed Jay'salan. The large man then turned to his fellow admiral, asking under his breath, "are you thinking of going in for Janise?"

"Yes," answered Jo'seph with resolve.

Hero took his eyes from the tactical display, leaning in to the conversation. "Who is Janise?"

Jay'salan answered. "His thirteen year old daughter." He gripped Jo'seph's arm. "I need you up here, Jo'. We're not out of his yet, nor are we down for good. But we need to keep those bastards from stealing any of our files or tech, and if the base is breached or they land troops in there, I may not be able to get you back out before we blow the place."

Hero's brow creased. "You have charges set to detonate the ship yards and instillation?"

"Yes," said Jo'seph. "But I'm going to get my daughter."

"I'll go."

"But you've never even been in there," Jay'salan stammered with disbelief.

"Show me where she is on the interior schematic. I only need to see it once. If you can get me pictures of her or anyone she may be with as well, all the better."

Jo'seph looked at him, hard eyes locked with Hero's in deep thought over a difficult decision. At last he gave in to the greater responsibility. "All right. But I'm trusting you with far more than I should, both as admiral and otherwise. If you were any other man..."

"Admiral, we're wasting time."

The ship docked with the large base, rock and alloy plating looming into view beside the bridge observation windows. Admiral Jay'salan ordered up direct communications with the base commander as Jo'seph showed Hero the schematics and pictures of the staff and Janise. "You're sure you've got all this?" The Triialon warrior nodded once, checking the rifle he had been issued. "You've got ten minutes from right now. Any longer than that, and we won't be able to get enough distance from the explosion."

Hero made for the exit. "Have Osmar meet me at the airlock." He pulled the sword from the Prizm, the energy discharge flashing over the inside of the elevator like a giant static shock as he stepped inside. The doors to the bridge closed in front of him.

"You called, master?" Osmar caught the plasma blaster Hero tossed to him midair. "What do I need this for?" He pulled the duster aside, revealing his usual over-assortment of weapons. "Not like I don't come prepared."

"Your choice," Hero quipped, working the airlock controls and preparing to enter the Coalition base. "Don't blame me when some cadet shoots you for trespassing on secret military ground."

73

"What, he's gonna be satisfied just because I have a Coalition-issue gun?"

Hero almost smiled. "Well, at least he'll think twice." He tossed a patch to his companion. "Slap that on, too."

"Oh, this looks familiar," Osmar said dryly. The Coalition patch consisted of a central triangular symbol surrounded by three circular satellites of varying size. Hero placed his own patch on his jacket's left sleeve, the right already occupied by the triangle symbol of the Triialon.

The inner hatch opened, and suddenly they were aboard the Norpan Ship Yard central installation. Alarms were sounding loudly and lights flickered each time the base rocked from any exterior explosion. Two soldiers were waiting just outside the door from the airlock, rifles held firmly in alert. They both looked at the emerging figures with masked interest, but quickly returned their gaze to their vigil.

A third figure stepped into view. "Commander Hero?" the lieutenant asked, an eyebrow raised. Hero nodded to him silently. "The admiral asked us to accompany you."

"Then you better keep up, lads," Osmar said. "We're in a hurry."

Hero was already leading them through the maze of halls he had memorized from the schematics. Rifle in left hand, sword in right, his eyes were always watching as he crossed each intersection. His group made fast progress, soon reaching halls closer to the central command. Officers and soldiers were running back and forth, grabbing the last of their things before the mass exodus.

Hero turned another corner and came to a room under guard. The man stationed there stepped aside to allow Hero and his team entrance, obviously alerted to his mission. Inside an attractive woman with an olive complexion was helping a young girl with long blonde hair into a jacket. A set of bags slung over one uniformed shoulder. The woman nodded to the entering strangers and left the room, searching for any final forgotten items.

The girl, no more than thirteen years of age, looked up at the tall interloper. She seemed fixated with this strange man and his battle-scarred jacket and long hair. Hero just looked back down at the girl, his mouth a hard line.

"Hello," she said.

"Hello," he answered.

"I'm Janise. Tykeisha says you're here to take me to my father." The girl picked up a large bag. "I'm ready."

Hero nodded, appreciating the girl's attitude and strength. The woman again entered, apparently ready to depart. "You must be Hero. Already the rumors are flying about you, my tall friend." She gave a sly smile as she sized him up. "I can see they're not all beyond belief."

"Can we go?" Osmar was watching the hall as it began to fill with smoke.

"There are reports of Lordillians entering the base, sir." The lieutenant watched a small wrist mounted screen. "Time is short."

"Lieutenant, you and I in front, the ladies behind us, the private and Osmar cover the rear."

"Aye, My Lord," replied Osmar, his work ethic again in command of his demeanor. The mercenary's lax attitude never affected his performance when serving the man he had sworn to fight beside. Knowing this, Hero continued to ignore Osmar's grin.

"I need a weapon," said Tykeisha.

Osmar handed her a nasty looking blaster, butt-first. "Careful, she kicks."

"Thanks."

"Does the girl know how to handle one?" asked Osmar, referring to Janise.

Tykeisha seemed uncertain, but Janise held out a hand, asking for a weapon. "I can manage small arms."

Osmar looked to Hero, who gave the briefest approving nod. "Very well," said Osmar, and gave her a tiny gun, showing her a few details before sliding it into her hand.

Hero led them into the now smoke-filled hall, followed by the lieutenant, his gun sights up at his right eye scanning the space ahead. Halfway back to the airlock Hero froze, holding up a signal that stopped his little column.

Through the smoke a giant set of figures loomed, tall of structure with wide torsos. The silhouettes were strangely featured, and moved in

75

ways Hero knew was no humanoid life form. These were too precise, too controlled, without life or form. The lieutenant beside him looked bravely down the sights of his rifle, waiting for his target to emerge, but Hero could sense the man's fear, and he spread his own feet and brought his weapons to bear, waiting for the Lordillians to join the battle.

Chapter Five

It has been said in some tomes that this was the Coalition's darkest hour. That the day the Norpan Ship Yards fell was nearly the day it all ended, and that if it had not been for Hero's presence then history would have taken a different course. I agree that Hero's involvement made a difference, but we must not forget Jo'seph and Jay'salan's brilliance when talking of the continued survival of Sparta and ultimately Coalition forces. It was from what came after Norpan that Hero's contribution can be measured.
Coalition and Triialon
- Dr. W. H. Redfield

Out of the haze stepped two Lordillian troopers. They easily stood seven feet tall, with long, ovoid heads beaked at the front - their lifeless, angular eyes lined by black, ominous markings. Great rounded plates of painted, smooth metal parodied the humanoid muscle system. The armored layers, moving and sliding over each other, were capped by jutting, angular elbows and shoulders. Their mechanical gauntlets were equally cruel, with razor-sharp spiked knuckles lining the clawed hands. The Lordillian's waists were thinner than their bulky chests, but the hips fanned back out into powerful, rounded thighs and sharply pointed knees, tapering down to angular calves and strangely pointed feet. Each trooper held a plasma cannon, bulky and with a muzzle like a grenade tube, the weapon being easily a two-handed gun in the hands of most men, yet the Lordillians held them one-handed easily. Even Hero was momentarily impressed with their aspect, knowing full well that the massive shells before him outlined the form of nightmares for simpler men. These machines were fear and death for countless worlds and peoples within the galaxy.

Hero was the first to get a shot off, taking the lead Lordillian square in the chest. The blast punctured a smoking cavity through the trooper's chassis, causing it to slump lifelessly to the deck. The second Lordillian got a off a few rounds before both Hero and the lieutenant took it out as well, Hero firing one-handed while deflecting a shot off of the Triialon sword's flat blade.

Hero looked down at their twisted, smoking ruins. "I had never seen one before," he told the Coalition soldier.

"First blood to you, then, I think," he said with a wry smile. "Count yourself lucky."

The group reached a three-way intersection of corridors when a hail of gunfire suddenly blasted towards them from their path ahead. They hugged the wall, each of them returning fire, their shots disappearing into the smoke and darkness. Flashes of light could be seen illuminating the black smoke ahead like lighting in night clouds, and Hero knew they were hitting some of their targets at least. Still, he still did not know how many enemies they faced. Just then a second volley of shots came from the side hall, and the young private fell, a gaping hole where his gut had been. Janise gave a scream of fear and anger, firing her small blaster at the four Lordillian troops coming from that direction.

"Osmar! Protect the girl!" Hero raised the Triialon sword, the lieutenant paused a moment, looking surprised at the electric energy that ran like a charge from hilt to the tip of the blade. Then Hero rushed into the smoke. "Cover me!"

The warrior slid in under the first Lordillian he detected through the haze. A blast shot over his head, but before the firing trooper could react further, its legs were cut out from beneath it. The Triialon sword sent it crashing to the floor in a shower of sparks. Simultaneously, Hero fired several shots from the Coalition blaster he cradled in his left arm, taking out a second Lordillian. He stood, spinning, the sword arcing around to decapitate another of the metal troopers and chop a fourth in half from shoulder across to opposing hip before either could even react.

By now the sword glowed with power, a blur of blue, green, and red emanating from the ancient weapon. Flashes of sparks sizzled into the air with each stroke. Again and again Hero's blade cut a path through the troopers that rushed to meet him, his gun firing in perfect unison, destroying those that tried to strike at him while his sword was engaged. Moments later he stood alone over the chopped and pitted shells of nine Lordillians, his gaze still searching ahead, his breath barely labored.

The lieutenant closed the distance behind him, followed by Tykeisha, Janise and Osmar. The Coalition officer, himself favoring a bleeding and scorched arm. looked down in disbelief at Hero's handiwork. "Still think it was just luck?" Osmar asked the lieutenant. "We've got the rear covered, My Lord," he called to Hero. "Let's get the hell out of here."

They crouched as they wound the rest of the way to the airlock. When they reached the final hall at last, the sounds of battle again reached their ears. Hero didn't hesitate, rounding the corner and picking off targets with his now-smoking gun. Coalition guards had moved from within the docked cruiser and were engaged with the Lordillian troops, trying to keep the squad from entering the ship. The warrior closed on the group in short order, dropping his blaster to swing two-handed at the remaining Lordillians. He ducked the clawed strike of his final opponent, slicing its weapons arm off at the 'bicep'. Then the crackling blade slammed through the torso of the huge Lordillian. It exploded, its separated halves flying about the hall.

The others were right behind him. With the opposition cleared, they raced past, Tykeisha ushering Janise and Osmar through the airlock first, her watchful eyes making certain no following enemy could cause the girl harm. "Clear!" came the call for OK from the injured lieutenant, and Hero backed through the airlock hatches and aboard the 'Sparta-one', followed by the Coalition guards.

The moment they were all within the ship's entry chamber, Tykeisha struck the controls to close the hatch, practically punching the button. She next hit the communications switch. "Bridge, this is Tykeisha. We're all safely aboard."

"Copy that," came Lise's voice. The airlock tunnel had not even finished retracting back into the ship before the craft lurched back into life, twisting away from the asteroid-based installation.

The cruiser continued to swerve sideways, moving out from the base. Hero watched through the airlock window as the base quickly fell away, analyzing the interlaced man-made structures that were built into the very rock. The others began to crowd around him to watch. Lordillian fighters passed into view, bombarding the complex, followed by Coalition *interceptors* and *bats* trying to shoot them down.

Their ship began a fast, forward acceleration, and the view port now passed docking rings and branching structures that had been blasted to pieces, the half-finished new-style cruisers in flames or being swarmed upon by smaller docking ships as the Lordillians tried to commandeer the more complete ones. They could then see the two forces' battle cruisers locked in battle, the older Coalition ships trying to run interference for the *'Sparta'* to escape. In the distance three more of the giant saucer-like Lordillian cruisers rained blasts from thousands of hull-mounted batteries down onto the central asteroid of the base.

A new-style cruiser, trailing a debris field as it lurched away from the base, came into range, so the enemy fleet fired on it instead. "It's the *'Return'*," said Tykeisha solemnly, watching as explosions rocked its graceful form. The huge main cannon, a gaping port on the front of the ship's body and beneath the outstretched neck of the vessel, began to glow in preparation to fire. A bolt of light and energy erupted from the main cannon's port, the giant beam striking the two farthest Lordillian ships. One blistered and exploded, disintegrating into nothing, while the other took the hit mid-ship, cracking it in two. Then there was a collective gasp in the room as the smoking *'Return'* slammed sideways into the closest remaining enemy cruiser. Both ships exploded, the wreckage incinerating in space.

The room fell silent as they all watched the carnage, and Hero could hear the young girl, Janise, weeping quietly.

Suddenly there was a voice full of hope from the back of the room. "Yeah, go, go!" Another new-style ship sped past the remains of the battle they had just witnessed, its forward Dimensionalizer emitters opening its own window into hyperspace and then disappearing from their sight as it crashed through the gate, the impassioned cheering-on of the lieutenant calling after the escaping ship. "Go, baby!" The *'Return'* had bought their freedom.

More ships could be seen escaping from normal space around the asteroid field, while others could be seen floating lifelessly through the metal-strewn void, many of them the hulks of old-style Coalition cruisers. Hero again returned his attention to the shipyards. Lordillian cruisers had moved in to help usurp the incomplete ships docked there. The fighters on both sides seemed to have all been destroyed or returned to their mother ships. For a moment it seemed as if they would get away with stealing Coalition technology in the form of its newest cruisers, but then the central rock exploded at last. A massive blast ruptured the base in half, and the energy wave shattered the structure, washing out to swallow the construction and docking pylons. It carried out as a rippling ring of red and white fiery energy, encompassing everything in its path and turning the entire shipyard and all of the craft there, enemy or not, to ash. As the wave reached out, rushing through ships and asteroids alike without prejudice, it looked as though it would catch up with the 'Sparta' before it could spirit itself away. But Hero could already feel the engines deep within the vessel again come to life, and instantly they were slipping through a tunnel of light and out of normal space, escaping from their own certain doom.

There was a sigh, and everyone around him finally relaxed, so many of them seeming to have been holding their breath. Hero at last turned away from the view port. Osmar was beginning to follow him out when a hand on Hero's shoulder stopped them. It was the girl, Janise, wiping tears from her cheeks with her sleeve, looking up at him and trying to muster a smile.

"Thank you," she said. She held out her hand to shake his. He took it, but instead held it as he bowed to her. He released her grip quickly and turned, unable to look into those eyes again.

"Secure from battle stations but keep the crew on watch until we're safely at our destination," ordered admiral Jo'seph. He ran his hands over his tired face, sitting back in the captain's chair and looking to Jay'salan, who had the same grim visage. They both turned as Hero and Osmar came from the hatch and onto the bridge. Jo'seph stood, wanting to shake the hand of the man who had helped save his daughter. Again he discovered the stranger's grip entirely too strong to hold for any prolonged time. "Thank you," he said genuinely. "I understand you ran into some opposition on the way. Were it not for you…"

"I simply insured that your daughter was safe, admiral." He said it plainly and without false modesty, and once more Jo'seph found himself intrigued by this man claiming to be of a race lost to the myths of the past. He was forced to smile. "Your men fight and die well, as warriors should. I'm glad she had the chance to come back to you safely."

"All the same, the whole day's been pretty touch and go. I'm grateful for your presence, no matter what." He nearly slumped back into the Captain's chair. "I just don't know what to do next."

Hero seemed thoughtful for a moment. "I may have someplace you can go next. A safe place where the entire Coalition can go and rebuild, if we can get everyone there and if... well, if the facility is stile viable."

"Facility?"

"Hang on a minute," broke in Jay'salan angrily, his nerves at an obvious end from the day's events. "I'm not about to make the entire Coalition one big target again anytime soon, I don't care what you say or what you've done for us thus far. It's tactically stupid!"

"Speak not of My Lord so!" Osmar practically had a weapon drawn; he was bitterly offended, ready to defend his master and instantly in Jay'salan's face.

Jo'seph held up his hands, stopping all parties, including the security team that had begun to move towards the command platform. "Hold it, gentlemen, please!" He sighed, sitting down again and forcing a smile as he scratched his bearded cheek. "I think that's enough excitement for one day, hm? Hero, Jay'salan, we can discuss all of this tomorrow, after a decent night's sleep. Two attempts on my life and the destruction of our shipyards are just about all the events I'd like to handle his week."

"I just hope the board members on the Coalition Council will be as easily placated," said Jay'salan, calming himself. "I know admiral Jo'seph would like to keep you around the high ranks for further assistance, Hero, but the senators who help run this Coalition may need convincing, despite Bevanne. Both as to your background as well as any plans that may or may not be best for our forces."

"Indeed?" asked Osmar, his mustache bristling with barely-checked anger.

"History is forged in this fire we call battle," Hero told them, "and yet I remain legend." He was unfazed by the high emotions surrounding him, but had said it with a power that communicated both resolve and perhaps even slight anger at the continued issue concerning his good faith.

83

Jo'seph nodded approvingly, trying to tell him that he understood something of his feelings.

Jay'salan sighed, his great shoulders heaving with exhaustion. "Still, I guess that's neither here nor there. We won't be rendezvousing with any of our forces for at least a day."

"This one's certainly been long enough already," replied Jo'seph. "Thank you both again. I suggest you turn in. Tomorrow promises to be equally lengthy."

The strange duo left, and Jo'seph and Jay'salan found themselves alone on the bridge save for the night crew. "Perhaps we should prepare some sort of speech for the fleet," Jay'salan said at last to break the silence.

"Yeah, but not until we've done damage control. We need to take stock and see what's left, check up on intelligence reports, and so on. Come on," he said, standing, "We've still got work to do." Jo'seph followed his friend down to an open command terminal, realizing with tired apprehension that it was going to be a long night.

Svea's ship came to land in the middle of Kordula city, landing on one of the many platforms that jutted out from the sides of the towers central to the capitol. The city had looked magnificent from the air, and now that she was departing her small craft and stepping upon the landing area of the very city her brother had been telling her of her entire life, she could barely manage her excitement. Still, she kept up appearances, smiling only slightly and adjusting her gown to show the greatest amount of cleavage available. She brushed a stray wisp of her brown hair back over her naked shoulder, the bulk it up in a beautiful arrangement fit for the heiress of the Seethlings.

A strange guard greeted her at the door leading from the platform to the inside of the building. It was the height of a man but covered from the neck down in thick robes. The head was masked in a large helm of silver or chrome, its surface cut into the angular relief sculpture of a horse-like head, capped with glowing slit eyes. "Svea Magdalene of the Seethlings," it bowed as it spoke her name, the deep voice sounding mechanical from within the odd helmet. "I am the servant of the immortal Gods, and I bid you welcome to the great citadel of Kordula"

"It is an honor," she replied, bowing in return.

"If you will follow me this way to the reception halls, I can then show you to your apartments."

"Are the Gods at court?" Svea followed the servant within, noting the small robots that were beginning to unload her luggage from her craft. She crossed the threshold into the bright interior of the tower, instantly awed and feeling at home.

"They are within the inner sanctum," it answered. "Some may join the court later this evening."

They reached a teleport dais and Svea felt a moment of dizziness as their surroundings changed to a different floor or room within the building. The room and wide halls that adjoined were awash in people and strange beings of every height, color, and shape. Many were lined up before a set of long counters being managed by small troll-like creatures of ill temperament. The servant led Svea behind these counters to private rooms for reception of VIPs, nearly every eye following her body as it disappeared into the offices beyond.

Svea was introduced to a thin, elegant looking being named Goursh. His chamber consisted of a fine wooden desk, advanced looking computer terminals and large, beautifully framed paintings. One glance at these confirmed to her that the artwork was genuine, and probably worth a fortune.

"Goursh will help you get settled in for your stay, and future visits, on Kordula," the strange servant said. "Currency exchanges, maps, personnel, gossip, locales, he is knowledgeable of it all. He shall also have someone take you to your apartments when you are ready. I hope you enjoy your stay on Kordula, Svea."

"Thank you, I'm sure I will," she told the servant. Svea crossed her legs as she sat at Goursh's beckoning. He handed her a folder full of documents and pamphlets, smiling cordially.

"Now, Madame Svea. I understand you are to be joining the ranks at court."

"That would be excellent," she beamed.

"I hope you find it to your liking, or at the very least to your use." Goursh sat, folding his long hands delicately. "Most do, but many newcomers also do not know exactly what to expect, especially as there are two courts that we speak of here in Kordula proper."

Svea's smile faded a little. "Two?"

"Yes. First there's the Court of the Gods, also called the Inner Sanctum. None save those of their race may enter this court. Then there is the Court of Kordula, which you have been invited to join. It consists of VIPs only from various worlds and trades or their representatives, all conglomerating, meeting, speaking, or trading within the Great Hall. There is often entertainment as well as business, and sometimes one or more of the Gods themselves may preside, but usually it is an open forum with the occasional decree handed down by one of the Servants such as the one you just met." He pointed to the pamphlet. "All rules, codes, honors, and protocols are within those documents."

Goursh briefly went over some of the finer points of court politics with Svea and then stood, shaking her hand. "Do you have any questions or is there anything else I can do for you?"

"No. You've been most enlightening," she answered coolly.

"Very well." He pressed a button on the desktop. "A servant will show you to your quarters, Madame." A beautiful girl, scantily dressed in fine silks, stepped in, waiting for Svea to follow. "I hope you enjoy your time here on Kordula," Goursh said with a grin.

Svea looked the servant up and down, then turned her eyes back to the shifty, if formal, Goursh. "Thank you," she said, smiling, "I think that this will all suit me just splendidly."

She followed the swaying hips of the obviously well-trained girl out of the office and down several halls and corridors, eventually arriving at a set of double doors. "These are your permanent apartments, my lady," said the young woman. She opened the doors and handed Svea the key. "They shall be here for you whenever you visit Kordula. Simply touch the servitor panels by the door for your needs." She began showing Svea around the very large, opulent space. With a graceful wave of her hand the girl introduced her to the enormous living room, furnished with alien plants on marble pillars, divans topped by velvety cushions, and chairs and couches made from the most expensive materials, all matching in their light colors and intricate prints.

Svea stopped the servant in the middle of her speech. "What is your name, girl?"

"Brithany, my lady," she answered cordially.

"Brithany," Svea repeated. "That's sweet. Tell me, Brithany, I'm still a little uncertain about some of my freedoms and privileges here as a member of the court. I'm told these apartments are mine for all of my future stays, but can I have it refurnished?" She motioned to some of the furniture and wall hangings around them. "All of this is a bit... bright for my liking."

Brithany's head cocked to the side a little and she clasped her hands behind the small of her back. "The servants and luxuries are here for you, my lady. You have but to ask Goursh and arrange whatever you want, whenever you want."

"Such a delightful mix of business and pleasure," Svea said, placing her hand on the servant's naked shoulder. "And what if I wish to have something right now?" she asked, looking deep into Brithany's eyes.

The girl was entranced for a moment, but she was able to pull her gaze away and, blinking, relieve herself of Svea's wandering hand by walking back towards the door and the servitor panels. "If I understand your meaning, lady, then there are always pleasure servants available for the asking. I'm afraid my duties require me to be elsewhere during the next few hours..." She was trying to sound as professional as possible still, but Svea could hear the waver in the girl's voice. She had unsettled something in their brief contact. Perhaps Brithany had never been with another woman before.

How sweet, Svea thought with an evil smile.

She sauntered over to the girl, slowly and purposefully, locking eyes with Brithany, the stare catching her mid-speech and causing her to leave her sentence trailing. Brithany was caught before she even had a chance for escape, staring back in wide-eyed panic yet unable to move or say anything. When Svea touched the girl again, her powers raced along Brithany's arm like a bolt of blue lightening, and she gasped aloud.

"Brithany, my dear," Svea said with a breathy voice, bringing her face very close to the servant girl's. "You have nothing to fear. Simply do as I say, and I shall be pleased." The words seemed to calm to nearly-hypnotized Brithany. The rapid rise and fall of her shapely breasts slowed, and her eyes began to close. "Now, do you really have to be somewhere so quickly, child?"

"No," Brithany answered slowly, as if in a daze. "I am not expected for at least another hour."

Svea smiled. "Good," she said, taking the servant's arm and leading her away from the door. "I believe you were about to show me the bedchamber."

"Yes," Brithany said, opening the double-doors to the master bedroom of the large apartment.

"And don't worry," Svea told the now-shaking girl as she put her arms around her neck. "If you don't like it, we can always find a nice young nobleman to help entertain us as well."

The winds blew dust and debris through the giant crack in the pyramid's wall. In the distance, the defense alarms finally stopped, but Hero barely noticed. Nothing mattered except the dying girl in his arms, her life's blood running like a crimson ribbon from the gashing wound that defiled her once perfect skin. He looked down at his princess, but she could no longer look at him. Her body had stopped moving, her last words spoken with her last breaths, her dark hair falling over a limp, lifeless arm. A sorrow unlike anything before or since overtook Hero at that moment. Nothing, not the death of friends or family alike, ever before had struck him like this moment, and his mind dreamt of it still, all these years later.

Hero turned his thoughts away from that tragic moment as one might turn a page, but to little avail, for the future was a sea of battle and carnage, his life lost to fruitless pursuits, his heart lost within the war he surrounded himself in. He emerged victorious from that war - victorious and alone. He turned away again, looking through the view port of his Triialon ship into the endless darkness of space. The black waste trailed away and became the flowing dark ringlets of black hair. Hero's eyes followed the flashing highlights within to the beautiful face the raven curls framed. The face was that of Lise, that perfect vision of a woman from the Coalition whose body was wrapped in the light brown cloak of a Triialon soldier. Her eyes stared into his own, and he had to look away, only to find his own gaze trailing down the barely-concealed curves of Lise's amazing body. Hero pulled his eyes from the sight, again trying to turn away.

The chime for the door rang just after Hero awoke from the dream. "I'll get it," Osmar slurred, and Hero turned to find him sitting on a chair by the desk, the bottle in his hands mostly empty. The mercenary got up and stumbled towards the door as Hero sat up in his bunk, trying to find the clock in the dimness of the room. He had barely been asleep an hour.

The hatch slid open, Osmar leaning drunkenly against the frame as he swept his arm wide in a fairly sarcastic half-bow. Jo'seph and Lise were in the corridor outside, and Hero stood up, grabbing a shirt to drape over the Prizm he always wore on his right arm.

"Greetings, admiral. Commander. You seek an audience with His Regal-ness?" Osmar turned on his heel and walked the few steps back to his seat, slumping back into the desk chair and taking another drink. "He's right there," he slurred as the bottle came away from his lips, his wavering finger pointing to Hero.

"I apologize if I am interrupting," Jo'seph said as he entered. Lise stood in the doorway, letting her gaze pass briefly down Hero's muscular chest.

Hero shook his head to clear it. "Not at all, admiral. Sleep is rarely undisturbed for me, and Osmar is a titanic drinker, so the evening is a fairly common one on that note." He ran a hand through his long hair before pulling it back to tie it and beginning to button up his shirt. "What can I do for you?"

Jo'seph looked at Lise a moment, who took the hint to excuse herself. "If you'll pardon me, sirs. It has been a long day and there's a bed with my name on it."

"Goodnight, commander," Hero said, studying her for a moment before she turned and left. The others echoed the farewell as the door shut.

Jo'seph motioned to another seat. "May I?" Hero indicated in the positive, and the man sat, resting his elbows on his knees. He looked tired and withdrawn, sitting there and formulating his thoughts after what might have been some of the longest days of his life. He glanced at Hero before looking at Osmar. "I think I'll take that drink now, if you don't mind."

Osmar's eyebrows shot up his bald plate. "Well, I *am* impressed, admiral," he said, genuinely surprised. He set his nearly finished bottle down on the desk and reached behind him to a crate full of the bottles and pulled one out, opening it. He grabbed the first, nearly empty bottle and handed it to Jo'seph as he began to drink greedily from the new one.

The admiral was so lost in thought that he barely noticed the switch, or was simply too tired to care. Hero, meanwhile, had placed a glass on the desk for Jo'seph to use. "Thank you," he said quietly, and took a drink. He closed his tired eyes and let the contents of the glass warm in his mouth before he finally swallowed the drink. He smiled a little afterwards, saying only, "at least Osmar has good taste in alcohol."

Hero frowned slightly, motioning to Osmar to pass him a drink, who offered the new bottle with hesitance and a great pout. Hero took his own swig before sitting on the lower bunk and handing it back. "Jo'seph," he said, breaking the admiral out of his reverie. "Why did you come here tonight?"

"Jay'salan and I have been receiving reports over the last two hours. We lost the base and twenty battle cruisers, including those at Norpan." He stared into the drink and sighed. "We don't think the Lordillians escaped with any of our technology or files, and the bulk of the fleet remains, but we don't think the Coalition council survived the attack. We know of one or two members beside Bevanne who are aboard other ships, but other than that, the people on this vessel are among the only surviving governing members of the Coalition."

Jo'seph sat back, wiping his face with his free hand. "You mentioned a place," he said finally. "A place where the Coalition might be safe." He leaned forward again, looking resolutely into Hero's gray eyes. "If you truly believe in this place and can show it to me, then now is the time."

Hero nodded. "Very well. We shall go tomorrow."

"What is this place?" The admiral shrugged. "Where are you taking us?"

"A civilization older than Triialon. Perhaps older than Kordula. A planet long since abandoned and forgotten."

Jo'seph was intrigued but dubious. "And no one's discovered it in two thousand years except you?"

"There is a city," Hero paused, amending, "a base, on that world that is still under power - power from the very core of the planet. It still projects a dampening field that creates false images of a gas giant on scanners. It has been ignored all this time for that reason."

"Distance?"

"Starting out tomorrow morning, your Dimensionalizer engines would have no trouble getting us there within the day. Once secure it would be a perfect fall-back site. From there you should be able to launch tactical offenses with little problem."

"And if we're followed?" Jo'seph asked. "If the Lordillians learn of this new base?"

Hero sat back, thoughtful. "This citadel, once we get it completely operational, will be safer than you can imagine. But until we can get it up and running, yes, you are in danger of open attack."

"Then we go in secret," Osmar put in. The other two men looked at him and, finding himself surprisingly part of the conversation, the mercenary continued. "We take the flyer, Hero's ship, with a team of soldiers and engineers and set up the base before anyone else knows where it is." Osmar sat there looking around him, as if searching for any further thoughts to complete the idea, and instead shrugged and took another drink. "And there you are."

Jo'seph scratched his beard and finally relented. "It's a good idea. A strike team, whatever scientists you think we'll need, engineers, and you to show us around. Can your ship get us there?"

"It is equipped with the equivalent of Star-Leap generators, but if you're men could fit it with Dimensionalizer engines our troubles would be lessened."

"Nothing that small has been officially designed with a Dimensionalizer," Jo'seph said, and then smiled wryly. "But of course a prototype has been created, secretly mated to a *bat* fighter." He leaned over to a COM panel on the desk. "Bridge, this is admiral Jo'seph."

"*Bridge here.*"

"Contact the captain of the *'Ranger'* and tell them to rendezvous with us in one hour. Have her top engineers at our disposal for a night job."

"*Yes, sir.*"

Jo'seph switched off the intercom. "Hopefully they'll be able to attach the engine to your ship. If not, we proceed anyway."

"If your men have any serious trouble fitting it to my ship, have them wake me," Hero said. "I might be able to help."

"Very well. As soon as the engine's attached, we leave. There will be a moment tomorrow morning when I make a speech to the fleet, assemble our team and then we go." He stood, invigorated. "If this base is all you say it is I'll shake your hand then. In the meantime, can I expect you to awake and report for duty on the first shift?" He said it with a smile.

"Of course," Hero answered, standing.

"Then I bid you goodnight, gentlemen. And thank you." Jo'seph turned to leave, nodding to Osmar's wave of his bottle and hurrying out of the room.

When the admiral was gone, Hero turned back to his bunk and swung himself up into it. "I hope you know what you're doing, My Lord," Osmar said in a sobering tone.

"If the Coalition survives the war with the Lordillians, then I shall worry about the power I have given them. Until then, it would appear it is anyone's game."

Chapter Six

'Remember the day when they took what you cared
for and destroyed it, took those you love from you.
Never forget those who have been lost. That rage will
see you vengeance. That anger will see you to justice.'
-Excerpt from the book of Triialon

Lise hugged Tykeisha. The woman had been at her quarters' doors just as Lise was about to leave for her usual early morning in the mess hall. "I'm glad you're OK," Lise said, not yet letting go of her friend.

Tykeisha simply nodded, trying to hold back tears as she smiled weakly. "I don't know how many people from the bridge decks actually made it out of there," she finally said. "I was assigned to getting the admiral's daughter Janise out, but I don't know if we'd have made it without your new friend. He's pretty incredible." She wiped the tears away, smiling. "Made me a believer." They both laughed at that.

Lise blushed a little, thinking of the night before. "Yeah, he's even better looking with his shirt off."

Tykeisha's eyes grew wide and she gasped. "Lise! You're joking!"

"No, no, nothing like that," she said, waving her friend's obvious thoughts away. Then she grinned. "I was with Jo'seph when he stopped by Hero's quarters last night and I think we woke him." Her smiled widened. "He's gorgeous."

"You're the Admiral of the Fleet's new best friend and you've got your eye on the unattainable stranger," Tykeisha said, shaking her head.

Lise frowned. "I know. That's what I'm worried about. And the last thing I should do is make it personal, but I just can't get my mind off of him." She sighed theatrically, brushing her hair away from her face. "I just hope its curiosity more than infatuation."

"Oh why? I say you should go for it." She elbowed her friend, sending Lise off balance a little as she looked away in frustration. "Come on, I'll join you in the cafeteria before I report to the bridge. You can tell me about every rippling muscle you saw."

"You're no help," Lise said, only half seriously, and locked her quarters' door behind them as they made their way to the mess hall.

Lise entered the conference room, once again finding the admirals, Osmar and Bevanne all sitting at the table. There was a camera pointed at Jo'seph's seat, and Hero was standing next to him, talking. When the admiral saw her, he motioned for her to stand near him.

"I'm giving a speech in a few minutes to the fleet," he told her, standing. "I'd like you and Hero to stand right over here. At the end of the show, I'll be telling of some of the recent deeds at which point you'll be awarded the Sparta Star medal." Lise obviously looked very surprised at that, and Jo'seph grinned. "I hope you don't mind. I could always give it to someone else, but then I've already promoted private Zhade to sub lieutenant."

Lise smiled and laughed a little, shaking her head. "No. No, sir, I think I'm not above accepting a medal from the Admiral of the Fleet."

"That's what I like to hear; commendations going right to my officers' heads," he laughed. "Now, if you please," he said, motioning to a spot just off-camera.

"Sir!" Lise snapped to attention.

Jo'seph sat back down, his eyes going over the speech papers once more.

"Sir, we're ready when you are," said the camera technician. Jo'seph nodded.

Hero came to stand next to Lise. He was in that ever-present jacket of his, but he held the sword with the Triialon symbol emblazoned on its golden hilt, cradling it easily in one mighty arm. She smiled to him, and he inclined his head in return, serious as always. Her curiosity and the need to speak to him got the better of her defenses, and she motioned towards the sword. "What is it called?" Hero only raised an eyebrow at her. "It must have a name," she concluded, grinning. "All great swords have names. You said Chebonka's blade was called '*Justice*', so..." She let the redundant question trail, waiting for him to open up.

"In the common tongue it would be called '*Strength*', the Sword of Kings," he answered at last, just loud enough for her to hear him. "Few have asked. Perhaps I had forgotten until you did."

"But the lost Artifacts," Lise said, nearly whispering, "you remember their names every day, don't you?" She didn't know how she knew it, but she did, even before he answered. He was looking deep into her eyes and had to pull her own away before she drowned in them. Or perhaps before he drowned in hers.

"Yes," he said grimly, "every day."

"Quiet everyone, please," said the technician. "Thank you."

The room fell silent, and Lise watched as Jo'seph stared into the camera, awaiting his cue. She looked for admiral Jay'salan and found him standing in a nearby corner, holding a metal box she assumed had her medal within it, and she found herself suddenly nervous. What was going on? What would this speech, directed at every remaining Coalition ship and outpost, address and do for its people? She was sure Hero would be formally introduced at last, and that made her glad, and she knew awarding her publicly was another intended morale boost, but it still put her on the spot in a way that made her a little more uncomfortable than she had imagined up until now.

"Good morning," Jo'seph began. "Just hours ago an attack took place that rocked the very foundations that this Galactic Coalition is built upon. The Lordillian fleets attacked the Norpan Shipyards and our secret base there, hoping to destroy the Coalition and steal our Dimensionalizer technology and drives, as well as our other advanced sciences. Admiral Jay'salan and I instead opted to detonate the Base's built-in charges and explode the shipyards before any materials that might aid the Lordillian army could be stolen. The attack was nearly a complete surprise and would have been a success if not for the quick thoughts and actions of our men and women, many of which are not with us today. Because of those actions, the Lordillians failed to appropriate any of our ships or technology. But the cost was high. A mass exodus was once again needed, and the vessels that could escape with as many personnel as possible did, or died trying. While the people of this army are no strangers to the need of escaping the terrible power that is the Lordillian horde, it is never any easier. We are still trying to ascertain the names of all who have fallen at Norpan, but the truth remains as bright as the shining example so many shone forth yesterday. And that truth is that the Lordillians scored no victory at the Norpan asteroid field, unless we let it destroy the Coalition.

"We stand on the very edge of infinity, ready to emerge victorious over the evil that has enslaved so much of what we love, or fall into oblivion, forever damning the very ideals we hold dear to be crushed under the metal boots of the Lordillian menace. The deaths of many of the Council members aboard the cruiser *'Vigilant'*, destroyed at Norpan before they could affect a Dimensionalizer jump, leaves a gap at the very summit of our hierarchy. The list of tragedies and triumphs within the last forty-eight hours would take me the day to recount. But a unique possibility is within our grasp. Should we win the day, and each day thereafter, then the future is ours. Should we fail, then it is not simply the Coalition that dies, but the whole universe within Chebonka's reach that will suffer for the next one thousand years. That future can be protected by the Coalition and all it stands for. The Coalition came together and exists because of this war. The conflict we have banded together to fight has made us a power this galaxy has not seen since the time of the Triialon. The ideals and symbols that so much of what this Coalition stands for is based on the legendary truths once defended by the Triialon. In their time, just as in ours, no one else had the power to do as they did and enforce what was good and righteous.

"For if there is one man alive today to remind us of the power and responsibility we wield and that we should fight to carry on beyond the confines of this war, then it is the man at my side today. Hero of the Triialon lived up to his namesake on the planet Moonshau and saved my life. He has since agreed to join us for a time and help us defeat this monstrous adversary. He has been granted an honorary rank and title that places him among the military and civilian leaders within the council of the Coalition, for already his council has proven invaluable and his power in battle unquestionable. He is the last warrior of his kind, and I believe in him, for he could not have come at a more needed hour."

"Also I have the pleasure of decorating one of my bridge officers today, commander Lise Decarva. She too saved my life on Moonshau, performing as an exemplary officer and soldier by defending her admiral and destroying an enemy agent. For those actions and more I award her the Spartan Star."

Admiral Jay'salan stepped forward and handed her the open box with the gleaming medal inside. Lise took it, unable to suppress her grin.

"I know many of you lost your home or loved ones yesterday," Jo'seph continued, "and we here feel your pain, for they were our friends and family as well, just as Norpan was also our home. And I promise you now, not only shall we work quickly towards finding a new and secure home for us all, but also I will not rest until the Lordillians have paid for their transgressions. If we all continue to work together, then we can do more than this; we can stop the Lordillians utterly and bring Chebonka to the justice that is waiting for him. The choice is ours. Thank you all, and may truth prevail."

There was a brief moment of silence, and then the camera technician gave the signal that the broadcast was over. The room erupted in applause, and Jay'salan shook his fellow admiral's hand, smiling. Lise felt a wave of emotion threaten to crash over and spill onto her blushing cheeks, so she clapped even harder and hollered out encouragement, her voice, hoarse with feeling, was drowned out by the noise of the room. Even Hero applauded.

The order was given to clear the room, and all non-essential persons quickly exited. "Congratulations, Commander," Hero told her, giving her his usual curt nod, this time with a hint of smile.

"Thank you," Lise said. Not knowing what else to say, she made to leave. "If you'll excuse me, I have to report to the bridge."

"Stay," Hero replied. With his eyes he motioned towards the admirals. "I think you will be needed here."

Lise turned, confused as to what might be going on next. She saw Jo'seph and Bevanne move to join Hero and herself by the door. "Have you told her?" Jo'seph asked.

"No, I was unaware you had made a decision." Hero's arms were crossed, his eyes studying the shorter admiral.

Jo'seph smiled. "I figured you would want her along, and her team would be good for this mission."

"Anyone going to let me in on the secret story we're all sharing?" Lise asked.

If Jo'seph was at all taken aback by the direct question, he barely showed it, instead simply broadening his grin. "We're going on a little trip. Top secret, just you, me, Hero, Osmar, your team, and a group of engineers and scientists, all aboard Hero's ship." He turned to Hero. "You were able to fit the Dimensionalizer to your ship?"

"It took a fair amount of adaptation, and more of my night than I would have liked, but we were able to finish the job, admiral. I think, if you haven't already assigned them, you should bring along at least one of the men who worked with me last night. We will be dealing with alien technology, and they did good work."

"Alien technology?" Lise's curiosity would no longer keep silent. "Sir, just where are we going?"

Hero was the one to answer. "A new home, we hope, for the Coalition and its people, for as long as they need it."

Chebonka entered the interrogation chamber, flanked by two Lordillian troopers. In the center of the room lay a man, beaten and bleeding, his Coalition uniform torn to shreds. The crumpled figure made no attempt to rise or escape through the open door, but instead whimpered and coughed up blood and phlegm when one of the troopers kicked him over onto his back.

"Have you nothing more to say in your defense, commodore?" Chebonka stood unmoving over the defeated officer. "Will you swear allegiance to the Lordillians and their rightful place as overlords, or will you die a traitor to both myself and your own race. You've already sold them out and lead to their deaths."

The dying man simply laughed, then coughed violently as his body was wracked by spasms. "If that were completely true, I would be dead already," he said, smiling.

"Tell me of their other outposts, where they might run, and I will make you immortal."

"You mean make me a slave, my mind trapped in Lordillian armor."

"You have nothing more?"

"Even if I did, I wouldn't be able to tell you much. I'm dying." Again the commodore's body wheezed, and he had to wipe the blood from his bruised chin with his good arm. "At least I will die knowing that the Coalition lives."

Chebonka gave a command to one of the troops via a silent electronic communication and a metal arm seized the Coalition officer from Nevartza 4. The Lordillian dropped to one knee, stabbing the man in the shoulder with the metal spiked ending of a paralysis device. The commodore went rigid, his eyes wide from shock and his teeth clenched in pain. "Take him to the laboratory, drain his mind of any further knowledge before he expires. If the process does not kill him, make certain he is terminated... after."

The Lordillian creator and leader could not purge himself of the emotional frustration that he had been afflicted with since he had intercepted the speech transmission of admiral Jo'seph. He was never able to fully remove that center of the mind from any of the humanoids he had converted to Lordillian cyborgs either, but the difference was always the slave circuit each of them had. Occasionally a lack of complete logic in his cyborg generals gave them an advantage in warfare, but Chebonka still despised the irrational welling of feelings that he carried within him. In many ways he had made the Lordillian machines into the image he wished for himself. It was an image he would never attain while still retaining the individuality that allowed him the hunger for power; to make the rest of creation into his ideal.

Chebonka entered his throne room, finding several of his generals waiting for him, kneeling before his throne. He sat before giving them leave to report. When each completed their task, he dismissed them all, reiterating his instructions of finding the remaining Coalition ships and destroying them. But Chebonka knew that the Spartan admirals would have dispersed their fleets in order to protect themselves. Hiding throughout the known systems like terrorist cells waiting to bite back, continuing to pester him like the faulty, fleshy mistakes of the universe they were.

His thoughts turned again to the Triialon warrior who had joined the Coalition. He had seen the man, Hero, again in the transmission, holding the coveted Triialon Artifact in his hands. To capture that man and drain away his secrets and power would be the culmination of greatness. Again the urge to simply hold his own weapon from that ancient and nearly lost technology surged through Chebonka, and he left the throne room for his own private chambers.

In the darkness he stared at the long, gleaming blade, its silence mocking him, yet its influence was still so tangible. As soon as he had entered the room, he could feel its call. Still, all these years since it had come into his possession, it remained a mystery to him. He was no longer fearful of releasing the Triialon artifact's power; he had lost that fear when he had donned his new metal body. But whatever means it took to ignite the energy within the sword had never revealed itself. No obvious buttons or catches had worked, and simple strength of will had no apparent effect. Yet still it called out to him with its baleful influence, begging to be set free.

Chebonka held the sword in his hands, lost in contemplation, waiting for the answer to simply come to him. Instead he finally slammed the sword's blade down into the metal casing that held it next to his charging throne. The thrill of rage surged through every synthetic fiber of his being and he had to stop himself from debasing himself in an act of blind anger and destruction. He turned instead to a communications port, activating a holographic display.

A Lordillian general appeared on the display, the markings on his armor and the prosthetic arms the only indication that this otherwise humanoid man was part of Chebonka's army, one his few such transitional cyborgs. "My lord Chebonka," the general said, bowing slightly.

"Deploy your squad of Battle Cruisers, general. Lay waste to Sagev 3. Its inhabitants, its moons, all life. Resistance should be minimal, but leave enough ships to defend against any Coalition raids."

"You are hoping to draw them out?" the general asked knowingly.

"Correct," Chebonka answered. "Keep me appraised of the campaign, but notify me the moment any Coalition vessels are sighted."

"Do I engage the Coalition should they move against us?"

Chebonka nodded. "Take no prisoners."

"My Lord."

The display faded, and Chebonka sat on the throne, letting its power flow into him and the influx of information from the computer net calm his decidedly overactive emotional responses

"Must so many of them accompany us, Lord?" Osmar practically whined it like a bored child.

Hero stood next to his companion, his arms crossed as he watched the busy Coalition crews prepare his ship and its crew for their journey. Lise and her team of seven soldiers stood nearby. She watched each item as it was set down next to Hero's Triialon gunship, checking items off of a checklist. Hero tried to avert his gaze from her shapely backside, shown off so effectively in her skin-tight body suit and armor as she bent over another crate. He tore his eyes away and looked at Osmar's pleading expression. "You would rather inspect an entire alien base the size of a city on your own?"

Osmar shrugged. "Between drinks."

Hero shook his head. "These are good people. Good warriors."

"But they're just so damned," Osmar paused, running one palm over his bald plate in thought. "*Military*," he finished at last.

"You'll not have to suffer their ways long, Osmar. I'll have another mission for you soon."

The mercenary screwed his face up, not pleased by either idea. "Ah, Your Grace. I can hardly wait." He marched up the ramp and into the ship. "I'll be prepping for liftoff, Lord."

Lise stepped up to Hero, a sly grin crossing her lips as she watched Osmar retreat into the ship. "Doesn't want to go?"

Hero tried to relax, admiring her candor. "He enjoys being difficult."

The young woman smiled, and Hero marveled at the way her face lit up. "I think I know the type." She instantly gained a seriousness, and he watched her body language change to a more formal stance as she gave her report. Once more he found his judgment of the young officer to be correct. "All the cargo is ready to be taken aboard, sir," Lise said. "My team is ready and I can call the science crews and inform the admiral when you are ready to depart."

"I am at your leisure, commander. As soon as everything is stowed, we can lift off. Inform admiral Jo'seph when you are ready to leave."

Hero watched her hazel eyes closely, staring deep into them. An unreadable expression came over her face, her head tilting slightly to one side as she watched him watch her.

There. There it was again; her mind's presence within his own. She could feel it too, he knew, and he grasped her shoulder as she almost staggered back from the sudden mental contact.

"Whoa," Lise gasped, a hand coming to her forehead. "Sorry, sir. Just felt kind of light headed for a moment."

"Lise." Hero's using of her first name came unexpected to her, and she locked gazes with him again. "Lise, is telepathy prevalent in your family?"

She just looked at him for a moment before stepping back and waving him away, Hero's hand slipping from her shoulder as she did so. "What?" She shot him a look of disbelief. "No. No, of course not." She seemed on the verge of being angry with him, her brow creasing. "What are you talking about?"

Hero stood his ground. "You fear it," he observed simply.

Lise stopped dead in her tracks, furious. "Fear," she repeated without looking at him. She was interrupted by the 'attention' command.

Everyone turned to see admiral Jo'seph step from the elevator and onto the flight deck. "At ease," he said, quickly moving to join the group near Hero's fighter. "Commander Lise, report."

Lise's face was a mask, the conversation with Hero seemingly put aside. "Sir, we're ready to load the Triialon ship and then depart with you and the sciences team. Strike Team Seven assembled and ready."

Jo'seph looked at her, then to Hero for a moment. "What's wrong, commander?" he asked her.

Lise almost looked at her shoes, caught off guard by the question. "Nothing, sir. Just anxious to get to our destination."

"You don't even know where our destination is or what is there. Neither do I, and I'm just as anxious." He moved past her, standing before Hero. "Are you ready to leave?"

Hero nodded. "Just say the word, admiral."

"Very well. We depart in ten."

Lise's team and the surrounding crew snapped back to work at that command, quickly loading cargo onto the desert gunship. Hero motioned Jo'seph to the ramp.

"Thank you," the man replied.

"You're entitled to a seat up front, of course," Hero told him.

"When we're leaving, I'll join you. I'd rather oversee the final preparations until then."

A group of men and women from several different races stepped aboard, each wearing gray plastic-like coats over colorful jumpsuits full of pockets and gadgets. Some carried briefcases, while others wore metallic backpacks. The lead man saluted. "Science and engineering team, reporting as ordered, sir. Lieutenant commander Sardeece leading the party."

"Very good, commander," Jo'seph replied. He inclined his head to Hero. "Our guide on this voyage, Hero of Triialon."

Sardeece smiled, shaking Hero's hand. "An honor," he said genuinely.

"Welcome aboard." Hero studied the slight man with his receding hairline and long face, taking him for a scientist only, perhaps worth only good marksmanship in battle. He seemed outgoing and brave enough, though, even if the light handshake may have said otherwise.

"Happy to be here, sir." Sardeece released Hero's hand, unslinging his own pack. "Where might we stow these?"

"If there are no special conditions concerning your equipment, then commander Lise is in charge of cargo."

"Commander Lise," the scientist echoed.

Hero almost shrugged. "She seems to enjoy organizing more than I." At that he felt Lise's eyes on his back, and he turned to find her overseeing the final loads of cargo, her attention squarely fixed on her job.

He made his way to the cockpit, hearing the whines of the heating engines through the cabin fuselage and feeling the slight vibration the vertical-take-off fans created. Hero sat in the captain's chair, ignored by the working Osmar. The mercenary flipped switches on the cockpit's ceiling and the exterior lights came on. The long cannon/engine-tipped wings of his battered brown craft stood out against the steely gray of the flight deck's floor panels, reminding him again of the ship's relative uniqueness. He resisted the urge to pat the panel's polished surface.

Lise stuck her head into the cockpit. "We're ready to depart, sir." She sounded very duty-bound suddenly. "The admiral's making a last check and then joining you."

"Thank you. We'll lift off then."

Lise nodded, but stopped before she could exit the cabin, one hand going to her headset as she listened to an incoming transmission. "There's some sort of commotion on the deck, sir. Some soldiers who demand to see you before you leave. Its probably just those idiots from the other morning, if you'd like me to take care of it..."

"I'll join you," Hero said, getting up.

"Very well." She led him back down the ramp. At its base three men knelt with their heads to the floor. They were Coalition soldiers dressed in the common uniform, but with brown armbands with triangular patches sewn on. Each had their foreheads touched to the floor with one fist down as balance. Jo'seph stepped up behind Hero as they arrived on the strange scene. "What's this all about, sub lieutenant?"

"They wouldn't say. They said they would speak only with Hero." Zhade shook his head in disgust. "Insubordination."

Before admiral Jo'seph could begin chastising them, Hero put a restraining hand on the man's shoulder. Jo'seph looked at him, surprised, but held out a hand. "After you."

"I am Hero of the Triialon," he said in a commanding voice that carried throughout the hold. "What do you want of me?"

The middlemost of the three soldiers raised his head, an expression of clear awe readable on his features. He did not rise from his bent knee, but instead lowered his gaze again before speaking. "My Lord," he said in a voice shaking with excitement. "We are of a holy order that has been

105

passed down through the ages and originating from the very temples of Triialon. We have come to see the truth for ourselves and pledge our services to you." He dared to raise his head again at last. "Lead us."

"You have two leaders worthy of your allegiance," Hero said.

"Teach us," the soldier said desperately.

"I cannot teach you. You must find your own path." Hero began to turn away.

The soldier rose and stepped forward, abasing himself at the back of Hero's feet, nearly grasping the buckles of his boots. "Please, My Lord! Your presence here is a miracle we dared not hope could come true. Do not turn us away. Do not leave us."

Hero looked down at the unexpected disciple. "I fight with all who would fight for honor and light. I shall not leave you." With that, he ascended the ramp back into his ship.

Jo'seph briefly studied the pious soldiers who lingered still. "All right, men. Back to your posts."

"Take over, Osmar." Hero released the in-flight controls and stood up from the pilot's seat.

"My Lord," Osmar answered, moving from behind Hero's pilot seat to take his place.

"Excuse me for a moment, admiral." Jo'seph nodded, not looking up from his calculations for the Dimensionalizer jump. Hero left the cockpit for the hatches just aft, moving towards the entrance to his personal cabin. He glanced down the cramped, dark portal leading to the cargo bay, seeing the geared up Coalition team members waiting there for the ride. Lise caught his eye before he could enter his room, and he stopped, knowing she wanted something of him. The young woman left another man in charge and hurried up the hall to meet the waiting Hero, a crease in her brow of deep concern. "Can I help you, commander?"

Lise stopped just before him, making certain no one in either direction could overhear. "I've grudgingly realized in the last hour that I can't stand the idea of you thinking I might be afraid of anything." She had a hard time meeting his gaze, but looked up at him through dark lashes nonetheless. She sighed, her shoulders heaving with the effort. "So tell me more about this telepathic episode you say I keep having."

Hero cocked his head to the side, interested. "Please come inside." He did not wait to hear her answer, but simply walked through the small hatch into his own quarters, switching on a single light and sitting down on a bunk. When she followed him in, he motioned for her to take the desk seat and waited for her to speak.

"So you think I'm telepathic?" she asked at last.

Hero absently scratched his chin. "No, not necessarily. It's just that I know it is not me, or at least not all me."

"What isn't?"

"What we've both felt. Some mental link in each other's presence that has caught both of our attention but no one else's. I cannot yet explain it."

Lise sat back, relaxing a little. "I've never heard of real telepathy among Spartans. And yet you asked about my family."

"Yes. I think it may have something to do with your lineage as an aristocrat."

"And that is?"

Hero looked down for a moment. "I do not yet know, but I'm forming some theories."

She stared at him. "You're not going to tell me, are you?" He just looked at her. Lise was forced to smile, shaking her head as she leaned forward again. She looked around the small, poorly lit cabin, her eyes briefly taking in the few strange objects that were laid out or hanging in what little space was afforded. "I look up to you, Hero. Already. I've known you but days and already I know I would follow you anywhere that battle called us to. Perhaps that bond is more than you think."

Hero stood. "Yes. Perhaps, if we can properly cultivate it, the link would serve as a great asset in battle."

Lise laughed.

Uncertain of her response, Hero asked, "Commander?"

Lise rose, stepping towards the hatch. "Nothing, sir. If you'll excuse me." She left the room, the waves of dark hair trailing after her as she moved away.

107

Hero watched the empty hatch for a moment before sitting back down, the controlled expression wiped away by a sense of confusion and loss as he tried not to think of her words.

The still barely familiar feeling of the craft around him breaking into the Dimensionalizer hyperspace rocked the ship, and Hero watched the cabin lights flicker momentarily. He opened a small drawer next to the bunk, taking out a golden ring fixed with a strange red gemstone, looking at the old gift a moment before placing it on his finger and digging deeper into the drawer. He found the data pad he was searching for and put it into his coat pocket, finally making his way back to the cockpit of his ship. Once inside the ship's foremost room again Osmar relinquished the pilot's seat allowing Hero to sit next to Jo'seph again.

"Incredible." Hero watched the colorful tunnel and floating apparitional gateways spin endlessly by. He'd had very little chance to study the Dimensionalizer effect when aboard the Coalition craft, and now that he was piloting his own ship's first voyage using the technology, he found himself in awe of it. "It is vast. Each window is a doorway to either one point in the universe or another?"

"In this universe, yes," Jo'seph answered. He too was watching through the large cockpit view port of the Triialon flyer. "We believe the ability for us to reveal and therefore navigate windows to other dimensions, or universes, is within the abilities of the Dimensionalizer Drive, but the correct application for true inter-dimensional travel still eludes us. This is simply the threshold of the cosmos, and we've taken but one baby step."

"A terrible power in the wrong hands," Osmar said quietly from his seat behind the two other men.

"That's why it must never fall into the hands of those such as the Lordillians." Jo'seph said without sounding defensive. "Norpan was an example of that; people died before they let our technology get taken." Jo'seph crossed his arms, suddenly reflective. "I admit we all felt the burning questions that creating something like the Dimensionalizer begs. How can you ever be ready for such power?"

"You cannot," Hero answered. "But you go forward anyway, for the right reasons. Or the wrong."

"Yes," Jo'seph said, his eyes lighting up. "That's exactly it. And it has saved us hundreds of times over. If we had not taken that chance, things would be far more desperate now." The admiral sat back, lost in though for a moment before he spoke. "I wanted to thank you for your handling of the situation in the hanger bay today."

Hero looked at Jo'seph a moment, then nodded, saying nothing further.

"It has been said you are the last of your kind," Jo'seph pressed, "Yet you feel no kindred link with those men? No responsibility?"

Hero's eyes narrowed as he contemplated the idea. "Perhaps I do not feel I have the time for such things until I have completed my own quest. But they are your men, with your cause, and that was what mattered."

There was a sudden flashing from the controls. The Coalition engineers had mounted a small display onto the main panels of the ship, and its small buttons and screen were flashing a bright red. "Window's coming up." Jo'seph pointed at the small screen. "This navigational display indicates your exit into normal space closest to the desired location. Preprogrammed, it will also fire the beam that allows us to exit the window to our destination point."

On cue a beam of light, as if emanating from Hero's entire ship, shot out and struck one of the ethereal floating 'windows' ahead of them. The speeding ship crashed through the energized barrier into real space, and then the stars of normal space surrounded them. Hero took a look at his navigational instruments, finding that they had emerged a few hundred million miles from their destination. "Engaging Star Leap engines," he announced. "Estimated time to arrival is five minutes."

"Confirmed," said Osmar, his own eyes trained on the panels decorating the walls and ceiling behind the pilots' seats. "I have to admit, that was a quick trip, given the distance covered. Remind me to toast your engineers."

"I'll do that," the admiral said dryly. "What happens next?"

"We're going straight to the Citadel on the planet's surface. Then we shall see what we find." Hero banked the ship towards the planet below, a cloudy green orb that suddenly filled the view port as the Triialon ship decreased from Star Leap speed and made for the atmosphere below.

109

Chapter Seven

*Once, long ago, before you were born, there was a
terrible war that lasted many, many years.
When it was over, two whole races were gone, wiped
from the very sands they had battled on.
The only man who survived that war is called a Hero.
-From a letter written by a Coalition
Soldier to his son.*

The gunship broke through the clouds and sped over the green mountains below. Hero looked down, getting his bearings and comparing them to the small data pad in his free hand as he piloted.

"What are we looking for, exactly, Your Regal-ness?" Osmar stared openly through the side of the viewing port, watching the landscape fly by.

"You've not been there?" admiral Jo'seph asked the mercenary incredulously.

Hero was the one to answer. "I am the only man to see the Grellion citadel in several thousand years," he said. "No one else has known of it since it was abandoned and lost to the mystery of time."

"I had no idea you were such a romantic," Jo'seph said with a smile.

"You have not yet seen the citadel," Hero answered.

"When we arrive, I want you to lead the strike team to secure the compound."

"That could take some time," Hero replied, shaking his head. "The base is the size of a large city, and as many stories deep."

Jo'seph smiled. "Then we'll do it one level at a time, just like a recovering sociopath."

"Very well."

The ship flew low over another range of snow-capped mountains and then came upon a grassy valley. Nestled at the far end of the plains were three enormous structures, strange buildings perhaps close enough to be connected. Their immense size was not lost on the men in the cockpit, even from this distance. Furthest to the left was an oval dome with three great rings encircling its width in intervals down its length. The centermost building was the smallest, and appeared to be the slanted, box-like command center. The largest of the three was what appeared to be an enormous hanger bay, its huge door closed to the outside world for thousands of years.

"My Gods," Jo'seph whispered, open-mouthed. He stared at the Citadel as they approached it, looking it over and studying the details as it loomed into view. A gray strip ran the length of the entire base in front of the three buildings, its surface covered in an overgrowth of plant life. "That runway must be nine miles long and a half mile wide!"

"That's a fairly close approximation, admiral," said Hero.

"What the hell did they land on it?" Jo'seph sounded amazed.

Hero cocked his head to one side slightly. "The hanger is over a mile in height. Perhaps closer to one and a half. You could hold and repair the entire fleet within it, I expect, if the bulk of the cruisers had their anti-gravs on."

"Or if they have docking arms within it." Jo'seph continued to stare at the alien citadel as they neared it. The closer they got the more details became clear, including the batteries mounted all over the building and the covering of soil and plants that had worked its way up the walls over the centuries. There was an enormous canon mounted on top of the hanger. "This is incredible." He studied it further, his brow furrowing. "It seems defensible and highly powered, but open."

"I think we'll find it has plenty of surprises."

"Such as?"

"If what I saw when I was last here is any indication, I believe this place throws up a defense barrier large enough to cover the entire facility." He brought the craft in to land, the ship lowering slowly onto the grassy runway near the centermost building. "Perhaps, given the energy source, an impenetrable one."

The ship touched down, and the engines' whine died away, leaving the cockpit suddenly quiet. Osmar was already on his feet, working his way aft, but Jo'seph sat still, looking to Hero at last, his features set in unreadable mask.

"You could have claimed this place for yourself. Made it the throne of the new Triialon."

113

Hero stood, checking his weapons and pausing for a moment before speaking. "Jo'seph. Should the Triialon return, this will not be their home. But they will need strong allies. Until then, the Triialon's place in this universe is uncertain, so the quest goes on." He considered his next words before returning to checking his equipment. "If you must wonder why I bring you to this place, then consider it a gift from a lost race to their successors."

Jo'seph stood, taking Hero's hand. "Be that gift from Triialon or Grellion, I thank you for it." The handshake was strong and heartfelt. "I just hope it all works out."

The two men joined the others in the ship's hold where soldiers and scientists alike were picking up their gear. They had not yet seen the amazing structure outside. One of the scientists was watching a small scanner he had set on the floor.

"Pre-disembarkation checks," the admiral commanded.

Sardeece read the display. "I've checked the atmosphere for constituency and contagious microbes. Levels are Sparta-norm." He looked up, shrugging. "Its fine, unless you're highly allergic."

Jo'seph's shoulders drooped. "Great."

Osmar pushed his way forward, getting aggravated looks from some of the soldiers. "Didn't His Lordship tell you in the briefing that this planet is clean?"

"It's standard procedure, Mr. Osmar. I expect no less from my people."

"Gods, man!" Osmar threw up his arms in anger. "You still don't trust him, even after Moonshau or Norpan?"

Jo'seph turned on the bald mercenary. "I will no longer tolerate your continued questioning of my commands, mister!"

"Osmar," Hero began, but they were all cut off by Lise's voice rising above the din.

"Excuse me! Gentlemen, if I may interrupt this little pissing contest." She stood there, her hands on those ample hips of hers, looking perfectly angry and maternal and decidedly sexy as hell. "I do believe we have a lot of work to do today." She lowered her voice a little, glaring at all of the other men in the room and carefully avoiding admiral Jo'seph's

114

wide-eyed stare. "Now, if I may be so bold; Osmar, the admiral is not impugning Hero's honor, he is simply giving his soldiers something to do, for their peace of mind as well as his own. Please take no offense as I hope Hero does not, but instead let us do our job." She turned to Jo'seph, looking up at him sternly. "Admiral, atmosphere checks out. Shall we disembark?"

The admiral found himself blinking and closing his mouth at last after the sudden change in subject. "Y-yes, Commander. Please proceed." Hero watched Jo'seph recover from his stammer and hid a smile, gazing at Lise who moved away, giving commands.

The Triialon warrior opened the hatch and the ramp automatically slid out onto the long grass outside. The sudden flooding of light briefly blinded the hold's company, but as they all blinked away the momentary flash they fell silent, staring at the massive structure that greeted them outside. "Impressive, is it not?"

Lise nodded without looking, then regained her composure. "All right, boys, we're not here for a picnic. Zhade, you're on point. McCarty, you're with the admiral and myself. Let's move."

"Commander, have your team head for that small door, straight ahead," Hero instructed. "You'll need me to get it open."

They all moved off of the Triialon gunship and out into the cool, crisp air of a brave new world. A slightly cool breeze washed over them, but otherwise the temperature was pleasant. Jo'seph watched the blue sky beyond the high top of the central building before them. "When were you last here, Hero?"

Hero walked beside him, with Lise and her soldiers as escort and Osmar trailing. "Several months since the first and only time I have been here, admiral."

"Scanner," Lise called out in question to her team ahead. A response in the negative was answered back to her. The team quickly reached the base of the building and ascended a small set of steps to reach a locked hatch, the overgrowth having been cleared off of its surface by Hero on his last visit.

Jo'seph sneezed. "Great," he said again. "COM officer?"

"Sir?" An officer turned back around to meet the admiral, a large equipment pack over his shoulder.

"Can we get a signal back to base via the scrambler?"

"Yes, I think so sir. The Triialon ship has been set up for dimensionalizer communications channels."

"Very good. Get me a link up."

The officer removed his hefty gear from his back and set it down, working its controls a moment. He handed the admiral a headset. "Channel open, sir."

Jo'seph sneezed again.

"Gods, man," came Jay'salan's voice over the linkup. The signal through the Dimensionalizer-space channel was loud and clear, and Hero could easily overhear the conversation.

"Like I need you to remind me how horrid my allergies are," Jo' replied.

"At least it's only allergies. You bring back some viral strain and I'll personally bust you down to private."

"Yeah, yeah," Jo'seph grumbled, waving the empty threat away. "We've successfully located the Grellion home world and citadel, and Jay', its amazing just from the outside. I'll have more to report after we secure the interior... which could be a while. This place is huge."

"Can you get back to me in six hours?"

Jo'seph nodded. "Affirmative. I'll talk to you then." He broke the link and handed the set back to his officer.

Hero stepped away from the admiral's side, moving to join the soldiers nearest the ancient door. Osmar nearly bumped into him as he followed his master. "Sure we can't get you a tissue, admiral?" the merc asked with an evil smile.

Jo'seph ignored the comment. "All right, commander," he waved Lise on. "Let's see if our friend can open this door." They followed Hero past the Coalition teams to stand before the tall hatch. For a silent moment they all just stood there, staring at it. "Right, how do we get in?"

"With this," Hero answered, raising his arm and pulling back his jacket sleeve to reveal the Prizm.

"You've rigged it since you were last here?" Lise asked.

"No, this is the same way I got in the first time, only then it took me several hours to find the correct combination." He waved the bracer at the door, its central crystal giving off an eerie glow. He pressed a sequence into the crystalline buttons around it and to everyone's surprise the door began swinging inward at a torturously slow speed, soon revealing that the bulkhead was easily three feet thick. "There are certain elements that are recurrent throughout the universe," Hero continued as they waited. "A few are rarer, and, under the right conditions, infinitely more powerful. In my journeys I've found that a few of these rare elements used to create the Triialon Artifacts are traceable via the

Prizm, helping me to track down the rest of the Twelve." He shrugged slightly. "In theory. It has helped me find an ancient trail of Triialon influence across dozens of worlds. It has also led me to find other interesting relics. The Grellion citadel is one of them."

"What made you try to enter the base if you weren't going to claim it yourself, then?" Jo'seph asked.

"Even I must succumb to curiosity every once in a while."

"Sir," came the nervous voice of one of the scientists. "The further the door opens the better readings I'm getting, and the power level in there is off the scale."

Jo' looked at Hero with a sarcastic smile. "Did you leave the light switch on?"

Hero's brow creased. "Let me see that," he said to the scientist. He studied the display, Sardeece watching around the warrior's shoulder. "No life signs?" The scientist shook his head. "This I cannot account for, admiral. It seems the citadel has become active somewhat since I was last here." He pulled his own blaster from its holster. "Whatever the case, we should be on our guard."

"Agreed. Commander, you and Hero take point."

Lise pulled her own weapon, marching to the front of the line and near the now open door. "Alright, boys, you heard the admiral. Zhade, McCarty, you're the honor guard. Strike Team Seven is with me. I'd like the science team in back. Any of you armed?" A few nodded. "Very well. Sardeece, I leave you in charge of your men and watching the admiral's back." She nodded at last to Hero. "After you, sir."

Hero moved on ahead, Osmar sliding in beside him without thought. Lise trailed behind them, watching intently even though she knew Hero would probably see anything coming first. Slowly and by the numbers, the group entered the Citadel of Grellion.

Memfis watched the room's occupants from his divan behind the two-way mirror. The ever-present displays of events and numbers from across the universe was reduced to a small floating hologram by his side. He knew Toapo watched from similar hidden chamber nearby as well, but he did not care. He had suffered the fool's ambition for centuries and with luck he would not have to for very much longer. He took another sip from his goblet, the motion stirring one of the slave girls that had passed out on the cushions beside him.

The room the God watched was filled with well-dressed members of countless races, all attending court. Today he paid few of them heed, for Svea had entered the room an hour before, dressed as elegantly and yet scandalously revealing as usual. From time to time she found her reflection in the mirror with those piercing eyes, and Memfis nearly thought she could see into his own black orbs through the glass. The woman moved with a deliberate slow sway, floating from table to table and looking over the shoulder of important men and women, or simply locking gazes with them from across the table as if to command, *'Remember me.'* The serving girl, Brithany, was by her side as always, her head bowed and hands clasped as she followed her mistress around the room, attending her needs. She was submissive, collared, properly conquered; Svea's first snare since arriving on Kordula.

Memfis shook the near-nude slave dozing against his left arm. "Awake and adorn me." The girl stood without a word and brought the jewelry and toga he had tossed aside earlier, fixing it around him and applying the accoutrements on his neck, arms, and face. "Dress yourselves," he commanded, "and then announce me. Today I join court, and be quick about it." He didn't really expect Svea to leave before he could reveal his presence, as she seemed to delight in the formalities and possibilities of court each day with some predictability, but he was also anxious to finally play his hand.

The two women wrapped thin veils about their hips, while a third left the room to enter the court from a side hall and announce Memfis, God among Gods and founder of the feast. With that, the mirror his cushioned observation point lay behind slid away and the platform he and his slave girls rested upon extended forward while Memfis sipped from his drink in a bored fashion.

Most of the attendees stood and applauded or rushed forward to bow and scrape and smile at his feet. A few of the more regular and therefore bored or disillusioned delegates ignored the pomp and circumstance, dining with careless demeanors while their tables emptied.

Through the crowd waded the slow and sleek form of Svea, wrapped in a black dress made of something thin and expensive. She looked up at Memfis through long lashes as she shouldered her way to the front of the group of beings now toasting his health or begging his audience. She was giving off a slight aura of transfixing power, enough to make many people near her turn to her with open lust in their eyes, but no where near the energy a Seethling could produce. Perhaps she didn't wish to be *too* obvious.

Memfis ignored the pleas from the fawning group, instead pointing directly to his intended target. "Svea of the Seethlings. Come forward." The noise around her died down at last, the crowd realizing that the God had made his only selection for the day, and quite possibly the week. Svea stepped up the dais, her long, shapely legs showing an exceptional amount of thigh with each stride. She stood upon the second to last step, as they were all instructed to do, and gave a deep bow. "You are enjoying your time with us?"

"Absolutely, My Lord," the dark-haired woman answered with a slight smile. Her voice was smoky and calm, quiet despite the noise of the enormous chamber.

"I am pleased." Memfis smiled, inclining his head in mock thought. "I have watched you; You work quickly. Already you have made allies," he paused, "and enemies. I like ambition."

Svea smiled seductively. "I am glad you are impressed. Perhaps I could make a request as long as I have My Lord's attention?"

"Please."

119

"As my Lord knows I just recently was accepted to Kordula as a member at Court. I was hoping to gain enough influence to eventually be able bring my brother and business partner Dahvis here as well. My apartments are certainly large enough."

Memfis waved away the issue. "Send the request to my secretary along with any pertinent information. I shall look the matter over personally and put it before the court." He smiled in return. "I'm sure we can reach an accommodation."

Svea gave a deep bow. "My Lord is too kind. I look forward to your decision, and," she continued with a knowing gleam in her eye, "any further agreements we may be able to come to."

Memfis nearly laughed, yet he could not deny being intrigued by her offer. Still, he had plenty of time for such desires, and he was not finished watching the moves of this woman, or her brother. He gestured to one of the servant girls and she stood again, controlling the dais to return to its hidden confines. "As I said, I like ambition. Unfortunately, I am very busy of late. The universe is at war, Svea. Perhaps the future will offer more serene opportunities. In the meantime, I look forward to eventually meeting your business partner at court." The dais began to again slide back into its place behind the wall, forcing Svea to step off and away from the moving platform. "I wish you good hunting, Lady Svea of Magdalene."

The wall and its mirror fell back into place, and Memfis stood, dismissing his slaves. He walked slowly from the hidden hall, past his chambers and eventually to the Gods' court, where some of his fellow immortals sat, studying their holographic displays or doing business over omnispacial transmissions. Toapo looked up, a glare, as always, evident in his eye.

"What news?" Memfis asked.

"Your pet android seems to have developed a temper, Memfis," Toapo said with distaste. "His Lordillian forces have attacked Sagev 3, laying waste to the planet." He looked to his compatriots. "I say they are bad business, despite their uses."

"As always," Memfis said, brushing the insult aside. "And the Coalition forces?"

Another God spoke up. "If Chebonka was hoping to flush them out with this attack, then so far it is not working. The Coalition fleets are scattered, in hiding. No retaliation is yet evident."

Memfis sat, calling up his own display. "How unfortunate. So many problems would be put to rest with the final destruction of that power."

"I believe that their recent ally may be leading them to a new base of operations. That Triialon could prove to be quite a setback."

Memfis looked thoughtful. "Yes. Yes, it would seem our plans concerning Hero may be a little tardy. Still, events are in motion against him, and against the issues he may bring to the table."

"What events?" Toapo stood, trying once again to plead his case with a loud voice as his only real backing. "There would *be* no issues if you had not already failed to kill him, Memfis. This probability has gone on long enough. The Triialon threat still exists, and this court is still banned from taking the matter from Memfis' hands and into its own." He stared at his leading opponent, lowering his voice to a hiss. "Hero must die, and the lost Artifacts must be found and destroyed."

"Such bold words in the face of so few of our fellow Gods," Memfis spat back. "Perhaps my lord Toapo would like to try this little coup' again when Court is in full session."

"Be that as it may, My Lord Memfis," Galatis broke in before the argument could escalate further. "Toapo does bring up a good point. The Triialon bears the tidings of trouble, and must be dealt with soon."

Memfis inhaled deeply, calming himself. "The Triialon world is dead," he said at last. "However, perhaps it is time to pay a visit to their former sect, the Sisterhood of Dailor, to see if they know otherwise. I shall have an agent ready for that task within a few weeks. In the meantime, we can discuss in court what next should be done about Hero," he paused, "and the Coalition. Perhaps by then both parties will have resurfaced."

"A pity that they have not taken up the Lordillians' challenge to defend Sagev 3," the other God said with almost a yawn. "I doubt their forces would have survived another confrontation with so large a force."

"Indeed." Memfis smiled slightly as he watched Toapo abruptly stand and exit the chamber in an obvious tantrum. How unworthy of a God, he thought to himself. Quickly his fingers worked over his controls while the others were watching the hasty departure of their fellow immortal.

He pulled up the files of Svea and Dahvis, posting and just as soon accepting the latter's submission to join his sister at the Court of Kordula.

Toapo waited in his chamber, dismissing the servants with a bark and pulling the secret chime cord behind the door panel. He paced the room, fuming silently in frustration and plotting furiously within his complex mind.

Kezeron appeared within moments, breezing into the room from another secret portal, appearing as if he were a huge, billowing shadow from within the wall. As always, the strange fighter was dressed simply but with elegance, his deep blue cape and hood made from the richest cloth he could afford, the light-absorbing material embroidered with beautiful detail. The cape flowed down over wide shoulders and chest, revealing form-fitting clothes of similar material beneath accented by a large belt hosting several blades and other weapons and tools. His face, hidden within the shadow of the cowl, had a blue tint of its own, topped by cropped blonde hair. His head was bowed slightly, his arms at his side as he came to stand before his master.

"My Lord has summoned me," said Kezeron with controlled coldness. "Why?"

"I have a task for you," Toapo replied with equal cool. "You will leave Kordula immediately and find Hero of the Triialon."

That got Kezeron's attention - his head snapped up and his shoulders squared. He smiled just a little. "Find the Triialon?"

"Yes."

"There are but Twelve Artifacts of the Triialon, yet so many remain lost. How does My Lord expect me to find one man?"

Toapo halted his pacing and turned on his personal Hand. "I'll suffer none of your inconsistencies this day, Kezeron Telbandith. I know how long you have waited to face him, how long you have studied his movements and ways. Cease your self-pity and find him, then inform me of his location. Do not approach nor engage him until I have given you leave. When the time comes, you will not only have him to face as desired, but you will have the means with which to destroy him."

Kezeron held out his hand, palm up, his eyes at last burning with the fire that made him so feared. "Give me the object! I shall take it and destroy him now."

"And call the very attention to ourselves that I would avoid? You do not use your intellect." Toapo began to pace along the marble floor again. "Soon the time shall arrive that our plans will be put into motion and not only will the Twelve fall into our hands, but with them the means to kill Memfis and take control of the Inner Sanctum."

"And what of the Forefather?" Kezeron asked.

"By then it shall be too late for him to detect the power we wield or defend his master, and you will have the weapons to bring him to your mercy."

The fighter and assassin stared off into space, his mouth spreading into a grim smile. "At last, I shall best the Triialon."

"Save your passions for the right moment. Now go, and tell me when you have found Hero. I shall send along any information gathered here as it comes." He waved away the departing shadow form of Kezeron Telbandith. "Be gone. Our destiny awaits." The fighter disappeared once more into the wall.

Inside the Grellion Citadel was amazingly clean and white. The moment they had all stepped foot inside of the structure a strange feeling, as though a gust of wind could pass through a body, overcame Lise, and she shuddered. She turned and saw the same effect cause each man to react the same way, save of course Hero who simply acted more guarded than usual, although whether he felt it also or simply reacted to everyone else's sudden jump, Lise could not tell.

"Which one of you just walked over my grave?" Sardeece asked quietly.

"That was a fair attempt at humor," Jo'seph called back with mock approval. "You're improving."

The scientist smiled. "I take no credit, admiral. Its entirely due to your influence."

"As it should be. Any theories as to what just happened?"

Sardeece leaned out of line to look at Hero at Lise's end of the hall, but the Triallon ignored the question, watching the openings ahead of them. "I'm inclined to reserve judgment until I have more facts, sir."

"I suggest we proceed more quietly," Hero grumbled over his shoulder.

The admiral nodded at that, and the whole group continued on in silence.

They finally exited the long hallway at a junction with another tunnel. Everything was very well lit within the interior, and it appeared that they were simply in a group of main corridors. Pipes, panels and hatches ran along the hall in either direction, lights embedded in the nine-foot ceilings giving off the illumination. The air was stale, but warm. Lise was unsure if the metal walls were painted white, or naturally that hue and therefore an unknown substance. She decided to remind herself to ask Sardeece for an analysis when she wasn't so worried about stealth. Despite that thought, she realized she'd have to chance talking if she were even going to ask Hero where they were headed, as she had no idea.

Lise gently placed a hand on Hero's shoulder, halting him in his tracks. He placed a finger to his lips as he turned to her, and when she looked up into his eyes, he touched his finger to his temple.

"Can you think it?" Hero's voice had sounded in her mind, surprising her. She nodded.

"Where are we going," she thought back to him.

Hero turned back around, leading her and her soldiers on through the mysterious tunnels. *"Up to the command decks,"* came the telepathic answer. *"Once we find our way to the lift."*

"So, you want me to tell the admiral you're lost," she thought back, the intended reaction curling her lips into a sly smile.

"I am not lost," his answer came back, the surprising anger behind the emotion lending a weight to the feeling that Lise could only interpret as yelling. Hero stopped when he finally noticed her smile, his face souring. He turned again to the portal ahead. *"Very amusing."*

Lise nearly laughed aloud.

Hero froze, watching, his rifle held at the ready. Lise brought her own weapon to bear, trying to see what had spooked him. Within moments she saw it; a shadow ahead, coming from just beyond the next corner. The figure casting that shadow moved quickly, with a strange gait and at a low height. Lise signaled towards the oncoming corner, and several rifles swayed in unison, awaiting a target.

A sleek white robot rounded the corner, stopping to look up at the figures that greeted it. It was short, at least a foot shorter than Lise, with a flat face showing only a single optic, and a head that swept back cylindrically, otherwise it was strangely bipedal. It just stood there, staring up at Hero's gun and the others behind him.

"It's an A.I.," Zhade hissed. "Damned Lordillians have already been here."

Hero surprisingly lowered his weapon, a motion that Osmar did not mimic, his own eyes and gun still locked on the strange little android before them. "I don't think so," Hero said. "Its a different technology altogether."

"It doesn't match any Lord design I've ever heard of," Lise said, following the Triialon's example and shouldering her rifle.

The robot looked at her, then scanned down the line of people it was faced with as each in turn put aside their weapons. Lise raised an eyebrow, grinning briefly to Hero as she relaxed and put a hand on her hip. Zhade was the last to lower his gun, and only then with obvious disagreement on his face. The robot seemed to make a decision then, and turned towards the entrance Hero had been heading for originally. It did not turn to face them again until at last it reached the threshold. It was waiting for them to join it, one arm extended to the control panel next to it. Hero took the cue and signaled the group forward.

The portal opened to a large elevator platform, the shaft above their heads extending up into the darkness without end. Once everyone was aboard, the robot pressed the panel, and the door slid shut in front of them. Instead of the upward motion Lise was expecting, the lift instead began to descend. A feeling of nervousness was suddenly quite obvious from most everyone around her, although Lise expected Sardeece was probably intrigued beyond excitable words.

"Where do you think it's taking us?" admiral Jo'seph asked quietly.

"Engineering or power decks, I would guess," Hero answered.

"Uh huh." There was a moment of complete silence, punctured again by, "Can you make this thing go faster?" A chorus of quiet chuckles greeted the admiral's sarcastic statement.

"Hero, sir," Sardeece asked aloud, no longer able to keep his curiosity quiet, "any thoughts on our host?"

The warrior continued to stare forward, simply waiting for the lift to reach its destination and the next step to be taken. "As you pointedly said before, Mr. Sardeece, I would rather reserve judgment until I have more facts."

Lise took the opportunity to study this stranger a little more closely for a moment, hoping that she could mask her mind as well as her eyes while she peered up at him. Of course, either notion was probably an exercise in futility where this man's nearly super-heightened senses seemed concerned, she mused. Lise had to keep from shaking her head to herself at that, wondering if such senses made the warrior that much more approachable, or less. She couldn't help it, though. Standing this close to him was like trying to lean casually on an electric fence. The attraction radiating off of him was simply that intense. She didn't want to be so enamored with him, and she began to wonder at last why she should be. Beyond an air of mystery caused by what was probably character flaws and a slightly shrouded and, well, let's face it, legendary past, he probably wasn't all that personable. She tried to reason that perhaps she was mistaking a bond of camaraderie and utmost respect for romantic infatuation. Then those gray eyes turned to burn into hers for a moment once more and she again felt that tremble run from her heart all the way down past the pit of her stomach.

Indeed, what was there to be so enamored with, she droned to herself, resisting the urge to cover her face with her hand.

Just then the lift stopped its downward motion and the door opened in front of them. The little robot stepped off of the platform and out into a huge room filled with tall, imposing machines, like an enormous energy plant. Lights flickered within the great machines and the noise from them assailed the small group the moment the doors had opened.

"Incredible," shouted Sardeece over the cacophony.

Hero led the group forward, following the squat robot as it walked purposefully between the great structures, heading for a set of large doors at the far end of the alleyway. The group of Coalition members stared about them in awe, looking at ancient feats of engineering that were working as though they had only been built yesterday. The machines and their walkways stretched high up to the ceilings above, perhaps ten stories. Even Zhade, desperate to remain alert for what might lay behind any corner, was inspired to look up in wonder between nervous glances. Lise tied her long curls of dark hair back as she looked up with the rest of them, amazed at what they had found. Or been led to.

They reached the large doors and the robot strode right through them, the bulkheads pulling apart to allow it access. The Coalition teams followed it into an obvious computer complex, and no sooner had the doors closed behind them did they find all of the noise of the previous room extinguished. Sardeece's mouth simply hung open to what greeted him.

A mass of robots identical to the one that had led them there suddenly swarmed into the room, surrounding the Coalition troops and scientists in a perfect circle. Lise's strike team members drew their rifles or leveled sidearms at them, but there was no attack on either side. They just waited to see what would happen next. Lise looked at Hero, who stood poised, the Triialon sword drawn and held at the ready. She gazed up at the huge mass of technology before them, perhaps the central computer core of the entire complex, realizing with growing certainty that the machine appeared to be giving off some sort of presence. It had become clearly evident since the moment the wave of automatons had come crashing into the room.

There was a minute of stunned silence, and then Lise felt a tugging within her mind, similar to the sensation she had experienced minutes before during her telepathic communication with Hero. *"You are not of Grellion,"* came the ominous voice within her mind. She knew they had all heard it by the sudden change of expression on everyone's faces. *"Explain,"* the voice boomed. *"Why have you come here?"*

Chapter Eight

Kezeron Telbandith had a reputation that would have
rivaled the meanest black sorcerer of ancient times,
and it was growing worse by the month. Few knew who
his master was, and fewer still dared to cross his path.
Any glory hounds who tried to take him on got killed
for their efforts. But even Kezeron had fame to
find somewhere, for while he was more infamous than
any other wanderer out there, there was still one man
more notorious.
History of the so-called Gods
- Dr. W. H. Redfield

Svea opened the doors to her apartments and found Dahvis waiting
there already, staring at her from a plush antique chair. She paused only
momentarily, smiling slightly as she waved Brithany away. The servant
bowed, her eyes never leaving her feet as she shuffled out of the room.

Dropping her bag onto a seat next to the entrance, Svea sauntered
over slowly, inching the cut of her skirt up her thigh. Finally she stood
before him, climbing into the chair so that her knees straddled Dahvis'
legs. Her hair cascaded down over them, trapping their faces, and she
looked down, grinning. "Hello, brother. I see you made it in record time."

Dahvis put his arms around her waist. "I'm so pleased with you,
Svea." She leaned down to kiss his lips, and he drank of her mouth deeply.
"You've been here merely days and already I am able to join you on
Kordula." He kissed her again. "I got the notice this morning, signed by
Memfis himself."

Something in that statement gave Svea pause, and she sat there over
Dahvis' lap as he nuzzled her neck, wondering at how easily he was given
such official leave to join her at Court. She would have been excited if she
weren't so perplexingly alarmed by the thought. Besides, she was not
expecting to see Dahvis for at least another week. As usual she hid all of
this from her brother, instead forcing a complacent look while running a
hand through his black locks. "Have you even had breakfast?" she asked
him.

Dahvis looked up at her, the darkness her curtain of hair afforded him giving a shadowed look to his features. "A wonderful idea. Perhaps you could call that scrumptious little slave back in here to join us, hmm?"

Svea returned his grin, stepping off of the chair and removing the straps of her gown to let it slide off of her perfect flesh and onto the stone floor. "Of course. But remember, brother, she is delicate, Kordula's property and therefore not breakable."

Dahvis feigned injury. "Would I hurt such a creature, My Lady, when already she seems so obviously under your spell?" Svea turned, naked save for the heeled shoes on her feet, to open the door to the servant's room and take Brithany by the hand. The girl emerged, returning the kiss Svea gave her with open passion, the look of loss within her eyes showing just how captive her reasoning mind was to the Seethling influence. Svea led her back into the room where Dahvis waited, sitting like a king upon his throne.

Svea pulled on a robe, watching her brother smoke a rather expensive tobacco. He sat on the floor, his back against the cushioned lounge. Brithany lay sprawled across the cushioned furniture, sleeping restlessly, her hair still plastered to her naked, sweaty back. Slight burn marks on her arms showed where Dahvis had let his powers become a little overzealous.

"You've not been here a day and already I must point out how you must govern your passions," Svea said, tying the sash around her thin waist.

Dahvis took a large drag and let it out slowly, staring at her through the smoke. "I have waited all our lives for Kordula." He snapped his fingers and a flash of blue energy flew from his hand and played across the servant girl's skin. She moaned in her sleep, straining through labored breaths before returning to her fitful dreams. "I'm celebrating, so don't let me hear any of your shit."

Svea's gaze locked with his for only a moment before she turned away. "Very well." She knelt to pick up his shirt from behind a chair, tossing it to him. "Would you care to join me at Court this evening?" The sulking man did not answer her, instead choosing to stare off listlessly as

131

his finger slid down Brithany's thigh. "It's everything you dreamed it would be and more, I promise you. The Gods themselves do not show themselves there as often as one might wish, but the contests are delicious." Her attempts to appeal to his brighter side finally succeeded, Dahvis looking at her with the hint of a smile curling his lips. "You must dress finely, of course," she told him.

"I suppose I could grace the Court of Kordula with my presence," he said at last. He stood, bending over the sleeping servant, and whispered into her ear. She awoke with a start, a look of near-panic in her eyes as she struggled to remember where she was. She looked up and, seeing her new master, quickly sat erect, covering herself self-consciously. Dahvis only smiled at her disquiet. "Brithany, go ready yourself. You accompany us to court, this evening." The girl nodded, her bare feet slapping quietly across the cooling floor on her way to her bedroom.

Dahvis dressed quickly in the master chamber, choosing his usual black apparel. He turned to stand behind Svea, who sat preparing her hair in front of a huge mirror. "Does anyone come armed?"

"There are those who wear ceremonial swords or knives, yes," Svea answered. She raised a sarcastic eyebrow at him. "*Civilized* weapons only. Wear the inlayed saber if you're concerned about it." She turned back to the mirror and fastened on her earrings, set for a night of intrigue and conquest.

Lise stood in her old room in her parents' house. The shocking reality of this returned memory was compounded by the sight of herself in the mirror, aged thirteen. The haze of time parted a little, and she found herself running out of the room and down the spiraling stairs, hugging her mother furiously just before greeting her father, Lord Decarva, as he came in the door from another day in the city. She held him close, releasing him only when she realized she was now standing outside, alone. The estate rolled out behind her, and she looked down the green hills into the glittering city and its harbor below. She had almost forgotten how beautiful a paradise Sparta had once been.

Memories poured through her mind like the sands of an hourglass, falling away to be replaced by each moment of daily life as the daughter of aristocrats on the wealthy planet of Sparta. She passed people on the streets, following her mother shopping in the capitol. She dined, watching the ships lift straight up from the waters of the harbor and into the dusky sky above. She smiled when a fleet of battleships passed over on their way out past the grasslands and into the desert to join their sisters at the skybase. There was no war, no famine; only the peace of an empire of tranquility.

She was seventeen now. She knew that by the cake before her eyes and the darkening sky of the horizon. Fear gripped her heart as she realized the fires from the city were coming from the buildings her father worked in. Soon the whole valley below was engulfed in the smoke of every burning street, and the flames would only grow, for the Lordillians had come. Each giant cruiser unleashed a swarm of destructive fighters like angry insects from a hive, the craft strafing the ground before joining the air battle against the overwhelmed defense forces. Landing craft unloaded their deadly cargo of the very same Lordillian troopers that would be occupying the planet for the following countless number of years.

Lise watched the house servants and her mother scurry around, trying desperately to get their affairs in order and escape to unknown places. Some of the staff left for their own homes and families, while others stayed to help their Lady and her daughter attempt to organize their belongings and find a route of escape. Lise's father never came home.

The explosions were suddenly much closer, and before anyone could even voice the question of what to do next, the door shattered inward. Lordillian soldiers, giant gleaming mechanoid killers, flooded through the gaping entrance. Their bird-like, ovoid heads looked for targets through the settling dust. Black-rimmed optics locked on targets and burned down innocent after innocent indiscriminately. Lise ran up the staircase, hoping to reach her father's guns locked away in his private study. Instead she froze in terror when she reached the top, watching the vast number of those evil creatures fill the great room and slaughter her friends.

Lise screamed when she saw her mother among the fallen, but was quickly shaken from her paralyzed shock by the blast that splintered the stair handle beside her. She leapt to the floor above, the tears, smoke and shrapnel in her eyes leaving her nearly blind. Knowing she would never find the key for the weapons cabinet, she hurled her father's chair through the glass case,

133

shattering it. She never even felt the pain of the shards scraping her arms when she reached in and took the two plasma rifles before hurling herself through the window and down the rooftop. Lise fell to the grass and bushes below, letting the sounds of heavy, metal feet pass before she again dared to move, trying once more to wipe the blur from her eyes. She made a dash for the estate's outer wall, scurrying over it to the hoped for freedom of her neighbor's yard.

Lise found her colleague's estate in the same condition, the houses left burning to their foundation, and she wondered if any of them had escaped. She had attended school with their daughter, Claussia, most of her life, and considered the girl and her parents friends. She coughed, the heat and smoke from the burning homes driving her further west, towards the grasslands.

Lise next found herself back in the city, months later. The apocalypse had past and now the few survivors who were not slaves or prisoners were the rebellion against the Lordillian garrisons. Lise was among their number, herself and a small group of boys around her age had found each other among the ruins and consolidated what weapons they had, but no one touched her daddy's gun. She had quickly learned to shoot and had learned where to aim and make it count on a Lordillian soon afterwards. They made guerilla raids whenever possible and foraged through the wreckage day and night for food and water. All of the boys quickly came to respect Lise, and one even claimed to love her. That boy would become her first, and together they would spend the next few years trying in vain to drive the invaders from their world.

Lise found herself alone, staring at the smoldering corpses of the young men who had been her friends and fellow fighters for so long. The tears came unbidden when she thought of all the time she had spent looking into the eyes of her first lover, now staring blankly back up at her from the ground. Her heart sank, lying there in broken pieces in the blood that still seeped from his wounds. This was the true face of war, and as horrified as Lise knew she was, she knew she could not turn away from it. She hugged her knees to her chest, silently weeping next to her fallen comrades. There was no choice left to her then but to leave Sparta behind, join up with the refugee ships and try to make her way to the Sparta war fleet assembled somewhere out in deep space. Those remaining battle cruisers were now rumored to be forming a Coalition against the Lordillian horde, led by admirals Jo'seph and Jay'salan themselves.

Time raced by again, and the young woman was now a raw recruit in the Coalition army, having served aboard a battleship for more months than she could remember. The thoughts of old friends and green fields were long buried within her psyche. Lise fought the Lordillians on her first off world battlefield with a ferocity that marked her quickly. Fear gave way to anger, and then to the numbness of duty. She rose from communications to second-in-command of her squad, and she soon commanded an attack group of her own. But the cold reality was ever present all around her, and despite her attempts to bury that feeling in her work or her smile, the Lordillians remained as a constant reminder; death was always close at hand.

Lise felt tears streaming down hot cheeks, her body shaking as she knelt on a cold, hard floor. She realized someone's arm was around her, holding her up, and she willed her hands to seek out the figure which comforted her. Large, warm limbs lay beneath the battered leather jacket that surrounded her, and she knew it was Hero. A feeling of heat washed over her as she opened her eyes to look into his, and her shaking began to subside, giving way to an unnamed desire. Lise's lips, already parted for want of air during the deluge of memories, now found themselves being bitten shamelessly by her own teeth. "Hero," she breathed.

The memories faded, and only Hero's concerned features filled her vision. "Are you alright?" he asked.

Lise nodded dumbly, and the feelings of warmth and sorrow combined gave way to cold reality as Hero stood up, leaving her chilled and barren, holding herself on the alien floor. She looked around her, finding everyone else within the group in a similar state of shock from the telepathic event, some still clutching their skulls in apparent pain. Even the admiral and Osmar lay stunned, shaking their heads to clear them as they tried to stand. Only Hero appeared unharmed by the psychic attack, standing watch over the group that was still surrounded by the army of small robots.

No, not an attack, Lise amended to herself. The sheer strength of the mental energy that had flooded over the room simply overwhelmed them all. But it had simply been the memories of her life as it had changed since the day the Lordillians came into it. She remembered now, in the

135

moments before the pain had entered her mind and they had all slumped to the floor, Jo'seph telling the Citadel, which was telepathically *speaking* to them, their plight and the Coalition's need for a new home. *"Make your case,"* the Citadel had 'said', and then the pain of the past had come.

Lise stood, still hugging herself to try and stop the shaking, wiping the tears from her face. She came to stand next to Hero and Jo'seph, the two men facing what she could only describe as the Supercomputer.

"The servitor robots act as a sort of amplifier," Hero was saying. "I believe the Base may have been trying to contact us ever since we entered, but as our brains work differently than those of the people who built this place, it needed to bring us here," he indicated the chamber, "in order to be heard."

The admiral didn't look happy. He was scowling as he held his head with one hand as though suffering a blinding headache. "And what about that brain-drain we seem to have all experienced?"

"All save you," Lise commented to Hero with a knowing smile.

Hero turned to look down at her. "No one gets inside a Triialon's head unless he wills it." He looked back up at the massive computer. "As for the effects of that psychic connection, it was probably the way the structure and the Grellions used to swap information regularly. You're minds simply aren't used to it."

"Then it's safe to assume that the Grellions were total telepaths." The three people turned to find Sardeece standing behind them, watching the computer in open fascination.

"Or synthetic themselves," Hero answered.

Lise tried to avoid the prejudiced thought that sprang from that idea, but still found herself asking aloud, "You really think a race of machines built all of this?"

"Anything is possible, commander. One thing is for certain - a race of machines is rebuilding this place as we speak."

"So now what is it waiting for?" Jo'seph asked.

"Digesting the information it has only just finished gathering, admiral. When it is ready, the interview will continue." Hero's expression turned thoughtful, like an arbiter who had just come upon a point. "Was the only memories it gathered from you pertaining to the war?" The three

Coalition members all nodded, looking at each other before Hero continued. "When it is ready, it will continue," he shrugged, motioning towards the 'supercomputer'. "When it has decided, it will judge."

"Judge?" Zhade and a few recovering soldiers were now also standing behind the admiral, looking sore and angry. "I refuse to be judged by any damned machine."

"That will be enough of that, sub-lieutenant," Lise commanded.

"It's a point, though," Jo'seph said under his breath. "If this is now a bargain, what's its end?" He folded his arms, staring at the floor as he thought out loud. "This is an unexpected turn of events. We're now trying to cut a deal with a living machine we would end up residing *inside*. That idea alone is obviously an uncertain one among a group of soldiers at war with machines."

"You have a choice then, admiral," Hero said simply. "Make it work here or move on to somewhere else. But I can tell you this; I can think of nowhere more secure than this base in any part of the universe I have seen."

"I will speak with you again, admiral Jo'seph Bel'ov of the Sparta Coalition." The voice boomed in Lise's head like an amplifier, and she knew they could all hear the telepathic signal. *"I have seen your plight,"* it continued, *"and must further consider your intentions. You are the first beings to enter these walls in years longer than even I know, and were it not for the trespass of the Triialon I might never have awoken. You may stay within this shelter tonight, and we can continue this matter tomorrow."*

"Do we have some unknown test to pass?" Jo'seph asked aloud.

"I believe we both do, admiral, given the reactions of some of your people to the true nature of this Citadel. Perhaps such circumstances will work against the bond you suggest and you shall move on and I will again rest, awaiting the return of masters who will never come. As your life forms are fond of saying, we shall see."

Admiral Jo'seph was silent a moment, his face an unreadable mask, perhaps wondering - as Lise was - whether the machines were reading their thoughts even then. "Very well," he said finally. "We shall encamp near the entrance we came in from originally and await your next envoy." With that Jo'seph motioned to fall back, and instantly a group of angry and confused looking soldiers and scientists formed ranks and began backtracking out of the large room.

Lise slung her rifle, looking in concerned wonder at the machine that watched them and the robots that parted to let her men through. She nearly backed into Sardeece. He was still staring at the supercomputer, his mouth a thin line and his eyes creasing at the corners as if lost in his study, concerned over a revelation he could not yet discover. Lise nudged him. "What?"

"Hero's right," Sardeece said without looking at her. "This is a unique opportunity we must not let slip away if we are to survive our own war."

She placed a hand on his arm, motioning to the retreating others with her chin. "It's been a long day," she said softly. "Let's go. We can figure this all out tomorrow."

Sardeece shook his head with disapproval, but picked up his bag and followed the group out of the chamber.

Hero sat with Osmar, watching the night's darkness beyond the hallway the group of Coalition soldiers rested within. The door leading outside the Citadel lay just beyond the little camp, cracked open slightly with a thick piece of steel jammed in as a prop; a safeguard in the interests of those such as Zhade who openly believed the robotic Citadel had asked them to stay only to trap them inside. Hero stood by one exit, left to guard there until relieved. A Coalition soldier guarded the only other hall entering upon the camp. The soldiers had complained about their fears and prejudices, and the scientists had weighed the options, but the admiral had simply wanted quiet, whether to sleep or contemplate, Hero did not know.

He looked back over his shoulder at the group of men and women huddling around the heating unit they had set up. Lise lay on her side under a thin blanket, the contours of her body faintly illuminated by the heater's red glow. Osmar sat behind Hero, leaning against a wall where he noisily dozed - a habit Hero had chastised the mercenary for on several occasions. He turned his head back to surveying the blank scene before him, listening to the darkness beyond.

A figure approached from behind, the footsteps not immediately recognizable, so Hero knew it was neither Lise nor Jo'seph. He was almost surprised when Sardeece came to stand next to him. The thin scientist was nervous and edgy, but his shoulders slumped as though he had already resigned himself to a terrible fate. "You have to let me pass," he said quietly.

Hero never looked directly at the man, instead remaining vigilant to his post. "That is a strange thing to ask a guard," he replied just as quietly. "Do you intend to desert?"

"I have to do something to save this mission," Sardeece said, frantically hissing through his teeth, yet trying to remain quiet. "This opportunity will never come again, and you know it." He looked down at his own feet, sounding suddenly somber again. "And we must help ourselves."

Hero was stone silent for a moment only before replying. "Try to be as quick as possible. I do not wish to have to lie about not having seen you."

Sardeece relaxed a little, smiling. "I hardly think it would be a convincing lie."

"Go."

The scientist nodded, moving off quickly into the gloom.

Hero turned to Osmar. "Are you awake?"

"My Lord," Osmar grunted.

"Follow him. Do not interfere unless he gets into trouble you can pull him out of."

Osmar groaned as he stood. "Aye, My Liege. Thy bidding shall be done." The mercenary practically stumbled down the dark hallway, rubbing his bald head to try and wake himself as he began to trot off after the brave Coalition officer.

"What's the verdict?" Admiral Jay'salan's voice came through the secured COM link distorted by static, reverberating like a distant echo.

Jo'seph stood just outside the open door of the Grellion Citadel, the transmitter held firmly in his hand as he stared up with mixed emotions at the alien stars that filled the cold night sky. "I don't know." He shook his head to himself in frustration. "I just don't know," he finally repeated. "The Citadel has reactivated since Hero's previous visit."

"Reactivated? How?" Jay'salan asked.

"The structure seems to be a living supercomputer, with what appears to be a minor population of servitor robots that are repairing its systems and structure."

"Robots," came the quiet, crackling reply. "That makes things difficult. What do you mean by 'living'?"

"It spoke to us telepathically, Jay'." Jo'seph rubbed the beard on his chin absently. "More than that, it probed our memories and now claims to be reviewing those thoughts in order to examine our claim to this planet. The only thing more I can tell you is that 'negotiations' will resume in the morning." Jo'seph sneezed onto his sleeve, the sudden allergy attack taking him by surprise. "Damn."

"And Hero?"

"Seems to be handling this impartially. I trust him, but I'm not counting on him to make this happen at this point. I honestly don't know what to say, but at the moment I am not optimistic, despite the amazing size and power of this facility. Even if this 'Citadel' does decide to favor our cause, and if it can be trusted, I don't know how we'll move a population of war weary Artificial Intelligence hating people into the belly of his beast."

Jay'salan's voice sighed. "Very well. Keep me informed. We do, of course, have more bad news in the meantime. The Lordillians attacked Segav 3's population. Jo', they've lain waste the surface of the entire planet. Nothing stands."

Jo'seph nearly choked. "Gods," he whispered. "And we can do nothing."

"A world under Lordillian rule for two years on the edge, but not the fringes of, enemy territory is suddenly deemed utterly expendable. It was an obvious trap to flush us out and finish us off. There was nothing we could do."

"Gods." Jo'seph could say nothing for a time, simply staring at the vine covered steps below him. "They shall not have died in vain."

"When the time is right, we shall will them," the admiral echoed. "But we can do nothing until our position is strong again."

Osmar had been walking nearly fifteen minutes in the dark, surprised that the lights were off this close to the control center they had been led to earlier that day. He was even more surprised he had never caught site of the scientist, but he headed for the computer room anyway, figuring it was the safest bet.

The vast chamber ahead of him was bathed in a weird green light, dark blue hues played off of the walls lending a further alien feel. By habit, Osmar's largest, meanest gun was in front of him, the wide barrel awaiting any targets that might need instant dismembering. There were none of the little servitor robots in sight, but he could hear the sounds of their tasks as far off repairs were affected. But a closer, stranger sound was what worried him; a bubbling sound mixed with the charge of electricity and the thumping of something against thick synthetic glass. He gritted his teeth, feeling uneasy and disgruntled that he had been put in this position. Osmar doubted Hero expected him to find such a strange scene, but he couldn't help but hold it against the Triialon warrior; it was in his nature.

Still, little could have prepared the old merc for the horror he perceived before him when he finally entered the main computer room. His sense had not deceived him, for there against the far wall of the room was the source of light and sound. Sardeece seemed unconscious, suspended in a large tank of green fluid, his body racked by spasms each time a flash of energy coursed through the thick, almost opaque juice. Osmar gasped in horror when he caught site of the few details he could make out from that far away. Quickly he grabbed a set of binoculars from a coat pocket and studied his findings. The Coalition scientist indeed was in surgery, with some sort of ugly technology being attached to his body and face. The mercenary increased magnification for a closer look, watching for a moment as small mechanical arms attached to the interior of the tank worked on the seemingly dead man, grafting some sort of prosthesis directly onto his body.

There was nothing he could immediately do for the man but run as fast as he could back to Hero. He would know what to do. Osmar turned warily, on his guard as he made his way back out of the horrific chamber.

"You let him go?" Jo'seph was obviously quite angry, although he controlled it well.

Hero did not feel well about betraying the admiral's trust, but he refused to take too much flak for it. "He made a logical point, and no one else would have let him pass, so he chose to ask me."

"Effectively voiding my decisions as the commander of this expedition, not to mention the entire bloody fleet, between now and whatever might have happened tomorrow."

Hero almost shrugged. "No. No power has been taken from you, nor do I wish to seem as though I was superceding your authority. Sardeece simply knew this mission was in jeopardy and wanted to do something about it in the hopes that tomorrow morning would not be too late. Perhaps he wished to plead our case further. In any event, I sent Osmar to follow him secretly."

The admiral visibly slumped, shaking his head. "I don't know how to feel about any of this." He turned on Hero, his eyes flashing anger. "No, I do. I'm pissed! Regardless of your purely honorary and temporary position in the Coalition I should have been notified of all important matters. The decision should have been mine, not yours."

Hero crossed his arms, about to argue his point further when running footfalls from up the corridor interrupted him. "My Lord!" Osmar's voice was labored from the long run. He came to stand before Hero and the now waking group of Coalition soldiers and scientists.

"What kept you? Where's Sardeece?"

"Unconscious or dead, I don't know which, but before I left him and became lost in this giant labyrinth he was being changed by that group of machines."

"Changed?" Jo'seph asked. "How?"

"I don't know, but he was fairly cybernetic by he time I finally found him. I can tell you this; he's not Sardeece anymore."

"On the contrary," came Sardeece's voice from just beyond the startled group. "I am."

Every weapon was suddenly trained on the tall figure that stood there. Hero's sidearm was out and pointed at the man's head before he even consciously reacted. He relaxed his stance just as easily, studying the man claiming to be Sardeece "Hold your fire," the admiral commanded loudly.

"Sir," Zhade nearly yelled the protest as he glared with open hatred down the sites of his blaster. "We heard the merc; those damn machines have taken him over."

"I said hold your fire," Jo'seph barked back. His narrowed gaze switched right back to Sardeece, though, and he studied the changed man.

Sardeece still wore the Coalition uniform, but from one sleeve protruded an arm replaced by some form of technological augmentation, and from neck to scalp ran further evidence of change, metal and circuits criss-crossing each other around his jaw, up next to his eye and finally under the hairline. From the back of his head and spine protruded tubes and other strange spikes of apparatus. His eyes were red discs on a field of white.

"What's the meaning of this?" Jo'seph asked the man who now faced them. His arms went up in near exasperation, the admiral nearly pleading angrily with the changed scientist. "Explain this, Sardeece. Why have you abandoned your post? Why have you put yourself in danger, and how am I even supposed to know it's really still you? What's happened?"

"Admiral," Sardeece addressed him like any subordinate officer. "I assure you, I am the same man who has worked under you for years. The same man who helped develop the Dimensionalizer engine. The same mind that realized how Dimensionalizer technology could work is the one that decided tonight to make *this* work; make the Coalition and the Grellion citadel form an alliance that could save our people and secure the future."

"You gave yourself over to them? Became something so many here would potentially hate and distrust?"

"Sir," the changed Sardeece continued calmly, "I was there when your daughter Janise was born. I was there the day we left Sparta behind. I
143

was there when the first ship made a Dimensionalizer jump. You had to trust me then, Jo'seph. You'll have to trust me again. I am here now because someone had to be a bridge between our two worlds, and it had to be tonight. Now I know what the Citadel is thinking, and it knows what I am thinking; always."

"You wanted to be a liaison." Lise strode forward to stand next to the admiral, studying Sardeece with open scrutiny and fascination. "Now you're in complete symbiosis with it?"

Sardeece looked at her. "Yes," he said simply. "I can never again leave this planet." He moved towards the admiral, cocking his head to the side a little. "But that's not important. I'm not important. What *is* important is the survival of the Coalition, and the key to that is Grellion." His face was alive again with the passion and excitement of a scientist explaining his greatest find. "Do you have any idea of the magnitude of this place? The Citadel itself stretches for miles. The power is unlimited, its shields able to withstand any attack save the destruction of the very planet. All this and so much more than you even know. And that is yours, but only if you wish to stay."

Jo'seph stared at the scientist that had now become so much more, a long moment of disquieting silence hanging in the tense air. "All right," he said at last, "and what does this computer ask for in return?"

"The Artificial Intelligence asks only that you do not abuse the power that it will give you. The Grellion were guardians of justice who disappeared long before the Triialon ascended, and fell from, their own power. But they had the same ideals in many ways as the Triialon, that much I can tell you. To become the very abusers that this technology was created to control would be unacceptable."

"If this place has the potential to distrust us so much, what are we to believe it gets out of this relationship?"

Sardeece shrugged. "Everything of sentience needs a reason to exist, to be, and you help fulfill that basic need."

Jo'seph nodded his head slightly, almost smiling. For a long, silent moment he stood, simply thinking. Finally he said, "very well; we stay." There was an instant murmur of both disapproval and relief among the soldiers and science team, which the admiral curbed with a look and voice that cut through the din. "I know it will be a difficult transition, but then all such changes are. I don't expect to get it any easier anywhere else, so I'll expect you to respect my decision while we all work towards making this happen. And we do *need* this to happen. This shall be the new Coalition base. The details will fall into place, one way or the other, but the longer we stand here arguing over trust, those metal bastards are out there plundering the galaxy. Since our mission began," Jo'seph paused, trying to keep eye contact with his people but suddenly seeming to find the task difficult. "Segav 3 has fallen. The Lordillians wiped out the population, hoping to provoke a response from the Coalition and finish us off. How long would you have us stay in hiding while such travesties go on simply because of our hatred of machine races? Maybe its time we had some of their technology on our side."

And with that, the hallway was silent, each man in turn looking to the other or at their own feet. "I stand by your decision, admiral," Lise said at last.

Jo'seph looked at Hero suddenly, as if awaiting the morality of someone other than an inferior officer. "You have made a wise choice, admiral," Hero said evenly, but nodded with approval.

"I stand, sir," said another soldier, then another until finally all present save Zhade had spoken his own pledge. Finally the young man nodded, forcing a tight smile. One of his team members slapped him on the back, and there was a murmur of laughs at that. Only Osmar remained silent, watching the display with half-hearted interest.

"Do you wish to take us back to the computer room, then, Mister Sardeece?" Jo'seph asked.

"I can show you to the bridge, actually, if you like."

The admiral looked a little confused. "Shouldn't we tell the... well, tell the Citadel the good news?"

Sardeece almost smirked. "It knows, admiral."

Chapter Nine

Undiscovered, the Grellion Citadel was a myth. Less than
a myth, as probably no one, save perhaps the Gods, even
remembered its existence. With the Coalition's finding of
the ancient structure came the fact that there was now a new
'Wonder' to add the universal list, as no one, anywhere,
knew anything about what had happened to the Citadel's
builders.
Not even the Citadel.
 Coalition and Triialon
- Dr. W. H. Redfield

The boy struggled in the vice-like grasp of the tall soldiers. Tears streamed down his cheeks and he screamed, pulling frantically back and forth, desperate to free himself. The uniformed troopers held him fast, another grasping his head and holding it fast. It was the tyrannical decree that all family present must bear witness to such punishment, regardless of age.

The boy's mother stood before him, merely yards away but unable to help her son for the bonds that tied her and the other prisoners to their posts as they waited, blindfolded, for their fates. The command was given and the rifles were raised. The boy screamed again, his struggles renewed with earnest. He tried to shut his eyes, but a leather-gloved hand pulled at his scalp and face, making it impossible. His vision swam through his own tears as the next orders were read and the drumbeats grew to a crescendo.

Finally the order to fire was given, and ten soldiers fired their fully automatic plasma rifles with unflinching resolve into the prisoners. The boy could have sworn that his high-pitched screams and wails were infinitely louder than the stream of unceasing fire that spat forth and burned down his mother before his eyes.

Chebonka awoke on his throne, a power surge through the charging apparatus answering his sudden jump from unconsciousness. The room's lights came up automatically, yet he still required several milliseconds to remember where he was. He tried to will his mind to calmness, but the sudden onslaught of the recurring dream he had not dreamt since his ascension to artificiality had left him disturbed.

A Lordillian trooper entered the chamber, signaled by the sudden interruption of Chebonka's sleep period. It signaled Chebonka, electronically asking him if he required assistance.

"It was nothing," Chebonka answered, offhandedly waving it away as he tried to regain his thoughts. "Only a nightmare."

"Define 'nightmare', Lord."

Chebonka felt emotion once again welling up inside him, threatening to hinder his judgment. "A nightmare is a subconscious event of negative imagery. A dream."

The metal, bird-like head cocked a little to one side. "Define 'subconscious', Lord."

Chebonka's hand swept the matter aside as he stood impatiently, pulling the Triialon sword from its cradle within the throne and marching past the Lordillian soldier. "Uselessness," he answered.

The soldier bowed.

Lise tried to shield her eyes from the glaring sun, watching the six ships slowly descend and land a few yards away. A day had passed since the evening Sardeece had appeared to them as the 'mechni-prophet', as some of the soldiers had taken to calling him. Much of the following hours had been spent huddled around him while he was given a medical examination, each soldier and scientist looking on during that time, alone with their own quiet thoughts. The mood between the examiner, the admiral, and Sardeece was unexpectedly jovial, at least in a strange ice-breaking sort of way. But while the others may have chuckled and laughed at each quip from the changed scientist they all knew that deep down it would take more than a medical exam to completely trust this man again.

Since then Lise had been left in charge of the camp while Hero and Osmar flew the admiral back to the fleet. Now they returned, escorting the first crews and garrison troops back to their new base. The location of the Grellion citadel was still top secret; no chances being taken until either the servitors or the Coalition scientists could repair the base's shields and weapons. Lise wondered how long it would take for the two groups to begin working together in proper unison. She did not doubt that that time would come, she just didn't know if it would be in her lifetime.

149

Hero's desert gunship touched down first, followed by the four Coalition ships, each one double the size of the Triialon craft. Scientists, engineers, designers, troops, cargo, weapons; all manner of life and supply began to unload from the ships almost the moment their gear had touched ground. Lise saluted as admiral Jo'seph walked up to her, Hero at his side.

"Commander Lise. You look none the worse for a day alone at an archeological myth on an alien world run by a race of machines." He smiled, looking happier than she could remember in some time. "At ease." Jo'seph handed her a packet full of notes. "Distribute these amongst yourself and your team, including the scientists, please, immediately."

"Yes, sir. Its good to have you back." She looked at Hero. "Both of you."

"I trust the day was uneventful?" Hero asked her.

She shrugged a little. "A bit of exploring, a lot of boot cleaning. Communication with the Grellion machines can be... interesting when Sardeece isn't around."

Jo'seph and Hero began walking her back towards the open front door of the base. "Where is Mister Sardeece?" Jo'seph asked.

"Attempting to oversee the repairs of the shield. He says he has a lot to talk to you about." Lise laughed, "If you can manage to pull him away from the task at hand. I think he's in love."

"The place is amazing, I have to admit," the admiral replied. "Which reminds me; admiral Jay'salan sends his gratitude for the images you relayed of the base interiors and exteriors. He was quite speechless."

"Miss Holsted's imaging class back at private school," she said sarcastically, then made a show of acting as though she'd just realized something. "Oh, you meant he was amazed by the base? I thought he just liked my photography."

Jo'seph's eyes narrowed, but he smiled. "Lise, if I didn't know better, I'd say that my sense of humor has become a bad influence on you. To your duties, commander."

"Sir."

Lise spent the better part of the day carrying out menial tasks for the admiral and instructing teams to different work duties. She was desperate for a shower and a change of clothes, but she hadn't the time to even think about it for most of the afternoon. She oversaw crews, using maps provided by the citadel on tracking tablets, to explore some of the closest and most important parts of what would be their new home and base of operations. One crew was cleaning and inspecting the large bridge levels. They began repairing the basics with the aid of the small servitor robots, the newly arrived team members casting the occasional odd glance at the small machines. Lise helped them to communicate with the servitors via the data tablets Sardeece had given her. They also looked at some of the more mundane areas, including the living quarters that ran the length and depth of one of the buildings and continued down into levels below the soil level. The Grellions must have been fairly humanoid and roughly the same size, if perhaps a little taller, given the dimensions of the rooms and their furnishings. A fine layer of dust covered most everything, but other than that most of it seemed in good condition, working or not. There were rooms where it felt things might be missing, but that was hardly surprising considering the place had been abandoned.

Finally Jo'seph asked Lise to escort him to Sardeece's position so that the scientist could report. She happily put Zhade in charge of her duties and took the admiral and the trailing Hero back down into the depths of the Grellion citadel.

Sardeece was waiting for them in an engineering bloc a few levels below the computer center. "Admiral," he said, saluting. "Hero; welcome. I have good news and bad news, gentlemen." He flashed a tired but excited smile. "Shall I begin?"

"By all means," Jo'seph replied, running a hand down his face in preparation.

"Very well. Good news; main life support and basic function power is restored. With a cleaning and repair crew I think we can have that hanger door open within a week and maybe even power up that main cannon on top of it at the same time. By my calculations, the cannon should yield about twice the blasting power the current Sparta battle cruiser can fire, so we won't be defenseless by any means. The bad news, though, is the base shields. The citadel's self-diagnostics aren't what they used to be, so we're having trouble finding all of the faults. I can't yet give you an estimate, but it could be months before we have a fully impenetrable umbrella."

"That's bad."

"We do have a lot of work ahead of us, I agree. But there may be an unforeseen compensation."

Jo'seph's eyebrows raised, interested. When Sardeece didn't immediately continue, the admiral looked to Hero to see if he knew what he meant, but the warrior made no move to indicate he did. "Okay, I'll bite. What possible compensation?"

Sardeece's mood changed, becoming deadly serious, his eyes narrowing as his voice took on a conspiratorial tone. "If you had the offensive power to wipe the Lordillians from the heavens, what would you do with it?"

"I would end the Lordillian reign," Jo'seph said with cold ease, "and make certain Chebonka was dead, his horde never to return again."

"And what then would you do with that power, once you had defeated the system which oppresses so many and become yourself such a dominant force in this galaxy?" Sardeece asked these questions not as a member of Coalition, but as the voice of the Grellion, of that much Lise was certain.

Jo'seph's face never even twitched. "I think I would have a drink." There was a pause before he smiled sardonically. "Other than that, I would do the same thing we were doing before the Lordillians came, if you might recall; the defense of the peoples and cultures of the Coalition, and beyond, and the exploration of those worlds we've not yet seen."

"And if others rose up against your power?"

Jo'seph pulled a face. "Every situation is unique, I should think, but I would hope negotiation would yield a positive solution to this hypothetical situation. What's your point?"

"The point is that the future is at stake no matter who wins this war." Sardeece turned to the control panels behind him, bringing up a picture of rolling hills covered in bushes. "These are the mountains outside the base, just behind us." He turned back to Jo'seph and the others. "Have them scanned; They are not mountains. You will find an enormous metal object the length of this citadel is buried there."

152

Jo'seph's jaw dropped. "But that's over eight miles long." Sardeece nodded.

"Its a battle cruiser," Hero said surely. He looked at the admiral with excitement checked under a proud warrior face. "You wanted to know what used that landing strip out front."

Sardeece smiled. "Yes. A flagship as powerful as it is ancient. The memory cores of this base may have been wiped when the Grellions left this world, but this much is known; the ship crash-landed there after its final battle. Either it was on fire or it was deemed irretrievable before the Grellions time here ended. In any case, mounds of earth were pushed over its hull and it was left there." Sardeece switched off the screen. "It might take us years to dig out and repair, and even then it may never fly again. But its cannons could defend against any attack, and if salvageable, the ship itself could just be the offensive weapon that could, hypothetically, stand against the enormous fleets of the Lordillians."

Jo's eyebrows were still arched in amazement. "We need to get a crew out there as soon as possible," he said at last. "Incredible." he muttered.

"I thought that might brighten your spirits," Sardeece said, smiling. "But you must remember your promise to the citadel, and entrust that promise to future generations."

Admiral Jo'seph scratched the beard along his jaw absently, but ended up grinning like an idiot. "I just hope it all works."

"I assume you're not moving the fleet here till the shields are up and at full strength?" Hero asked.

"That's the plan thus far, but I think we're kind of playing it as it goes."

"Well, you certainly have plenty of concerns," Hero replied, arms crossed as he followed the admiral back out of the room. "That aside, what do you think of your new home."

Jo'seph ran a hand through his blonde hair. "Its really overwhelming," he said, smiling. "It stretches for miles, most of it in pristine condition, and there's so much room above and below ground that not only will we fit the entire coalition compliment, but many of their families as well."

153

"If packed in tightly."

"But safe," Jo' stated intently. "A couple of the engineers have already suggested building a small town inside. No matter what we do its still so much more promising than where we left off. I owe you my thanks for showing us this place. We all do."

"Use it wisely."

Silence followed the two men for a moment, until finally the admiral asked, "Where's Osmar?"

"Back at my ship, I believe. Don't worry, he's nowhere that could compromise the mission here."

"You trust him," Jo'seph said simply.

"Yes. He's a simple man in many ways, but he understands honor despite his past professions. And he has an... enlightening sense of humor."

"How did you meet him?"

Hero raised an eyebrow. "A previous misadventure. I saved his life, he pledged it to me. He's a good fighter, I've found."

Jo'seph laughed aloud. "You're such a softy, Hero. Really pulling at my heart-strings."

Hero simply looked at him. At that moment, Lise, who had been trailing behind the whole time marking a checklist as she spoke into her headset, ran up and saluted.

"What is it, Lise?"

"Sir, shift changes are about to commence and nightfall is only a few hours away. I just wanted to make certain that living quarters were being prepared and assigned." She smiled a little and put her hands on her hips. "At least, I had been guessing we were staying in the base and not bunking it in the ships."

"And how many others did you tell this 'guess' to, commander?" Jo'seph asked with annoyance. Lise had the grace to look sheepish, and the admiral sighed. "Very well, I'll leave you to it, if the rest of your duties for today are complete."

"Yes, sir, they are."

154

"Good. Base the accommodations on the Norpan asteroid rank-and-privilege system. That, and what's been made available so far by the repair crews. I assume we have running water?"

Lise grinned. "Yes, admiral, thankfully."

Hero suddenly looked anxious. "Admiral, commander," he interrupted, "if you'll excuse me, I have matters to attend to tonight before I turn in." He bowed slightly to Lise, never taking his eyes from hers. "Good evening." With that, he turned and made for the elevators.

"That man is a true loner," Jo'seph said after he was gone.

"I don't think so," Lise said quietly, staring after him.

"Oh? And is that because you truly see beyond the warrior, or because you simply wish to see more?"

Lise turned, feeling found-out. She smiled at last, "Jealous," she asked, quickly adding "sir?"

The corners of Jo'seph's lips turned up tightly. "Are you kidding, Madame?" He looked around him. "I'm in love with this base. Just don't tell Sardeece; I don't know what the implications would be considering his recent transition. Besides, I couldn't condone such fraternizing."

Lise laughed and turned away, heading for the bridge levels. But once she was alone in the large lift, she found her thoughts again dominated by the strange warrior with whom she shared such a strange connection.

The cold water had felt surprisingly refreshing. Lise had initially spent a number of minutes trying to find the control that would heat the water, but nothing did. Then she had spent a half an hour looking around her new room and then floor for any object that resembled a water heater. When she finally tracked down a servitor robot and communicated her need to find such a device to the machine, the basic text reply it gave to her data pad had been something to the effect that 'things were missing.' She'd given up hope and taken the cold shower, letting the shock of it wash away several long days.

Now she stood outside of the quarters she had assigned Hero, rubbing the back of her long, dark hair with an all too small towel, trying desperately to combat the over-ambitious curls. She was disappointed to

155

find that Osmar was the one to answer the door. He stood there, trying to hide a bottle behind him, looking strangely normal without his weapon-laden duster despite his muscular, compact physique and bald plate. Maybe he just looked like any old soldier now.

"Oh, good evening, Osmar," she said cordially.

"M'lady."

"I thought I assigned you your own quarters," she said, trying to see past him into the room.

The old mercenary swished his moustache at her, his eyes squinting. "Yeah, but the alcohol is in his room."

"Ah," she smiled. "So, what do you think of all of this?" she asked, her eyes motioning to the base around them.

Osmar leaned against the door frame, looking around for unseen ears. "I dunno, lass. I am hopeful for you, but I have to admit feeling a bit like your friend Zhade. This whole deal with a talking citadel is a bit much to swallow for a simple man." He shrugged absently. "Robots make great pets because they don't talk. If it does, well, then its time to get a new robot." Lise laughed and Osmar seemed to suddenly see the joke, smiling at his own insight. "Still, if anyone can make it work out for you, its Hero."

"Can you tell me where to find him?"

"His Grace has gone to meditate. I'm certain that means the darkest, quietest place he could find in this great bloody place."

"Thank you, Osmar."

"You're welcome, lady," he said, closing the door.

Lise tapped her chin, thinking. She came to a decision and ran off, looking for the closest servitor robot.

He stood in the center of the vast room she had finally found after wandering through several corridors. Hero was right where the servitor had told her he would be. She was still learning the layout of the new base, and she did not want to alert him to her presence either by calling for him or by trying to use her mind to find him. Stealthily she had entered and found a place to stand in the dark, watching him.

The Triialon was dressed in loose linen trousers and top, with the sword in his hand and the ever-present Prizm on his right wrist. She was instantly entranced by the movements and the man who commanded them. The sword would stab out or arc, and then his arm and finally whole body would follow it through in a motion so graceful it belied the destructive cause of its origin. Then the sword would flash out, and his muscles would tighten as he began a series of strikes and defenses against an unseen opponent. He twisted and turned, his body in perfect harmony with the dance. He leapt, rolled, came up for another strike, turned and cut the air, stretched and stabbed at an invisible beast high above before coming down again to rest within the cradle of his arm.

Suddenly he stopped. Lise froze, thinking that she had betrayed her presence or otherwise disturbed him. But he simply held still, locked in a stance, before again turning slowly, following the point of the blade through space and over terrain. She watched his face, trying desperately to study every detail, decipher every thought he may have, read every line in his face from across a room. The darkness and space between them kept their secrets, though, and the man and warrior both remained a mystery to her.

She stood there, for how long she didn't know, simply watching. When Hero stopped again, she didn't think to stop her breathing and remain hidden, so lost was she in his meditation.

"I thought you were going to show me your customs, commander. Instead you see fit to oversee mine."

Lise smiled a little, caught, yet refusing to take the scolding from this man. She was much too fascinated not to take the bait instead. "I thought you had no customs," she said, stepping from the shadows to slowly cross the silent room. She stopped several paces from him and cocked her head with a mocking grin at his lack of reply.

Hero relaxed from his stance and faced her. He moved and the sword moved around him, graceful yet deadly strokes, and suddenly he was presenting the hilt to her. "My ancestors had customs. I only have this." The statement seemed detached, but his eyes grabbed hers and caressed them, inviting her closer still. "Take it."

The young woman straightened up. There was a sacred air to this moment, she sensed that easily enough, but more importantly she didn't want to disappoint his trust. She reached out and took the sword from him, turning it easily, switching to her other hand and bringing it to rest at her side. The blade was long, nearly three feet of the strange alloy, but the balance was superb, the weight almost an afterthought.

"Are you left handed?" he asked. She shook her head. "Are you my friend?" The second question took her by surprise, and for a moment she didn't know what he was talking about. Uncertain and desperate not to blush she nodded. "Then hold the sword in your right hand. You have the manner right, but on the wrong side. Carrying the blade at rest in your right hand means that you are at peace and bear me no ill will. Where you have it now, you are ready to draw." Lise had already made the sword change hands as he was explaining. "Very good."

She smiled. "You must change hands a lot," she asked, looking at the Prizm on his right wrist.

"I do. Now, hold it at the ready. Do you like the weight?"

"Yes," Lise answered.

"No, hold it here," he said, placing his hands on hers and showing her the stance. "This is called the Talenke'. It is the power of the triangle's peak. Hold the hilt here. Good. Now, bring the sword down to bring down the power of the peak."

She swung the sword with practiced precision, stopping at the arc's end but reveling in the movement as the blade snapped taut. She smiled openly, but a thought struck her as he began his next instruction, and she interrupted him. "What is your name?" The question was an honest one, and its significance had overtaken her with such suddenness that she had bluntly asked it aloud, albeit with a soft voice. When he simply looked at her, she continued. "Before you were called Hero, what was your name?"

He was silent only a moment before he answered. "My birth name was given up the moment the King gave me my title of manhood," he said. "It is no longer mine."

"But were you called 'Hero' by the King?"

"The Triialon pronunciation would be difficult for you, and I prefer the common tongue's translation after all these years. I'd rather put both of the old names behind me."

"Can you teach me the Triialon language?" Lise wasn't about to let him hide everything from her forever, and interest in his ways seemed to be the only icebreaker she could afford thus far.

His mood had darkened at the question, though. "It is a dead language." The man held out his hand to receive the Triialon Sword. She stood at attention again, doubling his maneuver which he had used to originally hand her the blade as perfectly as she could manage. The tactic worked, Hero's face relaxing as he showed a small smile. "Very good," he genuinely praised while taking the weapon. "Now, if you would excuse me, I have my meditations to complete yet this evening."

"May I join you," she pushed. "Perhaps I can learn your style."

"I would rather you d…"

But Lise interrupted him again, lithely turning away to leave him as she spoke over her shoulder. "Then it is my turn to show you our ways." She stopped, turning to bow slightly before departing. "Until next time, My Lord, when I might instruct you." She walked out then, leaving him standing there, hopefully more than a little dumbfounded in the echoing space of the training room.

Giant metal bodies barely shuddered despite the immense power their rifles unleashed against the forces before them. Their gleaming arms held each weapon out before them and unleashed hell upon a defense force that was hopelessly outclassed and outnumbered. Despite this, Memfis was almost impressed by Lordillian technology and form as he watched the spectacle on his screen. The images were already an hour old and he regretted not seeing it live, feeling as though he had missed something by not knowing the instant each power move was made.

The city under siege was on a small moon, the furthest, oldest and most independent colony of Moonshau. It had no real resources to speak of, no tactical positioning, no real place in the hierarchy of things. It was simply in the way, the next target on Chebonka's list of conquests. As specks on star charts go, it was putting up a decent fight. Humanoid soldiers marched forth and launched their own heavy artillery, cracking open the cylindrical metal limb casings of a group of Lordillians and exposing their inner machinations. The army of machines strode forth, undeterred, their sheer numbers giving them the confidence they might have lacked were they of flesh and blood. The mortals could do nothing but fight and die, then be marched over as the troopers made their way into the outlying towns, burning down anything they did not calculate as valuable. Buildings quickly turned to ash and people were herded like cattle or shot dead in the streets, depending on their age and size.

For an android, Memfis thought, Chebonka certainly was taking his inability to finally stamp out the Coalition rather heavily. Still, it provided such an unceasing spectacle of amusement, he almost hated the idea of one day having to put the Lordillian race to the flame. But he could certainly understand Chebonka's frustration; Memfis's own hold on the Court was slackening due to the current unknown whereabouts of Hero and the Coalition and the assessment of their current levels of strength.

Memfis sighed, turning off the VID display just as its picture slowly pulled back to view the entire colony on fire.

"Our lord is distressed by something?" Galatis asked. One or two of the other Gods briefly looked up from their own displays at the exchange.

Memfis made a show of looking relaxed. "No, no, just thinking of Chebonka's fate despite all of his brilliant fireworks displays."

A few of the Gods chuckled at that, but others were quiet, either lost in their own studies or simply not amused by Memfis' candor. That troubled him. Usually he couldn't care less what his fellow Gods thought of him, but it seemed Toapo's open challenge had touched a nerve of paranoia. He briefly contemplated calling the Forefather in to begin a quest for Hero, quickly setting the idea aside. If there was one thing Memfis could trust Toapo to do it was to be Toapo. The fool would make his own move, he knew, and when that happened Memfis would be waiting. Let Chebonka rage, let Hero fight on in vain, let the Coalition hide. In the end, none of it would really matter. Still, Hero and his past would have to be dealt with, but then issues like that were what Seethlings were for.

She had lain dead in his arms; his only love had been taken and would never again be waiting for him to return after battle. This was the gratitude the fates had for a man who fought for life, by taking so cruelly the very life that meant the most to him. He never even got to say goodbye. Instead he had found her already gone, a crushed flower among the ruins of the Triialon stronghold.

The King knelt beside him in the dust, slumping, a crumpled old figure with the very life cut from within him. He had been the only man that had loved her more than Hero himself. The warrior dared not weep, for his King shed those tears readily and openly in front of the silent and shocked masses that gathered around them. The mourning became a wail of pain and rage, echoing the same hole within Hero's heart. "She had the protection of her father and his champion, and yet even she dies," the King had screamed at last. The Princess was dead.

They had said it was the day hope died on Triialon.

The dream had repeated itself several times in Hero's sleeplessness since the night Lise had found him training. It was a memory he could never quite put aside, and for some reason the Spartan woman had reopened that wound enough for the past to flood in. He had since found a new room in which to train, deeper within the Grellion citadel. Despite these precautions, the past persisted and his own emotions seemed to call to Lise instead of defending against the problems she threatened to introduce. Refusing to give in, he had decided to approach the link he shared with the Coalition beauty scientifically, calling secretly for the personal charts and blood work of Lise's from the admirals' files. He had yet to bring himself to actually open them.

A chime at the door pulled Hero from staring at the unopened folder.

"Can you find what it is I need?" The citadel's voice rang in the minds of all of those present. "I did not know it was gone until I realized it was missing."

"We have another problem."

Sardeece looked as worried as Hero had ever seen the man during the last few trying days. This morning seemed to bring a new level to his relationship with the citadel, one which had left the young scientist quite disturbed, probably by a lack of being able to properly cross-communicate a need with the telepathic machine sentience. That and a lack of sleep. In any case, the dilemma left creases of near panic etched into his features, running under the strange augmentations on the side of his face. When no one else instantly grabbed onto the open statement, Hero decided to prompt the oncoming blow. "What is wrong, Sardeece?"

Sardeece began pacing. "The citadel needs something, and I can't figure out what it is. But whatever it might be, it's what is needed to power not only the shields but the main cannons and batteries as well."

"What?" Jo'seph nearly screamed the word. The scientists and officers standing nearby all jumped at the outburst. Even Lise looked surprised at the admiral's response, despite the obvious implications of what Sardeece was saying. "I thought you said you could at least get the hanger cannon working within a week? We're sitting targets until then!"

"I know, I know. All I can make out is that once the self-diagnostics came back online some of the computer's memory came back with it, and now it knows why some things aren't working around here. Or at least it has a better idea."

"And why is that?" Hero asked calmly.

Sardeece couldn't stop pacing, his motions becoming frantic as he tried to explain the lack of data to his superiors. "All I can figure is that sometime during the millennia that the base has remained dormant it's been visited by grave robbers, and the most valuable resource of the citadel aside from the very core of this planet itself was taken away."

"And what resource is that, mister Sardeece?" Jo'seph asked menacingly.

"That's just it," the mechni-prophet said exasperatedly, "it doesn't know. All it knows is that a very core element, or elements really, of itself are missing. Linkages, like crystal spheres, that help power critical systems at juncture points are gone, just inexplicably missing. Yet the strangest thing is the feeling the citadel keeps sending me, as if saying that you should be able to provide the missing elements some how."

162

"What do you mean, I can," Jo'seph wondered aloud.

"You. Us," he answered pointing to Jo'seph, Lise, himself, the others. "The new keepers of this place are somehow supposed to be a link the way the Grellions once were, and without that link nothing here works." Sardeece slumped against a wall, looking lost. "I don't get it."

"Let's start by looking at this from a logistical point of view," Hero interjected. "You can show us where crystal linkages are physically missing from the circuits for the shields and weapons?"

"Yes."

"And it's not something we can substitute, something else we can put in the space?"

"No. As I said, it's a critical element."

"And we're supposed to provide it somehow out of thin air?" Jo'seph asked with more than a little sarcasm.

"I don't know. I don't think the base knows." The scientist was practically pounding the wall at this point, unable to articulate his own thoughts now, much less the citadel's. "All it knows is that once, long ago, these elements were in place and that the Grellions were the ones who, I don't know, supplied them is the easiest way I can explain what its saying to me."

"And you think they were stolen," Hero pointed out. "Not taken by the Grellions, not dissolved by the passage of time, but removed at some point by scavengers as something of value."

"Yes, taken. Taken."

"What are you getting at, Hero," Jo'seph said, rubbing his temples roughly.

"I think I may have seen one of these crystals at some point in my travels," Hero said quietly. "Or at the very least heard of one."

"Not one, many," Sardeece mumbled. Lise moved to the scientist, placing a calming hand upon his shoulder.

"What makes you say that," Jo'seph prompted.

"The same thing that led me to this citadel in the first place."

"The Prizm," Lise realized.

"Yes. There are other things I have detected in my travels which have energy likened to that but ultimately different or unequal to the artifacts of the Triialon. Some of the basic elements can be the same, though, and that is what provides the false detection. Elements of that kind of power, if someone actually found this place during the last few thousand years, would end upon the black market. From there they fall into the hands of the rich and powerful or the traders with the greatest need. If what we seek is something I have seen before, then it could have been on the streets or in a palace."

"But you don't remember either." Jo'seph threw up his arms. "Great."

"It means I can backtrack and find, hopefully, something that will get this base's defenses online. I have been meaning to go to Okino again soon anyway."

"Okino?" Lise asked excitedly.

"Yes. Among other things I had hoped Osmar and I might start to get my fledgling information network working for the Coalition as well. In the meantime, I still suggest your scientists try and find the nature of these elements and recreate them if possible."

"Admiral: Okino," Lise smiled, walking over to Jo'seph and nearly grasping his arm happily. "Do we still not have a representative there?"

Jo'seph had to stop himself rubbing his temples, instead scratching his beard again. "No, we don't. And yes, we have been saying we need their support, but I was assigned Moonshau and the senator we had planned to send to the palace on Okino died at Norpan. Since then Jay'salan, Bevanne and I have been stretched a little thin." He had to physically keep himself from scratching his chin again, finally waving Lise away in frustration. "All right, yes, I agree."

"Agree with what?" Hero almost hated to ask.

"If you're going to Okino now, I'm sending Lise with you as liaison to the palace."

Hero winced. He sighed, crossing his arms. "You will need a dress."

Chapter Ten

Some said that he never existed, that it's impossible
for one man to have done everything they said he
did. Others, some historians even, said he was really
several people, the amalgamation of a group of
generals or fighters perpetrated by the common
religious and social need for a hero-figure. Of course,
I've seen the truth in my great, great grandfather's
notes and files...
Coalition and Triialon
- Dr. W. H. Redfield

The rain pelted them as soon as they stepped off of the platform of Hero's ship. A gray sky rolled above them, it's billowing clouds sailing past summer green trees. Lise smiled. The ground beneath her feet was moist, full of gravel and long blades of a bluish grass. Vara-Del was a small but pretty world, she decided, as pit-stops for dress shopping went.

The Triialon ship had landed in a field just outside of a large town, its buildings old but well kept, with decorations and trim accenting the brickwork designs. The place was quaint but obviously rich, with people milling about everywhere. There was a rumble of thunder that instantly brought sensations of real life forward from the subconscious of Lise's mind, and she couldn't help but run a hand through her long hair and wish she were in anything but a soldiers' uniform.

She followed Hero as he stepped over an old fallen tree on their way into town. "Goleida's last remaining unconquered colony," she mused aloud. "This place smells rich. I had no idea it was doing so well for itself."

Hero's eyebrow raised in surprise. "Few know that the Goleidans got so far out so long ago."

"I always enjoyed history class. Besides, we've been wondering how much longer it has before the Lordillians decide to cross the embargo lines and claim it as their own."

"Who's embargo?" the Triialon asked with keen interest.

"Kordula's, I'm told. Where's Osmar going?" she asked, noticing the mercenary heading in a different direction, dressed to the hilt in weapons as usual.

"He has business to attend to here."

She watched Osmar's retreat, shrugging. "Won't he be a little conspicuous?"

Hero smiled slightly. "No to the people he's looking for."

Lise picked up her pace to catch up with the tall warrior. She raised an eyebrow at him when she finally managed to catch his eye. "You're up to something, aren't you?"

"There are some old," he paused, finding the right word, "acquaintances here that may prove to have useful information. Some are more nefarious than others."

"So where are *we* going?"

"Reconnaissance and supplies purchase."

Lise grinned, throwing her arms up. "Shopping, Hero! We're going shopping."

That hint of a smile on his lips grew wider. "That's what I said, we're going shopping." She grunted in frustration at him for making fun of her, but he continued unabated. "I assume you'll first wish to find more appropriate clothing for today as well as for our trip."

She laughed. "Absolutely. I just don't know what I can afford in this town... it looks expensive as hell."

"I told you earlier, let me worry about that."

The first store they walked into was a strange mix of antique furniture and clothing, with displays that would have put some of the richer homes on Sparta to shame. Lise found she couldn't wipe the grin off of her face. She hadn't had an opportunity to be anyplace like this in years and hadn't realized just how much she had missed it until the moment she had stepped through the shop doors. "Oh I'm going to enjoy this." She turned to see if Hero had heard her, but he was already on the far side of the store looking through a selection of shirts absently. Lise doubted he was really doing much real shopping himself, but even if he was faking it she intended to make the most of what little time she might have there.

Within a half an hour she had tried on several items and was already wearing a tight pair of pants and revealing top, feeling strangely at ease with little effort. She moved on through the gowns, eyeing several different cuts and colors before searching for Hero. She found him dwelling in the doorway outside, watching the street.

"What colors will you be wearing to Okino?" she asked him.

"Why do you ask," he responded without taking his eyes from the town's people.

"So I know what color gown to buy," she said incredulously. "I should match my escort."

"Should you?"

Lise pulled a face. "I think you know more about customs than you're willing to let on. Yes, I should match you."

"Just wear black. There's black in what I'll be wearing."

"Ugh, you're impossible sometimes, you know that?"

"How much longer will you be?

"Never rush a woman when she's shopping." That got a laugh out of him. "Fine," she said, "I'll only be a few more minutes, but I still want to hit that store across the street." She motioned to the shop window with the sports, hunting and military equipment advertised in the window.

"At least we share some common interests," he grumbled, handing her a billfold.

"Stop complaining, you brought us here." Lise went back to the clothes and accessories, smiling to herself as she grabbed a copious amount of different garments and lingerie and made for the counter feeling like a woman again and not at all guilty for it. She joined Hero at the door and found herself studying the street and all of its tactical possibilities, hoping suddenly that it was simply Hero's influence that had caused her mind to act so militaristic in such a serene place. "Any word from Osmar?" she asked.

"No, not yet. We've not been here long, though. Ready?"

They crossed the street to the shop. Hero quickly starting taking stock of needed items for his ship's supplies. Meanwhile Lise had found the item that had caught her interest from across the street: a skintight bodysuit made of some sort of black flexible material. There was an armored metal-like corset over it as well, along with padding and boots. It stood out, and Lise wanted it for strike missions, which meant she would need several pair. She smiled, and went to find her Triialon host.

The rain had begun again in earnest as night fell. Hero and Lise had made a quick stop back to the ship to drop off their new bags and then headed back to the main street. He had gotten the call from Osmar finally a few minutes before, and now he and Lise found themselves ducking between shops and through alleys to keep a little dryer on their way to his location. Lise seemed not to have any trouble keeping up despite the heeled boots she wore, so he quickened his pace. Hero usually trusted the information the man they were meeting sold, but trusting the man himself was always a different story.

He looked back briefly, finding Lise still a mere step behind, her long black curls sticking to her wet face. He checked his blaster, making sure it was fully charged, and realized that Lise probably wasn't armed. "Lise," he called to her over his shoulder, "are you carrying?"

"You didn't say…"

"I didn't," he interrupted, "but you should always be prepared." He shook his head and continued on. "If anything goes wrong tonight, look to me."

He could practically hear Lise's scowl at that, and he certainly could feel her reaction to that remark, so he regretted the choice of words. "I can take care of myself," she said, and pulled a knife from inside of her boot.

"Very well," he replied.

"Who is Osmar meeting?" Lise asked, her tone now icy.

"An informant named Lek. I've purchased information from him before and I'm hoping to turn his ear to Lordillian news in future. Make no mention of Okino in his presence."

Lise paused, quiet a moment before calmly replying. "Understood."

Did she truly know how little he actually trusted the agent called Lek? Could she read his stronger thoughts now, or was it simpler than that?

The Triialon warrior stopped dead in his tracks at a junction from an alley out onto a street. His hand went up into a signal for quiet. He then pointed to the two objects that had halted his march.

There were two Lordillian troopers walking down the street, the rain bouncing off of their gleaming metal chassis. Each one had a blaster rifle slung over a shoulder, and they moved slowly, looking down each alleyway and peering briefly at each storefront window. People within range of the large metal creatures displayed shock and fear, moving off in opposing directions as quickly and peaceably as possible. Already they were past Hero and Lise's position, so he waited for them to move off further before he spoke to her.

"I thought this was a free world still."

"It is. That doesn't stop Lordillians from visiting worlds where they're not wanted." She looked at him then, her brow creasing. "But you're concerned beyond that, aren't you?"

"I am simply weighing the possibilities of this coincidence. Either way, you're in danger."

They had moved into a much shadier part of town. Hero hadn't really ever realized before just how much darker this part of the city was, but then he had never been there at night, either, much less during a storm. So many different kinds of people and beings came to this city as it was such a popular port; that was what made having an informant bankrolled here such a fortuitous thing. One corner of Lordillian occupied space was fairly close to this star system, as Lise had hinted. Hero shrugged. Perhaps, he thought, he was being slightly paranoid about the Lordillian troops they'd seen.

The rain made the lights streaming from the windows and signs of the dark buildings reflect brightly from the black streets with a multi-colored glare. Taverns and halls were the only things open in this quarter past sundown, the sounds of laughter and brawls carrying out from open doors. Hero found the bar where Osmar had indicated he was easily enough, and he and Lise entered, working their way back to a booth in a dark corner. There Osmar sat across from a scaly faced figure in a cloak. Lek was almost as ugly as Hero recalled: dark brown and green skin, matted, dread-locked hair falling out from beneath the cloak's hood, squinty, untrusting eyes. The lizard looked up at Hero's approach, frowning as he took a drag from a tobacco stick.

"I should have known where there was one there would be the other," Lek grumbled. His voice was like gravel, a deep rumble accented by the smoke pouring from his mouth.

Hero did not sit. "I just wanted to make sure you knew where the money was coming from, Lek. I want only the best information, as usual."

"So I've been told."

"Then we understand one another."

Lek leaned back, scratching one eyelid with his tongue. "You pay well enough, Triialon." He laughed, eyeing Lise in a way that spoke volumes.

"Lord, I've already told him about some of the information we seek." Osmar never took his eyes off of the informant while he spoke. It seemed he trusted Lek even less on this trip as well.

Lek shrugged. "I can only guess what you want with intelligence regarding the Coalition/Lordillian war. But hey, war is your business, and information is mine. We're old friends, Hero, so I figure you'll tell me when you're ready." Those eyes of his betrayed something once again, but quickly focused back on staring openly at Lise. "I've got all the time in the world. You sure your classy friend won't sit down and have a drink with me?"

Hero stepped forward, effectively blocking the lizard's view of Lise and forcing Lek to look him in the eye. "Of course you have time. You've provided such a wealth of information for me before." He smiled, handing a billfold to Lek. "This is a down payment. You know how to contact me." Osmar got up, knowing his cue, and tapped Lise's shoulder as they both headed for the bar's front door. "I'll be back here soon, though, Lek, so don't go out of your way."

Lek's lips twitched, as if he were cleaning his teeth under them with his tongue. "Of course. I'll be busy here collecting data."

Hero smiled a little at those squinting eyes. He nodded at last and turned away, following Lise and Osmar out.

"You don't wish to solicit him for part of the network, Lord?" Osmar's question was asked in a manner that suggested he didn't think it was a good idea either.

"No," Hero replied curtly. "Keep to the alleys."

"You don't trust him?" Lise asked quietly.

"Less than usual, M'lady," Osmar grunted. "This time he seems particularly full of attitude." He turned to Hero as they made their way quickly through a rain-drenched alley of brick. "You saw the metal beasties, my liege?"

Hero nodded.

Lise increased her speed, her heels clicking along just behind Hero. "What network," she called to him.

"There's a number of people I know in different systems that could be very useful to the Coalition if organized properly," Hero remarked in hushed tones, checking each intersection of alleys before leading them across. "And if the price is right."

"Are they all as charming as Lek?"

"No."

"Something's bolstered his confidence," Osmar observed.

"Only question now is whether or not he's already contacted those two Lordillians."

Lise gasped. "They were looking for us!"

"Yes, I believe so." Hero's senses were trying to alarm him of something, and with each step he became all the more certain of just what. "Hopefully there is only the two of them," he said, pulling his blaster from his side holster.

They turned a corner into a wide alley and came face to face with a squad of ten Lordillian shock troopers armed to the hilt. Hero had finished drawing and blasted two of the androids with direct hits to their heads before the Lordillians even had a chance to open fire. Once they did, the alley became a shower of light and noise, explosions tearing into the walls around them. Osmar pulled his long barreled cannon out from under his duster jacket, bellowing as he crossed the alley entrance to it's far side, all the while spitting blaster fire and curses at their attackers. Lise meanwhile threw herself against a wall. "Shit," she screamed. "There's more than two!"

Hero tossed Lise his blaster, then began to press the necessary sequence in the Prizm to release his sword.

"Lord, the rooftop!" Osmar turned to defend against the troops that had stalked from behind and above. The warning came late, the six or more Lordillians on the roof opening fire with fully automatic rifles, spraying their position with extreme prejudice. Lise leapt aside, flipping acrobatically across the alley to avoid the crossfire of blasts and landing next to Osmar to help defend against the Lordillians above. Hero, though was caught mid-action, momentarily distracted by the Prizm, he had to twist and jump to avoid the rain of deathly bolts while pulling the Sword from within the Prizm to help defend himself. He jumped, somersaulting up to the apposing rooftop, but the blasts from the ally below followed him up, and the crossfire finally caught him as every gun was trained on his fast moving body. He landed, deflecting a mass of plasma bolts with his sword, but before he could counter, a pair of shots from below caught him, and Hero fell.

Lise screamed, Hero's body falling with a sickening thud to the rainy street where smoke and steam arose from his still form. She and Osmar were now cornered, defending magnificently from their position as their rage wailed forth in the form of a hail of gunfire. The roof mounted troopers were quickly destroyed or dispersed, but the survivors easily found new positions from which to aim at the two defenders. Lise tried to poke her head out from behind the wall and answer the shots coming from the Lordillians in the alley, but an explosion sent her reeling back. She fell into a heap across from the alley, directly in the fire of the Lordillian troops.

Lise looked up in shock, amazed as the blast that would have finished her was deflected off of the Triialon Sword. Hero stood there, between Lise and her death, catching the next few shots on the gleaming metal blade before answering their challenge with a raised fist brandishing the Prizm. The energy poured forth in a gleam of golden light and blue electricity. The eight remaining Lordillians were all caught in the blast, incinerating instantly. Just as quickly the alley was left dark and empty, smoke rising from the blackened cobblestones.

"Are you alright," Hero yelled, turning to deflect another blast from the roof off of the blade. He fired back up at its origin with a smaller, focused ball of energy from the Prizm. The Lordillian was hit full in the chest, melting it from the waist up into a halved mass of molten alloys.

"Yes," Lise answered over the din. She took position despite her confusion and knelt near Osmar, each of them aiming shots at the roof-sheltered attackers. Hero ducked another blast, backing against the wall underneath the Lordillian. Lise and Osmar both let fly with another barrage which was answered by cracks and explosions. Lise leapt aside, a bolt smashing where she had just knelt.

"That last bastard's got quite the hiding place," Osmar complained. "Are you jumping up there, Your Regalness, or am I?"

Hero grinned. "Do not make me laugh." His fingers ran quickly over the settings on the Prizm's jeweled controls, and, still backed against the bricks, Hero raised his arm. The Triialon Artifact glowed briefly before a crack of blue-white lightning leapt upwards from it. It arced up over the rooftop, striking the head of the elusive trooper behind his cover. It fried there a moment before the Lordillian's head exploded and the energy stream ceased. Then it was over.

Lise instantly broke cover, running over to Hero and splaying her fingers over his chest. "Gods, how bad is it?" she asked with deep concern. She found the hole burnt in his white shirt just above the right pectoral. Confusion played across her soft features as she moved the shirt around, finding only a black scorch mark on his chest. She gasped, looking into his eyes, then back at the lack of wound, grasping at his clothes to turn him around. Her hands found the small hole in his jacket and shirt on his back, rubbing the burnt edges between her fingers but finding no blood or true wound.

"Such fuss," Osmar laughed.

Lise turned Hero back around, gazing into his eyes with the unasked question on her parted lips. He simply smiled down at her, taking her hands in his and removing them from his chest. "It takes more than that to harm a Triialon," he said.

"But how?" Lise asked Osmar as they followed Hero back towards their ship. "Those hits never even penetrated his skin!"

"No, not penetrated – absorbed." Osmar ran beside her, changing settings on his weapon. "I was a little amazed myself the first time I saw it. To hear him explain it, his people were amazing geneticists, and found a way long ago to help their bodies absorb a certain amount of many kinds of energies and elements."

"But those blasts would have torn the arm off of another man," Lise explained.

"Aye, he's not indestructible, but he can take a great deal more pounding than you or I, that's for certain." Osmar shrugged. "I can't fully explain it. He's the scientist, and he won't tell me all of it because he'd rather complain that he shouldn't have to rely on that ability."

"I heard that," Hero called back.

"Well it *was* a lot of blasters zeroed on you all at once, Lord. Nobody's perfect."

"No, but they certainly did pick him out," Lise said.

"Yes," Hero mused, "it certainly would seem I'm a Lordillian target. I will have to settle up with Chebonka soon." They crossed another alley, the drizzling rain spraying them during the moments they were in the open. "We have to get off this planet before they have a chance to track us."

The three finally exited the alleys and came to the field behind the city. Lightning caressed the far off mountain tops, illuminating the clouds, but the space ahead remained shrouded in darkness. Hero crouched low, using the sparse trees as cover and signaling the others to move forward quietly. The rain had stopped, but the wind was picking up, the electrical storm coming closer. He gave the motion to 'hold', waiting for the thunderhead to creep in closer. Minutes passed, Lise and Osmar exchanging unknowing looks in the dark. Finally the lightning flashed closer, the ground and trees showing up against the stark blackness for just a moment, and with them the gleaming metal of Hero's Desert Flyer and the Lordillian soldiers surrounding it.

The Triialon warrior smiled. It was just as he suspected. Fortunately they were still far enough out from the ship that the Lordillians' sensors hadn't yet picked them up. He motioned to Osmar and Lise, 'flank and cover me', then he stood up and, sword in hand, marched strait towards his ship.

There were another dozen of the metal murderers left to guard the Triialon ship. They stood motionless, watching the land around them. The closest one flinched visibly at the first signs of movement out amongst the darkness, bringing its weapon to bear. The others followed suit, keeping their positions but tracking Hero's motions. He walked calmly into the open, studying their movements and cover. When he entered the clearing and came into full view, the Lordillian troops froze, seemingly uncertain for a moment as to how they should react. It was all the time he needed to sprint forward, closing the distance between himself and the lead machine, cleaving the trooper in two with his sword. The sword glowed with power, shimmering streaks of light playing off of its surface as he maneuvered it to cut down the second Lordillian. All the while Hero was pulling a sidearm from within his jacket and using it to blast a third.

The clearing erupted in gunfire, blasts raking the ground at Hero's feet as he moved from trooper to trooper, cutting a wake of destruction. Meanwhile bolts of plasma shot out from the darkness, Lise and Osmar's own fire finding their marks, toppling Lordillians from their perches atop Hero's ship. The Triialon jumped, evading a closing Lordillian's blasts and flipping over the machine to land behind it, slicing away and decapitating it. Sparks fizzled from the headless body and it shuddered as motors and gears spasmed uncontrollably before it fell in a heap to the wet ground. He picked the last two off himself with his blaster. The battle finished, Hero peered through the lightning washed landscape for the signs of any further ambushes. Satisfied, he called out. "That is all of them!"

The others ran up to Hero and the entry ramp of his ship, the plank sliding down quickly as he worked the controls. "Lise, do you think you can fly this ship?" he asked her hurriedly.

Lise looked surprised. "Yes, I think so. Why?"

"Osmar and I are going back."

"That scaly bastard Lek sold us out," Osmar cursed.

"I need you to track and pick us up," Hero continued. "The controls will home in on the Prizm. Wait here as long as you can."

"More Lordillians will be here any minute, Hero," Lise said. "The moment this batch doesn't recall, a squad will be here to destroy the ship. There's no time!"

Hero held her gaze, not interested in her excuses. "There is always time for revenge," he said seriously.

The two men turned and ran off into the storm, leaving Lise with a look of shock on her face.

Chapter Eleven

The admiral's daughter. The description alone brings
connotations. But this girl was anything but following
in her father's obvious footsteps at age thirteen.
Introverted and possessing no obvious talents save high
scores on games, she was just another child lost in a war.
How things changed…
Coalition and Triialon
- Dr. W. H. Redfield

Osmar waltzed strait past the bar and the booth where he and Lek had been talking earlier. He pushed through the doors to the backroom of the tavern unceremoniously, eliciting an cry of anger from the bartender. Ignoring the yelling man, Osmar continued to wind through the hallway, looking for the back alley exit. He spotted it, seeing the silhouette of Lek standing casually in the open doorway. His back was turned to the hallway as he leaned in front of the falling rain, his hands pulling Hero's billfold out of a hidden pocket. The traitor opened the small envelope, the smile on his scaly face dissolving as he realized the billfold was empty. Hero had never trusted him. "Oh shit," the lizard muttered.

"Lek!" Osmar grinned widely, his arms opened as if to receive an old friend but his eyes squinted in open hatred. "Why would you ever do such a thing?"

Lek turned, pocketing his nonexistent cash and hissing. When he saw who it was his changed his demeanor, putting his hands up and smiling. "Osmar! What do you mean?" He began to back slowly out of the doorway and into the rain. "Did you have further questions or needs, old friend?"

"Oh, I think we have all the answers we came for," Hero said, stepping out of the darkness of the alley and blocking Lek's escape. He stood calmly, balancing the Triialon sword in his hand, gripped upwards with the blade parallel to his arm. The ominous weapon was nearly, but not quite, hidden behind his jacket's black sleeve.

Lek hissed again, crouching to spring at Hero and the freedom he barred. He produced a strange looking metallic weapon from within his cloak, the tube-like end suggesting it was a blaster. In a panic, he fired at
180

Hero, who easily dodged aside and swung his sword out into full view. Lek turned and blasted at Osmar. The mercenary wasn't in any mood to trade pot shots from any narcs, so he took the chance of staying open, ducking the blast but remaining in Lek's way. He returned fire, a warning shot if nothing else, making sure he didn't hit Hero in the cross fire.

The lizard was again forced to turn. Heading back towards Hero, he finally made his jump. Lek's legs carried him upward in a flash, and he tried to use his right leg to rebound off of the far alley wall and leap around and past Hero. The Triialon spun and slashed out with his sword, relieving Lek of his leg for the trouble. The lizard fell to the puddle strewn ground, screaming in agony as his blood began to mix with the rain.

"How much did you tell the Lordillians," Hero bellowed. "Talk!"

"Please! I beg!" Lek clutched the stub that had been his leg with one hand, holding up the other for mercy. Osmar stepped up next to Hero, looking down at the sad end of the traitor. "They just wanted to know where you were! I swear! Please, let me live!"

"Live," Hero sneered. "You don't even disserve *this* honor." With cold simplicity he drove the sword home, its tip crunching through sternum and organs to pierce Lek's heart and kill him coldly.

"Lordillians," Osmar yelled, firing instantly on the metal forms that entered the alley at its far end. The leader fell, its systems severed by a direct hit to the center of its head. Hero pulled the charged Triialon sword from Lek's body and prepared to charge the next group of enemies, but gunfire from behind the Lordillians quickly ended the fight before it could begin. The remaining three troopers fell, sparking and melting, and from behind them stepped two men into the dim light of the alleyway, their own handheld weapons still smoking. Osmar gathered from their uniforms that they were the local authorities, probably police. He did not relax his guard.

"Hopefully that's the last of them," one said, stepping over the silenced machines while the other covered him with his blaster. "Are you alright?"

Hero relaxed his stance a little. "Thank you for your assistance, though it was not necessary."

"We're not standing by while Lordillians walk around causing whatever damage they want as if they owned the place. Besides," he shrugged, "any enemy of a Lordillian..."

"Understood," Hero said, sheathing the sword inside the Triialon Prizm. "Will you be alright, or do you expect retribution?"

The officer studied Hero and the impossibility that was the Prizm a moment. If he recognized Hero by reputation or by the artifacts, he didn't say anything about it. "This colony is protected. Lordillians may be feared here, but they aren't in power. Our captain is making sure Kordula is notified of this even now. In the meantime though, you'd better leave while you can." Osmar watched as the officer's partner tried to cover his own shocked expression that these two strangers were being let go. The old mercenary smiled at that.

"Thank you," Hero said, shaking the man's hand. "What about the body?"

"We've known Lek to be dodgy for a while. Too bad how they killed him just for selling them information. Can't trust Lordillians." He shook his head, smiling. "Damn shame. Go on, get out of here."

Hero nodded, motioning for Osmar to follow him out of the alley. They made for the open street heading back out of town. Once they were out from under the street lamps and watchful eyes again, they started running towards the ship. The sound of its engines warming up could be heard over the wind and rain. They reached it with ease and Hero activated the hatch allowing the two men to finally climbed aboard.

Lise was in the cockpit, silent as she worked controls, her mouth a thin line. Hero sat in the pilot's seat. "I'll take over."

"Is Lek dead?" she asked.

"Along with a few more Lordillians," Hero answered simply.

"Pretty exacting justice, don't you think," she said. Her face was a mask, but Osmar could tell she was fighting down some anger.

"The Triialon have a saying," Hero said, lifting the ship off and into the air. "*'Take what grievances the evils give you and visit it upon them tenfold.'*"

Lise got up, obviously upset, and moved past Osmar on her way out of the cockpit. He placed a hand on her shoulder , speaking softly. "He is a warrior, and this is war. What would you have him do; allow Lek to continue selling intelligence to the Lordillians? If he'd had any suspicions about your Coalition origins he certainly would have sold that as well, if he hasn't already."

Lise's shoulders heaved a great sigh, and without looking at him she left the compartment in silence.

Hero was equally as quiet, staring straight ahead as he piloted the ship out of Vara-del's atmosphere and prepared to make the Dimensionalizer jump.

Osmar laughed to himself, shaking his head. "Nothing ever changes," he said, sitting in the co-pilot's seat. "No matter where you go in the universe, women are still a pain in the ass."

Hero ignored the remark, solidifying Osmar's theory regarding Hero and the Coalition girl.

Jo'seph sat on the new bridge in a makeshift throne, the few chairs that had been salvaged among the rooms explored thus far were all larger than what most Coalition races could use. The admiral sat with his feet practically dangling over the Grellion Base's metal floor. One of Lise's officers arrived in front of him and saluted.

"Sub lieutenant Zhade reporting, sir."

"Good morning, mister Zhade," Jo'seph replied, his eyes never leaving the data pad in his hands. "Stand at ease. I have a mission for you of utmost importance, sub lieutenant."

"Sir." The young officer never relaxed, still standing erect with head held high.

"Get down to one of the transports on the landing field. I don't care who you have to talk to, steal from or kill, just get me a new bloody chair."

Zhade stared for a moment, then dared to look down at the admiral's dangling feet, suppressing a slight smile. "Yes, sir," he said.

"Off you go."

"Sir," came a communications officer's voice from the dimly lit expanse of the bridge. The servitors and engineers combined seemed unable to get the shutters open. "The admiral's ship is in descent."

"Thank you, corporal." Jo'seph literally hopped down and followed Zhade to the lift.

It took only minutes to drop from the bridge located at the top of the center building of the citadel to its ground level and then follow a main hall to an exit hatch leading directly out onto the field. By then the gunboat had landed, Jay'salan exiting and stared up at the colossal form of their new base. Jo' was surprised to see his daughter, Janise, follow his co-admiral off the landing ramp. The girl looked worried as she was led by the hand of Lieutenant Tykeisha. She covered the last few steps between her and her father with a run, hugging him fiercely. Her right hand and arm was bandaged.

"It must have been important if you had to bring her here against my orders of essential personnel," Jo'seph said to Tykeisha.

Tykeisha stammered. "Sir, I..."

"Stop that. You've meant too much to my daughter of late to keep calling me that when its not necessary." He turned and motioned to the base. "You two can tell me all about it. Shall we go inside the house?" The girls began to step forward, but Jay'salan stayed unmoving, his mouth agape. "Hello? Control to Flagship. You there, Jay'?"

The gray-skinned admiral never took his eyes off of the staggering height and breadth of the place. "It's fantastic..."

"Oh I don't know, admiral. You see one multi-million year old stupendous sized abandoned alien citadel, you've seen 'em all." He grinned. "Come in, man. You're due back at the fleet in short order." The group finally made its way to the hatch Jo'seph had emerged from, flanked by several armed guards. "Don't let the robots take your coat; you won't get it back."

Janise looked alarmed by that. "The robots steal?"

"I just don't think they've found the coat hooks yet."

"Where's commander Lise?" Tykeisha asked.

"On special assignment with Hero. They could be gone some time."

"What works?" Jay'salan asked.

"The basics of life support, but not much else. Weapons and shields are still offline, possibly until Hero finds the missing elements or a substitute can be made." Jo'seph took them up to the command levels, the others always watching their large new surroundings with interest. "That's about it. I'll have Sardeece report to the bridge to confer and I'll meet you there soon. In the meantime I'm going to take the ladies to their quarters." Jo'seph scratched his beard. "Speaking of ladies, is Bevanne safe?"

"As safe as anyone in the fleet right now. She's aboard another cruiser, and we're all still on COM silence."

"Very good." The admiral led the two towards the quarters halls, many of the rooms still under reconstruction. He looked down at his daughter, the girl silently marching along side him, scratching her bandaged arm absently. "It could be dangerous here if we're discovered," he said at last, "but I'm glad to see you anyway." She smiled at that.

They entered the quarters adjacent to his own, its tall walls bare and the rooms empty, yet clean, with one simple cushioned bed in one room. "These will be your quarters, Janise, just next to mine." He motioned for her to sit next to the bed and, looking to Tykeisha, asked, "now, what seems to be the trouble?"

Janise didn't answer right away, so Tykeisha knelt down and took her good hand, smiling. "There was an accident. An event took place that surprised Janise and the rest of us." She seemed unsure how to continue, but finally asked, "admiral, what was Keri like?"

The question took Jo'seph off guard. Few still asked him about his wife. "I don't understand."

"She was not from Sparta?"

"No" he answered. "No, she never did tell me where she was from, or where she was going."

"And did she ever display any unusual," she paused, searching for a word, "abilities?"

Jo'seph was beginning to become worried. "What's this about?"

"I set the bed on fire," Janise said suddenly. "Mom never said I'd be able to do that."

"But she did tell you you'd be able to do something special?" Tykeisha asked, surprised by Janise's revelation.

The girl's eyes narrowed, as though she were looking into the very depths of the past. "I remember something," she said brokenly, "but I was

185

so little." The moment ended, and she was looking down at her hands again. "Then she was gone."

"What do you mean you set the bed on fire, honey?" Jo' asked.

"I was sleeping and awoke because of a pain in my hands and in my head. The bed was on fire around my hands. This one burned." She held up her bandaged arm. "I jumped out of the bed and when I screamed the flames jumped higher. Then the sprinklers started and it got put out."

"And you think you somehow did it?"

"I guess so." Janise shrugged. "How else do you explain it?"

Jo'seph sat on the edge of his bed in his own quarters. Tykeisha had remained with Janise to give her the painkillers the doctors had prescribed. A headache of his own was getting bigger, and he began rubbing his temples absently. The door chimed and Tykeisha entered.

"Admiral, are you alright?"

"I thought I told you not to call me that," he grumbled.

She sat down next to him on the bed. "And I thought you were going to relax?"

"I'm finding the concept of relaxation difficult at this exact moment," he sighed. "Suddenly I'm so worried about her, and suddenly I realize just how thin a cord the whole Coalition hangs on."

"Or how thin your own nerves have been stretched?" She smiled at him sympathetically. "It's only natural. I'm surprised you've been this strong this long under the circumstances."

"Do you think she's making it up?"

Tykeisha stood up and began to walk around the room slowly, thinking. "Something started that fire. She's at an age where any latent abilities might begin to flower, especially under stress. And something certainly scared her. She's been quiet since Norpan, but after the accident in her bedroom she's been almost silent." She shook her head, looking at Jo'seph. "She's frightened, and it's not the Lordillians."

Jo' sighed again. "Nothing's ever simple." The door chimed again. "Come."

An officer appeared in the open doorway, standing at attention. "Admiral, admiral Jay'salan requests your presence."

"I'll be right there." The young officer turned and left. Jo'seph stood, putting back on his uniform jacket. "We find one of the most technologically advanced artifacts in the galaxy and I'm stuck running officers between decks for messages."

Tykeisha smirked. "We might have to install our own intercoms. Weren't the Grellions telepaths?"

"That's no excuse." He stopped, irritated. "How do you know that the Grellions were telepathic?"

The young woman shrugged. "News travels fast, even in this fleet." She had the grace to look a little guilty. "Sorry."

Vines crawled along the intricate iron bars of the gateway surrounding the stone landing pad. Hero's ship had landed merely minutes before and Lise couldn't wait to get outside for her first glimpse of the planet. Everywhere she looked there was life, greenery and water surrounding the estates. Where the colony world had simply been well off, Okino was an absolute paradise.

Lise smoothed down the front of her new dress and pushed her long hair back over one shoulder, feeling elated. They had been in orbit, sleeping through the night before. When Hero had woken her and told her they were going to make their descent to the surface of Okino, she had been instantly alert and excited. Now she was calm yet happy, overwhelmed by her surroundings.

Her gown fell across he body beautifully. Lise loved every curve and every stitch. She was glad she had picked a simple but pretty necklace to enhance the rather plunged neckline that already revealed so much of her ample bosom. The soft, black material stopped just below her knees in the front and just above her heeled and laced ankles in the back. She smiled again and pushed a stray strand of her dark curls out of her eyes.

"Shall we?" Hero asked, offering her his arm. He was dressed in a way she had never seen him in before, but it suited him somehow, and by its design Lise assumed it was probably of Triialon origins. They weren't really matching in terms of color, but she didn't care; as much as she almost hated to admit it, he looked great. His hair was pulled back into a tight ponytail showing off those chiseled features of his. A long-sleeved top cut across his chest and buckled at one breast, while a long cape of the same sepia-toned material was fastened by a broach bearing the seal of Triialon at his right shoulder. He wore slacks that tucked down into tall boots, and a sash covered the tops of his thighs, falling lower across one hip. The material had a beautiful black inlay pattern and was obviously expensive, if aged. He had the Triialon sword hanging from one of the many belts around his waist.

Osmar followed, wearing the cleanest clothes he owned; simple black trousers, knee-high boots, a simple but nice shirt under a clean coat. A shining sword hung at his side as well.

They passed through the gates of the immaculate grounds and were soon led by a finely dressed servant through the gardens. Eventually they came to a long set of gradual steps that led up to an enormous house. Lise could only smile.

"You are in better spirits," Hero said, leading her.

"You're an uncommon man, Hero of the Triialon," Lise answered with a smirk. She shook her head at him, but held his arm tightly. "Maybe you're governed by more ancient laws in this universe. Maybe I'm just easily shocked considering my war is with those walking metallic scrap piles back there. And maybe you're just a stubborn bastard." She heaved a dramatic sigh. "I'm still trying to figure you out. That little connection of ours doesn't seem to be switched on all the time." She pulled a face. "Or is that only the case with me?"

"Perhaps." Hero had said it so strait-faced that it took her a moment to catch the mocking tone.

"I knew it," she said with a laugh, "You're a stubborn bastard."

"His holiness, stubborn?" Osmar asked from behind them with a sarcastic note. "Never."

"Herald," Hero called to the servant, and walked off to confer with the man and eventually sent him ahead.

"Still haven't heard your story," Lise said to Osmar as they waited.

"And you shan't, unless you've some real time to spare," Osmar replied, pulling at the buttons at his throat. "Quite a story to tell you how His Lordship saved my rump."

"Is that why you call him that?"

Osmar shrugged. "He's noble born as far as most of this galaxy is concerned. I give him no small amount of hell about it, but the truth is there's no man I respect more than Hero," he sniffed, "save myself."

Lise laughed. "Of that, I'm certain."

Hero walked back to where they stood, taking Lise's arm again. They began to ascend the steps leading up to the great doors of the white mansion. Lise watched the suns go down over the horizon, the land beyond the estates covered in thick forest as far as they eye could see. Two guards stood at the entrance of the house. The sounds of a party within could be heard echoing from the expansive ballroom.

The guards barred their advance, two large well-dressed men with calm demeanors and blasters sheathed in very ornate holsters at their sides. A young servant stood with them, a list of invitations and other allowed persons in his thin fingers. "Welcome to the house of Okino," the skinny man whined. "Please state your names."

"Tell your mistress that Hero of the Triialon is here," Hero said with authority.

The servant practically guffawed. "Certainly, sire," he snorted with a smile, "Hero of Triialon."

Osmar almost hit the young man. "Show some respect, worm!" He was silenced by Hero's restraining hand.

"It is all right," Hero said with calm ease. "She's on her way here. I took the liberty of having us announced."

As if on cue a woman stepped from the milling crowds in the room beyond. Two more guards flanked her, and her floor length white gown was embroidered with jewels. She was aging, her curves gone and her hair white, but the sparkle in her eyes and spring in her step belied her obvious years.

The servant also saw her, and the smug and annoyed expression on his face indicated what he thought his mistress would say of these strangers at her door. "Your highness," he whined, "this man *claims* to be Hero..."

"Of the Triialon," she finished. "Yes, I know." She pushed past her now-stunned servant with arms wide, the small, old woman taking Hero into her arms with a great bear hug. "It has been years since you've graced

189

this court with your presence, you old beggar." Hero genuinely laughed at that, and Lise grinned, watching the young doorman stare agape. The woman made a show of remembering that the servant was still there, finally exclaiming in mock surprise, "oh, I'm sorry, are you still waiting? You may return to your duties. I will admit Hero and his friends myself." And with that she led them into the ballroom of Okino Mansion, the servant left to stammer his apologies, watching the legend enter the room led by the hostess herself.

"Do you want a formal introduction to the court or are you incognito again?" the woman asked Hero, patting his arm as she led them to the center of the ballroom. All around them people of every race Lise had ever heard of danced and mingled in their finery. Not just a few stopped to openly gape at Hero or appreciate Lise.

"No announcements, please," the Triialon warrior responded. "Not until I've had a chance to know who would be listening."

"Very well," she said, and turned to Lise, her hand outstretched. "I am Krystka, of house Telisha, last royal queen of Okino. And you are?"

Lise took the queen's hand and bowed a little. "I am Lise, your highness, of Sparta." She looked to Hero for a moment, unsure as to how much more information she should divulge despite her orders from the admiral. "It is an honor to meet you."

Hero took up the cue, speaking in hushed tones. "Lise is a commander in the Galactic Coalition fleet, and admiral Jo'seph's liaison to Your Majesty."

"To me?" the queen asked with surprise. "Such a veil to bring her to me, Hero, when you are already aware of my current political position on Okino."

"Your Highness," Lise began, "I am aware of Okino's current democratic government. But I also know the love your people still hold for you gives you a certain amount of sway within the senate. I am simply here because Hero's mission brought us here, and while I have longed to visit Okino since childhood, it is my admiral's requests that brings me to you, and hopefully Your Highness's sympathies."

"Very well, young lady," Queen Krystka said with a smile. "I look forward to meeting you in court. If you would set up an appointment

190

with my secretary, then we shall talk soon. Make sure you set the date with Hero at your side; he has an influence over ink pushers. That way I'll be sure to see you this week. Now please, enjoy your first evening on Okino." She turned to Hero and his companion. "Osmar, is it not?" she asked, offering the mercenary her hand in greeting.

The old fighter took the queen's hand with only a little trepidation. "Aye, your ladyship. Thanks for remembering an aging nobody who's only been here once before."

"Nonsense. Any friend of Hero's is a friend mine. Besides," she continued with a conspiratorial grin, "the last time you made something of a spectacle of yourself. You did challenge me to a drinking contest, as I recall. Perhaps this time we can put our tolerances to the test."

Osmar actually looked a little shocked. Lise suppressed a giggle behind her hand as the merc nodded again and let the queen move off again with Hero at her side.

Lise watched Hero's figure and demeanor as he walked slowly with Krystka of house Telisha. For a man who so often claimed to have to no culture to speak of, he certainly seemed strangely at home in this palace at a queen's side. She wondered at his true past, how long had he been out here, traveling the stars in search of ancient artifacts and lost horizons. She sighed, an uncertain melancholy overtaking her.

A slight hand touched Lise's shoulder, causing her to start. "Oh, I beg your pardon," she said to the woman who stood next to her, smiling.

"I've seen that look before," said the middle aged and elegantly dressed woman. She wore a simple but sexy evening gown, and her hair was peppered with gray, but her eyes and figure were stunning despite her years. Lise could only stare in question. "I'm sure that it has graced my face at least once as well. So many get that lost, dreamy expression when Hero crosses a threshold."

"Yet he never ceases to amaze me," Lise answered, shaking the woman's hand. "For such a loner he certainly knows enough people. I'm Lise."

"Lorette," she said. "I'm one of the queen's secretaries."

Lise was a little relieved by that somehow. "Ah, that's how you know him. I thought perhaps you were yet another person who owed Hero their life or something."

"I do owe him my life," Lorette said, then waved the remark away. "Perhaps a better description would be to say that I owe him my *way* of life. If it wasn't for that man I might be dead, but I certainly wouldn't be the Queen's aide. I was neither of clean living nor of honest trade when he found me. In one night he had me cleaned up and introduced to our Highness." Lise's expression at that last detail must have given something away, for Lorette then placed a hand on her shoulder and smiled. "Nothing like that, though I certainly would not have minded. No, he simply reminded me of the person I could have been but was not yet able to believe in."

"And to think he only saved me from certain death at the hands of a Lordillian battle cruiser," Lise sighed. "How does one not fall in love with him?"

Lorette's manner became quite confidential and consoling at that point, the older woman steering Lise away from the crowds as they talked. "I think you've got it worse than even you know. Not that I can blame you. He's a living legend, a warrior, a wise man..."

"He's attractive, scientific" Lise continued, "he can't die..."

"He only seems immortal, dear."

"Oh, I know that. It's just that he's just that much further from mortality than the other men in my life."

Lorette nodded. "You're a military woman, aren't you?"

"I've lost a lot of good friends," Lise agreed quietly. "And I know it's not over." She masked the pain quickly, trying to again sound professional. "In fact that's why I've come here. The Queen said that you might be able to get me in to see her this week in court."

"For a friend of Hero's," Lorette smiled, "just tell me what time tomorrow would be good for you. Now," she said with a grin as she peered around them, "Tell me more about our elusive beau."

Lise smiled and began describing.

Hero placed his empty glass onto the servant's tray as Osmar took another full one.

"You see the guy in black?" Osmar asked discreetly as he tossed back the drink. A muscularly built man stood in one corner, staring back when Hero's eyes met his. His skin was bluish, offsetting the short yellow hair on his head. A black cape trailed over his shoulders and his demeanor was that of a fighter. Aside from his expensive clothes he was not a man that belonged in this room.

"Yes, I'll have to ask Lorette about him," Hero said quietly. "But first I want to talk to Durant."

Osmar looked confused. "I haven't seen him."

"That is because he just walked in." Hero turned towards the main double doors, watching as a thin, handsome but dangerous looking man walked in. He was flamboyantly dressed, covered in silks and velvets in the form of a long frock coat with frills at the sleeves and topped by a thin mustache and short ponytail in a bow. A sleek, bucket-hilted sword hung at his side. He was smiling when he walked in and grinned even bigger the moment he caught sight of Hero.

The smiling man walked quickly over and shook the Triialon's hand. "Hero, my friend! Our roads cross again, though I think by design."

"Durant, you are as observant as always." Hero smiled genuinely, releasing the smaller man's grasp.

Durant made a show of looking about the room. "My powers of observation are legendary, Triialon. Almost as legendary as you." He stopped, watching Lise and Lorette talking near the statue of a beautiful naked woman. "Note, for example, how quickly I catch the eye of the most lovely creature in the ballroom." He scooped a glass off of a passing servant's tray and gestured to the two ladies with it, grinning like an idiot. "I am certain she is as wealthy as she is beautiful."

Hero turned to look at Lise across the room, trying not to smile as he shook his head. "Perhaps, my friend. But I am certain that I can command her attentions more surely than you." It was Osmar's turn to hide a smile at that.

Durant looked surprised. "My lord Hero, at last you take an open interest in wenching after all of these years of covert romances and court

193

intrigues. I am impressed." He quickly regained his usual self-absorbed demeanor. "Though it will avail you not. Despite your status and apparent personality shift I am bound and determined to have her."

An evil smile spread across Osmar's face and his eyes winced as he spoke through clenched teeth. "You overblown dandy. I'll bet you thirty-five thousand that My Lord can call that lady from across the room without even speaking a word."

Again Durant took on the facade of being shocked. "The mercenary even defends this brave new womanizing Hero. This I must see." He stepped back, looping his thumbs through his sword belt and puffing out his chest. "Very well, Hero of the Triialon. Call to her."

Hero simply stared back at Durant, the corners of his mouth turning up mockingly as, from across the room, the beautiful Lise sauntered across the chamber. He did not have to look back to know each step was grace and sex in motion, every curve accented by the clinging v-necked dress that slipped and slid around her body as she slowly walked over and finally put her arm through his, looking up at him around her dark tresses of hair. Lorette had even followed her and took Hero's other arm, resting her free hand on his bicep.

"You called, My Lord?" Lise even cooed the words. It was nice to see that she had elaborated beyond Hero's telepathic request. The warrior smiled in triumph.

The look on Durant's face was finally one of true shock. Osmar let out a whoop of laughter, slapping his knee before holding out his palm. "Pay up, dandy! There's not one thing about *that* look that isn't worth thirty-five thousand."

A moment of silence followed Osmar's bellow of laughter, but Durant's face then split into that familiar smugness as he bowed. "I stand in awe, my friend." He raised his glass and took a drink while reaching into his coat for a notebook. "Once again you have proven that you are the better man." Despite that, he never took his eyes from Lise's, finally kissing her hand after handing the expensive note to Osmar who took it with a chuckle. "I am Durant of Julian, My Lady. I am at your service." Durant took Lorette's hand next. "A pleasure, as always, Lorette."

"Durant."

"Osmar, please take our slightly-less rich friend and buy him a drink," Hero said.

"Happily, My Lord," Osmar said, still grinning.

"I'll join you both in a moment. Durant, you may be happy to know that I can make you an offer that will easily replenish your checkbook."

"A pleasure as always," Durant answered, again raising his glass before following the mercenary away.

Hero turned to Lise, stopping when he saw the way she was looking up at him, studying his lit face. "What?"

Her eyes sparkled, and she was still holding his arm. "Nothing. I just don't think I've ever seen you have fun before. It suits you." Hero must have looked confused at that, for she quickly tried to throw him back off again. "What were you going to say?"

"I was simply going to apologize for using our connection to ask you to do that if it offended you at all," he said guardedly.

Lise looked bothered by that. "Stop it. If it had offended me, I wouldn't have done it. I knew you were up to something and it was fun. Now say hello to your friend."

"Hello friend," Lorette purred, and the two women laughed at Hero's obvious discomfort. "Ooh, I'm sorry. I know how unused to being outnumbered you are, Hero," she said teasingly, but hugged him closely and kissed his cheek. "It's been too long. You look well."

Hero took the open opportunity to change the subject. "As do you. Has Krystka promoted you yet again?"

"I'm one of her secretaries, yes. Pretty much top of the food chain, therefore among the first to catch hell from the senate." She made a gesture of waiving political talk away. "But enough of that. What brings you and your wonderful friend to Okino?"

"Battle."

Lorette smirked. "What else?"

"That man in black," Hero said without looking at him. "I do not recognize him."

Lorette took the cue and also spoke without calling attention to themselves. "He arrived a few days ago on a GCI pass, so his credentials are still something of a mystery but they're certainly enough to keep him

195

at court as long as he wants to stay. He's quiet, of sour disposition, talks to very few for very short periods, and seems to be looking for something. Or waiting. Personally, I think he's from Kordula. There are few other places that present such creds."

Hero felt something in the air, concentrating on sensing the shaded figure across the ballroom. He knew that the man was watching Hero's every step. "What is his name?" he asked coolly.

"Kezeron Telbandith."

Chapter Twelve

*There are few cases as sordid, or as interesting, as Svea of
the Seethlings. Who would have thought that the same
person capable of what happened at Dailor could also
perpetrate so much of what happened on Kordula?
History of the so-called Gods
- Dr. W. H. Redfield*

It was late. As usual, Svea couldn't sleep. She stood there in front of
the window, looking over the brightly lit city from her perch in the
darkness above it all. She was naked and trying very hard to get drunk. A
glass of wine sat warming in her jeweled hand.

"This city never sleeps," she muttered to herself, "like me." She
would have to close the shade completely in order to keep all of the light
from the Kordula signs and structures from flooding their chambers each
night, and each night she could not bring herself to do it. She would have
felt too lonely if she had. Dahvis was never home in the evenings to
complain about it anyway.

This evening's lover had already fled. The duke had left early,
smiling and exhausting his favors as he gathered his clothes and departed
before the bed was even cold. It suited Svea just fine that way in any
event; the thought of marrying him for his power had fled the moment
she'd had his shirt off. Besides he was no more a big fish than he was
gifted in bed, though he had acted otherwise on both counts.

Svea awoke on the lounge, still nude, her hair in her eyes. Brithany
shook her a second time. "My lady, it is morning."

Sitting up, Svea's head briefly swam. "Has my brother returned?"

"No, my lady."

She tried to keep from running her hands down her face. To look so
lost did not become a Seethling. "Shower with me," she commanded the
girl. She was certain the servant had already bathed that morning, but
Svea didn't care. She wanted company.

Whether the girl consented or not was immaterial.

"Yes, my lady," Brithany answered, and began removing her clothes
while heading for the bath chamber.

Svea's glass was still half empty, so she sat back a moment and took a drink.

When she heard the water running, she got up and made for the bathroom, certain the water would hide the tears.

Their lovemaking was furious and one-sided, the poor girl lost to abandon as always, a slave to the desires awoken within her by Seethling prowess and then battered down by its grasp along with the water that flooded over them both. Svea would have been disappointed if it wasn't that sexual conquest excited her so much. The look of that naked serving wench, hair plastered to her impassioned face, left panting and spent at the foot of the shower turned Svea on almost as much as being taken by an equally experienced lover. She left the shower already feeling better about the day ahead.

The window again beckoned to her, and she picked her glass back up and toasted

Kordula. "So many conquests await my time here," she told herself, biting her lip.

Happily, Svea began slipping into her new dress.

She had just begun brushing her hair when Dahvis stormed into the room with great strides, the look on his face a mix of anxiousness and concern. He was dressed in black leather and fine black silks, a short cape flowing over one shoulder. Certainly more formal and foppish than usual. Two beautiful serving girls in their skimpy costumes followed him in. They had been following him for several days, and she suspected they were under his influence. "Don't you ever check messages?"

"I just got out of the shower," Svea answered, her fingers tangling in her hair. "What is it?"

Dahvis's face lit up, all of his usual recriminations over her irresponsibility gone. "We have an audience with Memfis this morning."

Svea was elated. She jumped at him, throwing her arms around his neck with a squeal of delight. "I knew it would not be long!"

"Come, we have little time." He pulled her back into her rooms, calling for Brithany to serve her mistress. "Brithany," he called again, louder this time, while his own serving girls began to undress him.

199

Svea noticed the steam still pouring out of the bath chamber and she pushed open the door. Brithany still lay on the shower tiles, the water cascading down her motionless body. She was facedown and her eyes were closed. Svea touched the girl, knowing instantly that she was dead. Svea pouted. "I'm afraid Brithany will be unable to serve us any longer."

Dahvis paused only a moment, unmoving from where the girls were now dressing him as he stood on his toes a moment to offhandedly survey the scene. He went right back to looking at himself in the mirror instead. "Really, you would think that they could produce higher quality product on Kordula."

Svea was too overjoyed at the prospect of meeting Memfis alone at last to be depressed by the incident. She sighed melodramatically. "Pity."

Dahvis was almost completely dressed now in the cumbersome, high-necked and expensive formal clothing of Traditional Seethling design. He had never worn it out before. "It's all right, I've brought you a new one." He snapped his fingers, ordering one of the girls to quickly adorn his sister. "You'll have to be more careful with your toys in future, dear sister."

The most expensive jewels and elaborate make-up was soon set out and being applied, Svea stripping off the gown she was wearing and stepping into the traditional dresses and its weighty details with the young woman's help. She was soon looking her most ravishing and formal and joined Dahvis at the door.

"And dispose of that" he said to the two girls, pointing back to Svea's bath chamber.

Goursh, that shifty - if extremely informative - little secretary to the Gods was waiting for them outside of their apartments. His presence always made Svea's skin crawl, which was saying something. "My Lord, My Lady. I am here to take you to the Temple." He smiled a little at his own joke. "In case you've not yet heard of it, it is the rather eccentric name given to the building the Gods reside in, as well as the Inner Sanctum." He motioned for them to follow him.

A private transport took the trio from their building to a thick tower with jutting expanses and immaculate design. Their craft docked at a platform merely halfway up its huge side. "There has been no ground entrance to the Temple in millennia," Goursh explained. "The Gods live above the streets of Kordula, therefore those of the streets may not gain entrance. Even we must enter here and then be admitted to the levels above."

"And you, Goursh?" Dahvis asked wickedly, "Does your shuttle ever dock with the higher levels?"

Goursh shrugged the question off. "When the Gods will it."

Svea followed her brother and Goursh from the platform and into the magnificent building. It was as if she were arriving on Kordula all over again. The structure was ancient, she knew, but it was all so new and immaculate to her. "This is the very center of civilization in this universe," Goursh continued. "Its most ancient heart. This place is considered sacred, so please follow quietly." They came to the center of a vast circular room, empty save for the pillars that surrounded them and the art that adorned every inch of wall or ceiling. Goursh stood on the pedestal in the middle of the floor design, bowing his head as a column of light from above suddenly enveloped him. "My Lords," he intoned. "I have brought them." The words threatened Svea, and she had to fight down a primitive urge to run. She quickly pushed such fears aside, conquering them with the pure excitement of finally coming face to face with their goal. The ultimate seat of power in the universe was near their grasp at last; the Gods of Kordula.

"Enter," a voice boomed from above, and the light then encircled all three figures, transporting them to another, and Svea deduced higher, level of the building.

"Come," Goursh said simply. A long hall extended out before them, alcoves set incrementally along its length separated by pillars. Each of the alcoves was actually a small case, closed off by thick glass, and inside each case was the unique form of some man or monster, each in a dynamic pose of battle. "The Trophies of Chel'Zel," Goursh said with a wave of his hand as they passed down the hall. "The past winners and losers of the now defunct Decade Games."

"Glorious," Dahvis said, his eyes wide with power.

"Quite."

201

"They're real?" Svea asked.

Goursh gave another one of his shrugs. "I am told some of the more ancient ones are, if they were not victorious or if they chose to reside here as champions after their deaths. The others I suspect are representations of past glories on Kordula. In any case, they are the Gods private collection, and few others get to see such a museum. You are privileged."

They traversed the lengthy hall, coming to stand before a giant set of double doors. There followed a moment of silence, and Svea could tell that Dahvis, like her, was struggling not to fidget in the heavy, flesh covering fabrics of their old fashioned garb. At least hers showed *some* cleavage, she thought. Dahvis was covered head to toe. The doors quietly opened and Goursh held out his hand. "Please enter," he said, and stood aside as they swept past him.

The two siblings walked into the enormous room. It was furnished in much the same way as most of the estates, only all the more open and opulently. The ceiling was much higher then any other room Svea had ever been in, and the amount of doors suggested room after room of the same. A pretty young woman, topless and wonderfully built, greeted them. "This way," she said, leading the way to the foremost archway.

Memfis, God among Gods, waited for them in the room beyond. Sitting upon a cushioned divan, he was attended by several more such beauties. Dahvis audibly gasped at the scene, reminding Svea that her brother had not yet seen a God as none had been at Court since his arrival. Memfis size was impressive, even seated. A giant's body topped by the regal, horse-like head, he was adorned in the cleanest silks and finest jewels.

"Enter, and be welcome, Dahvis and Svea Magdalene, last of the Seethlings race." He waved the serving girls away, and they each swept gracefully out of the chamber. "At last we all meet under less formal circumstances." He looked them over for a moment. "Though you honor me with the dress of your ancestors." He smiled a little. "Well met, though in future such heavy garments will not be necessary."

"My Lord Memfis," Dahvis said, giving the deepest bow Svea had ever seen him dare. She followed suit.

"We are the ones honored to be in your presence, great Memfis," Svea intoned.

"Please, be seated and talk with me," the God said simply, and with a wave of his hand chairs appeared beside them, as though out of thin air.

"You can change energy to matter?" Dahvis asked, seating himself.

The corners of Memfis's mouth turned up a little. "Those chairs were in an adjoining room. I simply brought them here." Dahvis smiled back. "You have an inquiring mind," the god continued, changing the subject. "As well as a ruthlessness that you and your sister seem to share. While that is much of why I brought you here today, I do, on the other hand, hope that such carelessness with the servants here in Kordula city will not become habitual. The serving girls, while not really of consequence, do perform a function." The two seethlings were silent for a pause uncertain as to how to react, so Memfis filled the silence for them, smiling again to perhaps lighten the mood. "Still, its nice to see young people who enjoy their work."

"We can, of course, pay for the damages," Svea said as off-handedly as she could muster.

Memfis thought about that. "I'll make a deal with you," he said. "I will, shall we say, make the first one free if you will both do a little job for me."

Svea leaned forward, her ears pricking at the sound of a bargain. "You were going to let us off anyway. What else have you brought us here to offer?"

Memfis chuckled. "Shrewd. Very well, I'll tell you. But first, the assignment; There is a small moon called Dailor. There an ancient religious order of priestesses has survived for hundreds of years, its origins can be traced back to the height of the Triialon monarchy." Svea caught her brother's reaction out of the corner of her eye, her own heart jumping as he sat forward. "Yes, I thought that might get your attention. It has been such a very few number of years since the Triialon wiped the Seethling home world from the heavens.

"Dailor may perhaps hide the few surviving secrets of the Triialon. Such an order has long outlived its usefulness, don't you think? Its secrets must be discovered and brought to me, along with any artifacts, religious or otherwise," he said in a commanding tone. "If anyone resides there that does not seem to be of the Order, they should be brought back here, alive if possible."

"Vengeance over the ally of Triialon," Dahvis whispered, staring at their new master's throne.

Memfis stood, looking them both over. "Do this, and your place on Kordula and a prosperous future at my side is insured." He motioned for them to leave. "Go now. You will find coordinates and further instructions left with Goursh."

Svea stood, bowing deeply and began heading for the outer doors. She stopped after only a few backwards steps, cocking her head to one side. "My Lord," she said, her voice a controlled query. "Goursh did not seem to know whether the figures in the trophy room were real or not."

"Goursh is simply being formal," Memfis said. "He knows well that they are *all* real. They all serve me, now, in death as in life. The losers are the vanquished in my hall, while some of the winners were preserved in their moment of absolute triumph, for we as Gods wanted to remember them in that way only."

"'Some' of the winners?"

Memfis smiled, an expression devoid of humor. "The truly wise ones remain to serve me more… productively."

"I see. Thank you." Svea bowed again and backed out of the room. Dahvis copied the motion, but was only halfway to the exit when Memfis called to him.

"Dahvis, one moment."

Svea had no choice but to complete her departure from the room, leaving her brother alone with the most powerful being known.

The moments she waited in solitude in that outer chamber were like hours. She tried desperately not to fidget, impatiently brimming inside while she stood, calm on the outside, next to the doors to Memfis apartments. When Dahvis did at last emerge, a look of confidence and power etched in his features, she exhaled a breath of relief. She waited until they were alone in the hall of Chel'Zel before finally daring to ask him what had happened.

Dahvis grinned with an inner fire beyond anything he had ever shown, save for the day she had found their benefactor, the man who had taken them in after their parents death, slain on Magdala. "Our Lord Memfis simply gave me some instructions regarding the Priestesses of Dailor. The journey ahead is a lengthy one. But remember," he told her, "we report to no one save Our Lord on this matter, nor on anything of equal measure. None of the other Gods must hear of this." The way he had said 'Our Lord' twice, as though all of his loyalty had just been commanded, sent a chill down Svea's spine, though she dared not admit it. Instead she simply nodded, and followed Dahvis back to their apartments where Goursh waited to send them on their way.

Hero stood in the center of the ballroom, the area around him cleared, save for the queen, who stood next to him, listening intently. The entire remaining crowd stood in a circle around him, their attention commanded by the story he told. His dictation had been in part forced by Krystka's announcement that the most celebrated traveler, Hero of Triialon, must tell one of his adventures to her guests. Lise stood aside, remaining anonymous. She waited along with Lorette and her suitor, a man named Belfi', whose clothes suggested he was from the northlands of Okino. Like the rest of the mansion's inhabitants, they listened intently to Hero's tale.

The Triialon was used to this kind of treatment. He could never come to Okino without being coerced in one form or another to stand before the crowd and tell of his adventures. It was hardly as if he enjoyed being made a spectacle. Such storytelling had initially been reserved to Hero's youth on Triialon, back when there were still victories to crow about. Still, he found Okino and its Queen among his favorites. He returned to it annually when possible ever since he had first come to it only a year or two after leaving Triialon behind. The story he told now was from those early years of his quest, when he had landed on a primitive but cultured world called Waikamer following what he had thought to be the energy signature of one of the Triialon artifacts. There he had found a plot to overthrow a queen by a group of cultist followers whose temple was an underground labyrinth of forgotten catacombs. It was a story he had recalled in this room before, but it had been years hence, and the Queen did not seem to mind the replay.

"I arrived in the central chamber of the cultists, but found that I was too late. Already they had awoken the beast and taken it away, and the Princess was no-where in sight." Hero's voice carried strongly in the enormous ballroom, so he had no need for theatrics or elaboration. He simply stood before them as he had so many times before, his thumbs hooked through a belt around his waist, looking around the crowd as he recounted his tale. Choosing not to embellish too much, he simply told the facts of the adventure as he recalled them. On Triialon, in his youth, Hero's first teacher had been much more ornate during such tales. Hero had accused his mentor of being rejected from the capitol Opera, only to find that the man had indeed once performed for the stage – when there had still been a theatre to speak of. Other warriors had told their stories of battle at times to his fellows, but it had taken Krystka's persuasiveness to coax such meanderings from Hero.

"I stepped from the shadows," Hero continued, "meeting the remaining cultists head on, the first rushing forth so fast that I had to cut them down with my blade. The other gray-robes were slow to react, and I burned them to ash where they stood, leaving only their treacherous leader to stand before me. He revealed his true face and intentions from beneath his stone mask, telling me of the power they had prayed to harness through chaos. They had unleashed the Demon who had waited in those catacombs for so many generations."

Hero's eyes swept over the crowd. "*Power is an illusion*, I told him, and explained to him how such a creature would only consume him as well as those whom he hated. But he did not believe me. For the lives he had taken and the murder he had committed, his life was forfeit. He faced me, but his skill was nothing, his power broken mere moments after his greatest achievement had been realized. I swept his feet from beneath him and paused before finishing him. 'Where is the Princess?' I asked him. 'My master entertains her,' he answered." The crowd gasped again, as they had several times during the tale. "I ended his unforgivable reign and continued on into the catacombs. At last I found the Demon's room and entered. There, upon a dais as though she were a sacrifice, lay the Princess Jaslana, and above her was the vile creature the cultists had finally freed."

"What did it look like?" a woman breathed, her face ashen and amazed by the story thus far.

"Nearly twice the size of any man, with black scales of fire, huge clawed hands and a spiked tale. Whatever the creature truly was, 'demon' was an apt description. It did not take kindly to my intrusion and attacked. His talons burned like flaming coals, and his massive teeth snapped at my face. I was hard pressed to fight the creature to any sort of stand still. It was a glorious battle."

"What did you do?" asked another woman, less frightened than her compatriot but just as interested.

Hero smiled a little, bringing the story to a close. "I eventually won, finding that a Triialon blade could pierce even that vile creature's skin."

There was a murmur of relief and a lightening of the mood. A moment passed before the first, pale-faced woman asked, "Was the Princess alive?"

"Jaslana was returned to her mother, probably in better health than I at that point. The royal family was most… accommodating." A general laugh from the crowd followed that, and Hero bowed, closing his tale. There was brief applause followed by the Queen stepping forward and taking Hero's arm.

"Thank you, as always," Krystka said, and she pulled him down and kissed his cheek before moving away to thank her milling guests.

Hero scanned the crowd, finding Lorette and her escort, but seeing no trace of Lise. Before he could go looking for her, he noticed Osmar and Durant standing near one of the bars and joined them. The two men looked drunk and bored. Even Durant's usual gleeful expression was relatively sullen. "Tell me what you want, by the Gods, so I can go to my bed at last. Alone, I might add."

"Do you remember the conditions surrounding how we met?" Hero asked, taking Durant's glass from his hand and setting it aside.

Durant obviously had to think hard on that one, his brow furrowing deeply, causing him to bring a hand to his sore temple. "Yes, I remember, the…"

207

"Yes, it was a good story, was it not," the warrior interrupted. "When you awake tomorrow afternoon," Hero continued with no small amount of disgust, "come to my guestroom. If you can remember by then the rest of the story, and its final destination, then I think there may be quite a profit in it for you."

"Oh, you're making my head hurt, Hero," Durant complained.

"It's the drink," Osmar quipped.

"No, it's trying to remember the rest of the… story," Durant scowled, looking to Hero. "Very well, since you insist on being so mysterious tonight, I'll retire. Good night." He walked off, snapping his fingers for the attentions of one of the servants, no doubt to show him personally to his guest suite.

"May I retire as well, Your Regalness?" Osmar asked, belching as quietly as he could still manage.

"Make certain you are not followed." Hero watched the mercenary stumble away, scanning the room briefly again before making his way to the large balcony where he sensed Lise to be.

The balcony was layered, an initial landing offset by steps leading down to a more secluded spot under the stars. Lise sat there, a drink in her hands, staring at the moons above. "I knew it was you," she said without looking at him. "I couldn't tell until you were close, but then I knew." She looked at him, her hair spilling over one shoulder as she turned her head. "I don't suppose you've formulated any further theories as to why we share this little 'gift' yet?"

Hero sat down on a step a little higher than hers, but close. "No."

She turned back to the view. "Thought not." She sipped her glass, sighing. "I had no idea you could be so courtly. Does the Queen always make you tell those stories?"

"She is a good entertainer of crowds, and utilizes her guests effectively," Hero said. "I do not know why I indulge her."

"Its this place. Okino is wonderful. A treasure that should always remain an unblemished jewel in the crown of the universe." She laughed humorlessly, looking down at her drink. "I fight for these people and they don't even know it. Worse, I didn't know how tired I was until I came here." She rubbed her eyes and placed a stray wisp of hair back over her

208

ear. "Its so beautiful here. It reminds me of home, yet its so different. It makes me wish my life had been… easier."

"Perhaps that is why I return here so often."

She turned on him, her eyes hard and tired. "And yet you can do nothing but talk of battle. You've seen wonders and experienced cultures I've only dreamt of. You come from a world that was once the very spirit of this universe. And yet with all of this wonder around you, you still can be nothing save a warrior without a past on a quest to save an uncertain future. Don't you ever do anything accept train and fight?"

"I am a warrior of the Triialon. I have time for little else."

"Yes, but do you enjoy it?

Hero's tone became cold. "You disapprove of my lifestyle?"

Lise seemed about to throw her arms up in rage - but instead slumped forward, standing quietly. "No. I'm just very frustrated with a man who is fascinating beyond his apparent desire to reveal nothing of the greatness that makes him up." She began to ascend the steps. "Not to me, and not to himself." She left him alone on the steps, calling back to him. "I'm going to bed. I'll see you tomorrow, *sir*," she said in icy tones.

Hero crossed his arms, taking in a great breath of air to calm himself. It helped little, and he found himself staring out at the stars as Lise had been doing before him. A few moments passed before he heard another set of footsteps behind him. He did not have to turn to know it was Lorette.

"Lise did not seem happy," she said without scolding. "Is there a problem?"

"Nothing unusual."

"So then what's the excuse?" she asked mirthfully.

"Privacy," he grumbled.

"Oh," Lorette teased, sitting down next to him. "Don't you hate it when a girl wants to know something about you?"

"I do not have the time for frivolities."

She made a face at that. "Don't you mean trivialities, like becoming involved?" Hero growled a 'yes' at that. "Well don't give me any of your Triialon excuses. You've taken the time and care to have lovers before,

Hero. What makes her so different? Hell, she seems more compatible than most, in many ways. Or is that the real issue?"

"She expects me to know who the Triialon were and to be able to tell her, when I know almost nothing of who we once were. Our time was up before I was even born."

"You still know more than anyone else. What would happen if you told her that much?" He didn't answer that, but she still wouldn't leave him be. "You won't let anyone that close to you, will you? Even if you knew how." She ran a hand down her champion's cheek, though he did not acknowledge it. Lorette gave a sigh and stood, preparing to leave him for the evening. "Very well, keep your secrets. I know so little of you myself, so who am I to beg them of you? But ask yourself this tonight, if nothing else; how can anyone ever know what it is you truly seek on your quest if you won't even tell one person 'why'?"

Hero let her retreat to the quieting murmur of the emptying party. Taking out some paper and tobacco, he rolled it himself and lit it. He proceeded to take a long drag, letting the smoke fill his lungs before expending it into the night air.

At the top of one of the sets of staircases, in the gloom of one corner away from the retiring guests, Kezeron Telbandith opened the small communications device Toapo had given him and typed in a code on its tiny controls. His master's voice came through as a raspy whisper covered by static. "You've found something?"

"He is here, My Lord,"

The voice became more excited and demanding. "Where?"

"Okino," Kezeron grudgingly admitted to his master. He wanted his prey all to himself, with no interference from the Gods.

"Is there anyone with him?"

"The mercenary Osmar and a woman. I don't know where she came from, but they entered the mansion together. She is young, with long, dark hair."

"She's probably a Coalition officer," the voice replied. "There are those who would pay for that information."

"Let me kill him first, My Lord," Kezeron snarled. "Bringing others here would only force Hero to move on."

"You think of nothing save your own personal glory, Kezeron. Perhaps I shall let you engage the Triialon, or perhaps not. I will contact you when *I* decide. Until then, enjoy what Okino has to offer, stay out of site, and only contact me if Hero is moving again."

A bark of static and then silence told the fighter that he was again alone in the darkness. "*Enjoy what Okino has to offer,*" the God had told him. Kezeron grinned, winding his way back to his apartment where just such a diversion waited with already full pockets on sweaty sheets, sleeping blindly to the drama around her.

Chebonka sat in the throne room ignoring the usual busy activity of the command room. Instead the 'Android Born of Man' stared at the Triialon sword that rested on the arms of a servitor robot. Anger and bitterness over the disappearance of Hero and the Coalition and his continued inability to unlock the powers of the Artifact had driven him to this. He had deployed almost the entire fleet. Thousands of warships had gone forth into the galaxy to scour for the Coalition fleets, leaving only the reserves and garrisons to defend the home world and territories. Kordula had been just as disappointing, long since ignoring his requests for more materials to aid the war machine, much less his desire for Triialon knowledge. Finally he had demanded an audience with Memfis, the 'God' agreeing to send one of his agents.

The gleaming sword sat before Chebonka, unmoving as he regarded it. Chebonka knew now, somehow, that the Artifact of the Twelve was in some way alive, or conscious, and that it would have to join with its wielder on some level to work. Only that level continued to elude the Lordillian master. Chebonka still did not move, even when the Kordula agent was admitted into the room. History being made, a non-Lordillian creature entering the throne room of its own free will, yet still he did not move.

Legends persisted as to just what the agents, or God-Servants, were. The being swept into the room and up the steps to stand before Chebonka's dais. It was clad in a robe covering its limbs and body from

211

neck to floor and its head was a great metal helm, an angular parody of the Gods own horse-shaped head. Some said it was the final incarnation of what those who served the Gods closest became - the suit and helmet carrying on their life force past when a mortal body would have perished. Others said they were of the Gods own original race, the last few mortal beings from the same progeny that had spawned the immortal Gods, now trapped forever as undead servants. All claimed the creatures were indestructible. Whether it be machine, man, or God, Chebonka hated it and everything it represented, this day more than any other.

"It is customary to acknowledge the servants of the immortal Gods, Chebonka," came the hollow, metal voice from within the helm. "Even for you. You break tradition by calling me here, and call undo attention to the relationship you and my masters share."

Chebonka remained silent and still. Decades before, when he was still a being of weak flesh working as a soldier, politician, and scientist, he had been obsessed with perpetuating himself as the perfect being. He strove to change his race into a force that could not be defeated and would not succumb to the random opinions and wills that threatened to tear his society apart. That personal obsession had led to the creation of the Lordillian race as machines. Eventually, with his new army behind him and the strange alien sword in his hand, he had come to power. His own will was still subject to emotion and other inefficiencies, so he created a chassis for himself, a form based on his creations that he could download his own consciousness into and continue to rule his people for a thousand years. Chebonka was born, and hot hatred was put aside to further his cold new power.

"State your business, Chebonka. The Gods have no time for your games."

"Where is the Coalition?" Chebonka commanded at last.

"Hidden. Where, I know not. You are at war with them, not I."

"Why do I have an Artifact of power that I cannot even wield? For years, the Gods have held back knowledge I know they possess. It ends today. Tell me how to use the Triialon blade." The hatred that had remained behind the confines of his calculating mind now began to fire. What had become a dull ache now escalated towards an explosion.

"I have no knowledge," it answered.

"But your masters do. They made certain the weapon fell to my hands, I know. Contact them, now."

"You do not command me, Lordillian. I suggest you capture the Triialon and torture the information out of him."

Chebonka's fury overcame his machine mind, and he stood, snatching the Triialon weapon from where it lay cradled. "I said *it ends today!*" The red flame within his mind found its contact paper in the form of the Artifact held in his metal gauntlet. As though the emotion he had so long tried to confine within himself could travel down his arm and into the hilt of the sword, the blade suddenly glowed blue, a blast of power illuminating the room. The flash reflected off the silver plating of the Kordula agent's mask, actually startling the stoic being, making it reel backwards off balance. Before the creature could react further the blade had fallen with a powerful arc that split the agent from shoulder to breast bone. It screamed, a gurgle of failing respiratory system and artificial voice replicator that bled off into a warble of noise. A noxious black fluid gushed from the terrible wound, pouring down the robes and spilling onto the floor. Chebonka pulled the sword free, hacking down a second time. The lightning radiated off of the Artifact, catching the servant's robes on fire and stabbing invisibly through its torso. The second blow removed the agent's head, cutting the reverberating scream off suddenly and felling the creature at last.

Chebonka stared at the glowing weapon in his hand, at last obeying his commands. If he had still had a face, he would have smiled. The secret of the Servants of the Gods could have been revealed then, but the Lordillian leader was still testing his new ability. He aimed the sword's tip at the dead agent and let the same rage pour through him and into the weapon. The flickering lightening again took shape, radiating as a beam of energy that crashed into the corpse and decimated it, taking much of the staircase with it. Chebonka held the Triialon sword up and willed it back to a state of rest, the glow immediately fading to the dull shine of the strange metal.

"At last."

"I've just received word from captain Fazlu's fleet," Jay'salan said, a packed bag in his hand as he stood in admiral Jo'seph's newly refurbished conference room. The fellow admiral stood just inside the doorway, his ever present book under one arm. "They've had to change their position a third time now. The Lordillians keep getting close, Jo'. Close enough that the next time they might track our ships' withdrawal."

Jo'seph rose angrily, making certain the door to the conference room was secure from the rest of the bridge level of their new base. "We have to bring the fleet here," he said when he was sure no one was listening.

"That is unacceptable," Jay' said adamantly. "This base can defend no one. Our position here is still too weak."

"Precisely. We need at least one fleet here to defend this project the moment the Lordillians finally do find us."

"And we would endanger the entire Coalition by bringing further ships here. I agree we need to move the fleets somewhere more secure before we can either mount any kind of offensive or before we can bring them here once this place is a defensible position. But they need a more neutral location, or we risk everything." Jay'salan relaxed his massive shoulders a little and sat down at the conference table, turning on a tactical display. "You'll have ample evacuation time if any Lordillians head the direction of Grellion, Jo'seph. The fleets are still the only strength we have left."

"That would leave this place to the Lordillians if they do come this way. No, I still at least want something between us and them to at least make a stand."

Jay'salan contemplated the map a moment. "Very well, I'll move the second fleet here, to meet any force that might come this way before they even enter Grellion's neighboring systems. I'll take the first to the fringes of Nevartza, to watch their movements as best I can. That leaves the third through sixth fleets."

Jo'seph changed the display's angle, studying it intently. "What about the Abyss Field?"

"That's not a bad idea," Jay'salan said, scratching his square jaw. The Abyss Field was their somewhat pretentious name for a string of asteroids heading towards a large black hole, its position not all that remote, but the

214

gravitational pull was dangerous, as well as the threats posed by the asteroids, meaning that the surrounding area was mostly avoided by travelers, away from any Lordillian conquests. "All right, I agree, that's a good place for them to lay low." He groaned at his own words then, pounding the table in frustration. "I hate those words, 'lay low'. We need action. At least let me send out some minimal strike team assignments from solitary ships. We can get some work done and not endanger the other ships."

Jo'seph nodded. "Agreed. Now get going. You're already late for your rendezvous." The two friends clasped arms before Jay'salan took his bags and opened the door.

"Try not to miss me too much."

"I'll try to remember your rank once you're gone," Jo'seph replied dryly. The door closed silently, and Jo'seph was left to gather his own things before heading back to the control room. He was only halfway there when Zhade and another officer ran up to him.

"Sir! There's a Lordillian ship on the scanners!"

Jo'seph's heart sank. "Catch the admiral before he leaves, bring him back to the bridge." Zhade began to run off, and Jo' called after him. "Have him hide the ships on the runway!" He turned quickly to the other officer. "Have Sardeece report to the bridge immediately."

"Yes, sir!"

Admiral Jo'seph set off for the control room at a run.

Jay'salan and Sardeece entered the control room almost simultaneously, a servitor robot trailing the mechni-prophet like some sort of lost pet.

"What's their position and class," Jay'salan asked, tossing his bags and book in a corner.

"Lordillian attack ship," Jo'seph replied, watching the displays with trepidation. "It's sitting right between the Grellion moon and us. I think it just launched its compliment of fighters."

"That's another twenty ships that will be scouring the area. Fortunately I already hid our ships."

Sardeece said, "We managed to get the hanger door to open enough for that much, at least."

"Fantastic," Jo'seph said, relieved. "Now I need you to get the citadel to power down. The Lordillians will be looking for energy signatures."

As if on cue the lights dimmed and many displays failed, the officers at their stations confused as their controls went dark. The hum of power faded, the room's ambient noise falling to a deafening silence. "Already in progress," Sardeece said with a grim smile. His subconscious connection with the citadel had obviously improved.

"You're a little creepy sometimes," Jo'seph murmured. "Now we can only hope we're quiet enough for them not to notice us."

"Or that they haven't already noticed us," Jay'salan said. "What was the last report on those fighters before the controls blanked out?"

Tykeisha was stationed on the control decks. She stood nervously, looking up as though trying to see through the bulkheads above them to the stars beyond. "Heading strait for us and entering the atmosphere."

Jay'salan swore. "Guess it was a good idea not to clear off all the overgrowth on the base yet after all. Natural camouflage is the best." Jo'seph looked at him, wondering who he was trying to convince.

A bridge officer was reading off of a stopwatch, estimating the time from the last moment they knew the Lordillian fighters' positions to when they might have entered the atmosphere and be over the base. "Sixty seconds," he called out, quietly.

"What about life signs," Jay'salan wondered. "Can their scanners penetrate the Grellion bulkheads?"

"The dampening field that's hidden the citadel's power signature from space all these years wouldn't hide it from a close flyover," Sardeece mused, "but it should hide our life signs, being so few of us."

"Should," Jo'seph echoed. "That's comforting."

"Thirty seconds."

"Maybe we should evacuate to a deeper level."

"Too late for that," Jay'salan whispered.

"Twenty seconds."

"How the hell did they find us?"

"Fifteen."

"Quiet!"

They all waited in silence. Within moments a high-pitched whine could be discerned, muffled by the surrounding walls. The entire squad of twenty fighters must have flown directly over the bridge, a roar passing around the hiding Coalition officers. All of them watched the ceiling as though it were about to crash down upon them. The roar dissipated off into the distance, the silence returning to drown their ears again.

"They'll be around for a second pass if they came that close," Jo'seph said under his breath.

"Here they come," Zhade hissed, his ear against the shuttered view ports.

The metallic whine returned, followed by the roar of the Lordillian engines, lengthened this time by the tight circle the made around the base. They were probably examining the strange mass of metal and vines by visual as well as energy scan. The flyover lasted for what felt like hours, but Jo'seph new was merely moments. Finally the sound disappeared again, leaving them all to catch their breath.

"Are they gone, lieutenant" Jo'seph whispered to Zhade.

There was a pause before the young officer answered. "For now."

"Even if they didn't scan anything, they're not blind." Jay'salan sighed, sitting down in Jo'seph's new command chair. "Its only a matter of time now."

"Sardeece," Jo' called quietly. "Can we power up just the sensors so we can know when it's safe to poke our heads out, or do I have to go up on the roof with a telescope?"

"I suggest caution, sir." Sardeece started pacing, one of the more jittery character traits the scientist had developed since his transition. "I can get you minimal scan, so long as those fighters don't come back. Those fighters could just as easily scan us, though, when they head back over us to their cruiser."

"Then we wait," the admiral agreed. "Give the ships enough time to orbit. Less chance of getting caught, then. We give them an hour, then turn on the sensors and see if they've left the system."

"And if they don't leave?" Jay'salan asked. "What do we do if those fighters come back and park right on our doorstep and start snooping around?'

Jo'seph didn't have an immediate answer for that.

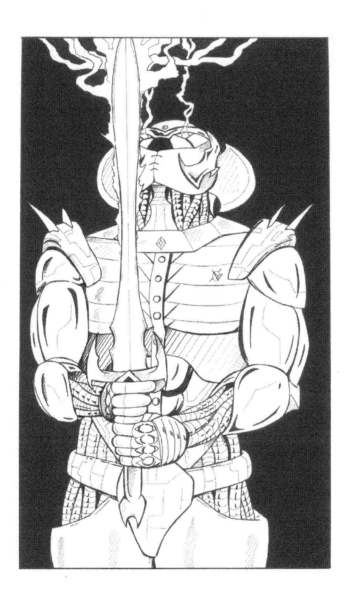

Chapter Thirteen

The importing of pop culture was a very difficult thing
if you were a soldier in the Coalition at that time.
Smuggled VIDs, often of year-old motion pictures
from Okino or some planet that had been under
Lordillian rule for five years, magazines and toys or
other items costing ten times the market value...
I'm surprised we found any ways to have fun...
-From the notes of a Coalition Corporal

Lise was just pouring herself a hot cup of cocoa when the door to her palace apartment chimed. "Come in," she said with some trepidation.

As she feared, it was Hero that entered, again in his usual garb. "I did not wish to wake you."

"I suppose you've been up for hours," she mused, blowing cool air over her mug. "Ow." She tried to sip, but it was still too hot, so she continued to blow over the surface of the liquid. With her free hand she pulled the white robe around her shoulders more tightly, hiding her bare skin. She had forgotten to buy pajamas on the colony world, and she wasn't about to spend her first night on Okino sleeping in rationed PJs on silk sheets. "Do Triialon even sleep?" She regretted the question even as she asked it, though she had meant it as a joke.

He did not answer.

"Ow!" Lise put down the mug, willing herself to calm down. She was frustrated with herself and the situation and wanted to make amends, not escalate the problem. She turned to him, her bare feet padding along the plush floor and coming to stand near him. "Look, I'm sorry for being rude last night, Hero." She hesitated when he just watched her, that emotionless glare of his threatening to steal her resolve. "I would like to blame the wine and stress, but I can't make excuses."

"Then why apologize?" Hero asked her. The question caught Lise off guard despite all her hopes to be resolute. He continued when she didn't answer the question. "You said what was in your heart. That is what matters."

"I... I guess I was just wondering what right I had to ask questions as if I were trying to change you. And it's not that in any case. I just resent

220

that wall you throw up in front of me whenever I want to know something about you. It somehow seems unfair to me because of that stupid psychic link of ours, as if I should be granted rights and privileges because of it. Now that I think of it, its probably *why* you close yourself to me as much as anyone I've seen you with. I'm in danger of getting too close, and a warrior can't risk that, can he?" Lise stopped, realizing that she had been rambling nervously. Looking up at him she smiled, sighed, and sat down at the wood-carved table. She ran her fingernail along its gorgeous surface, trailing the patterns in its surface. "Listen to me. I'm doing all of the talking. Again."

Hero relaxed a little, moving to the far side of the table. "Perhaps I have been too coarse with you."

With that, Lise was given leave to dig again, and she couldn't resist such a temptation. "Why do you hesitate to talk to me or teach me? We share some sort of bond that you won't tell me about and it must have something to do with the Triialon."

"I never said I would not teach you some things if I had the time…"

A moment of silence followed. Lise looked down at her mug of quickly cooling cocoa, finding it unappealing now. "You didn't answer my question last night," she continued almost meekly. "Do you enjoy nothing but training and battle? What do you look for in a place like Okino when you're the last of the Triialon?"

Lise was uncertain Hero was going to answer her questions at all for a moment. He was so silent. But then his voice came calmly and not angered. "I sometimes feel the thrill of battle, but war is seldom uplifting. Perhaps I too must be reminded what it is that I fight for."

Lise exhaled deeply. "A part of me wants to just forget the war and stay on Okino, stay closer to a life that should have been mine. But there's this other part of me, growing stronger by the day, that either out of desire or out of guilt wants to return to the only home that I've known these past few years; get back to the people I fight beside and make a difference with. I'm so torn by how much I missed the passions of a normal life, and didn't even know it, and how much the war means to me that I don't want to forget." Lise held the mug for comfort now, not even bothering to nurse it, fearing it may have gone cold. "When I watched you training the other night, it made me wonder how different or how similar we might be, you and I."

"The training relaxes me," Hero said.

Lise looked at him. "But do you enjoy it? Does it give you pleasure? I can see the ancient ideals working within your style of training or arts or however you want to refer to it, and I can see that its just as physically or spiritually appealing as it is battle-hardening. Do you even see that, Hero? Your culture was more than battle, I can tell. No race can thrive on war alone. Who were its artists, scientists, naturalists, architects...?"

"If they had a culture, I do not know what it was." Hero's tone began to become icy again. He strode across the room, standing in front of the morning sunlight that came through the large bay window. "It would have been before my time, when all that was left was the Great War that ended my race. What would you have me tell you of my people?"

Lise stood, trying to close the distance between them. "What about *your* culture, Hero? You've seen hundreds of worlds and ways and peoples, and I know you weren't fighting or questing or training every minute! I can tell by the way each wizened Lady or beautiful woman recalls your courtliness and charm from the last time you met. I can tell by the passion that frees you when you wield that sword, or the love you hold for the bustle of Okino or the lost empire of Grellion."

Before she could reach him, Hero moved away again. "There is no time."

"No time? What, for me? For you?" Lise finally dared to drink from the cold mug when the next moment of silence greeted her. It didn't really taste that bad, and she laughed under her breath. "What are we doing here then?"

" *'Can you find what it is I need?'* the citadel said. I'm here hoping to find at least a lead on what might be the missing power source of the Grellion base." Hero was giving orders at this point, reminding them both of their duty, just as a warrior should. Lise had to fight the urge to roll her eyes. "Hopefully something can be found before your friends are simply naked targets. *You* are here because you have an appointment with the Queen of Okino, to help present the Coalition's case before many respected galactic individuals. Lorette informed me this morning that you

222

can meet her tomorrow afternoon. Now I must follow up on my first lead." He stalked towards the door, as if to exit. When the door opened he paused, hesitant to leave. "However," he said, trying to sound slightly more pleasant and not doing a very good job of it, "perhaps you would care to join me for dinner this evening? It may prove to be our last on Okino and I would not want you to feel that it was wasted."

That was a surprise, though her mood only brightened a little. Lise put on her best formal face, nodding a little. "That would be most agreeable, sir."

Hero almost grumbled, closing the door partway again. "Very well. Eighteen hundred hours?" Lise nodded again. "Good. May I remind you, commander, to keep a low profile until we leave. I'm convinced there is at least one agent against us here and there may be more." With that he opened the door finally and departed, leaving Lise once again with mixed emotions and uncertainties. When she couldn't stand the inner conflict anymore, she finally decided that the elation over going to dinner with Hero that evening far outweighed her ruffled emotions over his attitude. Lise grinned like a school girl and leapt over to her closet, pulling out the remainder of her new clothing.

"He has killed one of our agents. Psionic contact cannot be regained." Galatis turned off the dull, void display. "The servant's death is confirmed."

"Chebonka's arrogance has increased," one of the other Gods sneered. "Perhaps he has finally gone over the edge."

"We know the Triialon Artifact was damaged even before it came into Chebonka's keeping. We also knew it might gain a mental hold on him because of that." Memfis' eyes raced over decades of notes and files regarding the Lordillians and their creator. "But the success factor of such an event was less than ten percent. I think it's more likely the 'android born of man,'" he said with a scoff, "finally lost his grip on the repressed emotions that mechanical mind of his always had such a hard time dealing with."

Toapo pounded the table. "And he may very well have finally gained control of the sword by way of those emotions. He is a threat to our plans and must be eliminated. The Coalition is scattered, decimated. Its power no longer threatens our plans."

"Even Chebonka still has his uses," Galatis intoned. "If Hero manages to turn the Coalition back into a strong opposition we will then have even bigger problems should they have no Lordillians to fight."

Toapo threw up his arms. "Again, so many of Memfis' past mistakes come back to haunt us. These forces are conjoining, creating issues that must be dealt with now!"

"It matters little," Memfis said at last. "The Coalition and Lordillian war is nearly over. When Chebonka finds their fleets his forces will overwhelm them. His time is limited."

"In any case he has opposed us openly and must be punished," another of the immortals elected.

"Agreed," Galatis said.

"This is ridiculous," Toapo fumed. "If Hero does lead the Coalition to some great victory, what then?"

"That will not happen," Memfis said in controlled tones.

"Chebonka and Hero are now in direct opposition." Toapo was standing again, his fists resting on the table. "Should they face each other one will prevail, holding that many more of the Triialon Artifacts because of it. If Chebonka has finally discovered the secret of the Artifact he will then be a threat, not only to us, but to the future itself. Memfis dares to let all of these factors continue unchecked, and you are all letting him, bowing and scraping like servants!"

"Toapo may be too outspoken," yet another God said, standing, "but he has a point. Chebonka and the Lordillians are in place to fight the Coalition, not Triialon. This is a wild card we should have seen coming. The Lordillians would hardly be a controlled factor if they wielded the power of three of the Twelve against us."

Others began to murmur agreement, nodding their heads and suddenly looking to Toapo for further insight. Memfis felt his lip twist slightly. Controlling his anger, he too stood up. "Have we forgotten every aspect of the board and all semblance of patience?" he asked of them. "It is not as though these are the only game pieces that remain. The Seethlings will soon be ready to take on the Triialon for the last time. The Forefather

224

simply awaits the word before he descends upon Chebonka like death itself. There are contingencies we have had in place for centuries, yet we sit here and squabble because one of us is simply malcontent with his feeble grasp on the situation around him."

"Bah!" Toapo's face flashed with rage. "You fear for your grasp on the Court, Memfis. The same fear that has kept you at the head of this table for millennia now threatens to topple your secret plans. You do nothing for the good of the rest of us any longer, only for yourself, and when Zone comes, the Gods will not stand beside him, only Memfis!"

"That's enough!" Memfis voice cracked like thunder. "His coming is close, perhaps less than a hundred years away, yet you dare to try and split this Sanctum in two with false accusations. We lose everything if we do not stand together when He comes."

"And we will not be standing if you are left to continue leading this Court with such feeble actions!" Toapo turned to the others, his outstretched arms sweeping over them all as he collected his speech again. "Memfis cannot even find Hero and deal with him more than thirty years after the fall of his empire. I shall correct this wrong and send Kezeron to kill this Triialon bastard," he declared, and many vocalized their approval of this idea. Toapo took full advantage of the dramatic moment, leaving his place at the council table and sweeping out of the room.

Memfis wasn't about to be left standing there a fool. He watched his opponent's exit, turning back to his fellow Gods and staring into their motley rumblings. "This is no time for rash actions with our destiny finally so close at hand. Calculated movements must see this thing through to its inevitable conclusion." He sat back down, smoothing down his robes. "Open a channel to the Lordillian home world."

The lights dimmed, leaving a spot shining down over Memfis' face. A hazy, globular hologram appeared above the center of the table, the visual signal not appearing till the connection had been established. Chebonka's face appeared at last. He was seated atop a throne, the Triialon sword in his robotic hands and the steps below his feet melted away. "At last the Gods contact *me*. Am I no longer forsaken?"

"Chebonka of the Lordillians, you have killed one of my servants, an act that would demand retribution."

"It was an act of defense," Chebonka said evenly. "No creature not of Lordillian design may set foot in the throne room, and the transgression was met with immediate action. It was not an act that could be controlled."

Usually the android man sat perfectly still when he was contacted by the Gods, encased in his metal armor like a statue. Something had changed, and now Chebonka held the Triialon Artifact to him, drawing the sword slowly across his opposing hand as if he were fingering the edge. *He has gained control of the artifact*, Memfis thought to the others, *or at least believes he has.*

"Perhaps it is best," Chebonka continued. "I would not want you to think you held complete dominion over me. I can act on my own, gain power without your approval."

"You are cut off from Kordula's support, Chebonka," Memfis decreed, "and that of its systems and assets. Do you hear me? Your influence does not spread so far as you think."

The Lordillian leader actually stood up in shock. "What? You cannot do that! I need those supplies to perpetuate the war machine. The Coalition are poised for the killing blow and you would turn away from me?"

"Your own conquered systems can more than handle the Lordillian need for war resources."

"Then I shall expose our dealings to the galaxy outside of Kordula. My influence is more absolute than you think. Okino and the systems beyond will know of your hand in the Lordillian war!"

"That would be a mistake," Memfis said. "Consider our business terminated, Chebonka. You have no proof that links your war to Kordula. If you ever expect to renegotiate with the Gods, myself or my power in the future, you will keep silent. Perhaps when the Coalition is finally destroyed, if you can indeed manage to find them, then you might be welcomed back into the society of Kordula. Dare to further this madness by even implicating the Gods in this dirty little war of yours and you shall learn the might of the Gods' hand."

The channel was cut, the hologram dissipating above him as Memfis brought the lights of the room back up. Some of the others nodded approval, others seemed to be less than satisfied. "Control over the Lordillians is no longer necessary. When the war ends, Chebonka will die. If the Coalition evades him, then we will fashion his destiny and make certain both armies are destroyed. Before then, our tools will have made certain the Triialon legacy ends." Those that had nodded before bowed their heads in agreement, but still the others stared, unmoved. The line had already been drawn - Memfis' support already wavered. He clenched his fists in silent rage.

The Triialon city lay in ruins around him, pillars and walls tumbled and strewn, looking, save for the scorch marks, as though an ancient civilization had passed there long ago. Hero climbed the steps of the central palace, one of the few large structures still standing. He looked up at the swirling, dusty sky before passing through the large doors. He stood alone in the great hall; most of his warriors were sleeping in their own homes. His bodyguards had by now all been slain. He dared not speak or breathe too loud, for the echoes would remain to taunt him with their loneliness.

The rooms and halls above were silent as well, Lance sleeping peacefully in a crib overseen by an equally sound-sleeping servant. Across the hall, in his own chamber, his bed lay empty. Verule had been missing all afternoon, but of late that had been the habit of his lover. He did not love the woman, he knew that now, but her presence had been soothing for a time, and he noticed whenever she was gone. Her own attitude had been equally cavalier, though no one among the Triialon could claim they had not lost someone close to them, so Hero and Verule hardly held a monopoly on desolation. Lance had been born merely months before, and would prove to be the last child born on the planet during the war. Even his presence brought little hope, though Hero did try to love the child.

Night was falling. Hero watched the darkness spread across the palace walls.

Only shadows remained.

Hero awoke. He had dared to close his eyes only a moment and thoughts of home had encroached upon his peace. The warrior almost fumed, but instead picked up his sword and began his training, starting with the *Talenke* stance. He watched the clock, knowing soon he would be taking Lise for dinner, but sooner Durant would call on him. Or Hero would have to find him.

A half hour had passed before Osmar entered the room from his adjoining apartment's side door. The mercenary scratched his bald pate and yawned, unaffected by the previous night's drinking save for the late wake up time. "Good morning, your grace."

"Good afternoon," Hero grunted, never wavering from his practiced moves. "Have you stretched yet?"

Osmar laughed at that. "Come on. You know I don't train on any given day, practice the totem bear position, or pray to any gods in the east." He poured himself some water and began to roll himself some tobacco. "When the fightin' comes, it comes."

"Fine. Get dressed and get back out there. If that Kezeron is watching me I want you watching him." The merc groaned, crumpling up the failed smoke. "Now," Hero commanded. "You've slept late enough."

"I know, I know, there's work to be done."

The front doors chimed, Osmar looking up as Hero paused in his movements. The mercenary nodded, exiting through the portal back to his own room, but never shutting the door completely. "Enter," Hero called.

It was Durant, overdressed as always and giving a theatrical bow. "Ah, Hero, 'tis a grand morning, equal only to the grand headache I sport. Where is your bald friend?"

Osmar slipped back into the room, pulling on his coat. "Here, you lightweight dandy."

"Ah. I knew there was a stench." He held the merc's gaze, grinning. "I do hope you're 'on the clock' dressed like that."

"Well I'm not off to a flower social," Osmar replied, squinting.

"Go," Hero reiterated.

Osmar returned his ugliest grin to the court blade, pushing past Durant and making his way to the door. "His master's voice," Durant mocked. The door slammed shut, cutting off the mercenary's rude retort. Durant sighed dramatically. "You called, master?"

Hero began toweling off, a mere gesture as he had barely broken a sweat. "Tell me about Kezeron Telbandith."

"What makes you think I know anything about him?" Durant asked, gesturing to himself with false innocence.

Hero stared at the man, pausing only a moment before returning to his dressing. "Do not play games, Durant. If things go the way I believe they will, you'll make plenty of money on this trip without the bribery of information you have already collected for yourself." He pulled on a shirt, buttoning it as he read off the mental list aloud. "You spent five years as a hired blade, informant, and senatorial bodyguard before finally being able to afford coming to Okino for work over three years ago. You worked both sides of the last war on Julian and defeated a very distinguished Belzchak in your last duel because you knew his blind spot. It is your business to know who people are."

"You knew about the Belzchak?" Durant swept his coattails over the side of a chair he had pulled out for himself, sighing again. "Very well, as you're such an old friend. But there's little to tell, save hearsay that has been gathering on this side of the galaxy the last few years. No one knows much save the reputation he's built." He absently played with the frill of one sleeve, looking thoughtful. "Word has it he's killed three Belzchaks himself, come to think of it. His fighting style is supposed to be unique, a mix of some very old, apparently effective methods. He's well off, obviously, but the source is untraceable. Whether he's stolen from those he's killed or just very well paid for what he does is unknown, but he's been an assassin, among other things. In any case he seems to only want the best, judging by the silks and women, and claims to be the best at everything he does. Bit of a showoff, really. He's dangerous as all hell, I'll say it. There's a reason he gets the jobs he does. But he's a hothead, so no one really likes him."

Hero snorted. "Have you met him?"

"No. No, he's been very reclusive here. Perhaps he's looking for work." Durant seemed to get a thought on that, his brow raising. "Perhaps he's looking for you. It would certainly explain a few things."

"Why?"

"He showed up just before you. He's known to take on reputed fighters simply for the glory of it. Yes, I think he is here for you. But you knew that, didn't you? That's why you asked."

Hero ignored the question, changing the subject. "Do you still use the same sword?" he asked, gesturing to the blade at Durant's side.

He smiled, pulling the sword out. "Stop being polite. You know it's the same weapon just by that crystal embossed bracer of yours. You've hardly forgotten the reason we met."

"No," Hero said, and took the offered sword, inspecting the swept hilt and the cloudy red jewel imbedded just below the slender blade.

"Three years ago you drilled me with questions regarding that sword every time you saw me in the Okino palace," Durant recalled. "Don't tell me you finally found out where it came from."

Hero studied the hilt closely, speaking quietly while lost within the jewel's contours. "Three years ago I was drawn to Okino not just by one of my visits, but by the recognized energy signature my *Prizm* picked up." His bracer glowed stronger as he brought the two crystals closer together, the clouds within Durant's jewel beginning to swirl like a gathering storm.

"You had hoped to come across one of the lost Triialon artifacts," Durant said grinning. "Instead you found me."

"The missing Artifacts of the Twelve continue to elude me," the Triialon mused, "But I find some of the same elements in other objects of either beauty or power strewn across the cosmos. This is one such object. Like another I have found, and just like the many you traded that are identical to this one. Tell me again where you came across them."

Durant shrugged. "I bought them off of a merchant, getting a fairly low price on them considering I was courting his daughter at the time. He had said he bought them off of a thief. The merchant got them from the guy for next to nothing. I guess the pilfering fellow was really superstitious and ended up with a bad case of the frights when he decided these crystals were 'alive', practically giving them to the merchant. You said yourself you felt it; that strange inner glow it has." He hooked his jacket lapels with his thumbs proudly. "I say it's good fortune. Certainly brought good fortune to me. Anyway the fellow was some crypt robber or something - easily spooked."

230

"Not a crypt; a citadel, more ancient than memory. The only things of any possible value still left buried there, at least to the untrained eye, were these critical elements. Thankfully he never disclosed the location of the city to anyone."

"But you've found more?"

Hero smiled slightly. "Not exactly." Hero sat back, breaking his reverie and handing the sword back to Durant. "Amazing."

"What?"

"The cycle of events that may just deliver the galaxy from the Lordillians." He locked gazes with the courtier. "How many did you buy, and did you sell them all to the same buyer?"

Durant's smile widened. "They're going to make me rich a second time, aren't they?"

Jo'seph watched the screen with trepidation as the main power came back online. Hours of silence had passed; the Lordillian fighters' positions still unknown and the low-level scans revealing no energy surge large enough to be any attack ships moving away. Finally the scans had come back positive; they were gone. But the admirals both knew the damage had already been done and that the ship would be back with others. Maybe not immediately, but soon.

"Confirmed," Tykeisha's voice sounded as relieved as they all felt. "Lordillian vessel has moved out of range. No fighters showing on scans."

"I can be spaceborn in ten minutes," Jay'salan said. "I'll take the biggest and fastest of what's on hand, a special ops team, and I'll go wait on the fringes of the system. Lead the next force away with some live bait, give your people, and hopefully Hero, some more time. Meanwhile I'll send the other ships to deliver orders to the fleets."

Jo'seph stood, holding his chin in contemplation, his brow creasing deeply. "Lordillians don't believe in coincidences, Jay'. Coalition ships in the same area as some derelict stronghold in a remote star system? They'll come here anyway, in force, and see what this place is."

"It gives us more time than we have now. I'll attack the first Lordillian ship I see heading back into his system, make them chase me. They'll expend a lot trying to track me down before they bother to check this dead hulk." Jo'seph was silent, staring back at his adamant friend. "I can do it," Jay'salan continued. "I can lead them off for hours, days, whatever we can buy to give you more time to either arm the base, defend it," he paused, his mouth becoming a thin line, "or destroy it."

Fortunately Sardeece was out of earshot for that one.

"Go," was all Jo'seph could say, hoping he wasn't agreeing to the death of both admirals. He clasped hands with his friend only a moment before Jay'salan grabbed his bags and left the bridge, heading down to the enormous hanger.

Jo'seph turned back to the useless displays, knowing he was powerless to thwart any major offensive against their new base. Status reports noted depressingly how there was still no power to the shields or weapons. Crews had begun to set up internal barriers with whatever supplies they or the servitor robots could find. A tiny crew had begun to dig their way from a lower level bulkhead, tunneling underground in the hopes of reaching what may be a crashed and destroyed giant battleship under a mountain of rock. He wondered momentarily how Hero and Lise were faring.

If the waiting didn't drive him mad the communications silence would.

"Anything?" Hero asked Osmar as he entered from the balcony.

Osmar stretched and flexed his right arm, as though he had pulled something climbing down from the palace roof. "Nothing. Either Kezeron's hiding spot is better than mine and his patience even longer, or he's content to wait elsewhere. I'll search the palace in an hour."

"Very well." Hero studied the mirror before him intently, never having even looked at his friend as he was so busy adjusting his rather formal attire.

"So are we going somewhere?" Osmar asked in mock interest. He crossed his arms and leaned against the wall.

Hero pretended to ignore his companion, straightening his collar in the large reflection. "I am," he said at last.

Osmar smiled. "Has she got a sister?"

"I do not believe so."

232

Osmar's eyebrow rose. "You're taking Lise out, aren't you?"

"Lise was a member of Sparta's aristocracy before the Lordillian invasion. I am simply being cordial."

Osmar poured himself a drink from a crystal decanter sitting on Hero's desk. "Yeah, cordial." He laughed. "Gods, man, that girl is so gorgeous, and a proven fighter. Anyone can see that..."

He was cut off by Hero's exhale of frustration, the warrior's temper becoming short. "She is beautiful, I agree," Hero said, turning back to the mirror and calming himself. "But you know I have had no time of late for the matters of women's hearts. As it so happens, her company tonight may in fact aid my quest. In a way."

"You think she's of Triialon heritage?" Osmar asked around over the top of his goblet.

Hero stared off for a moment before answering at last. "It is possible. In any case there's something about her."

Osmar shook his head, finally turning to leave. "Fool yourself all you want, Your Lordship. All I have to say is that just because you're frustrated that you can't find ten swords scattered across space doesn't mean you shouldn't use yours from time to time."

Hero turned, now openly antagonistic. "Is that some sort of metaphor?" Hero demanded, tired of this conversation.

"Aye, Your Regalness," Osmar replied on his way out. "It means you need to get laid." He waved as the doors began to shut behind him, smiling sweetly. "Let me know if she has a sister."

Hero glared at the closed door. The anger quickly washed away, though, replaced by uncertainty. It was a rare feeling that the Triialon did not relish. He sighed, putting all thoughts aside as he tied his long hair back and inspected himself and his standard formal attire before confining himself to the fate he had fashioned by asking Lise out for the evening.

Lise's room was next to his own, on the opposite side of Osmar's, though not adjoining. He stood before the closed door momentarily, finally deciding to knock. Within seconds Lise opened the door and smiled. She was dressed spectacularly, as always of late, in another form fitting and low-cut dress.

"Good evening," she said. "Would you like to come in, or are we stepping out?"

"We may go, if you are ready," he replied, his negativity gone the moment he had seen her. "You look very beautiful."

Lise seemed surprised, though he wasn't sure why. It was not the first time he had complimented the young woman. "Thank you," she said, beaming.

They were stopped in the main hall when trying to avoid a milling group of dinner guests by the Queen. "Hero, my dear. Just the chap." She said it with her usual glowing smile. "I was hoping I might be able to talk you and Durant into perhaps showing off a little of your fencing skills after dinner this evening?"

Hero mustered a smile. "I am afraid not. I have sent Durant on an errand and he may not be back for several days."

"Perhaps I can fill the space of your missing sparring partner," came a voice from the crowd just behind the pouting Queen.

The black cape and blue skin of Kezeron Telbandith turned from the circle of guests and came to stand before Hero, looking up at him with fire in his eyes despite the smile on his lips. Hero was shocked that he had not sensed the man before this moment. He chided himself inwardly, attributing the slip to the distraction Lise posed.

"I'm afraid you're not on tonight's dinner list," the Queen said to him coldly. "Close friends only."

Kezeron smiled, showing perfect teeth. He did not bother to look at the queen. "A shame. I am certain it would have been a spectacular battle."

"There are few in this mansion that would dare make such a statement," Hero said, glaring back.

"And there are none that could hold their own against you, much less defeat you as I could, I'd wager."

"A pity, then, that all the finery and silks you've bought or stole to get in this house cannot buy you the friendship of the Queen as well so that we might settle the issue tonight."

"I take what I want and I own what I take," Kezeron spat, his mood now openly hostile. "I've earned every bit of respect and money I have."

234

"And look at the reputation it has garnered you," Hero said, remaining outwardly calm. In truth, his body was primed, muscles ready to explode into action as needed, protecting the Queen and Lise should Kezeron so much as move in a way that displeased him.

Just as quickly, Kezeron's mood switched again, and he leaned back on his heels as he crossed his arms and grinned. "You're right. My reputation is not complete. I should not expect to be invited to the Queen's table until *after* I have killed you in single combat." His lips curled, his expression hard while his head jerked to one side slightly, like a man that was trying hard to swallow something down. "But my master has not yet given me leave to slay you, and our mistress has forbade my joining you for dinner."

Hero's voice dropped to nearly a whisper. "I'll be waiting."

"And I will be ready." Kezeron paused, then took a step back, bowing as he again grinned at Hero, Lise, and the Queen. Then he was gone, lost among the crowds.

Hero reproached himself a second time for being so distracted the he had not sensed the slime in the first place. He looked at the Queen, apologizing. She shrugged, making little of it as she moved away to ferry her guests into the dining hall.

"Perhaps my original idea of eating out tonight was not such a bad one," Hero said to Lise, watching the groups of people as they filtered away. He let her take his arm and walked her down the palace steps and to a hovering vehicle that waited for them by the main gates. In minutes they were whisked to one of the towns nestled just beyond the enormous tree lines. A servant opened the door for them to exit, informing them he would be waiting when they returned. A lamp-lit little city greeted them in the hazy dusk, an old and detailed three story building looming from the corner before them. Hanging vines adorning its hallowed walls and from within came the sounds and smells of a bustling restaurant.

"You wished to see Okino," Hero said, trying to put the stresses of the day behind him. "This seemed a good example."

Lise just looked at him and smiled, letting him guide her into the front room where a host showed them to their seat. A table for two, complete with candles and a window view of the street from the second floor was in a quiet corner. The two uncertain diners were seated, giving them the last few rays of sunlight to fall behind the forests while thinking of something to say.

"This is wonderful," Lise said at last. "I don't know how I'm going to repay you for this."

"Unnecessary," Hero said, trying not to lose track of his surroundings by getting lost in her glinting brown eyes. "My heritage has allowed me to afford a lot of things others may not have the chance to." They were interrupted briefly by a server asking for their orders, which Hero took the liberty of giving when it was apparent Lise was unfamiliar with the dishes. "It is actually about heritage that I wished to speak to you this evening."

"Oh?" Lise turned a glass of wine around with her fingers, interested. "Are you going to tell me a story?"

The corners of Hero's mouth turned up, "Very well." For a long moment he stared out the restaurant window, watching some unseen event on a faraway horizon. Then at last he began, leaning in while speaking in quieter tones. "Centuries before I was born, the Triialon's influence over the galaxy was at its height. Other worlds and their nobles or politicians wanted to improve their own standings, so marriages were often arranged. Triialon blood mixed with those that were lucky enough to be compatible."

"Compatible?" Lise interrupted.

"Yes. A Triialon individual's influence is not just his prowess in battle or his social standing or knowledge. Our lineage has been genetically engineered. That is why I am able to withstand a certain amount of plasma energy impacting my physiology, and that is why not all beings of the opposite sex may be able to withstand," he paused, deciding to go the scientific route, "mating with a Triialon."

Lise smirked. "You sure you're not just trying to propagate some sexual stamina reputation?" she asked, half-joking.

Hero shook his head. "There is a telepathic as well as physical influence that can take place. That same energy is used to intimidate and anticipate our opponent, but it becomes something else in the case of cross-mating, something that can be… overpowering."

236

Lise was silent a moment, contemplating this new information. Finally, she asked, "And you think this may have something to do with our psychic link?" Realization dawned on her features. "You think I may be the descendant of one of these arranged marriages?"

Hero nodded. "It is possible. You said you were from a royal lineage, but I would need to do some tests to be certain. Though I am not sure what it would mean should the results prove positive."

Lise seemed almost ecstatic. "This is wonderful! You can train new warriors to wield the Artifacts when you've found them all. Don't you see what this means? You just have to find others from the lineage..."

"No," Hero interrupted. "The Twelve must never again have the chance of falling into the wrong hands. I must find them to keep the past from repeating itself."

Lise looked angered by that, but cast her eyes downward and clenched her fists to keep those feelings to herself. "Very well," she said quietly, "it's your past to do with as you see fit. I just wish you would consider the alternatives."

An uneasy quiet descended then, broken only by the arrival of their food. Once their server was again out of earshot, Hero tried to calm the situation. "Thank you for understanding. I wish to ask something else of you."

"Yes?"

"Cancel your date at Okino's congressional session tomorrow."

Now she was openly shocked, though controlled when she asked, "Why?"

"No one here yet knows who you are or why you are here, save the people I trust. To openly and publicly declare your identity would make you an instant target." His voice became even quieter. "That man who confronted me, Kezeron Telbandith, poses a threat to this whole mission. Whether he is an agent for someone else or just a fighter, he has also been a paid assassin. He could sell you and your knowledge of the Coalition's current whereabouts to the highest bidder."

Lise released a deep breath, visibly slumping in her seat. "Then my coming here serves as nothing but a compromise. I won't accept that, and neither will the admirals."

The Triialon smiled. "You will not have to. I can get you in to see the queen privately. You can convince her of the importance of your mission and record a VID file for the congress that she can display after our departure." Lise's face calmed and then spread into a pretty smile of satisfaction. Hero returned the gesture and scooped up a portion of his meal. "Now eat up. Its some of the best food in the galaxy."

He walked her back to their rooms. A strange quiet had settled over the pair since the moment they had again entered the palace grounds, both sensing that their evening was over yet neither seeming to want its end. Hero had taken her to shops and gardens after their meal, the conversation turning from his lead on the element crystals and the details of the agent Kezeron, to idle chat about Lise's childhood on Sparta. So much of Okino reminded her of home. "Smaller in scale than my home city," she had said, "yet more important and grandiose than Sparta ever was," its ornate structures still rarely built higher than the trees despite its growing culture and population.

Now they stood outside her apartment door, uncertain where the time had gone or how their evening had taken them there. "Well," Lise said offhandedly, "here we are." When Hero didn't answer, she brazenly motioned for him to come nearer. The warrior hesitated a moment, then bent closer, allowing her to put her arms around his neck. Their faces nearly touched and he could feel the warmth of her body, smell the light fragrance of her skin. "I don't know how to feel about you, Hero," she said, shaking her head. Then she smiled. "But you're right; being this close to you does begin to drown my senses."

"It is probably not something we should put to the test this evening, Lise."

"No?" Her eyelashes drooped only momentarily before she again met his gaze. "No, I suppose not. But don't think it means there aren't a lot of things I'm going to keep trying to convince you of." She stood on her toes, kissing his cheek. "Thank you for an amazing evening." She avoided his eyes, for her own benefit or his, he didn't know, and turned around and entered her room, leaving him alone in the hallway.

Osmar was waiting for him in his own chamber. "I might have needed privacy, this evening," Hero said, setting his dinner jacket over the top of a chair.

"I doubted it," Osmar replied, crossing his arms and grinning. "Lise entered her own room alone. I was on the roof."

"Yes, I know."

Osmar got back up, taking off his own jacket to pour himself a drink. "Did it go that badly?"

"No. She's a very interesting woman, in fact, if persistent."

"And does she carry Triialon blood?"

The warrior sat, suddenly exhausted. "The issue requires testing."

"But she's interested? Promising."

"I don't know why *you* are so interested," Hero grumbled angrily.

Osmar snorted and got up to leave the room, taking his drink with him. "Fine. Act that way if you want to, Your Lordship. But ask yourself why *you* should be interested. I think that's the better question."

"Everyone here thinks I need to ask myself questions as if for my own good. I know what it is I am doing and why. Any movement from Kezeron?" Hero asked before the mercenary could leave the room.

"I caught site of something maybe once. For all I know it was an Okino guard checking the palace roof. If this Kezeron is up to something, he's good. Real good. Do you want me to go out again tonight?"

Hero ran a hand down his face. "No." By the time Hero had added "Thank you," Osmar was already gone.

Chapter Fourteen

*Legend has it that the last son of Triialon was cast
asunder by his mother. It is said that before Hero could
catch him, the last great Javal Eagle came from a flash
of lightening in the sandy sky and snatched him from
Death's hands and took him to a goddess and her
priestesses. There he would grow strong until the
day he could leave and quest the stars like his father.
Legends can be very disillusioning.
But they are also based in truth...
Coalition and Triialon
- Dr. W. H. Redfield*

The temple of Dailor was an oasis in the middle of a vast wasteland,
lost on a small moon with an orange sky. The wind howled around the
tall brick structure, as it had howled around Svea and her brother since
they had landed. Night was falling, the vast expanse of stars had become
purple and black like a festering bruise. She looked up at the far away disc
of light in the sky, wondering if the legends were true and that the planet
above was once the home of the Triialon.

Dahvis, more then anyone, had taught her to hate the Triialon. Not
even their long-dead benefactor had taught her that ideal with such
loathing. Before them now lay one of the last known ties to that ancient
culture, and even then Svea had never heard of this forgotten place before
Memfis had sent them to it. Her brother, on the other hand, salivated at
the mere mention of Dailor and the revenge he could exact against it. The
Triialon had wiped the Seethling world from the heavens years before, and
no one knew the reason why, save the Triialon edict of 'destroying evil'.
The Seethling empire was not allowed to prosper any further, finally
obliterated for its own ambitions. It was a family and home she had never
known, so it mattered little to her, but Dahvis felt differently about it.

She studied the building, watching the treetops that poked out from
the courtyards nearest the top rustle with the gusts of strangled air. A
main gate was at the base on the near side, with several levels of windows,
terraces and what appeared to be arboretums jutting out from different
points all the way up. Plenty of ways in, and the priestesses who resided

there had few known combat skills. Still, the siblings were going to be searching the entire compound, so they quietly agreed that one of them would go in somewhere near the top while the other would take the front door, which would probably have to be blown.

Svea nodded her willingness to take the front door, and her brother gazed into her eyes, the lust of revenge evident in his stare. He kissed her lips and headed down the crags of gray rock. Svea's worry increased; not over the mission, but the implications of taking it on and her brother's reaction to all that had happened since she had arrived at Kordula. The power and recognition they had always desired would soon be theirs, he had told her. She shook the sensation away and followed him across the gulf between their cover and the temple in the valley below.

Dahvis was already scaling one wall, using the terraces as mid-way points of cover on his way to the top. She waited, crouched by the front door, until she saw him slip over the topmost wall, then she picked what ended up being a simple, ancient lock and slipped inside. The initial hallway was dark and narrow, the stones barely illuminated by the torches far ahead. She listened and watched a moment, then carefully stalked forward, reaching a silent dining hall. Movement caught her eye, and Svea turned directly into the path of two surprised figures. She grasped the closest by the throat, sending a charge down her arm and shocking the figure severely with her abilities. At the same moment, she lashed out at the second figure, slamming her powerful elbow into its head and sending them both crumpling to the ground.

Svea regarded the two prone forms after making certain no one else was in the room. The first was a young maid, dressed in simple, unrevealing linens. She was pretty, barely of age. Her breathing came ragged, lost in whatever fever of unconsciousness Svea had dealt her. The second was an old woman, draped in the robes of a priestess. The blow had killed her, breaking the dry bones easily. *The Priestesses of Dailor*, Svea thought to herself. *What sad lives they must lead, trapped alone with an ancient, dictating religion based in such filth. How celibate and boring.* Svea moved the bodies behind a large pillar and continued on.

She entered the first arboretum, noting the darkness of the now dominant night. No one tended to the trees in this place; the terrace was

243

empty. She moved into a stretching corridor and wound around the corners and up stairs, passing empty rooms with their simple furnishings. She at last found what must be one of the higher priestesses' chambers. Old books lined one shelf, which she quickly threw into a satchel she was carrying with her. At the far end of the room lay a small stone alter, the prongs that jutted up from its top suggesting it had once held an object or weapon, but that item was now gone. Her curiosity rose, and she removed one of the tomes she had just pilfered, opening it to quickly scan a page. The text was illegible, written in a language that resembled nothing she had ever seen before.

The next room revealed more of the same, only this chamber was occupied. The middle aged woman was searching through her books intently, not noticing the intruder who had just stepped over the threshold. Svea pulled a blaster, waiting until she was at last spotted to fire a single shot, not wanting to damage the texts with blood or fire. The priestess fell with a single gasp. Svea took the books, adding more weight to the already heavy satchel. Slinging it over one shoulder, she left the room, closing the door behind her. The Seethling then crept past other rooms, some with women, young and old alike, kneeling within, lost in prayer. These rooms were like the first, drab and without items of interest.

On the third story landing she was forced to sneak by more of the clergy, hiding as they came the opposite way and headed down the stairs. Slowly she worked her way along, passing another terrace and more apartments, then coming to the far end of the floor. A set of double doors barred her way to what must be a shrine. Svea put her ear to the door, hearing from within a body strike the stone floor, then the gasps of a female voice struggling against an unseen force. She quickly peered through the lock and saw her brother in the torch-lit corner at the far end of the chamber. Svea tried the door, finding it unlocked. She entered, closing the doors behind her again and setting down the satchel.

Bodies were strewn around the room, blood pouring freely from killer wounds left by Dahvis' blades. He had obviously come upon a group of the women performing some sort of ceremony and his vengeance had taken its toll, quickly and quietly slaughtering priestesses young and old. He knelt where she had seen him to be from the door lock. A beautiful young girl was splayed out on the floor beneath him, resting her arched back over one knee. He grasped her chin in one hand, the blue sparkling fire of his Seethling abilities flowing from his fingertips and onto her skin. Her face was a mask of horror and pleasure at once, her eyes captured by Dahvis lingering gaze, locking her to him, form and soul. His other hand was searching somewhere up her raised dress, doing as he pleased with her now more-than-willing body.

"Such pliant, pure flesh," he said. "She's never known a man's touch before now. Such inexperience has left her a slave to her buried desires, so easily awoken and manipulated. Though perhaps she has known a woman's touch, eh?" Dahvis looked at his sister, hunger evident in his expression. "Svea, would you like a taste?"

Svea stepped closer, watching in muted fascination as the scene played itself out.

"This place has held many secrets," Dahvis continued, "But most now are gone." He grinned, closing his eyes as he delved deeper into the woman's mind. "Mm, yes. This one likes the feelings I bring her. Many times when she was alone has she used the memories of the young man who stayed here. He left before she came of age, but now lust stirs within her, and the only man she has seen haunts her dreams. But this one, this Lance, is long since departed; gone to seek the ways of Triialon." Dahvis' eyes sprung open like shutters, locking his vision with that of Svea. His hands returned to their ministrations of the girl's flesh, renewing the young priestess's moans of pleasure. "We could kill the old ones and keep the young. We could train them as our own personal harem to take back to Magdala. No one would ever know."

"But you won't," Svea answered. "Memfis gave you different orders, didn't he?"

Darkness and disappointment spread itself over Dahvis face, and he dropped the girl unceremoniously to the stone floor. She continued to stare out blankly, her breath coming in labored gasps, her senses still inflamed, possibly on the verge of climax from the Seethling's mere touch. "Yes," he replied at last, standing. With one hand he reached out, sending the full intensity of his power down onto the prone girl beneath him. She screamed, convulsing a moment before lying silent amongst her own smoking clothes and skin.

Within seconds the doors crashed open. Two priestesses dressed in the shorter garb of guards burst in, armed with spears. They screeched battle cries of sadness and rage, rushing the two assassins who waited eagerly for their engagement. Dahvis and Svea both pulled their own short blades, catching the thrusting spears and pushing them aside. The guards countered, using the spears as staffs to force the two siblings back. The Dailor women presented a good fight, momentarily putting the Seethlings on the defensive, but ultimately proving no match for their battle-hardened skills. Dahvis ducked the next blow from his opponent, then savagely lashed out at her exposed midriff, nearly slicing the woman in half. The death beside her shocked the other guard into letting her defense down. Svea turned her own blade and used a combination of punches to disarm her and then drive the tip of her weapon deep into the woman's heart. The Dailor guard gasped, her eyes widening as she slumped to her knees and finally fell over, dead.

Dahvis pulled his blaster, aiming it at a point somewhere across the building. Svea turned, catching sight of a priestess near the far stairwell. She stood frozen with fear, having watched her guards struck down by the intruders. Before she could scream or run, Dahvis coldly shot her down. He then knelt in a corner, picking up his own laden satchel. "I have everything of value from the upper levels. We leave via the terrace – now."

The windstorm had increased since they had entered the temple. They dropped their bags to the ground below and leapt into the wind, Dahvis landing nimbly first and then continuing on without looking back. Svea landed with more difficulty, nearly twisting her ankle as she touched down. She followed her brother's example and re-slung her own satchel. She looked back up at the terrace she had just jumped from with mixed emotions, then followed him. She had to run to keep up, finding herself happy to soon be leaving this doomed place.

When they both reached the cover of the rise they had started out from, Dahvis dropped his bag full of books and items and removed a small transmitter from within his black costume. He smiled to himself, depressing the switch with his thumb and then closing his eyes in

246

satisfaction as the temple exploded behind them. Svea turned, watching the ensuing fireball light the cold blackness and then recede into the collapsing structure. The howling gusts of Dailor's winds kicked glowing embers into the air, just as quickly extinguishing them with their brutal force. Bricks toppled and timbers cracked, the only temple of Dailor wasting away into nothing.

"As you said," Dahvis remarked, "Memfis had other plans."

Lise entered when she heard Hero's voice through the door. He did not turn to her when she strode in, but instead sat facing a painting sitting on an easel, the morning rays pouring through the balcony doors giving a slight glow to his large physique. She looked about the apartment, knowing instantly that this place had been a temporary residence of his many times over the years. It was larger and more open than many of the other rooms she had been in thus far. The furniture was aged, more stylized and old fashioned, and objects, weapons, and decorations of every fascination littered the tops of the tables. It was much more finished and lived in than her own basic guest room, not that there was anything basic about any chamber in the Queen's house. How long had he known her, she wondered. How long had he been coming to Okino?

"Is all of this yours?" she asked, running her fingertips over the edge of one tabletop.

"Most of it. To be honest, I do not recall what is and what is not mine. The Queen is most gracious to let me leave many old things here." Hero had still not turned to her, and she realized that he was running a brush along the canvas surface.

He was painting.

Other works lay half covered at his feet or leaning against the lounge. Tenderly, she stepped up beside him, gazing at the work he was doing. Her breath nearly caught in her throat when she realized that the impression was that of her. She stood frozen a moment, unwilling to break the spell, as though it might disappear like a dream the instant she acknowledged his creativity. When she couldn't stand it anymore, she spoke anyway. "It's beautiful."

"You wanted to know what cultures I had picked up in my travels," he said quietly, immersed in the painting. "There are certainly those with better hands than I, but I found out years ago that this was calming in a way very different from meditation or training. Ironically I had nearly forgotten the paintings and the past-time." He glanced at her. "Until you reminded me."

"I'm flattered," she said genuinely, looking down at the dusty older works. Most were color works of great warriors, either locked in battle or standing proudly. A few were of women, either simple face studies or whole portraits. One bore a resemblance to Lise, she realized, but the dark-haired woman wore the garments and symbols that marked her as a Triialon. A study of a small hand, like that of a baby's, lay tucked behind another piece on the floor. "They're wonderful. Are they all real portraits?"

"Essentially, though not all were living models and some others have long since passed. The one who showed me the basics of this art convinced me it 'alleviated the stresses of questing tirelessly by getting something done,'" he quoted, "It has, at times, released a creative energy that I had been unaware I even had. Perhaps the last few years have been more than any simple painting could alleviate."

"Perhaps," she agreed, "or perhaps you simply chose to forget." Hero nodded honestly at her assessment. Lise took the time to look at each piece while he painted, studying the powerful images, but finding no self-portrait. She stopped, looking at him a moment before smiling with admiration. "Thank you," she said, hands clasped behind her back. She waited a moment before deciding to let him to his work, leaving for the door.

"Tomorrow morning," he said, stopping her. "Be here early. If you can sneak in without waking Osmar then we'll begin."

"Begin what?" she asked, confused.

"Your training."

She was certain he could feel her smile on his back from across the chamber. She said nothing, turning back to the door.

Admiral Jay'salan had taken the small gunship and its crew to the edge of the Grellion star system and sent a coded message to the *Pulsar* during the flight. The new style battle cruiser was waiting for them at the designated coordinates by the time the admiral's ship arrived. He had his crew land the gunship within the vessel and assumed command of it from the captain, quickly informing the ship's compliment of the danger and secrecy of their mission. Long range scans began immediately. Orders and information were then coded and sent out to the other portions of the Coalition fleet by the communications team. In the meantime, the ship was placed in orbit around the system's furthest planetoid, but hours passed with no further sign of Lordillian activity. Jay'salan had finally resigned himself to relaxing during the wait, and was passed out in his quarters with his book in his hands when the alarm sounded.

He returned to the bridge, finding the crew was already tracking a small squad of cruisers and their fighter compliments, coming from the direction of Lordillian-held space. "Estimated time to arrival?" the admiral asked.

"Five minutes at maximum Star Leap speed," a bridge officer answered. "Their heading puts them on target with the Grellion planet."

"They're definitely Lordillian ships, sir," another said.

"All right," Jay'salan commanded, "We wait here and pretend we haven't seen them. We take only as much damage as necessary for it to appear that the Dimensionalizer engines have been hit, then we bolt, using Star Leap generators and we hope they follow." *And hope they don't really cripple us*, he thought to himself.

The minutes passed quickly, officers and crew scrambling to their stations the moment the alert was sounded. Jay'salan watched the tactical display, counting the number of enemy units that inched their way closer to their position. Two full size Lordillian battle cruisers and three small destroyers were now coming into visual range, their fighters fanning out to help corral the target they had obviously sighted. The admiral absently rubbed his angular cheek with a gray hand, the fingers feeling numb as his body tensed in anticipation of the coming battle and chase. "Bring us about, helm, and head into the open, point zero one. Engineering, bring the Dimensionalizers online, quietly please."

The main view screen was suddenly filled by the enormous Lordillian craft as they slowed and faced off against the lone Coalition ship. "Fighters coming in from aft and below," tactical announced.

"Change heading," Jay'salan commanded, his voice booming now that the battle was being joined. "Dive at the lower attack group. Ready main cannon."

The ship's nose pointed down towards the incoming fighter craft. Twenty or thirty of the strange Lordillian ships came into view, their stabilizers looking like sleigh runners sweeping out in front of the cockpit and main bodies of the ships. "Ready; Fire main cannon," the admiral ordered. A giant beam of irradiated plasma spewed forth from the gaping cannon portal mounted on the underside of the vessel's body. The weapon strafed the inbound Lordillian fighters, vaporizing the entire squad in moments, leaving no trace of the ships. "All batteries, open fire!" Just as the *Pulsar's* many hull-mounted cannons and missiles began to fire, the blasts from the now openly antagonistic cruisers and gun-ships in pursuit began to reach them. Each burst of energy slammed into the Coalition ship's shields, weakening them quickly with their sheer numbers.

"Second fighter group breaking off, sir." The officer sounded confident despite the odds. That stony resolve was part of the reason Jay'salan had chosen this particular crew. "The cruisers are pursuing and moving in, with the gun-ships flanking."

"They'll want to capture us, helm. Make sure they don't get out in front of us." The admiral turned in his seat to another portion of the bridge. "Damage report."

"Aft shields weakening. We're taking quite a few hits back there." The Lordillian ships had no main cannons the size of the new Coalition vessel's, but their hulls were simply littered with batteries. All Lordillian tactics relied on overwhelming numbers. "We're trailing debris."

"Prepare for Star Leap speed. Ready main cannon." Jay'salan regarded his tactical display one more time. "Helm, change heading seven point two four. Take out that gunship trying to overtake us, then get us the hell out of here."

An explosion rocked the ship, sending even the giant admiral scrambling to keep his balance on the command deck. The communications officer, blood streaming from a gash in his scalp, continued his duty with resolve. "Sir, engineering emergency! Leap generators have been hit. Dimensionalizers threatening to overload."

"Fire on the gun-ship!" The main cannon's beam exploded from underneath the view port again, striking the rapidly approaching Lordillian warship direct center. It exploded spectacularly, and the admiral afforded himself a brief smile. "All stop!" He had to gamble that the damaged Dimensionalizers would at least get them away from the immediate harm, but still be a traceable escape that might drag the Lordillians' interests along with them. He decided it was his only choice. "Bring us about, helm. On my mark, engage Dimensionalizer engines, but change the heading to half of the original distance."

"Admiral," the communications officer warned, "engineering isn't sure the D-jump won't destroy the ship."

"That's a chance we'll have to take," Jay'salan answered, watching the remainder of the Lordillian squad bearing down upon them. "Ahead full." He could hear the now familiar hum of the Dimensionalizer engines coming to power, see the intensity and uncertainty in the eyes of his crew. "Ready... NOW!" A blinding flash of white-hot light surrounded the ship, and then they were gone.

"Good morning," Jo'seph said over the loud speaker. Nearly the entire compliment of the Grellion Base's skeleton crew of scientists, officers, soldiers and pilots was assembled before him in the gigantic hanger. The rest of the personnel would be listening over the now-working intercom system. He stood on the makeshift podium, with Sardeece and a few of the servitors on one side, and some of the bridge officers on the other. Above them loomed an endless darkness, as the ceiling of the vast bay was lost in the dimly lit chamber. "We can only assume that admiral Jay'salan's decoy has worked. As expected, we've lost contact with them, and the Lordillian ships that were entering the system have dispersed." A brief cheer went up at that, but the admiral plowed on. "This does not mean more enemy ships won't come to investigate this spot, and soon. We must be as ready as we can be for any eventuality while this facility goes through the process of being brought on-line after uncounted millennia.

"You will be ordered to work in teams, along with servitor robots which mister Sardeece will assign, to fortify this place, inside and out. I expect every one of you to give this one hundred percent, and to put aside any reservations any of you may still have lingering regarding our relationship with the Artificial Intelligences of this citadel. It is a simple matter of survival; if the base isn't defensible by the time the next Lordillian squad comes, we're dead, and the Coalition could die with us. We're counting on you, so good luck. That is all." Jo'seph's closest officers moved forward, handing orders out to each of the next levels of command. The admiral turned to Sardeece, whispering just loud enough for the scientist to hear him over the echoing voices around them. "What do the scans show?"

"Difficult to tell, admiral," Sardeece answered. "In all honesty, we don't know how many ships were destroyed nor whether the *Pulsar* was one of them, but for whatever reason their Dimensionalizer was activated."

Jo'seph scratched his beard pensively. "Very well. Continue scan. What news on the digging crew?"

Sardeece smiled a bit, the skin around the eye now framed by the Grellion augmentations stretching strangely. "They blew a satisfactory hole in the rear-most wall of the underground level we decided they should start out from. They're now digging through both soil and sometimes solid rock in the direction of the flagship. They're making decent enough time, but it could take days just to tunnel to it, much less find an entrance… or make one without collapsing the tunnel."

"Keep me informed, please. I need to oversee the fortifications. If you'll excuse me."

It was time to tour the battleground, for admiral Jo'seph knew this place would become one before very long. He just hoped they would be able to withstand any sort of attack. His thoughts turned towards Hero and Lise for the hundredth time, trying not to feel so anxious about their progress and their possible fates out there among the silence. The isolation and covert nature of his position was beginning to take its toll, and another defensive battle was exactly the opposite of what his emotions were begging for. Jo'seph rode a secret, threadbare line between hope and hopelessness, praying inwardly that the Grellion citadel's prospects would pay off in time.

The first line of defense would be the obvious entrances of the base. Generators for artillery and cover for troops were being placed in the main hall adjacent to the doors the Coalition had been using. As many weapons as possible had been taken from the ships that were parked in the hanger and used to defend this position. If the Lordillians breached this point, they would be loose in the same labyrinth of passages and levels as everyone among the Coalition had been for the last few days. Traps would be set at choice intersections, rigged to blow anything that came through that way into atoms. From there the only other positions that would be manned and fortified would be the entrances to engineering and the command decks. There they would have to hold until reinforcements came, the Triialon showed up with a miracle, or they all perished.

Jo'seph smiled and nodded to the soldiers who worked frantically to arm the cannons salvaged from their ships. The guns and covering positions now filled the wide hallway pointing at the main doors and joining hallways. "Digging in," he thought. He hadn't fought a trench war in years, and had spent much of that time trying to put aside the casualties of that battle.

The admiral checked his data tablet, marking his route to the command decks and watching for the as-yet unarmed booby traps. The same activity surrounded the openings from the stairs to each level under the bridge. Sardeece and the citadel were working on a way to disable the elevators when the attack came in a way that would not leave them irreparable. Meanwhile engineers and soldiers worked to block passages and set further traps. The few who could defend would be concentrated at these points, hopefully to do the most damage to the enemy with the smallest effort. Despite these assurances, the admiral felt comfortable nowhere save the bridge at this point, where at least he was in command. He entered, trying to look more confident than he felt, and sat in his new chair overlooking his officers' positions, watching the view screens and windows, waiting for the attack to come.

Tykeisha was suddenly standing next to him, saluting briefly before turning to watch the same scene that the admiral was surveying. They both stood there, silent, perhaps thinking the same thing, perhaps not at all. "Janise is sleeping peacefully," she said at last.

"Thank you. I assume you're on duty?"

"I relieve the COM officer, yes."

"Good," he smiled. "Then I'll stay a while longer if you promise to show me that smile of yours from time to time."

"Such fraternization," she said dryly. Her expression turned to light concern. "You all right?"

"I will be soon," he said, his voice almost a whisper. "Or we'll all be dead soon and it won't matter anymore."

"You really expect an attack to come that soon?"

Jo'seph nodded. "Chebonka would appear to be consumed with finding and destroying us. He won't overlook a find like this base, whatever it leads to. If they attack before this place is operational, then we defend it to the best of our ability. One way or the other, they'll never have the Grellion technology, I promise you that."

Tykeisha said nothing, finally nodding and briefly placing her hand on his shoulder before she turned away, heading over to her station to begin her shift.

Lise checked her hair one more time before joining the valet at the door. She smiled at the older man, allowing him to guide her though the palace and eventually to the main wing. Lorette was waiting for her in an office leading to the Queen's private chambers.

"Lise, you look lovely," the secretary said genuinely. The woman waved the valet away, thanking him. "I trust the last few days have proven productive for you?"

"I'm not certain," Lise answered. "I don't believe Hero ever tells *anyone* everything."

Lorette pouted a little. "No progress on the whole romantic front, then?"

254

Lise shrugged. "I wouldn't say that, exactly. Dinner was candle lit, incidentally, but never the romantic fires one might hope for." She thought for a moment before asking, "Did you know he painted?"

Lorette's eyebrows went up a little at that. "I didn't, no. Perhaps he's let you in a little more than you initially thought possible."

"He had a bunch of old pieces he'd done strewn about his room this morning," Lise said, smiling inwardly. "He was working on one of me. He told me he had learned the art form years before and that I reminded him of it. Anyway, I guess he's had them stored here all these years."

"I wonder if the queen knows," Lorette said conspiratorially. "She's left that room for Hero in the palace since before I started working here. I'm certain that when she's gone and this castle becomes the property of the republic and no one remembers any of our names anymore, his room will still be reserved here." The secretary stood, making a sweeping gesture towards the inner doors. "I believe you have an audience with the queen, commander. Shall I show you in?"

"Thank you. I'm looking forward to it."

"War effort support would be a binding start. The civilians and admirals that have made up the Coalition's leading delegation realize that not everyone has the ability to fight the way we have." Lise stared into the camera before her, wondering if she could will her eyes into the hearts and minds of those who might listen with the same intensity of the lens that bore her down even now. Queen Telisha sat just off-camera, having already given her own speech while a trusted technician recorded the event. The woman smiled reassuringly as Lise continued. "But to stand mute only invites the hastening of all our fates, as the refugees of races and worlds that are now a part of the Coalition can attest. Non violence is powerful and just - we have all believed that. But a culture that stays mute and refuses to stand beside its brothers and sisters for what is right eventually dies. It dies as surely the day it decides to remain immobile as the day the enemy finally overruns its cities and homes. Even if it takes years for everyone to understand the urgency of this matter and finally rally together, the call to arms should begin here. Only then will all of these worlds begin to understand that they need to stand together against the Lordillians now before you are simply the refugees that make up the Coalition fleet, fighting for your lives.

"I wish to thank her majesty the Queen of Okino for this opportunity to address so many important peoples and their representatives at this time. Okino and its neighboring tributaries are unique in their current standing political and economical powers and long standing peace treaties. With our concerted efforts, I hope we can keep it that way. I thank you for your time, and hope that my words have been worthy of such generosity as well as worthy of the people who have placed their trust in me."

"And we're clear," the technician announced, switching off the camera.

"Very inspiring, dear. I feel there are those that will rally to our cause." The queen stood, beaming as she took Lise's hands and kissed her cheek. Lise was pleased at the way the aging woman already referred to it as 'our cause.' The Queen's concerns regarding the growing threat of the Lordillian horde had become apparent, and she had quickly understood the danger of Lise's position. She'd agreed to record her speech in secret and even supplied her own words to introduce the situation. The VID file would be presented at the next Okino court, as well as sent to the leaders of the respective worlds belonging to it. "I'm sure that if nothing else it will begin a debate that will bring this war to a forefront of discussion, and that is much-needed."

"Thank you again, your majesty. I am so glad you believe in what I have said. I only hope that your people listen. The admirals are expecting more from me I think than encouraging words."

"But they have been good words. Strong words. Your admirals will be proud." She deftly moved the two of them out of the room and back into her private antechamber. "Has Hero committed himself to your cause?"

Lise shrugged. "He has, but I don't know for how long. He quests for the Twelve, and Chebonka holds one of those Artifacts where no one may get to it."

"He has helped others before. Many a sway of power and rebellion have had a tale of the Hero-lore within its pages."

"But how long does he remain in any one given place?"

It was the queen's turn to shrug. "Who can say? But he may surprise you."

"He never ceases to surprise me," Lise said, smiling.

There was a quiet knock at the doors. Hero put down the files he had been reading and walked towards them with caution, un-holstering his blaster from where it sat on a table even as the second knock came. Unlatching the lock, he slowly opened the entrance to his rooms and peered outside, confirming what had expected. Osmar was standing there in the hall with Durant and a robed figure. "Why did you not simply come through your room?"

"I didn't want to startle you, Lord," Osmar answered, leading the others into the room.

"As if you could," Hero said, smiling.

Once they were all inside and the door was secure again, Durant turned, gesturing to the figure beside him. "May I introduce Master Wollhaw, a cleric of the holy order of Moonshau."

The cleric removed the hood of his robe to reveal the simple, aged face of a balding man in his twilight years. "It is an honor to meet you, sir," he said in a surprisingly powerful voice. "I hope you don't mind this face to face meeting, but it was the only way Mister Durant could even begin to convince me to be a party to this deal."

"Of course, master Wollhaw," Hero answered, shaking his hand. "It is a pleasure to meet you. I hope we can reach an accommodation, for all of our sakes."

"Yes, ah, I'm afraid mister Durant has been rather lax on details concerning this issue." The old cleric sat, prompting the others to join him at the table, save Osmar who excused himself to his duties. "Perhaps you could explain why it is you think you need the crystal spheres housed within in my temple so urgently?"

"I shall try to do just that. I would like to start by asking if you could tell me a little about them and the function they have in your holy order. You brought one of them as I requested?"

Wollhaw reached into his robes and pulled a small, cloudy, black and red ball from within, its shape and texture an exact match to the one embedded in Durant's sword. "In the years following our procuring them from mister Durant here, they've become a subject of study and interest as well as the decoration they were purchased for." Even as he spoke, Hero could see the grainy interior of the sphere coalesce like gathering energy, the effect stronger when he moved it near the Prizm. "Our order is not a poor one, Hero, though it is a devoted one. Still, we like our house to look good for guests, just as anyone would, and we wanted something special: spiritual. So when such unique objects came along we bought them up, simply noting at the time the strange properties they seemed to have."

"I should have charged more," Durant laughed.

"Since then most of them have been fitted into the walls and decorations of the inner temple, while a number were kept free for future projects and study. Now we're all but convinced the objects are blessed with a life force. The physical manifestation is obvious," he said, pointing at it, "the swirling clouds within. And it becomes more prominent at prayer time, especially when there are large numbers of people within the shrine. But there is a mental connection as well, as many of both my fellow clerics and the temple patrons will attest to. They speak in a whisper."

"The physical and kinetic properties are even more amazing than you know, I can assure you." Hero reached into a satchel next to the table and pulled out a medium sized device made from a strange metal. One end had a transparent sphere that stuck out, while the center of the other end had an empty socket the size of the cleric's crystal. "This chunk of technology is from an ancient citadel built by a race long since disappeared. They were called the Grellions, and they were masters of a power that ruled over this galaxy, creating devices that served them in their fight for freedom until the day they were no longer needed." He placed the sphere in the socket, the crystal turning a light blue. "It is my belief that the spheres were stolen from the lost citadel and by a twist of fate ended up in your temple." The strange device began to hum, coming to life as power coursed through its circuits for the first time in eons. The transparent globe at the far end sparked and began to glow the same blue

258

tint. Hero's eyes studied the effect for a moment, the three men sitting in silent awe of the reaction. He placed his hand on the globe, letting the strands of energy flow to his fingertips, giving him a slight shock. Hero gave a quiet laugh.

"Amazing," Wollhaw breathed.

"What this object is," Hero said at last, "is an element of their technology. Based on your own findings I'd say some echo of the Grellion race themselves resides in these somehow. It provides a link between the user of the technology, those around it and their own life forces, and the power source it derives its motor functions from. That is why nothing at the citadel works, and that is why the Grellion A.I. knew that it was missing what would not only link itself with its new owners, but return power to its functions; this crystal completes a circle of symbiosis that could never be filled by any other object."

"What new owners?" the cleric asked. "I don't understand."

Hero finally took his eyes off of the working technology he had set before him on the table, turning urgently to the old man. "You know of the Galactic Coalition's plight against the Lordillian horde?" Wollhaw nodded. "The Coalition was nearly destroyed several days ago, its fleet and peoples scattered when the Lordillians destroyed their shipyards. Most escaped death, but they cannot regroup for fear of discovery and eradication. Instead I led them to the Grellion citadel in an attempt to find them safe haven. But that place is just as deadly to them without the elements that would arm the structure and allow them to raise defenses. Master Wollhaw, their future rests in your hands."

The cleric was overwhelmed, his face draining of color as he struggled momentarily for breath. "What are your terms?" he managed to ask at last.

"This is an historic opportunity for your order. An allegiance with the Coalition could begin here by releasing the vast majority of the elements to them, keeping a few for your own further study." Hero studied the man before continuing. "In the meantime, I will not only pay your temple what it cost for the crystals initially, but I will also triple that amount."

259

Wollhaw's eyebrows went up at that, knowing full well the inordinate price he had originally paid Durant for the crystal spheres. He stood, walking slowly to the window, hands clasping and unclasping behind his back. "My order does not condone war, Hero," the cleric said carefully. "Still, this issue has been brought before me by the last of the Triialon, perhaps the only race of warriors the temple has ever mentioned with any favorable note." He laughed a little, turning to look at Hero. "Did you know the legends of your people is part of our litany?" The cleric sighed, shaking his head. "The Lordillian horde now threatens Moonshau, and there are those that believe only the Coalition could save us. Now you tell me it is in my hands to save them. It is not as though you could not take the spheres by force yourself."

Hero nodded. "That is so. But it is not something I ever *would* do. There must be another solution."

"And yet if I do, it will mean people will die."

Hero stood. "And if you do not, than even more people will die. Some things must be fought for. Just because I am not using my blade does not mean I am not fighting for what I believe in right now."

Wollhaw smiled again. "I know. No war is right, but at least a fight for the future has its basis in the just. Very well, Hero, I agree to your terms."

Hero crossed the room, shaking the cleric's hand. "Thank you, sir."

"Now what?" Durant asked, finally breaking his silence.

"Now I pay you half of your finder's fee. The full amount, equal to what the order of Moonshau paid you for the elements, will be delivered to you when we meet you at the temple. I need you to take Master Wollhaw back there and immediately begin removing and collecting the elements."

"Immediately?" the old man asked worriedly.

"I am afraid so," Hero answered. "Every moment counts."

Chapter Fifteen

*Indeed, by all accounts admiral Jo'seph was a
most remarkable man. Before Sparta was attacked
he collected sculptures of varied mediums. He was
one of the few surviving members of Sparta's democratic council and was literally the driving force
behind the very formation of the Coalition. What he
lacked in faith he made up for in strength and hope.
Everything else was covered by that sardonic wit.
-Creatures of Virtue, a biography of admirals
Jo'seph and Jay'salan of the Galactic Coalition*

Lise sighed. She was lounging in a plush piece of expensive furniture
that was probably a hundred years old, watching the stars over lush
treetops on a beautiful planet, and she wanted to leave. "I'm beginning to
feel pretty guilty about being here, I think," she told Hero. The Triialon
had entered only moments before, asking how her meeting with the queen
had gone. "I love it here, I really do. But my friends are out there, fighting
and dying or running for their lives. I should be beside them."

"Then I have what I hope you will find to be good news," he said,
standing by a nearby sofa. "I've found them."

She looked at him, startled and a little confused. "Found what?" she
asked hopefully.

"The Grellion elements. Durant had sold them to a cleric on
Moonshau whom I met today. I have already brokered a deal and they
have left to begin collecting them at the temple."

"That's wonderful!" Lise leapt from her seat, jumping into his rigid
arms and throwing her own around his neck to hug him fiercely before he
could think to object. "Hero, you're amazing," she said, leaning back from
the embrace a little, and instantly becoming locked in his eyes. The two of
them stood there, frozen, uncertain, like the smile still plastered on Lise's
lips, staring at each other. His hands were big and warm, closed
precariously on her sides just above her hips to catch her. He was easily a
head taller than her, and she suddenly found herself swimming in his
sheer size and magnitude, her face flushed with onrushing passions she
almost couldn't control.

Then the spell was broken, Hero releasing her supple body as she slid back down his rigid stomach to land tip toe. Lise could only hope her cheeks weren't as red as they felt, and she cleared her throat as innocently as she could muster. She held the smile through it all, and, hoping to hide the moment, walked away to find a bottle of wine in the small kitchen. "This is cause for celebration."

"I must decline."

"And I must insist," she said, pouring the red finery into two crystal glasses. "You can lightly sip and humor me while you tell me how it is you're certain our quest is over."

"Our quest is not over. We will not leave until tomorrow night or the following morning, allowing for unfinished business here and the travel time it takes for Durant's ship to reach Moonshau."

"Cheers anyway," she said, practically forcing the glass into Hero's hand and touching her own against it, providing a satisfying ping of glass on glass. "Another finery," she said after the first sip. "I wish I didn't feel so guilty for loving it."

They were both quiet for a time, watching the night sky from a plush couch. Hero sat leaning one elbow on his knee, holding the glass and just staring. "Not long after I left Triialon for the last time," he said solemnly, "I came to the city of Waikamer. It was primitive, lush, and backwards by the standards I had been used to, but it was so alive and colorful and new. I was alone; more so than ever before. I tried to ignore the planet's beauty; I only wanted to replace grief with rage and let the quest take me where it willed. But I could not deny the citadel of Waikamer and the way it made me... wish my city could have been like that. The people had life in their eyes and simple dreams in their hearts. Everything was done personally, right down to their home spun and dyed garments. Their weapons were simple pieces of metal forged in flame, and their royalty lived in a palace above it all, never having to pay any of it heed. And I was a stranger there, as I always am to such places."

Lise had watched him as he lost himself in the past, the feint breeze brushing his brown hair over muscular shoulders. Moisture had collected in the corner of her own eye, and she quickly wiped it away, attributing it to something on the wind. "Perhaps we might both have it that way someday?"

He seemed to smile, but never took his gaze from whatever past he found there in the night sky. "I hope someday you can." He took a drink and turned his back on the view that had so captivated him. The barely scratched surface of what Lise now understood to be a very deep man was just as easily glossed back over, and Hero stood before her again, a proud warrior. She realized that she was staring and blinked the moment away, having to clear her throat to find her voice and tell him of the hopeful support she had begun to raise with the Queen that afternoon. He listened, nodding, asking a question or two that instantly brought new ideas to her reasoning. By the time she had concluded her recapping of the meeting she'd added a half dozen new points to her mental list of things to bring to the table the next time she or the admiral sat before the Okino court.

Hero explained to her his day's events and the test he'd performed using the Grellion technology he'd had brought from the citadel. He told her of the crystal elements' trip in the hands of thieves from their home world and eventually the hands of Moonshau clerics. He also told her of his theories surrounding their properties and purposes. Lise listened intently, genuinely fascinated and excited, and also desperate to cloud her mind with as much alcohol and techno-babble it took to make certain Hero knew nothing of the feelings she had nearly let boil over into his arms minutes before.

When he finished he set the barely half-empty glass down between them, standing to excuse himself. "Can you contact the admiral with this information?" he asked her.

"Hm?" Startled, she had to force her eyes off of the reflection of his body in her glass. "Oh, yes, I should be able to contact them briefly on a coded channel. At least I hope so."

"Very well. You can tell me how that went in the morning." He stopped, fixing his gaze on her in a way that made her giddy. "You are still joining me in the morning?"

Lise's mouth went dry, her jaw nearly falling open for a second before she remembered what he was talking about. "Yes. My first day of training. Don't want to miss that." She was certain she had said the last bit just a little too loud. Her head was beginning to hurt. *What is* in *this,* she wondered to herself.

"It is the Queen's wine," Hero answered, leaving. "See you at dawn, commander. Good night."

Lise sat in shock for whole minutes before finally groaning aloud and burying her face in the lounge cushions.

When she had finally regained a semblance of her composure, she willed herself off of the seat and opened the cabinet that had been hiding her gear and the transmitter within.

It took a few minutes for the coded transmission to set up and then find sufficient link up. The main transmitter was actually aboard Hero's ship, broadcasting via hyperspace to ghost coordinates and eventually bouncing their way back to a receiver on Grellion. After another ten minutes of waiting, Tykeisha's voice finally came over the speaker. "This is Nest One. Go ahead, Eagle."

Lise let out a breath she hadn't realized she had been holding. "Its good to hear your voice, Nest One."

"Its great to hear yours," Tykeisha said. "I'll patch you through to the Mother Hen. Keep it short, though; bandits are on the horizon and could enter our nest's forest. If cut off, maintain communications silence."

"Understood."

Admiral Jo'seph's voice came next. "Report, please, Eagle."

"Mystery elements being collected and soon delivered, so says my Fearless Leader." Lise almost laughed aloud at her joke code name. "Returning to nest within two to three days, providing all goes well. Understand bandits are close?"

"Affirmative. Expediency of utmost importance, Eagle. Please make certain 'Fearless Leader' understands."

"Copy that, Nest." There was a crackle of noise from the speaker, the connection going silent at its seizure, the sound sending a chill down Lise's spine. "Nest? Come in, Nest, do you read?" She knew the link was gone, but the lack of information only deepened her worry. The transmitter gave back negative information, uncertain if the link had been terminated by the source or jammed by something else nearby. Lise didn't hesitate, switching off the transmitter and running out of the apartment to knock on Hero's door a second before opening it.

"I think that the Grellion base is in trouble," she blurted. She froze in her tracks at the site that greeted her; Hero was kneeling on the floor, facing the open bay window and the stars without, wearing nothing more that a thin pair of shorts and the Triialon bracer. His posture suggested meditation, and he did not turn to greet her.

"Shut the door."

Lise complied, unsure of how to act in the given situation, so she simply decided to stand at attention behind him. "Communications were cut off within moments of contacting the base. I don't know if they cut it due to ships entering the area, or if they were suddenly jammed, but the Lordillians are close. They're running out of time."

"The admiral knows what he is doing." Hero's voice was calm, commanding. "He'll hold off of direct confrontation as long as he can, then he'll fight from fortified positions."

Lise felt frustration and anger beginning to fester within her, and a constriction in her chest that left her feeling ever more uncertain. "With all due respect, sir, the admiral was adamant in my communicating to you the need for immediate action."

He finally looked over his shoulder at her, his expression becoming hardened. "Calm yourself, commander." He let out a controlled breath, gesturing for her to come stand before him. "Kneel." Lise's shoulders heaved, but she obeyed, copying his posture on the floor before him. "Close your eyes," he said at last. "Good. This is the most basic form of the Triialon art, so learn it well. Are you listening?"

Lise nodded.

"No. You are not listening. You're distracted by what your emotions and preoccupations are trying to tell you. Listen to nothing. Do nothing."

"I need to work my way though what I feel, Hero," she bit back.

Hero's tone came back stern. "You cannot do that until you have cleared the path for concentration. That is the point. You cannot think without clouds while you are lacking shelter, just as we cannot leave Okino before Durant and the cleric reach that destination first. Besides, we have unfinished business here. Now, meditate on whatever it is you need to meditate on, but do it unimpeded by the rest of the noise."

Lise tried to think of nothing, set aside her feelings and fatigue, but found her mind was still centered on her troubles. "May I concentrate on something outside of myself if it helps to calm me?"

"So long as it is not a distraction."

She listened to the open window and the breeze rustling the leaves and branches of the dark forest. "The trees," she said. "I can hear them move, back and forth, rocking gently in the wind."

"That is good," Hero said.

Lise was unaware of how long they sat there like that, but then she did not care. Soon she gently felt the touch of Hero's mind within her own. "Good," he said quietly. "You can easily find your own technique, I see. Done every evening, you will find the days pass easier."

Lise rolled her head and sighed, relaxed, her eyes finally opening to find Hero still in meditation. She found herself openly studying his physique in the dim light, then wondering if he could sense that fact in any way. "I guess my training has begun early."

"I still expect you here in the morning. Despite the loss of hours, you should sleep well after this evening." He opened his own eyelids, his gray eyes capturing hers.

Not as well as I would like, she thought, returning his gaze.

Jo'seph knocked on his daughter's door. He heard a brief "Come in," as though she were preoccupied. He opened the hatch, finding Janise kneeling on the floor, her waist-length blonde hair falling down perfectly flat against her back. She had her entertainment system in her hands, playing a simulator game there on the floor. The young teenager barely seemed to notice his entrance, so the admiral quietly closed the door and sat on her bed, overlooking her progress.

Janise's game was one of her usual fighter SIMs, her own ship flying through a perfect graphic of the gaseous atmosphere of some unknown planet, blasting away at the multitudes of enemy fighters swarming around her. "What level?" he asked her quietly.

"Twenty-five," she answered through tight lips. Her hands furiously worked the controls, but she wasn't overwhelmed by the game by any means. Her bandaged little hands, her father thought. Janise's fighter banked and dove, coming up again through the clouds and firing a volley of missiles that vaporized another seven targets.

Jo'seph looked at the top corner of her screen, watching the points rack up faster than he could count. "That's got to be a record score for you." He was genuinely interested, amazed at her technical ability, but he was still forcing his tone to sound light. He'd had very little sleep of late.

"Its nice to be good at something other than setting beds on fire," she retorted. Obviously she wasn't getting much rest either. She swore when her ship took a hit, Jo'seph's eyebrows going up at the sudden expletive.

"I'll shut up," he said.

"Doesn't matter," she said, her teeth grinding together as the game's enemies began to regroup and attack with a new intensity. "I'm not going to last much longer." Her ship broke through the first wave anyway, destroying more fighters than Jo'seph even had known were on the screen. The second wave bore down, blasting away. She took two more hits and then finally exploded in a spectacular display of 'game over,' but not before destroying at least a third of the second wave of ships with her final volley. Janise dropped the remote, watching the screen. She looked at her father, her mouth a hard line, but her eyes twinkling. "That beats my old record by a million points."

"What're you going to do with that skill of yours?"

Janise looked away, shrugging. "I don't know." She quickly changed the subject. "What's up?"

"Nothing," he lied. "I just wanted to see what you were doing."

His daughter smiled, glancing at him as she changed games. "I know, daddy. I hate waiting for the attack too."

He smiled at her candor. "Do you want to wait on the bridge with me?"

She seemed nervous at that prospect, shaking her head and starting the new simulator. "No."

"You sure?"

"No. I'll be fine in my room."

She was adamant and would not be moved, he knew. He placed a hand on her shoulder as he got ready to leave. "I'm scared too." Without looking, she placed her hand on his for a moment. "But we're going to be alright."

"I hope so, daddy."

Jo'seph left the girl's room and passed his own, making strait for the bridge. At the end of the hall he paused in front of the saluting guard. "I want you to find a guard for my daughter's room, private. Make certain extra arms are placed in her quarters, enough for at least two people." The soldier saluted and began radioing his superior as the admiral began climbing the steps to the command deck, passing the other soldiers at their covered positions.

The bridge was quiet save for the occasional murmur of orders and the sounds of the computers. He sat in his new chair, scratching his beard and studying the displays. Within minutes of Lise's transmission a claxon had sounded, view screens switching automatically to long-range sensors, telescopes, and tactical displays. The admiral sat forward in his chair, studying the sudden inrush of information. "Report."

"Two squads of Lordillian cruisers have just entered the system from Star Leap speed," an officer said. "They're at the sixth planet and heading strait for us."

"Sir, do I power down?" another of the bridge officers asked.

Jo'seph watched the long range scans, his eyes narrowing at the first visual of the fast coming fleet, the dots of light becoming vague shapes. They weren't slowing down.

"Sir?"

"Negative," he ordered at last. "They're here for us. Might as well welcome them with open arms."

No one left their post, but every face was turned towards the open view ports as the first group of landing ships sank into view and then touched down on Grellion soil. The Lordillians were now less than a mile from their position.

"I wish you were here now, old friend," Jo'seph murmured to himself.

The attack ships began unloading their cargo of rows upon rows of marching Lordillian shock troopers. There was very little in the way of heavy artillery, and the full sized battle cruisers were still in orbit above them, but the threat was no less imposing. "Either they didn't bother to scan the power source here or they just don't care," Sardeece said. The scientist had come to stand next to the admiral's chair as they all watched the scene play out.

"Chebonka may suspect we've been here, but he certainly doesn't seem to be sending in the guns you'd expect he'd throw against us." The admiral looked at the changed officer and the strange mechanical implants on his face.

"They probably didn't bother with a second scan after they initially detected this place."

Jo'seph smiled. "They think they got here first. Then they're in for a surprise." He stood, his arms gesturing to each station as he gave orders. "Get me the commanding officer at the front door." The communication was patched through, and the officer's voice flooded into the room. The man was captaining the forward position, awaiting the moment when the first group of Lordillians would spill into the base and begin their attack. "Captain, they don't know we're here. Their interest appears to be the citadel. We may have the advantage of their wanting to take the installation intact. Make certain they have a warm welcome at first, would you?"

"Yes, sir!"

"After that, keep them baying at the door. No one gets in until we want 'em in."

"Understood."

"Very good." He turned back to Sardeece, reinvigorated. "I believe you're needed below. Make certain you get to engineering unharmed, mister Sardeece. You have an important role here today, and it will only become expanded when Hero and commander Lise arrive."

"That's a leap of faith," Sardeece replied, leaving for the lower levels, "but I hope it proves to be clairvoyance."

270

"They're almost to the doors, sir," came a warning from the tactical officer.

"I want a visual of the main hallway," the admiral ordered. He had found himself near the view the window afforded the command deck, watching the different ranks of metallic, red and black Lordillian robots march in lines from the ugly ships that had parked on the beautiful green grass. He turned away, knowing that the landscape would soon be changed forever, no matter what. He sat back in the command chair, watching the displays mounted both on his armrest and the screens around him.

The view of the troops waiting behind their cover in the dark hall was a tense one, the sounds of the base' systems suddenly apparent as the crew held its collective breath. Then light could be seen through a crack forming between the main doors at the front of the citadel. The light widened, the camera adjusting and filtering out the brightness spilling in to reveal the Lordillians framed by the clouds and grasslands beyond. A mass of the mechanical killers was gathered there, waiting and watching as the gap slowly widened.

When the doors finally stopped being forced open, a Lordillian gave the signal to advance, and the marching line obeyed, the first rows stepping into the hall before beginning their scan. The figures they must have detected in the dark would have been the last thing they saw. Someone bellowed an order, and the large cannon the crew had set up fired, the blast filling the hall and slamming into the rows of troops. The rest of the Coalition soldiers opened fire, slicing to pieces any remaining Lordillians that were near the door and tearing through them to whatever waited beyond. Answering shots began to slip through and slam into the cover and walls, then the picture went blank.

The siege had begun.

Hero had just finished dressing when the door chime sounded. He answered it personally, stretching out with his senses first to make certain it was Lise before opening the doors. She stood there in the hall, wearing the black, skin-tight bodysuit that she had bought on the colony world. It covered her from neck to toe, with a large inverted triangle design

271

exposing a fair amount of her ample cleavage and a metal corset around her middle. She had braided her hair in the back and was looking up at him with those piercing brown eyes of hers, a sword in one hand. "Borrowed it from the wall decorations in my apartments," she said in answer to his unasked question. "I assume I won't be striking anything with the queen's property?"

"Not unless you are a much worse student than I think you are."

"Oh, thanks," Lise answered dryly, closing the doors behind her.

"You know what I meant. Stop antagonizing me and begin stretching." He almost regretted the command the moment he had said it, forced now to watch that perfect body of hers bend and flex in the glove-like material. When he thought she might catch him looking, he tried to hide it with a compliment. "That uniform suits you. It is certainly more pleasing than most."

She had paused mid-stretch, looking at him from behind her own legs, her hands still pulling at the toe of her boot. "It *is* you I have to thank for it," she said. "My sense of style is placated after years of meager sustenance. Now you give in to my desires to learn your ways as well. I really don't know how I'm going to repay you."

"You can begin by paying attention," he said at stonily as possible. "Pick up your blade. I am going to teach you some of the basic forms, most of which are just as effective in hand to hand combat. Hold like this." Using both hands, he brought the hilt in close to his middle, spreading his feet and bringing the sword tip up, ready to thrust out. "This is called the *Palatade*; the spire of the cave. It is the most balanced form and allows for the greatest range of actions. You can thrust out," he said, demonstrating, "bring up the blade for defense or to draw-slice or hack, and a number of other attacks. But its original position also guards against attacks to your sides. Try it."

He watched as Lise mimicked his every move, bringing her own sword back around to guard. He showed her again, adding new turns and movements to the repertoire, then commanding her to repeat the motions. She did, nearly to perfection. When he nodded his approval, she smiled. "I can see your movements in this. It feels good." She commenced a third time, the blade slicing the air, her body turning to face a new direction and guard, then cut again.

Hero's eyes never left her form, and he marveled at the mere site of her. "When she finished the set, he told her to do it again. "This time," he said, showing an additional set of moves, "include the *Talenke*." She obeyed, and he watched, his arms crossing and his mind raced. He did not even realize the betraying smile that had begun to curl the sides of his mouth until Lise had stopped to regard him. This time he did not turn away. "It must be true," he said proudly. "You have the blood of a Triialon warrior."

Lise was silent, uncertain of how to respond. Her head cocked to one side, her hands suddenly fumbling with the cumbersome blade in her fingers. "What do you mean?"

"I have seen your Coalition files, Lise." He stepped closer to her, motioning to the folders on his desk. "I've studied them during our stay here, comparing blood samples to my own. There are traces of Triialon heritage in your DNA, suggesting that you are indeed descended from the marriage of old Sparta royalty and a Triialon house."

"I don't understand. What does that mean?"

He was standing right in front of her now, looking down into the shimmering brown orbs of her eyes, deftly taking the decorative sword from her hands and placing *Strength* within them. "Let's find out." He walked around behind her, his arms wrapping around her body to place his hands on hers and the hilt of the Triialon sword. "Close your eyes. Feel the power of the Artifact. Let your mind touch that power." Watching over her shoulder, he could see her chest rise and fall, her lips parted slightly as the moment threatened to overtake her. "Be calm. You and the artifact can be one, but not through anxiousness, or darkness. The blade is but a shadow of your light. There," he said, his own eyes shut tightly as his mind found hers, his hands working her own along the silver and gold metal. "There is the Balance. Now, brighten that light. Let it cast a shadow over those who would stand against you and those you fight for."

He heard her sharp intake of breath, opening his own eyes to find the familiar power radiating along the length of the Triialon sword in their hands. Bolts of charged plasma flung themselves briefly along its tempered edge, while the entire length of the blade glowed the changing hues of blue, green, gold, and red. Hero released her hands but kept his own fingers pressed to her arms. Lise was holding the sword out in front of her, uncertain of what exactly to do with it or how much she should fear it. Yet she was smiling excitedly, her eyes large discs of awe that she dared not take off of the weapon. She was gasping, trying to regain some semblance of composure.

"What do I do now?"

Hero let go of her arms. "Continue," he said simply. He watched, amazed and inspired as again her graceful movements commanded the basic Triialon forms. With each swing of the Artifact, the trailing light and energy played briefly around her figure. The wonder of a mere alien girl wielding the activated Triialon Sword of Kings, perhaps the first ever non-Triialon pureblood to do so, was suddenly put aside. Hero could not keep Lise's body from his vision, and he found himself staring at the sway of her hips, the strength of her legs, the subtle bounce of her heaving breasts. She spun and cut and twisted at the air enclosing her, her hair whipping around her magnificent form. She was nearly laughing aloud in wonder and surprise, and he studied every move, every smile.

The grin never left her face. "How do I turn it off?" she asked, still swinging at the air around her.

Hero's own movement was a flash, his body stepping into the path of her next cut. He did not watch the down-swinging weapon but instead the light within her eyes. The sword finished its arc, coming through to strike down at Hero's body which was suddenly in front of her. In that same instant, his right arm came up to guard, the edge of the sword striking the now-glowing Prizm bracer and stopping dead just as the embedded crystal drew the energy off of the sword and into itself, leaving it still and quiet again save for the ring of steel on steel.

"With practice," he answered.

Lise's body and lips were quivering, the sweat from the exertion and excitement plastering stray wisps of hair to her face and forehead. They stood their ground, lost in each other's eyes as they slowly lowered their locked-together arms, the again gray metal blade sliding listlessly off of the

274

bracer. Her lips were still parted, but the smile was gone, replaced by a look of longing that echoed the same feeling Hero still denied he felt. At last her free hand shot forward, grasping Hero's jaw within its gloved fingers. She reached up with her full lips, standing on tip-toe to kiss him hungrily before he could move away. But he had already brought his own mouth down upon hers, matching that kiss and opening her mouth with his tongue to taste the sweet secrets within, his own free arm holding her to him by the small of her back.

The universe stopped.

For that brief moment they were as one, yet lost to everything around them. The room was silent except for the sounds of their kiss and the tiny noises that came from the back of her throat.

Finally he broke the embrace, resting his forehead against hers. She gasped for breath, not letting go of his face. "Don't stop," she said. "Please."

"No," he whispered. "You will lose yourself."

"I don't care."

"No!" He had to hold Lise at arm's length, not wanting to let her go, but having to distance himself from her. "You cannot allow yourself to be overpowered by this." He forced himself to release her at last, trying to ignore the look of anguish in her eyes the moment his fingers left her body. "And neither can I."

"But we both want this," she pleaded. "Don't deny it, because I felt it too."

"And neither of us is ready for it." He turned his back to her, trying to reason with himself as much as her. "I cannot let this be, not when I am so close."

"So close to what? What is it you think calls you away from something that is so right?"

"*Everything* that is important to us. A distraction such as this would only harm us both."

"I don't believe that and neither do you…"

"Nevertheless I forbid it," he interrupted, his voice harsh and raised. He willed himself to be calm, turning back to her with as much sympathy he dared muster. He reached out his hand towards the sword that she still

275

held. She stood there a moment, still shocked, but finally moved towards him. She tried to turn away the moment he grasped the Artifact, but he had caught her wrist. "Wait, please."

Lise's shoulders slumped in resignation, but she agreed to look back at him through the veil of her damp lashes and stray hair. "What?"

"Do not think I am without a heart, Lise. As you said, I felt it to. But there's a war out there that we must fight and a quest I must finish. I would rather give you nothing than simply one hollow night, given the nature of your feelings."

Lise nodded meekly. "I know what you are saying, Hero. But you're the one faith that's come along in a long time that I've given myself up to. The last thing I need is for you to turn me away. At least if we could have one brief moment it would be worth the pain of the rest of this war."

Hero said nothing, and when the silence was again unbearable, Lise resumed her exit, making it all the way to the door this time before Hero called to her again. "Lise I am sorry. I only want things to change." She did not answer or look back at him. "We leave for Moonshau soon. Please be ready."

"I will."

"Lise." She finally looked at him, her body nearly halfway out the doors. "I would like to continue your training, if it would please you. Perhaps with your help the future can be different."

Lise smiled sadly at that, replacing the stray wisp of hair back behind her ear before leaving the room and closing the door.

Chapter Sixteen

Many great duels have been fought in and around
the palace grounds of Okino. Most were sport or
spectacle for the royalty that resided there. Few drew
blood or ended in death. All such events of the past
were quickly forgotten the day of Hero's epic challenge.
-Anonymous source

Lise wiped the tears from her eyes at last once she was in the hall. Leaning against the doors she had just closed behind her, she reflected on the words and feelings she had experienced only moments before. The kiss had been amazing; an all consuming fire that had spread itself into her soul before their lips had even touched. But that fire was washed over by cold reality when he had pulled away, and for a moment she thought she could not exist without him. That must have been the empathic intimidation Hero had spoken of before, threatening to wipe away her very sanity. She could have been lost to it, and she still agreed with what she had told him; she would not have cared. The seemingly heartless denial of what she now realized she'd wanted so desperately had almost been too much to bear at first. But Lise was a woman of strength and class, and now the hope that his actions and final words had brought beamed within her. A hope she had not dared to fight for in years.

She smiled to herself again. Yes, she thought, she would continue her training of the Triialon ways. There was always the future.

Lise found herself standing in front of her own apartments, having traversed the hall in silence and in thought. She squared her shoulders with a new determination. She would have more time to reflect later, after she had packed and at last begun her trip back home.

The room was trashed. Furniture was overturned and her belongings were strewn about the apartments. Before she had even had a chance to curse out loud a figure was upon her, moving with the same speed and agility Hero had demonstrated a few minutes before. A fist slammed into her jaw with just enough force to help throw her off balance while a boot-covered foot tripped her. Lise found herself on her behind, a blade point nearly driving itself into her right eye. The hand holding that sword was that of Kezeron Telbandith.

"Don't move," the assassin hissed. His eyes roamed down her body. "Nice outfit. I thought perhaps you were only an envoy for the Galactic Coalition. Seems you are a soldier as well. I could get a lot of money for the information you could provide me. But I don't care. I want Hero."

Lise glared at the muscular alien. "You're not even a shadow of Hero, Kezeron. How long have you trained for today? Months? Years? All out of the envy you carry against a man who is a legend. What are you except just another assassin? Hero knows who you are and he was right about you; you're nothing until you have everything *he* possesses."

"Up," Kezeron snapped.

Bracing her back against the wall behind her, Lise began to slide up, but before she was completely standing, she kicked out, catching the assassin in the groin while side-stepping his sword point. She stood, briefly finding her balance while Kezeron reeled off-guard, and then punched at him with a combination of moves, both Triialon and Sparta, knocking the sword hand away and striking his chin with her palm.

Kezeron rolled backwards, coming back up on his feet just as quickly and finding that his sword was some several feet away. He pressed the attack anyway, easily deflecting her next batch of moves. Lise was astonished at the man's sudden speed. She thought she had learned the Triialon moves well, but Kezeron anticipated each action, finally catching her arms and twisting them painfully, causing her to fall onto her knees, gasping in anguish. He held her there, hissing into her ear. "Don't! You're not even in my league, and I will kill you if I must."

Kezeron grabbed her wrists, securing them behind her back with a cord. Lise tried to cry out but found her lungs refused to grasp enough air. "Still," he said behind her ear in a voice that sent chills down Lise's spine, "You are an astonishingly attractive woman. Perhaps you have *other* skills." She could almost hear the smile spread across his mad face, feel his hands begin to caress her flesh. "If what you say is true, and I must possess all that would be Hero's, then maybe I should start with you." Lise wriggled and kicked out, unable to break his vice-like grip. Then she felt a blade at her throat, and realized Kezeron's sword was there, recovered

279

from the floor during the struggle. "Relax. You shall have plenty of time to prepare yourself for my attentions. I am a hunter, and carnal pleasures come only after the kill of the hunt. Now - call to him."

"No need," Hero said from the door. Lise dared to let out a sigh of relief, finding that he had indeed heard her telepathic call. Hero tugged on the sleeve of his jacket to reveal the ever-present Prizm bracer, and pulled his sword from within it again, the crystal's energy bathing the room in that strange white light. "I believe you have a challenge that I am due to answer."

Kezeron almost laughed in glee, tossing Lise onto her side as he stood up and poised himself for the coming battle. Lise quickly used her feet to push herself out of the way, watching the maniacal grin of victory-within-grasp smear itself across Kezeron's features. "I've waited a long time for this moment."

Hero was calm and cool. He moved away from the door and Lise, crossing the room over the fallen furniture, ending up closer to the balcony doors. The sword began to shimmer, lightning spreading itself along the blade and into the air around it, causing a crackle in the atmosphere as he stood ready. Standing with the Triialon Artifact poised above his head in the *Talenke'* form, he simply waited.

At last Kezeron took Hero's invitation, crossing the space between them in a single bound. Hero blocked the arc that would have opened his chest, and the crossing of the two blades sent out an explosion of energy that surprised Lise and knocked over even more items in the already destroyed room. The two fighters seemed unfazed by the event, now engaged in a furious battle where the two traded blow for blow, matching the other's every combination of moves, cuts and parries. They moved around each other, the speed of their attacks increasing and decreasing like some strange dance accentuated by the power jumping from blade to blade. The sounds of the swords clashing together got louder and more fearsome as Kezeron moved in again, the smell of charged air permeating the room as Hero's own weapon answered each challenge.

Some of the alien fighter's movements were precise imitations of ones Lise had seen Hero perform, which made her wonder where Kezeron had learned such skills. Other moves were foreign to her, but just as

280

effective, for he was more than holding his own against the Triialon's style. Lise wondered with impending dread if Kezeron might actually be able to beat him.

Kezeron cut a wide arc, trying to take Hero's head. He only succeeded in destroying the doors to the balcony in a shower of energy and glass when Hero ducked the swipe. The assassin then had to bring his blade back around to stop Hero's point from eviscerating him. He jumped back onto the balcony, but Hero was less than a step behind him, kneeling again and bringing the Prizm to bear on its target. The Triialon fired a volley from the powerful Artifact, but Kezeron caught the energy wave on the strange blade he carried, somehow refracting it back at Hero. He leapt, narrowly avoiding the returning crackle of power. The blast landed where Hero had stood, and the balcony was blown away from beneath him by the resulting explosion. Before Hero disappeared down into the fissure below, he lashed out with his sword mid-air, the same type of energy arcing out to disintegrate the remaining balcony from beneath Kezeron's feet. The two warriors fell into the unknown.

Just then the door crashed open, a frantic Osmar entered, preceded by his hand-held cannon and followed by a group of palace guards. When the mercenary caught site of the destruction he began to head for the ruined balcony, but Lise called out to him first. "Cut me loose!"

"You alright, lass?" the old mercenary asked while making short work of the cord around her wrists.

Before she could answer, Lise's attention was grabbed by the sounds of the recommenced battle and the sounds of amazement coming from the guards standing in the sunlight, peering over the side. "Gods," one of them said. "I think he's got him on the run!" She stood, running with Osmar to view the continuing battle, now playing itself out on the winding steps and planters that zigzagged their way down the cliff-face towards the misty waterfall that spilled from beneath the lowest back level of the mansion. The two men would meet, crossing blades, then dodge their opponent's next move by leaping to the next lowest level, all the while leaving a trail of wreckage from the waves of energy their swords would give out. Then Hero fell back, avoiding the pressed attack that came next. He jumped, spinning mid-air over Kezeron and disappeared again, this time into the fog of the rushing waterfall that spilled between the green cliffs and trees. Kezeron easily followed him down into the misty chasm.

Hero found himself on a gray slab of overhanging rock, watching through the haze for any signs of Kezeron's retort. He heard the strange fighter before he saw him, faint laughing and the rustle of cloth slipping through the wind, then the figure of a man coalesced out of the gray nothingness. Hero caught the intended blow just in time on the Prizm bracer, returning the favor with a slice at Kezeron's chest from his sword arm. But the fighter simply bounded back, grinning. Both warriors regarded each other in the mist, blood seeping from several small wounds on each man's body.

"You might as well give up and die, Hero. I've followed your every move for as long I have known of your existence. I have forged a weapon that can withstand Triialon energy. I've have learned your ways easily and mastered the styles that will counter them. I am better than you."

"Half truths and hollow words will not win this battle," Hero said, beckoning. "Stop stroking your ego and come and die."

The two clashed again, balanced precariously now on the slippery rocks beside the falls. Each bone jarring sword stroke was met by the other's equally ferocious parry and then countered. They circled each other again, the fight carrying on for minutes on end with no clear victor in sight. Hero studied his opponent's moves, looking for the perfect moment when Kezeron's guard might be down long enough to strike. The abilities the assassin were showing were formidable for one so young, and that fact coupled with the disturbing properties of his enemy's sword and its mysterious origins worried Hero.

"Whom do you serve, Kezeron?" Hero asked between the striking of blade on blade.

"I told you, I take what I earn."

"You gained little of this merely by chance. Some unseen master has heaped such teachings and weapons on you." Again, he turned away a cut that would have skewered him, and smiled knowingly. "You are a liar and a fool."

282

Kezeron began striking with redoubled force. Hero had to move twice as fast to avoid taking a fatal hit. Nevertheless, the assassin scored a mark, slicing open Hero's thigh, causing blood to seep through the black pants he wore. The attempt to anger his foe had backfired thus far, and Kezeron grinned. "Then I am glad that 'master' agreed to finally let me kill you. I was tired of waiting."

Hero parried the next swing – just. In that instant, he stepped in and caught the upswing with the Prizm, leaving Kezeron open. Hero's sword point buried itself into Kezeron's chest, slicing through muscle and bone to find what Hero could only guess was the being's heart. Kezeron Telbandith fell to his knees, the sword falling from limp fingers. "Then the wait is over," Hero grunted into his shocked face. "You have failed your master's test."

Hero might have wanted to force any final admissions as to who this master may be out of Kezeron, but the time was already past. The barely audible gurgling from Kezeron's red-rimmed mouth spoke volumes. Hero pushed his boot into the dead man in order to more easily free his blade. The corpse fell back and pitched over the edge of the cliff, and Hero watched as it careened into the misty river below. A dark stain began to spread beneath the churning water.

The victor watched the spray where the body of the vanquished had disappeared for a few moments before finally turning away. Hero inspected the fine slash across his upper leg. The bleeding was beginning to slow, Triialon physiology already answering the body's need for healing. He limped back to the edge and picked up Kezeron's sword, inspecting the strange metal that had somehow deflected all the Triialon energy he had thrown at it. Checking the Prizm, he found nothing registered, so the mystery blade had none of the elements that made up the Twelve within it. The alloy itself might be a synthetic one, but that still begged the question as to where Kezeron had obtained it in the first place. Hero put aside his suspicions and began the climb back up to the mansion.

Once he had reached a point where the others could see him again, Lise, Osmar and some of the Okino guards and staff raced down to meet him. "You're hurt," Lise said, reaching him first and kneeling down to inspect the wound.

"It is not serious," Hero said, sitting down for a moment on a railing.

"You're full of it," Lise replied, concern etching lines in her forehead.

"I simply need to clean and dress it. I have the needed medical supplies in my ship."

"Don't worry, lass." Osmar was sitting now as well, shaking his head. "His Royalness is a quick healer. That damnable Triialon blood, again."

"And Kezeron?" Lise asked expectantly.

Hero held up the strange sword. "Dead. You were supposed to be watching him," he said to Osmar.

The mercenary shrugged. "As I just explained to the commander, I think he slipped past me while I was watching the other side of the house."

"That fight was spectacular," one member of the excitedly milling house staff finally interjected.

"He knew Triialon moves," Lise muttered worriedly.

"Apparently not all of them," Hero replied flatly.

"Who the hell was he?"

"The question is: who was his master?" Hero froze, watching with grim fascination as the sword he had taken from his conquered foe began to shimmer and disappear from where it leaned. "Damn," he said under his breath.

"What the bloody…?" Osmar reached for the disintegrating weapon, but his hands passed through it, and they all observed it vanish before their eyes, dumbfounded.

"I am a fool," Hero muttered. "I never should have let the body fall into the river. Now my only link to where Kezeron came from is gone."

"Did it self-destruct?" Lise asked in awe.

"Either that or it was teleported away, the effect triggered by Kezeron's death."

"If the body went over those falls…" a guard said, "then its as good as gone. A servant of the Queen could still search his apartments, though."

"He will have left no clues." Hero stood again, limping his way past the crowd, ignoring them as best he could. "Nothing we can do about it now. We have a mission to complete. Lise, Osmar, gather your belongings. We leave in an hour."

The Triialon desert flyer was preparing for takeoff, Osmar in the pilot's seat going over the final checks while Hero was patching himself up after the duel with Kezeron Telbandith. The warrior watched Lise, whom he had instructed to contact her superiors. She had been busy at it for nearly twenty minutes, with no results.

"Someone should have responded by now," Lise said, exasperated. "I don't understand it, and it has me worried as hell. I can't raise Grellion and a call for admiral Jay'salan is also going unanswered. I think enemy forces are jamming Grellion. I'm cut off, Hero. I don't have the positions or call-codes for any of the rest of the fleet because of the dispersal, and the admirals are now missing in action."

"Put out a call for Bevanne of Goleida," Hero suggested.

"Councilor Bevanne? Of Goleida?" Lise seemed stumped by the implied association. "But I thought she was from some far-off colony world?"

"You are on a secured, scrambled and coded Coalition transmission, trying to find the fleets. Some good COM officer may hear and figure it out."

Lise smiled. "Right," and got to work sending out a new transmission. Within minutes and answer finally came through. "This is commander Lise Decarva of the first fleet with an emergency transmission for the commanding officer or Councilor Bevanne if she is there. Do you read? Thank you." There was a moment of silence while Lise waited. "It's Bevanne," Lise said with relief.

"I wish to hear," Hero said, standing to test his field dressing.

Lise hung up the headset, turning the incoming transmission onto speakers. "Councilor; it's wonderful to hear your voice. I've been trying to raise the admirals for nearly a half hour."

"Our attempts to raise them have failed as well," came Bevanne's voice over the static-filtered signal. "Given the nature of admiral Jay'salan's instructions, the Grellion garrison is probably under attack by hostile forces at this point, commander. Has your mission been a success?"

"Nearly. We're on our way to what we hope is the final destination of the needed elements, then on to Grellion."

"Good. A fleet is being deployed to admiral Jo'seph's position to help defend as needed." They could hear a sigh of resignation in Bevanne's voice. "I'm going to take a risk to help insure your eventual safety – what is your position? I wish to send a ship to assist you."

Lise looked to Hero, who nodded. "Bevanne, this is Hero. How long have we known each other?"

There was a laugh. "Ever the pragmatist, my Lord Hero? We met twenty-five years ago, my friend. Does that satisfy your security interrogation?"

"Enough for now," hero answered. "If this transmission is picked up, I doubt it would be decoded by the time your ship meets us on Moonshau."

"Moonshau?"

"That is where we are going, Bevanne. Have your ship meet us there, and make certain it is Dimensionalizer equipped."

"Very well. A small attack cruiser will pick you up there. Our fleet is ready to make the jump to Grellion. Good luck, Hero. And to you, commander."

"Good luck, Councilor," Lise said, "and victory."

Jo'seph could hear the sounds of battle ahead. He and the team assigned to his protection were heading towards the defensive barrier near the front doors, passing the as-yet unarmed traps that the soldiers had set along the routes to the upper and lower levels. They reached the adjoining hallway very near where the attack was under way. "Place the camera and transmitter here," the admiral detailed two troops, "then rejoin us." He tried to see around the next corner to the fight itself, but the fire was too heavy, and risking a peek nearly roasted his face off. "Captain, this is admiral Jo'seph. We're rear of your position and I've brought some relief troops. How goes the defense?"

"Sir, I'm certainly glad you're here," came the officer's voice over the noise, "but if you want this position held any longer then they'll simply be replacements. We're taking casualties here."

Jo'seph was aware that already the medical teams had been in and out of the battle zone several times, taking away the few wounded when there was a break in the heaviest fire, but the attack was growing in ferocity, and the blasts that had hit home were fatal ones. It was then that a large explosion erupted very near where he sat. Jo'seph could see bodies fly back from where the defenders had been positioned, burning and shredding mid-air. They landed in twisted lumps some distance away, still caught within the line of fire from the hallway. More flames and plasma bolts flew over them, but their forms were motionless. They were already dead.

"Captain," Jo'seph called. "Are you alright?"

"Yes, sir," was the reply over the static-charged line. "That was closer to your position than mine."

Jo'seph leaned back in momentary relief, the bodies just beyond the reach of he and his men again catching his eye. The sounds became dull in his ears and the light faded to the bleakness of a smoke and dust-laden landscape. For a moment, he thought he was looking once more at the terrible battlefield that Sparta had become years before. The VID files that had been brought to him in the weeks following the invasion of his home had seared themselves into his mind so strongly, that he awoke some nights in a state of near-panic, dreaming he had been there. He had vowed never to let it happen again, though he knew the promise to be beyond his means even then. None of them would have any sort of home to return to ever again if their defense failed this time.

"Right, we're coming in. Give us covering fire." He signaled his men forward, un-shouldering his own rifle and leading the charge. The soldiers already pinned in the hallway increased their own fire, and the admiral's troops rushed in, taking positions and adding to the storm being cast against the doorway.

Jo'seph took cover next to the battered officer. "Well met, captain," he yelled over the cacophony of noise. He was then forced to duck a blast, returning fire quickly, and his shot found a Lordillian's metal head. "As requested, these men are here to help defend. We'll need this position held as long as possible."

"I've been lucky, sir. We've stopped them at the threshold because they've brought no artillery against us. Unusual for Lordillians given the length of this defense."

"I agree. We're lucky Chebonka is showing such a curiosity." Jo'seph briefly popped up from his cover, taking aim and watching two more Lordillians fall before surveying the scene as best he could in an instant. One of the fresh soldiers he had brought fell, a precise plasma bolt catching him square in the chest and killing him instantly. The nearby cannon emplacement answered the insult with a volley that tore through the machine killers threatening to spill into the hallway, knocking their forces back again.

"I don't understand, sir. Curiosity?"

"Captain, I'll need you to gradually fall back, but keep them pinned at the doors as long as you can. The Lordillians don't know what it is we're defending, and they're not interested in destroying it just for the sake of killing a few of us. That's why their fire has been relatively light."

"They want to capture the citadel," the captain realized.

Jo'seph nodded. "They'll want to take the base with as little damage as possible, it seems, but that means killing us all, so be prepared for their next offensive by pulling your men back. Understood?"

"I'll keep them down here as long as I can, sir."

"Keep me posted. When they finally press in, fall back to relieving positions and arm traps. We'll destroy more of those tin bastards once they're inside, so no heroics. You're simply buying defense time." The admiral's communicator went off, and he removed it from his belt to answer it. "Yes?"

"Sir, Lordillian troops are preparing to break through a second entrance west of your position! They could be through in moments."

Looking at his portable tactical display, Jo'seph swore. "We have no one near that position?"

288

"Negative."

"I have a suggestion, admiral," came a voice over the COM unit.

"Sardeece," the admiral said in surprise. "What are you doing on this channel?"

"The citadel AI can monitor them all, sir. Quickly, the enemy has nearly breached the second entrance."

"Very well, what is your suggestion?"

"I can send servitor drones there within moments," Sardeece said carefully, "if you'll give the order to arm them."

Jo'seph found the captain next to him staring in disbelief. The admiral understood the implications; arming machines to fight machines – the idea was still too new and unacceptable for most of the Coalition forces to agree with. "Bridge, what's the status of that second force?"

"They've cleared away any exterior debris and have nearly finished cutting away the seals," the officer declared. "They'll be through within two minutes, then able to attack your position freely."

Jo'seph never broke the stare his captain had locked him with. "Sardeece, there's a cache of weapons near the servitors' position."

"Sir, *no*," the captain at last dared, grasping the admiral's arm.

"Captain, there's no other way. We'll be trapped without help, so it's a moment of truth or we all die here." The captain released him with resignation, but said nothing. "Go ahead, Sardeece."

"They're on their way."

"Keep me posted, Sardeece. Bridge, I need an escort force to get back to command." He turned back to the captain of the forward defense. "Keep them at bay. I'm counting on you and your people. Begin your retreat to the next position when my escort arrives."

A far off explosion could be heard through the bulkheads. "Admiral, bridge," came the familiar voice through the COM. "The enemy has breached the second position."

"Sardeece," Jo'seph called. Silence answered him. "Sardeece?"

Svea disembarked her ship following her brother's anxious steps with her own uncertain ones. The sound of her boots once again touching a Kordula landing platform was a familiar one, but not immediately comforting. Secretly a part of her wished for her home palace on the Magdala moon, but she dismissed such thoughts, resigned to the fate of Kordula, which she was forging for herself.

The trip home had been lengthy and quiet, Dahvis spending much of the time alone in the ship's small living space while Svea had watched the streaks of the stars flitter past the cockpit, lost in contemplation. Something had changed, but what exactly she could not put her finger on. Usually the two were jubilant after the completion of a mission, reveling in the carnage of their tasks. They would make love on the way home if the flight was a lengthy one, the excitement of the moment not to be lost. After the night on Dailor, though, the two had been separate and silent, and Svea's own feelings over the events were strange and alien to her. More than anything, though, she wondered less why her brother did not feel the need to be close to her as why she felt no desire to be close to him.

Goursh was waiting for them at the entrance to the building the platform jutted out from. "Please," he said, holding out his arm to a craft waiting off to one side, "Our Lord Memfis awaits your report. I shall take you to him."

Dahvis smiled wickedly, happy to have so much attention centered on his knowledge and tasks. Two men stepped forward, taking the satchels the Seethlings had brought and placing them in the craft. Svea simply followed obediently, sitting on the white leather seats and feeling the rise of the transport as it lifted silently from the platform and up to the higher entrances of the Temple. She found herself once again following Dahvis and Goursh down the trophy hall and finally to the doors of their new master, where Memfis waited with his usual entourage of beautiful serving girls of varied race and color. She bowed automatically, her body going through the motions.

"At last you return," Memfis said with a smile. "Be gone," he said to the females, and they hurried away, following Goursh out of the echoing chamber.

"It is done, Our Lord Memfis," Dahvis intoned, bowing again. "The temple of Dailor is burned, its priestesses are as ash on the wind. I have brought back records and objects detailing their last activities there, as well as the mental knowledge of events that had taken place before our arrival."

290

"And what precisely have you brought me?"

"As you suspected, the witches were indeed harboring someone there for some time, possibly even while in a form of cryo-stasis. But I could only glean images and feelings from the priestess, for the man they harbored had left some time before."

"Do the records give any further details?"

Dahvis shook his head. "I have not read them."

Memfis stood and descended the steps from his dais "Just as well," he said, snapping his fingers for a serving girl to come and take the collected items from the Seethlings. "And what did you find in the minds that you touched?"

"The image of a young man," Dahvis said off-handedly. "He was trained in their ways, many of which seem to be knowledge and styles passed down by the Triialon. The man had dark hair and eyes, spent a number of years at the temple, mostly in secret with the higher-ranking priestess, and then left less than a year ago aboard a supply ship. As to his destination, there were no details that I could discern."

Memfis seemed angered, but he kept that emotion out of his voice, instead sounding matter-of-fact. "Such a mystery man. I will have to see if I can learn more from the records you stole."

"Was this person a Triialon?" Dahvis had asked the question suddenly, menace in his voice.

Memfis stared only briefly at the breach in protocol before saying evenly, "Perhaps. It would not conform to our known facts, but anything is possible." He returned Dahvis' look with promise in his tone. "One day you may have to kill this stranger for us so we may both be certain. You have done well," he said then, changing the subject. "Both of you. You have my gratitude, as well as that of the Court, although events have transpired since your departure."

The open opportunity for information intrigued even Svea despite her gloomy mood. "My lord?"

"Toapo has advanced his stubborn and self-centered moves to usurp power of the Inner Sanctum. He has openly challenged my authority and sent agents to kill Hero."

291

"But *I* want to kill Hero," Dahvis hissed, standing with fists clenched. "My Lord, his people destroyed our race."

Memfis snapped his fingers, making certain any servants still lingering within earshot left the immediate chambers. "Toapo's actions place the entire Court in jeopardy. But if he succeeds in this, many of my problems will die with Hero. That would leave only one pressing issue: Toapo." He smiled. "Can you accept the death of the last Triialon at the hands of another if it means I give you the power to destroy a God?"

"At last, you honor us with your presence," Galatis moaned as Memfis swept into the room. The elder God ignored the complaint, standing behind his place at the table and resting his hands upon the seat's back.

"I have new information that you should now be able to access," he said, looking around the room and finding Toapo not among their number. "My agents have returned from the Temple of Dailor. They were forced to raze the building to the ground, but not before taking as much of their records as possible."

"What is the bad news?" one of the Gods asked even while his fingers commanded his console to begin downloading the topic of discussion.

"The legends regarding a Last Son of Triialon may have some basis in fact." Memfis reached forward, bringing up his own display of the reports. "The good news is that the Sisterhood is gone and many of their secrets are now ours. But some of the events that have transpired there remain cryptic. Lance, if he truly does exist, may have been harbored within the temple for most of these many years."

"Why would a Triialon's son spend over thirty years in a temple full of celibate women with only limited teachings regarding fighting?" Galatis was smug and contemptible, staring at his fingernails while waving away Memfis' findings with his free hand.

Memfis's lip twitched at his contemporary's attitude, but said the next with calculated intent. "Because he may have spent more than half of that time in cryogenic stasis."

There was a collective surge of interest from the present Gods, each scrolling faster now down through their shared reports. "What would cause him to need such a sustained healing time?" Galatis asked aloud, his attitude completely gone.

"It begins to finally unravel the nature of the relationship between the Triialon and Dailor," another chimed in. "Obviously their medical skills were quite advanced. One question at last answered only to produce another."

"My guess is his mother," Memfis said at last. "Her plans against her own people were in motion the night before the final battle on Triialon, but somehow Hero found out and was able to take Lance to Dailor in time to save his life."

"A poison," Tannek suggested.

"Who can say?" Galatis shrugged. "The rest may have been lost in the sands of the final battle."

Baletto waved both Gods' comments away. "This is still only conjecture. A theory we are amassing here today based on sketchy facts."

"But still a theory that answers a lot of old questions," Tannek said, raising a finger.

"Leaving two very important ones," Galatis said. "Where is Lance now and what are his intentions?"

"Could Hero have smuggled him off of Dailor in one of those transports?" Baletto asked.

"I've cross-referenced every known record of space traffic in that system since the end of the war until today with the known positions of Hero; he was never anywhere near Dailor." Memfis sat at last, pulling up further screens. "If Lance was indeed there he left at a time of his own choosing, apparently of his own accord."

"Another wild card," Galatis sneered.

"One revealed only by my order to finish off the line of Dailor," Memfis glared. "This matter has not come to light until now because of our laziness and desire to be distracted, pointing out yet again how we must resolve to see these matters through as one under my guidance." There was a rumble of agreements and denials from the small group, but Memfis pressed on. "If Lance does indeed exist, he has certainly kept a

293

lower profile than his kith, and we will have to work hard to find him. But we cannot do this while bickering because one of us is unhappy with his place."

"The clock is apparently ticking, Lord Memfis," Galatis said with a hint of taunting in his voice. "It would seem there are now many issues that we must face as one. *His* coming draws near. What would you suggest?"

"I say we begin the reinstatement of the Games," Memfis announced. The Court began to nod and rumble in agreement, and Memfis stood again to be heard over their voices. "The Decade Games would once again bring our allies close and our enemies closer. If we act now we could have every possible threat in every corner of the universe here within five years and be certain where everyone stands. Let the people of Kordula begin the preparations now. Let the rebuilding of the coliseum commence and the word go forth. We shall reinstate the Decade Games. Let them all come to Chel'Zel!"

Toapo left the teleportation chamber with a grin on his face. In no way upset still by his initial setback, he now knew the plans he must set in motion with all haste. Entering the next room he stood at its center, the inky blackness that surrounded him clashing with the clean whiteness of the chamber he had just exited. The doors shut, and he stood in total blackness until the column of light from above began to illuminate him, glowing brighter as the secret transmission he was sending became clearer. At last Chebonka appeared in a floating holographic display in front of him, and Toapo's smile widened.

"The other Gods have abandoned you, Chebonka, but I remain. My faith does not waver."

Chebonka's metal helm coldly regarded the face that hung before him, the features unmoving despite the words that ushered from its visage. "I have no need of your kind, Toapo. I have again found what a power hate can be, and that power has given what the Gods themselves forbade. Leave me."

The God feigned a pained expression. "Such harsh words for the being that handed you the very sword you wield. Were it not for me, you

294

would have no weapon to power with such hate, no governing of a race that conforms to your vision."

"What you have done was the will of the Court, just as the order to withhold knowledge from me was their will. I am through being the puppet you would say you have made of me or the tool that you simply are."

Toapo's brow raised in interest. "Your newfound power has made you philosophical as well as short tempered, I see. Yet you sit there while the Coalition still lives, evading your grand army like a child that you cannot bring under control. How long can you sit there while they still live, Chebonka? How long can you wait to find and kill the admirals? Or Hero? Your paltry inexperience with one Triialon Artifact is barely the beginning of power, yet you are somehow able to fool yourself while you wallow there in your artificial sanctum, safe… until they come for you. Or until Kordula comes for you."

"What do you know of power?" Chebonka's digitized voice came back, the volume now raised an ominous decibel. He was yelling, enraged. So it was true; the machine born of man had somehow found emotion. "You and your fellow Gods waiting at the center of your web, trapped by your own impotence! Meanwhile my forces bear down on a Coalition outpost, promising their heads, the path to the death of their leaders, and new power."

"And just like the Gods you hate, you wait in your lair for your plans to unravel in the hands of your subordinates."

"No. I shall lead my regime to victory, Toapo. I can take my Flagships and go even now, while you must simply watch. I will kill Hero myself. Soon I shall have the strength to take the galaxy, even Kordula!"

The picture went blank and Toapo had to suppress a laugh. Adrenaline fueled his body, the rush of such direct manipulation not felt in years now coursing through his ancient veins. He was still grinning when he stepped out of his private chambers and almost directly into Memfis who waited in the hall.

"And what plots keep you from Court today, my lord Toapo?"

Toapo's grin became barred teeth as he went nose to nose with his rival, resisting the urge to physically challenge him right there. "Your
295

failed schemes that would only benefit you are nearly over, Memfis. What I do, I do for the greater interest of our Court." He felt giddy, the promise of what might soon be flashing before his vision like forgotten riches. He stood back, again feeling haughty. "Oh, I am going to enjoy your fall. One way or another, I will soon have both the political and physical might to see you ground under my boot heel, Memfis, and when that happens, I shall enjoy every sound of your agony."

Toapo locked his chambers behind him and walked away, heading for the Court of Worlds with a bounce in his step he hadn't felt in what must be eons.

Jo'seph watched as the troops broke from their cover behind his position, hoping their aim proved as true as the training and battle statistics had shown. The two soldiers knelt down next to each other, both quickly taking aim through viewfinder sights on their rocket launchers and firing. The two missiles sped over the bodies of both living and dead Coalition defenders and down the hallway, striking the advancing group of Lordillians and obscuring them in a haze of smoke and fire. The explosion stretched out, reaching forward towards the soldiers and shaking the whole room. The fire subsided before it could hurt those it sought to defend and became black smoke as the soldiers quickly picked up their gear to fall back as the order was given. Jo'seph ran with them, keeping his own rifle's sites trained on the smoke behind them to cover their escape until they reached their new positions.

At last the admiral's people reached their liberators. "Good work, corporal. Leave your APR team here to join the captain. The rest of you, come with me."

A smaller group of soldiers began following Jo'seph away from the immediate action and back along the labyrinthine corridors of the Grellion citadel they now worked so diligently to call home. "My COM unit is damaged," he said, unbuttoning his officers' jacket.

"Here, sir." The corporal handed Jo'seph his own communicator, procuring a replacement from a subordinate.

"Sardeece, this is admiral Jo'seph. What is your position?"

The admiral was almost surprised when he heard the reply, the scientist's voice suddenly clear over the COM signal. "I am less than fifty meters from the second front, sir. The servitors were able to reach the weapons cache and their current position in enough time, I'm pleased to say. I'm glad to hear your voice; when you went offline I feared the worst."

Jo' didn't know how to reply for a moment, conflicting emotions of relief at the report and guilt regarding the moment he almost believed Sardeece or the citadel's servitors might have somehow defected churned his gut. "I'm fine," he said at last. "What is your status?"

"Lordillians are holding at this position, but are not able to enter. The line that passed the entrance and were nearly ready to spread down the adjoining corridors were quickly destroyed, as have been any followers." There was that familiar voice of a scientist amazed by his findings. Jo'seph was forced to smile. "We've sustained no casualties, though; it would seem the Lordillians are either unwilling or unable to target the servitor drones."

The admiral's jaw nearly dropped. "Would you repeat that?" he asked haltingly. Even the soldiers around him looked shocked at the prospect.

"The Lordillians cannot target the servitor robots thus far, sir. We're holding them at the entrance, blasting any that enter and, I repeat, we've sustained no casualties."

"Sardeece, that's incredible. You're promoted."

"Don't get too happy yet, admiral. Its taken every drone I could spare to hold this position, and indestructible defenders won't be much use against sheer numbers once the Lordillians regroup and begin to march. Save a nuisance."

"I'll take it. Get back to the lower levels and stay safe. Inform me if the servitors begin to encounter resistance they can't hold back."

"Understood, sir. Sardeece out."

"Are we heading to the command decks, sir?" the corporal asked.

"I'm not certain." He thumbed the COM unit again. "Command deck, this is admiral Jo'seph. Any noise?"

"Still safe and sound up here, sir," came the reply. "No other breaches, and the Lordillians seem to have resigned themselves to a ground assault thus far."

"Let me know of any status changes, bridge. I'll be remaining here to help the main defense." The soldiers around him smiled at the admiral's sentiments, ready to fight and hold their position, not wait for an attack that might not come for hours to the upper decks. "Corporal," he said.

"You heard the admiral, men. About face! Lieutenant, take point." The group turned around, heading back towards the main entrance with renewed vigor. "You think we have a chance now, admiral?"

"I think we might be able to make all the difference when it comes to time – if our luck holds, corporal."

Chapter Seventeen

Little has been written, comparatively, about Hero's
oft-time companion and mercenary friend Osmar. A
titanic drinker, the man somehow also managed to be
a dead shot with an assortment of weapons, almost all
of which were nearly perpetually hidden under his coat.
Coalition and Triialon
- Dr. W. H. Redfield

The open grasslands around the large, opulent shrine and its tall, pointed towers overlooking the city on the horizon were a stark contrast in many ways to the confines of the stuffy Okino palace and the dense forest that had surrounded it. Osmar resisted the urge to shrug himself out of his long duster jacket that suddenly felt so heavy in the warm Moonshau sunshine. He forced himself to pull his eyes off of the shapely roundness of Lise's behind in that black jumpsuit of hers and instead regarded what Osmar presumed was Durant's small ship parked next to the towering church. The doors leading into the temple of the Holy Order of Moonshau were open, and beckoned Hero and his companions to enter. He resisted the urge to clear his throat, remove any caps he wasn't wearing, or swear off drinking and entered with trepidation.

Inside it was cool, the darkness of the stone walls and high ceilings leading into the open lit main shrine. There stood the cleric and some of his fellow robed zealots. Wollhaw and Durant were both standing on some sort of scaffolding, using large pliers-like tools to pull more of the crystal 'elements' out of niches in the walls. Osmar studied the strange decorations, the swirling patterns of raised lines in the walls ran up and around the interior of the temple, looking like the relief print of some strange tree. The reddish elements were set into them at even intervals along the surfaces.

Durant stopped to regard the trio as they entered the shrine. He stood there in his rolled up shirtsleeves, covered in a fine layer of dust. "How much were you paying me for these menial services, again, Hero?"

"Enough to buy yourself into any court in the galaxy you wish."

Durant redoubled his efforts visibly, Osmar laughing at the sight. "Has he complained this much the entire time?" he asked the cleric above them.

It was Durant who answered with a grimace. "It may have been a little while since I dirtied my hands, but I've done my bit for king and country in the past, old man."

Osmar felt his moustache bristle at the comment.

"We have made progress, but extra hands would be appreciated nonetheless," Wollhaw said.

"Lise and I shall assist you," Hero said, grabbing another set of tools and beginning to climb a scaffold. "Osmar..."

"I know, I know, your greatness; I'll stand guard." The mercenary did an about-face, heading back towards the large hall that led into the temple.

Osmar cradled his hand-cannon. Standing watch, he peering through the darkness to the green grass and purple sky beyond. The wind whistled up through the stone corridor and rustled his jacket. From behind him he could still hear the sounds of chisels and hammers, the clerics and others talking as they collected each item from the walls. "There must be hundreds of them," exclaimed Lise, her voice echoing sweetly from the shrine. "Why didn't you detect the elements here on Moonshau when we were last here?"

"You might recall that I was distracted at the time," Hero answered. "Besides, Moonshau capitol is on the other side of the planet, and I have never been here before."

Lise's small laugh followed the exchange, and Osmar groaned, rolling his eyes. He strode away from the distracting conversation, deciding to stand guard closer to the doors. He leaned against the frame, removing a flask from one of the inner pockets of his coat and took a drink. As his lips came away from the nectar within he froze, his gaze caught by a small bird landing not three feet from his boots. Red and brown feathers bled beautifully into greens and pinks, and its wide black eye regarded him momentarily from the side of its head. The creature picked up a small morsel, lifting again into the air, but dropped its prize in flight. The breeze caught the morsel of food, dancing it through the air

301

in front of the bird. Its aerodynamics allowed it to follow its prey in circles, up and down through the air, finally catching it and zipping off while Osmar stood in mute fascination. He barked a laugh when he was certain the bird was gone, finding himself strangely amazed at the sight that had passed.

Soundlessly, something fifty times the bird's size landed where the creature had flown from seconds before. The mercenary dropped his flask, suddenly springing into a stance, his feet wide apart and the barrel of his gun coming to bear. The gun was knocked aside before he could even get off a shot at the man that had appeared so stealthily. Osmar backed off, narrowly avoiding a slice that would have removed his head from his shoulders, while pulling weapons from his coat with both hands. He stopped, ready to face his enemy with a blade and a blaster in each grip. The figure stepped from the blinding light and into the shadows of the temple's hallway, kicking the second gun from the mercenary's hand and bringing a large sword down. Osmar parried the swing away, but the next swipe came from the side, and Osmar's short sword proved too inflexible, shattering as it connected with the larger blade. The sharp edge bit into Osmar's gut and he screamed in pain, falling back. The enemy wiped the blood from the sword edge with his fingers and pulled back into a battle ready stance all in one fluid motion, and at last Osmar got a good view of his opponent.

"You!" Osmar couldn't believe his eyes, instead attributing the sight to pain and drink, remembering then how little he'd had. Nonetheless, Kezeron Telbandith was the figure that stood against him, grinning with that same interminable smile. "But you're dead!"

"Then it seems the fates serve me better than you," the enemy said, and began to step forward, the point of his sword reaching for Osmar's heart.

Osmar's hand shook from the pain, but he still managed to slip the small grenade off of his belt, though sticky with blood. He used his thumb to help propel it, making sure its first bounce was just behind Kezeron's feet, knowing that it would explode on the second. The assassin sensed the explosive and leapt aside before it went off. Still, the desired result was the same; Osmar had the extra seconds he would need to escape immediate death. He rolled in the opposite direction, still clutching his opened stomach with one hand. He threw the other arm over his head as the grenade went off, then scrambled to get onto his feet and get a gun in his hand. "Hero!" His legs failed him, and he slipped again. The movement saved his life, his body falling from the height where Kezeron's sword would have pierced it. He instead kicked out, tripping the alien fighter while he called out again. "*Hero!*"

The next sound was that of blade on blade. Hero had jumped over the now prone mercenary and stopped Kezeron's attack. The timing was less than he would have liked, but again the desired effect was there. "You fight without honor," Osmar heard the Triialon growl at their unexpected adversary.

Kezeron advanced upon his hated foe. "Nobody kills me and gets away with it," he spat.

Osmar tried to breathe a sigh of relief at the sight of the two figures now engaged against each other, but found the sharp exhale to be more than his threshold could bear. Suddenly two pairs of hands were on him, Lise and the cleric pulling him out of danger. "Good lass," he tried to say, but instead he blacked out.

Hero stopped each attack from Kezeron's sword with equal rage. His surprise at seeing his defeated and seemingly dead foe was put aside by the discipline of battle and fury at his companion lying bloodied on the temple floor. "I shall have to make certain I kill you this time. You prove resilient."

Kezeron almost shrugged, but instead chose to parry the next attack and answer with a stabbing slice before pulling back away and catching Hero's arm with the back swing, ushering fresh blood. "Perhaps it is I the Gods favor."

"I wonder." Hero did not even notice the gash, but moved in, blocking a nasty downward attack and reversing it, knocking the alien's blade away and raking the edge of his own sword along Kezeron's ribs. The assassin howled in anger and spat through gritting teeth. "It matters little," Hero continued. "I shall have your head on the point of *Strength* before the sun sets this day." He thrust again and the other man dodged, giving Hero a chance to let power flow along the length of Triialon steel at last, igniting the weapon and lighting the temple in eerie light. He backed away, leading the now fuming Kezeron through the echoing shrine. When next their swords struck, the power that flashed off as a report struck pews and flung them through the air, setting the wooden seats alight. He chose a moment at last when the others had fled the room and there was a brief opening in Kezeron's defense to fire bolt of energy off the edge itself. The enemy deflected it and the surge instead smashed down part of the far wall. Hero took the opportunity to lead the duel outside and leapt away from his opponent.

"Your obsession led you here quickly, Kezeron Telbandith," Hero taunted as they battled. "You waited many years to stomp out my legacy, only to continuously find yourself in my footsteps." The swords clashed again, sparks flying as the sound became deafening. "You are nothing."

"I am your death," Kezeron hissed, attacking again and again. "If you think your barrage of insults will coax any secrets or mistakes out of me, then think again."

Hero could feel Lise's mind nearby, and he dared to look at the temple to spot her standing near the smoking hole the fight had created. "*Take my ship*," he thought to her. "*Take as many elements as you can and get to the Grellion base and the admiral, now.*"

"*I won't leave you,*" her thoughts came back.

"*That would serve nothing except the wasting of more time. Go!*"

Again the two figures danced, spinning and twisting, moving to an unheard song of death, each step in time to avoid the one that preceded it. The dance moved out onto the hill, where a city of silver spires stretched into the air along the curving horizon, the haze of midday and the power that shot out of their blades obscuring the details of the far off view. Perhaps no one now watched this ongoing struggle for the final supremacy, yet all would hear of the outcome should Hero fail and Kezeron's wish at last come true.

The next set of moves was fierce, and Hero had to move with all his speed to defend against the combination. He could feel each blow rain down with greater power than the last, could sense the next move only just in time to evade it. "You see it? Do you see it, Hero?" Kezeron's face

304

split into a sneer of defiance and triumph as he pressed the attack. "I am your *death*!"

The point of Kezeron's blade pushed aside Hero's and jabbed into his right shoulder, paralyzing the arm that held both Triialon weapons. He grunted in anguish and Kezeron laughed. Hero could not pull away, couldn't escape the stab that held him fixed in the final move of their dance. His left hand still gripped *Strength* below his right, but the latter extremity would not release. For that last moment he felt trapped. "I no longer care *what* you are," he bellowed through clenched teeth. With all of his might he at last freed the hilt of his sword from the grip of his right hand and sliced across Kezeron's chest with its edge as he pulled it away. Kezeron gasped, blood flowing copiously from the devastating wound. He fell away, pulling his sword with him, only to drop it onto the wet grass among the crimson of his own lifeblood. He stood reeling, watching with shock as Hero was once again able to move his damaged arm and stand erect and powerful before him, gripping the Triialon blade. "The penalties for evil are final and exact," he quoted evenly from the Book of the Triialon. With a sweeping arc he slashed out at Kezeron's neck, completing the promise he had made inside the temple by decapitating the assassin and watching as his body slumped lifeless to the ground.

Hero sighed, his hand coming away from his right arm wet with his own blood. "Interesting move," he said to himself, staggering. "I shall have to remember that one." He regarded the headless body a moment before moving back towards the temple, not bothering to take the sword or head. He assumed nothing of the dead alien or his weapons would remain on the hill for long, possibly returning to their true master or some other point in space at some time after the assassin's death. He hoped against it, wondering if he had simply failed to kill Kezeron the first time, but fatigue won out over even that pragmatism. Hero returned *Strength* to the confines of the Prizm's central crystal. The sword disappeared in a flash of white light.

Master Wollhaw ran out to meet him as he neared the new temple entrance. "Osmar?" he asked of the cleric.

"I had him taken to a medical center, my Lord. You are hurt."

"Nothing I cannot take care of. Did Lise leave unharmed?"

"I assume so," Wollhaw said. "A ship arrived just before she could lift off, but she seemed quite relieved to see its occupants. She left with them, taking the bulk of the crystals."

"Bevanne's transport arrived," Hero mused. "Master Wollhaw, I would take any remaining crystal elements and leave in my ship. Your payment along with extra is in the bag I arrived with. I hope to return soon, but if not, would you please look after Osmar for me should he not survive?"

"Of course." The cleric turned and hurried into the ruined temple, Hero following slowly as he clutched his arm.

He stood in the clouded shrine, the smoke from the extinguished fires rising into the pointed gray ceilings. The destruction he had helped cause was disheartening but not unrepairable. He regarded the strange church in a melancholy light, musing at how the giant relief of a beautiful goddess in the ceiling above the entrance hall remained untouched. He stared at the woman's eyes, noting their red centers and the way they stood out from the gray stone the goddess was carved from. "Master Wollhaw," Hero called. The cleric appeared from an antechamber, a look of question at Hero's tone obvious on his features. The Triialon warrior pointed at the statue with his good arm. "Were those purchased from Durant as well?"

The eyes of the goddess bore down upon the two figures standing amongst the destruction with benign indifference; two giant red orbs, each more than twice the size of their sister Grellion elements.

Jo'seph's entire body ached. He didn't know exactly how many hours had passed since the siege had begun, and he wasn't sure he wanted to, fearing the knowledge would only add to his growing fatigue.

He and his troops had been forced back from the main entrance hall at last. They were now falling back, corridor by corridor, sending runners to set traps and auto-guns in adjoining hallways. His force had met up with surviving servitor robots, the small team having finally been shoved aside by massive numbers of the invaders. Explosions rocked the rooms around them as Lordillian squads ran headlong into the traps and other positions. Again Jo'seph's soldiers held, now reduced to the middle ground, not far from the shafts that would take them either up to the command decks or down to engineering.

Suddenly the corridor was quiet save for the sound of fire and injured men and women. "Have they found another way?" the captain asked.

"No, they're just regrouping," the admiral answered. "That's fine. Gives us a chance to prepare a surprise for them. Corporal!" Another soldier ran up, saluting. "Get the rocket team together. Set up a mid position ready to respond when called. Have them stagger three lines in the hallway for quick repeats and reloads."

"Contact!" A soldier, bleeding slightly from an arm wound was watching the spectral analyzer. "Movement. They're coming soon."

"Ready, people." Jo'seph was suddenly struck by how confident he felt and sounded in the face of almost certain death. He had been in critical situations before in his career, but nothing ever so desperate. He and the other officers and soldiers, each from so many creeds and races within the hunted Coalition, might still stand for days or maybe only hours. But he also knew that they would fight to the last man if necessary, unwavering in the harsh storm of destruction, doing their job and doing it well. He only hoped it would not be in vain – that the promised salvation Hero and Lise had searched for would arrive in time to at least secure the Grellion citadel as a Coalition base, even if every defender had died.

The next wave came, filling the hall with more of the hulking Lordillian bodies than many might have thought possible. The defenders hit the deck at the captain's command, and the first volley of missiles sped over their heads to strike the metallic troops en masse. The second volley sped through the smoke to strike any behind that had survived and waited to rush forward. "Hold," came the command, the captain studying the display of his scope. "Wait for a target." Moments later the next wave came, and then the next, each one being mowed down by the combined firepower of rifles and missile teams. The sound was deafening and the smoke threatened to choke them all where they stood, but the Coalition soldiers simply kept firing, some falling as blasts from Lordillian arms that had gotten through, others taking the chance to reload whenever the explosions filled the corridor.

Three more times the attack came and three more times the invaders were repelled, but the strikes were beginning to take their toll. Jo'seph slid his communicator from his belt. "Strike Team Seven, this is the admiral."

"Sub lieutenant Zhade here, sir. No contacts at the command decks."

"We need reinforcements here, lieutenant," Jo'seph said, trying to hear. "Bring your team and one other squad to relieve our position."

"On our way, sir."

The next wave of Lordillians came, and Jo'seph found himself joining his comrades on the front line a row of pulse rifles blasting a hail of plasma as suppression while the missiles waited for the greater need. Bolts of searing energy flew past the admiral's head. The sounds of the dead and dying could be heard behind him, but he simply battled on, firing as he had been trained years before and leading simply by example. He fell behind his cover for a moment when his weapon jammed, handing it back to whatever soldier waited. "Overheat! New weapon," he called, finding a fresh rifle placed in his hands quickly and returning to his position on the line.

"Contact! They're bringing up an artillery position!"

"Captain." Jo'seph called for the missile team to be ready, and when the next group of Lordillians appeared in the hall they had their right arms replaced by large cannons. The squad of shock troopers were accompanying a tread-mounted mobile mortar tube. The Lordillians opened fire, but the mortar never even got off a round, decimated by the silencing volleys of missiles that sped down the now blackened corridor. Each heavy-mounted machine that followed found the same fate ready for them, in turn destroyed by the well-prepared group of defenders. When no further resistance was encountered, the sudden silence seamed just as overpowering as the terrible noise that had preceded it. "Captain?"

"Scanning." Again the tense silence followed, then, "They're beaten for now, sir. They've fallen back to regroup." A cheer went up from the bloodied group of men and women, a moment of joy awash in the bleakness of battle.

Janise waited in her room. Tykeisha had entered some time before, standing near the door with rifle in hand and the occasional reassuring smile on her lips. At least one guard waited directly outside the door, with a full squad in position at the far end of the hall leading from the highest level of living quarters up to the command decks. Janise looked down at the large pistol in her hands, wondering what good it would do if Lordillians did indeed enter the room.

"You alright?" Tykeisha asked, breaking the girl's reverie. Janise nodded slightly. "That's OK, I'm scared too. I am every time we come under fire."

"How do you deal with it?" Janise asked. "The fear."

"Oh, you put it aside as best you can and do what you have to do to get through it all," Tykeisha said with a shrug. "You'd think I would get used to it. In a way I guess I have, but it still sucks." Both of them smiled at that.

Moments later the sounds of battle erupted from the far end of the corridor. "Some of them must have slipped through." Tykeisha, who had been leaning lazily against the door, was suddenly alert and poised. She backed away from the closed portal, waving Janise back behind the bed to hide.

"Sounds like more than just a few," Janise said nervously. A series of explosions rocked the room, and she knew that the soldiers posted in the hallway were dead. Tykeisha looked at her as she dove behind the bed to hide, and Janise could see naked fear in the older woman's eyes, filling her with dread. There was a scream, followed by the sound of another body falling. The guard posted nearby must have been killed by whatever waited in the corridor.

The door exploded inward, smoke and debris flying across the room to impact in the wall above their heads. Janise could feel her heart pounding with such ferocity she thought it might burst. Silence followed the explosive entrance, long seconds of terrible quiet as they waited to know if they had been discovered. Then a rifle burst shattered the tranquility, the blast tearing through the top of the bed and striking Tykeisha's arm. She screamed, falling back, the woman's face a mask of pain.

309

Janise's heart caught in her throat in the next moment when a Lordillian giant ripped the entire bed aside with one arm. The bulky machine stood above them, its black, glassy eyes staring lifelessly down at the cowering women as it raised its weapon. Janise clenched her fists involuntarily, her fingers closing around the gun in her left palm tightly, but she knew she could never aim it in time. Instead her mind simply screamed; a blackness encroached the peripherals of her vision as she stared at her death in fear and rage. Her mind and extremities exploded in a sudden and surprising pain, the darkness becoming a fiery light that seemed to change the color of the room.

Janise heard Tykeisha gasp at the sight of even more Lordillians in the hall beyond, but in that same instant something appeared between the two groups of machines – a black dot hovered briefly in the air. Janise could just make it out at the edge of her vision, yet she could not pull her eyes away from the Lordillian poised to strike her down. Suddenly the room exploded with a gust of powerful air, hot and smelling of sulfur. She could feel her long blonde hair whipping around her face, stinging the skin. The gust did not push them back, but instead pulled forward, sucking in towards the center of the room, towards the expanding dot. The Lordillian was propelled off its feet, flying backwards, nearing the gaping portal of black light the dot had grown into. Their would-be killer flew through its yawning entrance, its arms flailing as the blaster it held fired randomly. Yet even the plasma bolts did not escape the fully-grown whirlwind as it spun and twisted, pulling next each Lordillian from the hall into itself. Just as quickly as it had expanded, the portal shrank, closing with a mighty pop of the in-rushed air being cut off, as though someone had slammed the largest door known within the same room.

Janise's quarters were now quiet and perfectly still, nothing remaining within its small confines save the two startled, yet alive, young women. "Did you do that?" Tykeisha asked at last, her mouth still wide with shock.

Janise stared at where the portal had closed, just as shocked and amazed. The girl raised her bandaged hands up slowly in front of her face, gaping at them as though they were completely strange to her, wondering to herself what she had done or how she had accomplished it. When she could stand the silence and mystery no longer, her brow creased with renewed purpose. "Come on," she said, taking Tykeisha's good arm to help her stand, "we've got to get upstairs." She led the injured woman out of the room carefully, looking around the corner to make certain no further enemies awaited them. But there was nothing in the corridor save the silent bodies of their fallen comrades. "It didn't touch them. Or us."

Tykeisha squeezed her hand slightly. "We need to go before we get cut off. We can figure this out later."

It was always later, Janise thought to herself, her lip twisting in frustration. Her elders did not understand it and did not have the time for it because of this infernal war. Janise's own fears kept her from deciphering any of it for herself. She held back the tears that now wished to come unbidden, a surge of emotion that had somehow been silent until now, and yet again there was no time. She forced her head to nod, a broken, halting expression that seemed to take every remaining ounce of her strength.

They worked their way up the corridor and then to the stairs as quietly as possible. When it seemed a clear path up to the next defense position, they half ran, half hobbled their way up. They reached the top, finding themselves in the welcome arms of two scouts that had detected them. "What happened?" one of them asked.

"A squad of Lordillians must have slipped through somewhere," Tykeisha grunted. They were taken down the hall to the waiting group of soldiers and a medic who sat them down and began to check them out. "They wiped out the entire group stationed on our living quarter level. They're taken care of, but I don't know how many more might be behind them."

"You finished them off yourselves?"

Janise's eyes turned nervously to Tykeisha, a feeling she couldn't quite explain washing over her. Suddenly the thought of being some sort of freak to the others was a horrible fear that she could not bare.

The woman returned the look, but nodded reassuringly. "We took care of the stragglers and escaped."

"Go and check it out," the sergeant said, waving the scouts back down the hall. "Get these two up to the bridge as soon as they're fit to be moved."

"I'm alright," Tykeisha muttered. "I've got to get the admiral's daughter out of harm's way. Nobody expected forces to reach where we were as fast as they did."

"So much for false senses of security," Janise said with a smile she could barely muster.

Lise and Bevanne watched the eerie lights and shapes of the hyperspacial vortex become shattered by the exit that formed in front of their cruiser as they crashed through it into normal space. There was a collective gasp as the view port was filled by the sight of entire fleets of Lordillian ships hovering in the stars over the naked orb of Grellion. "Battle stations," the captain ordered. "Prepare to engage."

Lise turned to look up at Captain Taneere's command platform. "Sir, I need a ship. Something that can cut through as fast and as unnoticed as possible to get these elements down to the citadel."

"Request denied," Taneere said, a scowl briefly passing over the ridges of the Segavian's features. "I can spare no craft while we're so outnumbered."

"Captain, if you don't let me get these crystals down to the planet's surface, then the whole battle will be a moot point; the admiral and the citadel he's defending will be laid waste without them."

The captain only gave her the briefest glance while still tapping commands into her controls. "Councilor Bevanne?"

"She's telling the truth, captain. The nature of her mission was to retrieve these elements in the hopes that they would somehow restore power to the citadel's systems."

Taneere scowled again. "Very well. Get below to the flight deck and be ready to leave immediately. I'll have a ship standing by."

"Thank you, captain." Lise wasted no times on goodbyes, simply dashing through the exit and into a lift to take her down to the hanger bays. Once there she found the bags of Grellion elements already being loaded onto a *Bat* fighter. "Who's piloting?" she asked aloud.

"Me," said a young lieutenant, stepping forward. He gave her an obvious once-over and, finding no rank insignia on Lise's strange, skin-tight outfit, decided to salute just to be certain. "May I ask why I've been pulled away from my squadron, ma'am?"

"I'm commander Lise, sub-lieutenant, and its so you can help me save the admiral's forces on the planet below, providing she's fast," she said, motioning to the fighter above them, "and providing you're one of the best pilots we've got."

"That sounds like a challenge, commander," the pilot said, still at attention.

"This is a challenge. We die, the Coalition dies with us."

The pilot only looked more determined at that. "Then I'm your man, commander."

"Then get her warmed. We leave now."

"Need a blade?" The voice was Durant's. He had been with Lise when Bevanne's transport had suddenly swooped down to pick her up from Moonshau, and he had opted to come along, since then apparently waiting in the now frantic hanger bay of the battleship.

"It will be dangerous," Lise told the smiling courtesan. "Once we fly through an entire fleet of Lordillian ships both up here and in the airspace below, we have to somehow get this ship inside the base on the surface, then possibly fight our way through any hostile forces that may try to stop us from getting the elements to the right locations, deep inside a structure that's nearly eight miles wide."

Durant's smile barely wavered. "Anything for a beautiful and fearless lady, my Lady. I might as well earn my keep while I'm here."

Lise nodded. "Very well, welcome aboard. Now why don't you go use that charm somewhere its effective, like rustling up a few soldiers to accompany us down there."

Durant bowed and quickly turned away, running over to where a group of soldiers stood attending their gear. Lise dragged the satchels full of the Grellion crystals towards the *Bat*'s ramp, the short plank between the front landing gear and the tail gun providing a rather steep angle to have to move the heavy bags up. She decided to wait for a hand, regarding the sleek ship for a moment. She found herself hoping that its advances, such as the heavy tail cannon, would be enough. It was an either manned or cockpit-controlled gun, mounted on a swiveling pod at the end of the long tail that curled underneath the craft, a feature unique in the Coalition fleet to the *Bat* fighter. Soon the small group was inside it's cramped interior, awaiting liftoff out into the battle that had already begun to rage around them. "Hang on," came the pilot's voice from the seat above them. "We're cleared for our run."

The fighter shot forward into space. Lise was suddenly a ball of excitement and anxiety, her fate for the moment in someone else's hands. She had to look though the tiny window next to her space and watch what was happening just for the briefest moment to fool herself into thinking she was in control. Their battleship fell away with astonishing speed, and Lise watched as it and its sister ships began to engage the fleet of Lordillian destroyers. Fighters from both sides flew past them, each trying to knock the other from the heavens. In the distance the inky black of space was peppered by small bursts of light followed by blossoming explosions. Then the blackness gradated away, slowly replaced by the pale blues of the Grellion atmosphere and the fire and turbulence of their ship buffeting its way down. The *Bat* fighter dove down, then began to slide back and forth through the sky as it slowed, reducing the hull's temperature after the fast descent before resuming its course to the planet below.

The plains running the length of Grellion's immediate surface gave way to mountains, and soon the landscape seemed familiar to Lise. She knew they were closing in on the citadel's position. Her heart quickly sank, though, when she spotted the cluster of Lordillian battle cruisers hovering over the base, awaiting the signal to wipe it off the face of the planet. Surprisingly very little smoke arose from the enormous structure, and she was hopeful despite the odds that they might be in time.

"Hang on, we've been spotted." Lise and her makeshift team could hear the high-pitched whine of the pilot's computer telling him there was a lock on. The whole craft rotated ninety degrees and then slid sideways, down through the air. Angry bolts of energized plasma from a pursuing Lordillian fighter sliced through the atmosphere where they had just been. Then came the sounds of their own underside tail-gunner returning fire,

314

followed by a far off series of thuds. The gunner gave a whoop of excitement. "He's so gone," the pilot confirmed with a smirk.

Lise looked again, noting with alarm how close they were coming to the hulking wide masses of enemy battleships. "We're going to be in battery range any second," she called up to the lieutenant.

"Its the only way to punch through, commander. We're a target no matter what. I was going to ask you where we might land."

"Give me a COM line out," Lise said, pulling a headset out from a small locker and plugging into a jack just below the pilot's seat. "Nest One, this is Eagle, come in, please."

"We read you, Eagle," came an officer's voice from the ground below. "Go ahead."

"We're directly over your position and under fire in a single fighter. Need immediate docking."

"Negative, Eagle, wolves are at the door."

"Patch admiral Jo'seph through, now," Lise yelled, all patience gone. "This is a code gold emergency."

"Stand by, Eagle."

There was a moment of radio silence; the time filled by the sounds of incoming blasts from the Lordillian cruisers that they were even now attempting to fly past. "Commander," came Jo'seph's voice, the echoes of a battle garbling the signal he was trying to send. "Is that you?"

"Admiral, I have the package," Lise said quickly, "but I need immediate entrance into that citadel."

"I've been apprised of your situation, Lise. Head strait for the base of the giant hanger door. I'll make certain they get you in somehow."

"See you soon, admiral."

"Glad to hear it," came Jo'seph's relieved reply.

Lise called up to the pilot. "Head for the hanger door, the largest building on the right. Strait for the base of it."

"And then what?" the lieutenant asked nervously.

"Then hope to the gods that it opens before we crash into it."

The fighter sped towards the soil encrusted door, the giant wall soon filling their entire forward view. All the while blasts of enemy fire flashed all around them, rocking the ship back and forth. A series of rounds

315

impacted against the left wing, tipping the craft and eliciting a cry from all of those aboard. The whining sounds of their dive towards the citadel's enormous building became a deafening cacophony when combined with the explosions that chased them. The *Bat* fighter shuddered as it fell through the air. Lise's grip on the bulkhead above her became viselike, and she leaned towards the viewing port again, watching with increased alarm as the ground rushed up to greet them. She leaned back against the small piece of glass, gasping in terror when she saw how close they were getting to the still-closed gate. "We're not gonna make it," she breathed, clutching one of the satchels full of the Grellion elements to her breast, ignoring the weight.

Lise held her breath, bracing herself now with both hands yet unable to tear her eyes away from the structure that loomed before them, even as the ship's wings passed so close to the ground beneath them that they stirred the long grasses. Then something happened that made the entire group of people caught within the *Bat* fighter to jump; a crack, like the clap of thunder, bellowed forth from the building before them. Lise couldn't believe her eyes even as the giant door, its top now beyond her line of sight, began to open. Her fingers bit into the steel they held as she stared at the black maw now waiting to swallow them, hoping only that it had opened far enough to allow them entry. An instant later she had her answer as the craft flew right over a squad of Lordillian soldiers and through the opening into the darkness beyond.

The *Bat*'s nose lurched up, the ship just barely clearing the top of a parked Coalition transport before it finally dropped its speed and circled around, landing roughly in the echoing chamber. Lise finally found that she could breathe, and her lungs gasped to life at last. "Holy shit, we made it," she cried, and the men with her called their praise to the pilot even as they stood and slung their packs over their shoulders and picked up their rifles. Within moments they were prepared to exit via the ship's belly mounted boarding plank. "Ready?"

"Wait!" There was a new tone of worry in the pilot's voice, and Lise knew that they had another problem. "I can't open the *bat's* bay door."

"Why not?"

The loud rattling of the tail gunner below them answered her question. "Because then the gunner will be blocked from engaging that squad of Lordillian troops that got in before the hanger door closed again." The gun squealed forth another series of rounds, only to be answered by a returning group of blasts that smashed into their hull.

"We're trapped in here," Lise droned. "We all go out the canopy we'll be picked off one by one."

"Can't we lift off again?" Durant asked. "Turn the ship at an angle to allow the gunner a clean line of sight while we disembark?"

"There's no time," Lise said. "We go now; do or die."

Chapter Eighteen

There are few battles of such importance and possible
finality in the history of modern war craft that are so
sudden and so unknown to the universe around them
- at least while they were taking place - as the battle for
the Grellion citadel.
Coalition and Triialon
- Dr. W. H. Redfield

"Good thing you've got back up," the lieutenant called from the
cockpit, "or we'd all be fried."

"What?"

More noise of far off blaster fire could be heard, but without the
resounding thuds against the *bat's* sides. It was joined by another burst
from the tail gun. Someone else was in the hangar, Lise could tell, and
they were shooting at the Lordillians.

"Go, now," the gunner called up, "while there's an opening."

The boarding plank fell, and the troops moved out, firing at the
closing group of Lordillians as they stomped down the steep grade. They
jumped from the ship to let its hatch close again, allowing the tail cannon
behind them a clear shot once more while they ran for cover. Lise caught a
glimpse of their support before ducking a shot; Sub-Lieutenant Zhade and
Lise's strike team were pinned near a doorway leading from the hanger's
interior to the next section of the citadel. Despite this, they had laid down
enough suppressing fire to allow Lise and her men to exit the *Bat*. She
smiled, hope finally allowing itself to creep into her soul. *Hell yeah*, she
thought. "Grenades," she ordered, a new sense of urgency overtaking the
cold fear of battle.

Even as the Lordillian squad was being decimated by the fire now
coming from three fronts, one still managed to break away and try to pick
up the grenades that landed nearby to toss them back. The action was
futile, the resulting blast enveloping the metal killer in a flash of smoke
and fire before fracturing the cases of the rest of its squad, felling them all.
The shooting stopped.

"Clear," came McCarty's voice, and Lise looked over at Zhade and her familiar team and smiled.

"Well timed, lieutenant. I'm grateful." She stood, checking her blaster while her shipmates sounded off. The two groups of soldiers met near the door and Lise grasped Zhade's hand after he saluted. "Where's the admiral?"

"Holding the line. Lordillian troops have infiltrated and we've been hard pressed to keep them at bay."

"Its paramount we get these crystal elements to Sardeece," she told him.

"You'll need me to navigate through our booby traps in any case," he said. "Just give the word, commander."

"Move out!" Lise waited as Zhade opened the door leading into the citadel's interior and sent men ahead before she signaled the march.

The corridors at this far end of the structure were dark and quiet, no signs of life or Lordillians, though Lise knew Coalition forces had been down it recently when they had left their ships in the hanger. Zhade and the others brought Lise and her makeshift team up to speed, telling them of the siege and the efforts of the small Coalition force to thwart their advances. The Coalition ships had been almost completely cannibalized for weapons and supplies, and those preparations had been all that had kept them defended this long. Hobson mentioned the news that admiral Jo'seph had led the defenders since early in the fighting, battling alongside his soldiers to hold the lines. The others took up the praise, talking of how strong a moment it had been to hear such events. Lise asked what news there was of admiral Jay'salan.

"He met up with the *Pulsar* to lead any Lordillian ships that came this way out of the system," Zhade said quietly, guiding them into the next group of hallways. "We're pretty certain he bought us a day or so, but I don't think anyone's heard from him since."

"Gods," Lise breathed.

A scout signaled a halt. There was movement ahead, and Lise and the others prepared for the fight to come. She looked back briefly over her teams, silently making certain the satchels were still slung over her compatriot's shoulders. Durant was an odd addition to their group, his strange clothes and elegant sword out of place next to the armored soldiers despite the standard issue rifle he carried in the other hand. The scout's signals came back; Lordillians were near, cutting them off from their next intersection. Lise ordered the squad to fan out and find positions. They would wait and ambush the roving group of androids. Hopefully there were no more than the twenty five the scout had so far counted.

The wait was short; the Lordillians rounded the next corner and came instantly into range. "Fire," Lise commanded, and their rifles opened up in unison, fully automatic chatter suddenly filling the hall. The first round of blasts found their marks easily, slamming into the lead machines and shattering them in fiery explosions. The next group of Lordillians answered the call with a hail of their own fire, and suddenly the battle was joined. The enemy rushed into the corridor the Coalition soldiers occupied, shooting some of their score at point blank range and then engaging others with their razor-like, steel claws. Men screamed, while others had not the chance to make a sound before they fell to the hot floor, dead, with vacant eyes. Lise ducked a blast from a Lordillian that had closed in on her, then moved aside to avoid the following swipe from its metallic gauntlet, shooting a pulse of rounds off into the thing's chest before moving on. She looked around, peering through the smoke that now filled the hall to try and see how her squad fared. She caught site of Zhade, moving ahead with Hobson who was leading a group of five Lordillians away. Behind her she spied two more from her team, and along side them was Durant. The courtesan stepped forward when a Lordillian moved to take him, his blade flashing out with surprising agility in the cramp space and easily removing the enemy's hand before following suit with its head.

An explosion suddenly shook the corridors ahead, the sound coming from the direction Zhade had just been going, and she feared that Lordillian artillery had been brought against him. Anger threatened to overwhelm her, but she continued to concentrate on the task at hand, dispatching each target that came into her sights with extreme prejudice and felling each metal giant with practiced speed and skill. The tide seemed to have turned back in their favor at last. "Regroup," Lise called, and through the haze of battle her fighters returned to her. "See to the wounded."

"Where's the Lieutenant?" McCarty asked.

"Here," came the answer, Zhade helping a limping Hobson back down the corridor towards them. "We managed to lead that group towards a booby trap I knew was just ahead, but the private here got caught in the blast."

"I'll be alright," Hobson complained. "Its not bad."

"Where do we stand?" Lise asked, trying to make a head count despite the smoke.

"Five dead, two wounded," Durant answered. He had discarded the rifle in the firefight, opting for the sword in the close quarter battle. He picked a fresh one up from a body, shouldering the weapon with indifference.

"That just makes the eight of us," Lise scowled. "How much further is it?"

"We can bypass most of the real fighting from here," Zhade said, wrapping a bandage around Hobson's leg while the young man rested. "With luck the majority of any further roving squads will still be on the other side of the trap line. There's a stair case ahead that takes us down to the engineering levels, but its going to be a long walk. From there it's a straight shot to Sardeece."

"And whoever's in our way down there." Lise put a fresh energy clip in her rifle and checked her sidearm. She looked back at her remaining team, noting with a renewed sense of urgency the slight glow coming from within the satchels the troops carried. She stared a moment, realizing that the elements had not been glowing earlier.

They were getting close. "Are we ready? Right, move out."

Admiral Jo'seph backed away from the fireball that lit up the intersection in front of him and raised an arm against the heat. His forces had finally been pushed back to the final lines of defense before the command decks, but he had made the Lordillian invaders pay for each step, corridor by corridor. For the most part their attackers were still being funneled towards them by the traps laid at the other cross sections and by

323

the servitors they could bring in for added strength, but occasionally a surprise attack from a flanking position had caught the Coalition forces off guard. Each time the odds became harder to overcome and the amount of blasted bodies and trampled servitor robots got too high they would fall back again. The gradual retreat had brought them at last to the heavily armed and almost entirely fresh group of troops they had just joined, defending the hall above the living quarters from guarded positions with small arms and the remaining artillery brought from the transport ships. Jo'seph ducked behind some cover midway down the hall, avoiding the next barrage. He popped up when the shooting stopped, lining up his sights and firing a burst of energy at his target. The Lordillian at the far end of the corridor fell, sporting several smoking holes in its chest panels. The admiral smiled before pulling back further, letting a soldier take the relieved position.

"Admiral," came Tykeisha's voice over the COM, "you'd better get up here."

Jo'seph's brow creased with concern. "Janise?"

"She's fine, but there's a new group of Lordillian ships entering the atmosphere."

"I'm on my way up," he said hoarsely. The earlier news that Lise was in the base with the missing elements had been uplifting, but time was running out. The fate of the Galactic Coalition would be decided within the next few minutes, not hours, and the enemy had just called in reinforcements. He patted the captain's shoulder as he passed, sneaking through the fortifications to get out of the battle zone and up to the bridge. He wound his way up the stairs, trying to ignore his aches and pains while changing frequencies on his COM device. The unanswered call to commander Lise and her forces only increased his worry, but he knew there was any number of possibilities as to their fates.

"Admiral on the bridge," came the call from near the door as Jo'seph entered.

Tykeisha looked at his strained features with deep concern. "You're hurt?"

"What? No." He scratched his beard. "Well, yes, but its a good kinda hurt. What horror has befallen us now?"

Jo'seph followed Tykeisha to the windows, giving his daughter a brief hug along the way. "They've just been spotted visually," she said.

"How many?" the admiral asked, all humor gone from his facade.

"Thirteen more ships have joined the three already above us," she answered. "Bevanne's cruisers are still engaged with two more in orbit, but we think they've destroyed four others. But its that big one that's got us jumpy," she commented, pointing to the group of descending shapes hovering in the atmosphere. "Scans indicate it may actually be three Lordillian cruisers joined as one flagship, combining shield power as well as firepower."

"I doubt they'd simply lose patience and destroy the whole site," Jo'seph mused, "so the question still begs 'why combine three cruisers?'"

"Could it be Chebonka himself, sir?" an officer asked.

"A fair guess. I wouldn't put it past him to want to see this." Jo'seph again resisted the urge to run coarse hands down a weathered face. "As soon as you can get confirmation of what's aboard that ship and what they're up to, let me know. Let me know of all developments immediately. Tykeisha, keep trying to reach commander Lise. She should be nearly to Sardeece by now."

"Where are you going, Daddy?" Janise asked.

"Back to the lines. We have to hold as long as we can."

The ambush had come just before the staircases leading down into the depths of the citadel. An advance unit of Lordillians had made it through to that point and lay waiting for other forces to back up their advance. Instead they had pounced on Lise's team in a surprise attack, forcing the group to dive for cover and defend themselves as best they could. The moment had become desperate quickly, for they had all been separated, left to fend for themselves from their own vantage points. Bolts of searing light cut through the stale air in every direction, causing smoke and noise and death.

"Sardeece, come in," Lise yelled into her COM device from the corner she had managed to retreat to. "Do you read? We're above your position and taking heavy fire, over." There was no answer.

A blast knocked McCarty off his feet, throwing him into the open. Lise gasped and tried to provide covering fire, but she knew it would only be a matter of moments before he took another hit. She gritted her teeth, preparing to dive into the open battleground to help her subordinate to safety, but out of the haze came the form of Zhade, springing to action faster than she could have managed at that point. The lieutenant grabbed McCarty by one arm, dragging the dazed soldier to safety. The time they were exposed was minimal, but it was enough for a shot to catch Zhade in the back. The blast threw him onto his face. He lay, unmoving, beneath Hobson and two men where they tried to provide more covering fire.

"No." Lise could see the blood collecting on Zhade uniform even from where she sat. "Regroup!" Lise bolted from her position, making strait for Hobson and the others when a Lordillian jumped out of nowhere, bringing its blaster to bear on her.

"Look out!" It was Durant who saved her, slashing out with his blade to behead the machine before it could fire on her. Lise returned the favor as she rolled, letting fly a group of shots down the corridor to strike the two Lordillians that were about to take advantage of Durant's moment of exposure. She completed her run, diving behind the next wall where Zhade lay bleeding.

The sub-lieutenant groaned when Lise touched him. "Shit," she hissed.

"W-where's Hero?" Zhade asked. Blood spilled from his lips, sticking to his face and the cold floor it was pressed down upon.

Lise thought about Hero, left behind on Moonshau to fight that madman. "He's coming," was all she could say.

Zhade smiled. "I was afraid to ask. He was the only thing I really dared to believe in." The newly promoted young man coughed and sputtered, then his eyes rolled up in their sockets as his body shuddered. He was gone.

"Damn," Lise whispered, tears gathering in her eyes.

"We can't hold here much longer, commander," came the urgent voice of a corporal.

326

"Damn," she said again. She tried to gather her wits, put aside her fear and emotion, but suddenly the stakes felt overwhelming. "Can we fall back? Find another way down?"

There was an explosion from the Lordillian side of the hallway. Two of the large machines flew into pieces, preceding the smoke that then bellowed out of their positions. The other visible Lordillians seemed confused, but continued to pour fire towards the only targets they could detect: Lise's diminished strike team. Another explosion rocked the corridor, destroying another handful, and then another. The few remaining Lordillians left their cover, coming out into the open hall to advance on Lise's group. Lise's squad quickly took up the call, bringing rifles to cheekbones and opening fire on the walking machines, taking them down quickly. Suddenly there was no one left to fight.

Six of the small Grellion servitor robots waltzed out of the smoke, each carrying blasters and grenades while they searched for any remaining targets. One motioned to Lise specifically, waving them in its direction. Lise almost laughed, wiping her nose on the back of her glove. Sardeece had gotten her message after all. "I wish Zhade could've seen that," she said with a sniffle. "Let's get everyone downstairs, people. Double-time it."

A team of Coalition troops met them down one flight, pushing aside more Lordillians from the group that had attacked Lise's force. They had been forced to make their stand there and send the servitors ahead to assist her strike team. The rag-tag group and their casualties made their way down together from there. Sardeece and a small garrison of soldiers, scientists and robots were waiting for them down at the base of the stairs. The sight of Sardeece and his strange prosthetics standing with open arms and a smile was mildly shocking, despite having been present for his 'transformation'. She had been around him in one way or another for years aboard the Coalition ships and shipyards, so it was still odd to see him as the mechni-prophet.

"Commander, you are amazing," Sardeece said, taking her hand and shaking it vigorously, all the while looking right past her to the satchels full of Grellion crystalline elements her troops were setting on the floor. "It would seem communications in your area were being jammed.

327

Fortunately the Citadel's Intelligence was able to forward your call to my mind." His smile faded. "But where is the Triialon?"

"He bought our escape so I could bring you these," Lise said, stepping aside as the scientist knelt down to inspect the strange orbs, now glowing a bright, vigorous blue being so close to their proper place in the universe. "Now I hope you know what to do with them."

"Amazing." He just stared at the few stones in his hands.

Lise cleared her throat, trying to get his attention. "Hero has already tested one of them, so we know they're the real deal. They certainly weren't glowing like that before, though."

"Really?" Sardeece asked, turning away from them at last.

Lise explained to him briefly the chain of events that had led to the elements ending up at the temple on Moonshau, all the while a group of servitor robots were unpacking the crystals. She explained Hero's theories regarding the essence of their power, noting the evidence of their renewed inner strength the closer they had brought the elements to the center of the Grellion citadel.

"Amazing," Sardeece said again. "The further they were from where they belonged and the more time that passed since their purpose was at hand, the duller and more subdued the elements became. They became silent with age. Now they swell with power and reason; a collective of energy as well as the consciousness of Grellion past." The scientist opened a large machine, a giant door weighing tons swinging easily on perfect yet ancient hinges. The interior looked like a carved puzzle; lines cut through the surface of the two open halves of the insides, like a giant circuit board digging troughs along from one end to another. In the center lay the perfect cup to hold a crystal sphere, and Sardeece placed the element in his hand into the socket. Instantly power flowed through the completed lines, and the machine came to life. "Home," he muttered, watching it with relief and awe. "Power; energy from the very core of the planet, un-dammed at last and allowed after eons to pass harmlessly through the citadel and bring it finally back to life."

The other machines nearby were coming to life as well, Grellion robots placing more of the crystals in them, while more still were being taken to the lines of computers and other apparatus in the next rooms.

"*You have found them,*" came the voice of the Citadel's Artificial Intelligence in Lise's mind, and she wondered if they had all heard it.

Jo'seph pulled the wounded man out of the fire quickly, and dragged him back to the rear guards. Tykeisha was waiting for him, a strange mix of emotion evident in her tired but pretty features. "What is it?"

"I'm not sure," Tykeisha said. "Some of the systems are just, well, coming to life." The admiral followed her back up to the bridge, asking her just what the hell she meant. "Systems that have been dormant since our arrival are now working. We're trying to figure out just what they do, exactly, but waiting for the servitor robots to translate while we're all busy at our posts is getting frustrating. My guess is that Lise made it; Sardeece must have the elements."

Jo'seph hurried to the observation windows, noting with alarm as he came closer to the expansive view the large number of Lordillian battle cruisers that hung in the air less than a mile away. The ships were preparing to launch landing craft that would bring thousands more Lordillian shock troops to invade the Base. "What about the main cannon and shields?"

"Nothing yet, sir."

The flagship hovered closer still, and Jo'seph found himself squinting, trying to see across the distance into the eyes of Chebonka himself, if he did indeed stand at the front of that monstrosity. A claxon began to sound, breaking the admiral's reverie, and drop ships began to pour out of the bottom of each of the newly arrived battle cruisers.

"Did you sound that alarm?" he asked the executive officer.

"No, sir. Must be automatic."

The clear expanse of sky between the front of the enormous citadel and the enemy ships that waited before it was suddenly broken by a thousand blasts of light that crossed the distance and slammed into the drops ships as they fell. Each of the craft carrying their cargo of Lordillian invading forces exploded, showering the grasslands below with debris.

"Well, that's something," Jo'seph said, and found himself genuinely smiling for the first time in what must have been days.

329

"Auto-guns all over the base's surface are coming to life," Tykeisha reported. "The batteries on the front and top are firing on random enemy targets. Initial reports, and I don't know where this information is coming from, are saying that the accuracy is sixty-seven percent."

"I'll be damned!"

"More drop ships," she said. "A few are getting through and landing troops."

"That's better than all. Are COM frequencies still jammed?"

"Affirmative, sir."

"Keep trying. I want to know if Bevanne's forces are still active as soon as possible. There's a big fleet out there and apparently no way to shoot them down, as yet." A thought struck the admiral, and he nearly slapped himself for not having seen the obvious idea earlier. "And somebody sit down with a servitor robot and a data-pad. Write out whatever conversation with it you need to that gets me a message through to Sardeece. I want to know what's going on down there."

"I can tell you one thing," Tykeisha said with a smile, sitting down at the COM station now that the tension was beginning to lessen. "The interior security measures are starting to work too. The front line just reported one of the corridors suddenly threw a field around the assailing force of Lordillians."

The admiral's eyebrows went up. "Wow," was all he could say. A shockwave caused the whole room to shake. Jo'seph and the others who were standing fumbled to stay on their feet. The blast was followed by another. "What was that?"

"Sir, the flagship is firing on the citadel's hull-mounted batteries," came a tactical officer's wavering voice. "Its trying to pinpoint them and blow them off the surface of the base, sir."

Tykeisha looked at him, one hand on her communications headset as she listened to the next set of reports coming in. "The auto-guns are returning fire, but drop ships are slipping through the net now because of it."

"The stakes just got raised," the admiral mused, freely raking a hand through his blonde locks.

The sensation of dropping out of the strange hyperspace that Dimensionalizer engines traveled through was beginning to become familiar. Hero ducked back into the cockpit of his ship, watching as normal space suddenly flooded the view with the giant orb of Grellion. Several battleships of both Lordillian and Coalition design faced off, but the immediate advantage in space seemed to have turned in favor of the defenders with the diminished numbers of attacking ships. A Coalition cruiser fired its main gun, the giant beam slicing the closest enemy vessel along its arching topside, ripping it open to space. Debris briefly began to float out as it listed, but quickly its systems failed and the flammable fuels within caught fire. It exploded into a ball of light, further damaging its counterpart that drifted nearby. Hero smiled at the brief victory, knowing full well the fighting below would be much more desperate.

He fastened the clasp of his cloak over his chest, sweeping the flowing cloth over one shoulder plate of his armor. He had tried his best to forget the Triialon armor stored aboard the ship since the Final Battle, but it was not just necessity that had made him begin strapping the ornamented plates back on after all this time. A sense of purpose filled his vision, and he knew a moment of trial and honor approached. He might not survive the coming battle, and his quest might then die with him, but he knew that this was something he must do.

He pulled on his gauntlet, the edge coming over the black under-suit to meet the rest of the armor, when suddenly his eyes glared. Hero smiled at the meaning of this moment. It had taken him years, and yet still he did not fully understand the properties of the Prizm; but he knew now without a doubt that the glowing bracer meant more than the gathering of the Grellion technology below - Chebonka was down there. If he had the chance to face him, the *Sword of Warriors* would be his at last. He fastened on his other gauntlet, marveling for a moment at the swirling patterns cut so exquisitely into the armor's design. He placed a knife in a sheath on one belt, slung a sidearm over another and closed the final buckle on the armor before finally donning the shining helm, letting his hair fall around the collar from beneath its edge. He lowered the faceplate, obscuring his visage behind its blank mask, and stared at himself for a moment through the ominous eye slits in the mirror lining the locker's door. He stood,

331

armored just as that day on Triialon. Its last warrior coming home one final time.

The ship began to shudder, entering the planet's atmosphere as it made its way down to the citadel's coordinates. Hero sat back down in the pilot's seat, taking the ship off autopilot to try and land it amongst the battlefield. He slipped over the mountains, trying to keep low and avoid detection, watching as the sun dipped over the distant horizon. The mountains opened up to the expansive valley where the Grellion Base sat, a fleet of Lordillian warships hovering in the air around it. The clouds and surrounding hills were a strange mix of color. Pinks deepened to purple from the sunset, highlighted by reds and golds from explosions and gunfire.

The Triialon desert flyer dipped even lower, skimming along the grasslands scant inches above the blades. He did not delay detection long, though, for soon many of the weapons above him were trained on him, and Hero found himself fighting to keep the ship airborne. Blasts streamed down on and around the craft, quickly weakening the shields. He tried to increase speed, but the sheer number of guns using his craft for target practice was too much. A shot tipped the left wing into the ground, and it caught in the soft earth, dragging the ship down in a sudden spinning skid. The flyer came to a smoking halt after a few moments, and Hero leapt from the cockpit and back through the ship to disembark, grabbing the small pack with the oversized missing elements and flinging it over his shoulder. By the time his feet hit the ground, the shooting had stopped, but the flyer wouldn't be able to take off again without considerable repairs. He was still on the far side of the buried runway, more than a mile from an entrance to the citadel. He began to make the crossing by foot.

Hero's legs took great strides, running easily across the plains despite the heavy burden he wore. Ahead he could see the figures of Lordillians in the dim light; the rows of synchronized metal soldiers marched down exit platforms from landers and headed for the Coalition base. The batteries on the citadel's surface were firing, which meant that Lise had managed to get in alive and deliver the majority of the elements, but the cruisers above him were beginning to blast those cannons to pieces. He would have to be fast, he knew, so he quickened his pace despite his fatigue, heading strait towards the army that had landed ahead of him.

At last he stopped, still a good distance from the looming base, but no longer directly beneath the fleet. Hero stood upon the battlefield, raising his fist towards the sky. His other hand passed over the glowing Prizm and its embedded crystals, pulling the Triialon sword from within. The energies coalesced into the shape of the sword *Strength*, and he drew the blade out of its mystical sheath. Lightning passed between the two weapons despite the growing distance between them. He lowered the sword's point to the ground while raising his right wrist further. Hero aimed the ancient bracer at the lead ships above him, each a hovering black mass of alloys and power nearly half a mile wide, and each firing on the base with hundreds of batteries. He felt his own power flowing from within, thoughts and emotions melded with training and ancient science as they gathered within the metals and crystals of the Prizm. The glow became a flash, and the combined force was unleashed, spewing forth a wide arc of energy every color of the spectrum, the shot stretching instantly from the Artifact to the ship above. The vessel exploded instantly, the shrapnel striking many of the other close ships. Parts fell from the sky in clumps, but nothing larger than a small house remained.

Hero's aim turned to the next craft within range, and the power stretched out again, a flashing ray of light that slammed into the cruiser and cracked it in half. It fell to the base of the mountains in a funnel of fire. Another, and then another, each time his power brining down an entire battleship and silencing its guns forever, yet each time diminishing the Prizm's strength. The next target was further away than the others, and Hero's shot only seared off most of the underside hull, laying the superstructure bare, but it would be enough to down the ship. The fleet was in disarray, moving away from its exploding sisters. Finally each ship lifted away, halting its reign of death.

Through the giant clouds of belching smoke came the menacing shape of the Lordillian flagship, the odd site of three battleships somehow joined. There was little or no obvious damage to the craft, and a giant forward platform seemed to be open to the sky, covered apparently by a combined force field. Chebonka, creator of the Lordillian race stood upon that platform. Yet even as Hero spotted the evil form from so far away the flagship opened fire on him. Superheated plasma strafed the ground where Hero was standing, but he dodged the blasts, taking only minor residual hits. Hero countered with the Triialon sword. Slashing at the air above, the power came as a flash of light; like the briefest extension of the blade itself, yet yards wide and crossing the distance between he and the craft. The brief arc of energy struck the vessel mid-ship with a resounding thud. The Lordillian flagship dipped, its engines and shields flickering and then failing. The behemoth fell, descending in what seemed for a moment like slow motion, then suddenly it nose-dived and crashed into the ground with a deafening roar and resulting explosion. The quake along with the debris and chunks of dirt and dust it threw into the air slammed Hero aside like a pile of bricks, and he fell at last, buried beneath falling chunks of smoldering cruiser.

Chapter Nineteen

I too know the legends of the Triialon. Jay' and I both grew up with those stories. At the height of their power, clad all in armor, the Triialon were the most terrifying force for good ever known. No blaster could fell them, no blade could cut them, no army could stand against them. Now the last of their kind stood in that armor on what may be the final battlefield for freedom… fighting for us.
Personal journal
-Admiral Jo'seph Bel'ov

A metal hand pulled itself free from the twisted steel that surrounded it. It pushed aside the rubble encasing its arm and then worked to free its other limbs. Hero arose from the dust and smoke, battered but not beaten, though he was uncertain how long he had laid unconscious. His helmet was gone, lost somewhere under the debris, and the now-howling winds caused by the raging battle and the Grellion evening whipped his hair furiously. He stood, making certain that the case with the Grellion elements was still fastened to his armor. Night had nearly fallen, but the twilight was brightened further by the moons above and by the floodlights the Lordillian cruisers were throwing on the target of the citadel. Explosions both distant and near could be heard following flashes of the still raging battle. The citadel's cannons continued to pick off enemy troops making their way into the base, while the occasional one would be destroyed by a precise Lordillian shot that would hit its mark.

Battleships were again clustering together, filling the sky near where Hero stood. He could see their underside bays opening, preparing to launch even more drop ships. He needed to get inside the citadel quickly. As it was the odds were not in the warrior's favor. He checked the Prizm and the sword, *Strength*, finding neither to have had a chance to recharge due to his own weakened state. It had taken much to get this far.

Hero turned, about to resume his run towards the base entrance, when something behind him caught his eye. Back at the site of the crashed flagship, a group of dusty Lordillian troops of varying colors worked diligently on digging something out of the wreckage. Nearby, a dome of flicking energy peeked up from beneath even more rubble and figures moved around inside what must surely be a still-functioning force field.

Chebonka.

Chebonka and the sword were somewhere in that smoking heap, possibly trapped behind his own protective shield wall. Hero's fatigue vanished, replaced by the quest. The hollow feeling of age and loss suddenly swelled with meaning and strength. Even as he began running towards the site, he could see the force field fail at last, and a Lordillian help its leader from the pit that had nearly been their grave.

As the figure of Chebonka rose to stand atop the wreckage of his flagship, Hero crossed the distance. The one they called the 'Android Born of Man' was a hulking mass of gleaming metal, strange angles and sharp edges jutted out over twisting cables and smooth panels, and a spiked glove held the long blade of an Artifact of the Twelve.

A war cry in the Triialon tongue escaped Hero's lips, and he held his own still-charged sword high, closing in for the kill. He jumped, soaring the last few feet to his enemy through the air, his hair and torn cape whipping in the strong winds while the blasts of late-reacting Lordillians soared past his head. Chebonka brought the weapon he gripped up to block, and the two swords of Triialon clashed for the first time in recorded history. The power was unexpected; a flash of lightning sparked off of the impact that radiated a shock wave, sending both combatants reeling. Hero spun, preparing to swing again, but instead found himself defending against the surprising wave of power that had been flung at him. Chebonka had unlocked the abilities of the Artifact, firing blasts of raw energy from his stolen Triialon blade with ease!

The damage to the ancient lost Artifact was worse than Hero had suspected; no being not of Triialon blood should be able to wield that weapon's power. That miscalculation had nearly cost Hero his life.

Hero caught each blast on his own blade, gripping the hilt with both hands and using it channel the energy as well as deflect. Chebonka's mechanical voice came from behind his angular mask with its slit-eyes and metallic cowl. "Now I wield the power of Triialon!" He advanced as he spoke, the language a guttural dialect, similar to many Hero had known but with tones and origins hinting at a lesser upbringing. This man had been trash even before he made himself this disgusting creation. Hero's rage flamed higher, burning away the amazement he'd felt at this initial demonstration of Chebonka's new abilities. "You shall not have the Artifact, Hero. The new order of Lordillian shall sweep away the old, and I shall become master of all life and death. The Universe will finally know logic and conformity, or it will perish beneath my boot heel!"

Even as Chebonka moved closer, loosing more of the out-of-control energy with each step, the nearest Lordillians fired their own rifles. Most of the bolts ricocheted off of the Triialon armor, and what shots did get through were ignored by Hero; the pain was put aside and the inconvenience disregarded. "You do not own that sword, Chebonka," Hero said with vehemence. "You wield its awesome power like an errant child and its reaction shows just how unbalanced you are." He chanced a look, again getting his bearings of the field while waiting for his chance to go back on the offensive. Above him the Lordillian battle cruisers in all their amazing girth closed over the battleground. Beyond lay the encrusted shell of the Grellion citadel; already coming back to life after eons of sleep, it would be home to the new masters of justice – but only if this battle could be won.

"My people have a saying," Hero smiled. "'Those who do evil must be stopped from hurting again – those that take must be punished.'" Hero watched every move his enemy made, studying the way this strange creature and its mesh of mechanical logic and blind anger moved. "' The penalties for evil are final and exact.'" Hero quoted, waiting as each moment brought the sword once called 'Justice' ever closer. He brought himself up to his full height, grasping Strength *and waiting to thrust again, standing proudly and ready for the kill. "I am Hero, last of the Triialon, strongest of that race and the doom of all that is vile.* Now you will know true despair, for I am the light."

The distance was closed again at last, and Hero stepped in to engage the Lordillian leader sword against sword, attacking before the next wave of energy could erupt from the glowing blade. Again the two weapons flashed with the impact, but both warriors held their ground, even while the wreckage and bare field around them began to ignite under the terrible waves of the Triialon artifacts' combined strength. Multi-hued lightning and sparks danced between the weapons and shot out in random spikes as the battle was joined, and both swung away with all their might. Each deflected the other's blow with agility and speed, then clashed again, making certain neither could step away long enough to get off a shot.

Finally the series of strikes ended, Hero sidestepping a swing from Chebonka and kicking the metal figure's legs out from beneath him. The android fell hard, turning to make certain he didn't fall upon his own sword. The Triialon warrior twisted and brought down his blade with a mighty stroke, severing the left arm Chebonka had instinctively brought up to guard against the next attack. The forearm and gauntlet separated, falling away in a shower of sparks and unraveling metals. Chebonka continued to roll, and Hero's completed swing only bit into the ground where his opponent had just been. Noise of rage and agony buzzed from the audio slits in Chebonka's helm, a sound akin only to a scream. Stolen sword still in hand, Chebonka got to his feet. Hero lashed out, severing a portion of Chebonka's chest panel from his body. Chebonka fell again, but sliced at Hero's open guard as he staggered. The pain and anger had only fueled Chebonka's fight, causing a surge of energy to radiate from *Justice* that nearly slammed Hero off of his feet.

Lordillian troopers that had been slowly advancing during the battle suddenly surrounded their master and began dragging him away. Meanwhile, those that had flanked the duel opened fire again, forcing Hero back.

A waiting Lordillian drop ship seized the opportunity to sweep down from where it had been, hovering for the last few moments above its leader's struggle. It positioned itself in the path of the retreating form of Chebonka, opening a hatch and preparing to pick him up. Hero staggered, dodging and deflecting the suppressing fire coming from the wall of Lordillian soldiers that had gathered, quickly calculating his options. The Prizm and the Sword retained little of their charged power, and while he knew he might get the troops between he and his real target with the next blast, he couldn't be certain the energy would carry through to destroy Chebonka and the transport. That would leave him with little or no power to face the army that still lay between he and the desperate defenders inside the base. It would all have been for nothing if the citadel fell into the hands of the Lordillians, yet he was so close to at last retrieving at least one missing part of his past.

He instead turned away, facing the future and the lives he knew deep within that only he could save. He did not have to look to know that the drop ship had successfully picked up its injured master and his stolen blade and even now flew away to freedom.

"Admiral," came the excited voice of Tykeisha from the corner where she sat with the Grellion servitor robot. "I've got commander Lise on, well, on the line."

Jo'seph pulled himself away from the viewing port where he had stood watching the battle. From the moment a technician had called out the word "LOOK!" in utter amazement, he and many of the others had been rooted to the spot, watching with wonder as two titans faced each other in single combat. Hero had nearly killed Chebonka in the fight, he could tell that much, but the strange warrior had been forced back, and was last seen heading towards the besieged citadel. Even during that legendary struggle, Jo'seph was forced to tear his eyes away to watch the number of enemy battleships increase as even more fell from space. He assumed many had orbited before their descent, bypassing Bevanne's small fleet, but he could not be certain; the Coalition forces in space may have already been shot down.

"You've established communications?" the admiral asked, coming to stand over the kneeling woman and the idle servitor.

"Confirmed," she nodded. "That's Lise alright." Tykeisha pointed to a message appearing in a holographic font, hovering just over a small panel mounted on the robot's arm. "The servitor's acting as a translator. Just tell it what you want to say, and it sends it to the servitor Commander Lise and Mister Sardeece are using, and they see it as text like this. You were right; the A.I.'s are a sort of hive mind, so they're not affected by the Lordillian jamming."

"What's their status?"

"They've successfully delivered a large number of the missing elements to the systems in engineering. Main power restored, systems functioning… They're trying to find some way to bring anything more than basic shields and weapons online, but thus far are having problems."

"Tell them to rig whatever they have to," Jo'seph said. "We need those shields. We need something."

A soldier had come to stand at attention next to the admiral, waiting patiently to give his report. Finally acknowledged, the young officer never dropped his salute, speaking quickly and nervously. "Sir, the Lordillians are sending more troops into the citadel. The base auto-defenses are holding them at bay now that the booby traps are exhausted, and most of the forces within the citadel seem to be taken care of…"

"But its only a matter of time until they break back in and overwhelm us. Yes, private, I get the picture. Tell the captain to be prepared for another assaults, but to hold position and let the auto-defenses handle the front lines."

"Sir." The young officer rigidly snapped out of salute and marched off.

The moment to moment details of the command deck again called to Jo'seph's senses, but when a tactical officer reported that several Lordillian craft were breaking formation and heading back up into the stratosphere, the admiral found himself back at the view port, watching the lights recede in the night sky. "How many have left?"

"Five Lordillian cruisers have broken off and are heading up into orbit to intercept three new signals."

"New signals," Jo'seph mused to himself, wondering what kind of news that may mean; bad or worse. "What's the total number of ships still off our front porch?"

"I don't know what they're waiting for, admiral," the exhausted tactical post answered. "There's still a total now of twenty five battleships."

"Meaning…"

"Admiral!" Jo'seph had been cut off by the near ecstatic cry of the communications officer. "Jamming's clear! Admiral Jay'salan is signaling!"

Jo'seph couldn't believe his ears, finding a moment of surprise replaced by an irrepressible grin. "When the very seas threatened to swallow us." He jumped up to his command chair and slipped back on

341

the headset he had discarded earlier and brought the mouthpiece up to his chin. "Admiral, you'd better have a good excuse for keeping your date out past curfew."

"And to think I'd catch you sneezing or begging for help," came Jay'salan's familiar voice. "Now I'm not so sorry I'm late."

"I assume that's you those five Lord cruisers just headed up to meet?"

"Actually I think they're coming up to replace the ships Bevanne's wing just finished off." Jay'salan's voice was obscured for a moment by static, but then the channel was clear again. "Her ship's damaged, but still in good shape, as is one other. The third of her wing is retreating now that we're here to relieve. My wing consists of the *Pulsar* and two fresh ships. We just took out the vessel that was jamming your communications and are moving the combined fleet down to assist. What's your status?"

Jo'seph gave a quick run-down of current events. "Jay', I'm glad you're here. Attacking the Lordillian fleet is probably the only course of action open for you right now. But I don't think your five ships and our ground forces are going to be able to beat back this entire siege without a miracle."

"Nor do I. I can call in the rest of the fleet, but I'm sure the Lordillians are doing the same thing right now. We'd just be giving them more targets."

"Any chance you might have seen where that transport that was carrying Chebonka went?"

"No sign, and we've just entered the atmosphere," Jay'salan answered with disappointment. "Where's Hero?"

"Damned if I know," Jo'seph quipped. "Last I saw he was headed *towards* an army of shock troops massing outside of the citadel entrances. Better hope they don't do anything stupid like shoot at him: it will only piss him off."

Again the cry of battle carried in the Triialon tongue upon the wind. Hero rushed headlong into the staggered rows of Lordillian soldiers before they even knew he was coming. He waded through their giant metal bodies, slashing and hacking left and right, and firing blindly into them

342

with a plasma rifle until its power pack was exhausted, lost in a wild rage. The residual energy still left in the Sword served to crush aside multiple enemies with each wild swing, and his armor and Triialon physiology took the brunt of the few bolts from Lordillian guns that got through. When he reached the group massed closest to the mangled interior opening of the Grellion citadel, he loosed the final shot he still had stored within the Prizm. The blast radiated out like a giant searchlight, melting those directly in its path down to molten puddles while simply bowling over others. Hero leapt past them all, leaving tens destroyed and hundreds damaged in his wake.

He entered the citadel, instantly aware of the presence of the A.I. mind, now much stronger and more aware of its own parameters. The Lordillians on his heels were quick to react, a group of them reinterpreting their orders to hold at the entrance and instead following this new target into the citadel. The internal defense that had been silent at Hero's passing instantly opened fire, dropping each metal soldier that set foot inside in a hail of beams raining down from ports near the ceilings. Hero ran on, oblivious to the gauntlet he had just passed or the fate they met as they tried to follow him.

The Triialon's mind reached out, searching for the familiar shade of Lise. He found her, the strange link between them opening easily despite the distance. "*Lise,*" he called out, "*have admiral Jo'seph meet Sardeece and I near the central computer room, where we first found the Artificial Intelligence.*"

"*Hero,*" came her reply in his mind, "*I'm glad you made it. We can't get the shields or main cannon to work.*"

"*I know. I am on my way.*"

Hero rushed though the endless corridors and down the darkened stairwells. Blood seeped through tiny cracks between the plates of the tarnished and scarred armor. He wiped his hand along his brow as he ran, the fingers coming away wet with sweat. Hero had not exerted himself this much in years. If he hadn't been so angry over the choice Chebonka had forced him to make, he might have admitted to himself that he was having fun.

He reached the bottom at last where a defensive barrier had been hastily erected. Coalition soldiers propped up rifles and artillery behind the makeshift cover, and instantly those weapons were trained on him. A member of Lise's strike-team stood, recognizing Hero instantly. "They're waiting for you, sir," Hobson said. "Good to see you."

Hero nodded, jogging past. Beyond the defenses and rows of giant machines lay the central computer room. Servitor robots were still working on faulty mechanisms or banks of computers, with small teams of Coalition technicians beside them. Lise and the scientist Sardeece stood in the A.I.'s main chamber, studying a large machine's inner workings and the empty alcove within it. Lise took one look at Hero and her expression went from relief to concern. "Gods, are you alright?" She looked over his beaten armor and dirty, blood encrusted face. "What did you do, fight your way in from outside?"

The warrior shrugged. "It was the only way in at the time."

"Gods," she breathed, running her fingers down the scarred plates.

"There is no time for that," Hero grunted, un-shouldering the pack he had carried from his crashed ship. "The cleric and I found these last two oversized versions of the Grellion elements before I left. I believe it is what you are missing in order to power the shields." He scooped one of the large, perfect spheres from within the pack, and held it out to Sardeece.

"Fantastic," the scientist whispered. He gestured to the giant apparatus behind them. "This is exactly what was missing from this machine. I believe the completed circuit will also power the main cannon atop the citadel." He placed the glowing element into the socket, watching with eyes wide open as the interior of the machine began to pulse with the same glow. "This is historic."

Hero looked around the brightening chamber. "Where is Durant?"

"Gone above to hold the lines, not that there's too many Lordillians still inside the base." Lise stood near Hero, each watching Sardeece intently while Hero unhinged the Triialon body armor and stripped each piece off. He stacked them neatly nearby, removing all of the plates until he stood only in the lighter, black under-armor, its flexible, ribbed substance covering him from neck to toe. "I brought one other element of equal size, though I believe it may belong to the flagship."

Lise's communicator unit screamed static. She removed it from her belt, checking its instrumentation. "The jamming's ceased. We've go a clear signal from the bridge."

"That does not mean the enemy is not listening."

Lise smiled. "Doesn't matter; we've been communicating by servitor robot signal."

"The systems are coming online," Sardeece exclaimed. "By these readings, I believe we have full power."

Hero's own scientific curiosity was piqued. "Can the shields be raised?"

Sardeece shrugged. "Ask the bridge."

Lise looked confused. "Why don't you just ask the citadel?"

The scientist blinked. "There's a thought." Sardeece closed his eyes, the strange tubes and prosthetics crowning his head briefly illuminating. "We're raising the shields," he said, eyes still tightly shut, speaking as though he were intoning a magical chant in symmetry with an unseen conspirator. "The power is raising, expanding out... From deep within the core it spreads out, past this room, out past the citadel and the lands. It moves out to cover the planet..."

Lise's eyes opened wide with amazement. "The planet?!?"

"Yes," Sardeece muttered. His speech had become quiet and halting, as though he were in a hypnotic trance. "The shields protect the entire planet, not just the citadel and those within."

"That means we are still under threat from the enemy vessels within the atmosphere," Hero sternly reminded him.

"Wait," Sardeece said. "We have the main cannon still. I shall attempt to move it." There was a moment of suspenseful silence, then he smiled. "Admiral Jay'salan has made it. His ships are engaging the Lordillians. The fight is valiant; primary weapons tearing Lordillian ships to pieces... but the enemy numbers are vast."

Hero leaned over to Lise, speaking in a hushed tone. "He can 'see' now though the citadel's senses. With the elements returned, his link with this place is complete as well. He speaks through Grellion."

345

Sardeece's smile vanished. "The cannon will not move. It – it is damaged somehow." His eyes snapped open. "The cannon will not fire."

"How fare the Coalition ships?"

Sardeece spoke quickly, flustered again by the reality that threatened to crash down upon him. "The sheer size of the main batteries of Coalition battle cruisers is a direct result of the inevitable numbers involved when speaking of the Lordillian war machine, Hero. The firepower will decimate the Lordillian fleet trapped in the planet's atmosphere with us, but ultimately, I fear, at the cost of our entire force."

"Can the cannon be repaired?"

"There's no time!"

"Hero," Lise called, "The admiral demands a report."

The Triialon warrior shook his head, frustrated. "Please tell me that you have had a team digging their way to that buried flagship all this time."

Sardeece shrugged. "I know Jo'seph sent a team, but nothing's been heard of them since. We've been too busy defending the citadel. They were digging towards a likely entrance, but..."

Hero snatched the last giant element from where it lay in the vast A.I. chamber. "Then that our last hope. Tell the admirals to hold out as long as they can."

"Oh no," Lise scolded, "I'm coming with you."

Hero's brow furrowed, readying himself for the backlash from the lecture he was about to give her. "Listen, we have no time..."

"To argue," she interrupted, "I agree. Let's go. Sardeece, inform the admirals of the current situation. Hero and I are going to find a way into that Flagship."

"But you don't even know if it will fly," a panic stricken Sardeece screamed.

Admiral Jo'seph, co-founder of the Galactic Coalition, watched the burning skies outside the window of the citadel's command deck. The room was a cacophony of noise, the giving and sending of commands from each post mingling with the rumble of the battle outside. He was partially responsible for the gathering of some fifteen worlds, be it the remnants of fleets or civilizations, and forming them into one great fighting force. Since then others had rallied to their cause in the hopes that the same fate would not befall their peoples. But the vanity of accomplishment was crushed now by the vain battle that raged without, a final and inevitable extermination that had simply been withheld until the events of this fateful evening.

He watched as Coalition battle cruisers attacked and then regrouped, aligning in a formation against their overwhelming opposition and preparing to fire a combined volley. The dark masses of the Lordillian cruisers against the misty night sky broke their own formation, dozens of giant ships suddenly scattering as if they were one-man fighters, only at substantially slower speeds. The Coalition ships fired, their giant blasts spilling out from the main cannons mounted at the belly of the ships. The beams pierced the enemy lines, destroying hundreds of the just-launched Lordillian fighters before dicing their mother ships. Some exploded, others were gashed and fell from the sky, but most evaded or suffered minimal damage.

Next the enemy fighters moved in, strafing the hulls of the defenders' battleships. The *Bat* fighters that had moved away to avoid the previous friendly-firestorm swooped back down, trying to drive off the swarm of angry ships. The groups of vessels were strangely contrasted; The white, graceful sweeping hulls of the Coalition cruisers turning and diving to blast at their black, ovoid and angular Lordillian equals. Meanwhile the dark, down-and-forward swept wings of the *bat*s versus the industrialized Lordillian cutters and the cannons they bore raged as a fantastic dogfight. The ships themselves might be evenly matched if not for the limitless numbers of their foes. Each tactic and act of desperation was put to the test in the air above Grellion that night; attack groups became separated and then engaged in close combat, ships rammed each other, nets were formed, and ultimately men and women died. Meanwhile the Base's own anti-aircraft weapons fired away with their own regular tattooing of sound and fire, swatting down ships and affecting occasional damage to the enemy battle cruisers.

"The citadel's power readings are now off the scale," Jo'seph thought to himself, "and yet there's so little we can even do with it."

He had watched as each new miracle had suddenly appeared from the sky, one following the others. Lise had brought hope in the forms of the crystals, yet still they were besieged. Hero had appeared and battled against the very skies with ungodly powers, yet even his strength had its limits, it would seem. Jay'salan had ridden down upon the increasing numbers of Lordillian battleships, only to turn the battle into a sky war rapidly becoming a massacre. And still they battled on, for hope was not lost. Sardeece had said that the shields now covered the entire planet; an amazing and noteworthy feat, save that this may have not only locked all ships out, but locked the swarm of the Lordillian horde in with them. The main cannon atop the base's giant hanger would not fire, despite the elements that Hero had brought. But there was still the tiny hope that lay within a giant battleship, buried for eons beneath a mountain and powered by lost technology.

Right.

Janise came to stand beside him, holding Jo'seph's hand tenderly. "What's happening, daddy? What's going to happen?"

"We wait," he told her, watching as the skies turned to fire once again. "We hope for one more miracle."

The pair of nearly exhausted warriors had found the tunnel Sardeece had instructed them to enter easily enough, running as best they could at a stoop, fruitlessly chasing the search lights they shone ahead of them. Lise had voiced her concerns about a cave-in, and Hero had verbally brushed such fears aside, secretly hoping that the makeshift engineering of her crewmates would hold up as well as he had given them credit for. "How much further?" he called back to her, changing the subject.

Lise ran close behind him, searchlight and blaster ready in one hand, a hand-held scanner in the other. "I'm not sure. The rock and minerals are dulling the range. Based on calculations, though, we should have less than a quarter mile before we either run into the buried ship or run out of tunnel."

The man-made cave turned slightly, and suddenly Hero could make out faint light ahead. Seconds later the light vanished. "We've found them."

"Halt," came a man's voice from the far end. "Who's there?"

"You had better answer before they take us for cybernetic agents," Hero told Lise as they slowed.

Lise cupped her hands to her mouth, calling ahead. "Commanders Lise and Hero, sent by Sardeece and the admiral."

"'Commander'?" Hero asked of her. Lise shrugged.

The pair jogged the rest of the way up to where several people dressed in varying Coalition uniforms waited, each covered in dirt and dust. Beyond them lay the end of the tunnel; a sloping, polished surface made from the same alloys as the exterior of the citadel. The excavation team had dug a large cavern out, uncovering as much of the side of the craft they had found as they could, obviously looking for a way in. Seams and some sort of revolving lock mechanism broke the otherwise smooth hull at one end of the cavern, and two members of the group were busy trying to crack it open. The one who had called out to them saluted. He looked Hero and his strange uniform over once, uncertain, then his gaze caught on Lise and her own outfit. "Sergeant Pel'gent, commanders. You'll have to forgive me a moment; we've seen no one else down here the last few days. I assume by all the noise that we are under attack?"

Lise forced a smile, nodding. "What's the situation down here?"

"We've located what we believe is a hatch leading within the ship, ma'am. What little surface area we've uncovered or have been able to scan seems intact." He gestured to the two working at the hatch. "Very intact. That door won't budge. We were contemplating blasting."

"That will not be necessary, I hope," Hero said, shouldering past him and waving the others away as he approached the unyielding hatch. He raised his arm, feeding the same combination of commands into the Prizm that had opened the citadel's front 'gate', and to the surprise of everyone present the hatch twisted of its own volition and opened, gently swinging out towards them. Hero did not hesitate, ducking through the circular opening to be the first to stand within ancient spacecraft.

The air was sparse and stale, barely breathable to the others who made faces at the musky smell as they followed the Triialon in. "Masks," Pel'gent ordered, handing a small oxygen cylinder and mask to Lise, who placed it over her nose and mouth. Hero waved the one offered to him away, his own lungs having negligible difficulty with the atmosphere.

"Which way is the engine room?" Hero asked aloud.

Pel'gent stepped forward, shining his light onto the corridor wall nearby. A diagram was etched there, the sign seemingly some sort of diagram of the ship. He compared the apparent directory to his own scanner, and then motioned off to the right. "Back that way, sir. About a mile." He smiled. "Bit of a walk."

Hero shook his head and handed the sergeant the satchel he had been carrying, opening the top flap to show him the crystalline element within. The man's eyes opened wide at the site of the strange, glowing orb in front of his chin. "No – a bit of a run. If you do not get this Grellion element into the main power drive's systems and if I cannot get this craft's weapons online somehow, then the Coalition's war will end within the hour in the skies outside of the citadel."

The surprised sergeant looked to Lise, alarmed by this profession. She nodded to him. "That's the whole damn war you hear up there, sergeant. The Lordillians are here in full force, along with part of our own fleet to defend the citadel. They're buying all of us time with their lives."

Pel'gent nodded grimly, saluting. "You can count on us. I assume you'll be heading for the bridge?" Lise briefly looked to Hero, then indicated positive. "Take one of our data scans, then. Its by no means a complete diagram, but its better than running blind. We'll contact you once we've arrived in the engine room. Come on," he said to his team, and they all disappeared into the darkness.

"Good luck."

Hero could feel Lise's eyes on him as he compared the data pad they'd been given with the schematic on the wall. "Yes," he said, answering her unvoiced question, "it is just the two of us who will have to pilot a craft nearly eight miles in length."

"Providing it will even lift off," she pointed out, following again as he began to run down a corridor to the left.

"All that matters is the main weapons systems. We will improvise the rest."

"Comforting."

He could tell she was studying him again as they ran together in silence, past junctures and rooms long-since forgotten and hollow. Their lights briefly created shadows as they jogged past each chamber. Eerie shapes and hollows illuminated ghostly recesses of what once was, then faded again to blackness. They hurried past these lost wonders with barely time for a glance, Hero mostly watching the schematic in his hand, hoping to shorten their time to their destination. He could hear Lise's breathing becoming more labored as they ran. "Are you fatigued?"

Lise ignored the question. "How is it you are doing so well with so little air?" she asked between breaths.

"Good breeding." He glanced back at her, noting the sweat that had begun to bead on her forehead. "Remember the Triialon teachings; calm yourself. Control your breathes or they shall control you."

"I hope we aren't already too late," she said.

"As do I."

Chapter Twenty

*We were all doomed; we knew it. Myself, I just
hoped to all the gods each of the others prayed
to that maybe admiral Jay'salan had one last
trick in that book of tactics he always carried that
just might save our asses.*
- From the personal journal of
a Coalition private.

The lights came on even as they neared their goal, and Lise pulled her communicator off of her belt as she got her first look at the interior of the ship finally lit up. "Sergeant Pel'gent," she called into the COMlink, "what's your status?"

"Took us about five minutes to find the lights, commander, but we've arrived in what appears to be the engine room. Power's building; we're really just flipping switches at this stage. Give us a minute while we see if anything matches your description of where this crystal ball of yours goes."

"Make it quick, sergeant. We're nearly at the command decks."

"This way," Hero said, suddenly turning a corner and leaving the hall to climb a set of steps leading up. Lise followed, each step making the anticipation and stress levels rise within her. Her thoughts threatened to be overwhelmed by the imagery she had already seen and the idea that those Lordillian bastards might be killing those she considered friends. Worse – if they failed, then everything that had once been like Sparta and its way of life would fail with them. The cold, calculated history of Lordillian files might not even bother to mention how her people had once lived, or what they had given up.

The air was becoming cooler. She lowered her mask, tasting the atmosphere briefly. Hope dared to puncture the wall of Lise's depression with each gasp of fresher air that Lise gulped. If the air conditioning worked that efficiently, then perhaps other systems, like in the citadel, would still work just as well despite the centuries. But they still had no idea what damage the Grellion flagship had sustained that had caused it to be left behind, buried until they had found it. Sardeece had guessed that the shield now surrounding the planet was impervious to nearly all attacks, yet the citadel and the flagship both seemed to have been left for dead. A mystery that even the citadel Itself seemed to have forgotten the answer to.

"Here," Hero said urgently, leading her to a wide hall winding off from the next level of stairs. They ran with renewed speed down the white corridor, heading for a set of secured double-hatches at the far end. Once there, Hero turned the manual release and pushed the sliding doors aside, at last giving them their first view of the Grellion flagship's bridge.

They were standing on a wide command platform overlooking a huge room full of command seats and their control panels. Two sets of steps curled down from either side of the platform to the deck below, and the ceiling above stretched out only half-way towards an enormous view port. It was a giant pane of some form of glass that curved up and back beyond the deck suspended above them. Outside the glass lay the dark soil and other elements making up the mountain that had covered the vessel.

Hero hesitated only a moment before stepping forward to begin working the panels on the command platform. Instantly controls near them as well as on the panels below began to come to life. Lise had to will her jaw shut long enough to swallow and find a voice. "Any idea what this stuff says?"

Hero studied the displays even while standing over yet another set and turning those on as well. "We would have been wise to bring a Grellion robot, but I think I can manage." When the next bank of controls came to life, the sounds of battle greeted their ears. "COM stations arc up." The room was filled with voices from overlapping channels being broadcast outside. Orders and reports from fighter groups and cruiser commanders bantered back and forth, yet even those sounds were soon being drowned out by the screams of the dying. The Triialon looked at her, worry evident in his features in a way that made her own blood run cold. "We must hurry."

Lise brought the COM link to her trembling lips. "Sergeant, talk to me."

"We think we've found it, commander," came the static-filled reply.

"Hurry!"

Hero was stooped intently over a group of controls and their displays. "I think this is propulsion and this the weapons."

"What can I do?"

"You can work this bank here for lift-off, if I can get anything to work at all."

"We're installing the crystal now," said Pel'gent. His voice was nearly drowned out by all the other sounds of criss-crossing communications channels. Each piercing explosion and every blood-curdling scream made Lise grit her teeth harder. She stared at the display Hero had placed her in front of, trying to quickly decipher the systems. "Damn," came the sergeant's amazed voice, "I think its working! Crystal is in place in what appears to be main drive systems. At least it's the only bracket we could find that matched. The whole damn thing is glowing! What do I do next?"

"Pray," Lise said, her voice breaking. She could feel a single tear plot a course down her cheek even as her fingers fumbled with the strange, unknown controls.

"Sergeant, try to find some way of regulating the power," Hero said. "Make sure there are no fall-offs as well as no overloads."

Pel'gent sounded uncertain. "How do I know what's normal? This is already off every scale I'm familiar with."

"You'll find a way," he answered. His own hands worked frantically at the panels before him, crossing over to Lise's station as well, yet still nothing further seemed to be happening. "I am not getting any response from thruster or anti-gravity control. Main cannon is also unresponsive."

Lise tried to understand the messages overlapping her own screen. "Maybe they were damaged, like the base cannon."

"No. Nothing major is recognizing my control. We have no interface. Perhaps we are missing further Grellion elements; I don't know."

Lise could feel defeat pooling in the very pit of her stomach, yet she refused to give up. She looked over the platform's systems again, then watched Hero's displays, marveling at how fast his hands sped over the alien technology. The ever-glowing crystal of the Triialon Prizm glinted back at her, and she smiled. "Open the door," she heard herself say softly.

356

"What?"

Lise grasped Hero's arm, nodding to the jeweled bracer he always wore, the very technology that had gained them both entrance to the citadel and the flagship in the first place. "We can't control its interface because it doesn't recognize the link; the critical element is missing as far as the computer is concerned. So maybe you can fool it into thinking you're interfacing, that you're connected to the ship properly."

Hero looked into her eyes a moment before smiling. He turned his now purpose-filled gaze to the panel, triumphantly ripping aside a cover-piece to reveal a socket. The half-sphere cut into the console panel was roughly the size of a missing Grellion element. Hero did not hesitate, turning his wrist over and slamming the Prizm crystal into the socket. Suddenly the ship lurched, sparks shooting from the violent connection that had been made, landing on Hero's bare hand. He did not flinch, even when the escaping power began to strike at him from the panel like a viper. Instead, he closed his eyes, letting his mind and will flow into the brain of the ship itself. Lise watched in awe as man and machine began to interface. His mind was soon closed to her, lost within the alien software, and the power threatened to burn and tear at his flesh and rend his mind, but she knew that he would not break the connection this side of death itself.

Another Coalition battle cruiser fell from the smoke-filled sky, plummeting through the acrid clouds caused by the battle and crashing into the ground below to explode when the graceful neck snapped and the main cannon and drive systems collided with the planet. A few more escape pods managed to break off before the rear of the ship was engulfed in the ensuing fireball, but within moments nothing that was still aboard was alive. Jay'salan's cruiser was desperately trying to free itself from an engagement with two more Lordillian battleships and route its sister vessels back into formation. "Come around, mark three-five." Jo'seph could hear the other admiral's voice cut through the COM signals as he watched the scene – he could imagine his friend standing on the bridge as was his rightful place. "Jo', can you get the Base's auto-guns trained on that lead ship, lay down some covering fire?"

Jo'seph gave the order, his officers having soon figured out how to manually control some of the citadel's exterior batteries since the place had come to life. Once more fire rose forth from the ancient structure, tearing into its enemies. Jay'salan's ship finally broke free and headed back up into the atmosphere, the remaining ships joining him. But the smoke that leaked from the majority of the Coalition ships told the truth; soon they would all fail.

The Lordillian ships also began to move, grouping into a new formation. Their own weapons opened fire again, a million bolts of plasma flaring out towards the admiral's ships, dispersing against shields or cutting their way into their hulls. The *Bat* fighters dove, strafing another run along the new line of enemy ships. But another volley from the black cruisers tore out before the Coalition line could get its bearings, and one more of the new-style battle cruisers was shot out of the sky. "Ready main cannons," Jo'seph could hear Jay'salan say. "Transfer all power to auxiliary systems; we're going to hit them with everything we've got." But deep inside both admirals knew it was not going to be enough.

A rumble began deep below Jo'seph's feet, almost unnoticed at first. The rumble became a quake, vibrating and shaking the entire command deck. Jo'seph looked at the displays around him, watching the picture signals coming from the cameras both within the base and from the cruisers still transmitting. "What's happening?"

"Sir!" Tykeisha stood bolt upright from her station, pointing at one of the screens. The picture was a bird's eye view of the citadel and the surrounding land, transmitted from one of cameras on Jay'salan's ship. "The mountains!"

The hills behind the base began to crack and burst and angry red light poured out of a sudden gash as though a volcano were opening up. The soil that had covered it exploded out into a cloud of dust and hot ash. The light cut the two mountains lengthwise, excavating a trench from within, then it ceased. The dirt surrounding the enormous gash began to rise and fall away to either side. Jo'seph thought that perhaps the planet could no longer take the full measure of power that they had awakened and was at last splitting asunder.

And then something began to emerge from the devastated mountains.

Jo'seph could not believe his own eyes. Illuminated only by the light of the moon filtering through the smoke and ash and the fireballs of the war ships still sparring so close by, it rose like a floating mountain. Covered in the mounds of soil and plant life that had buried it for years, the flagship slowly ascended from its grave atop billowing thrusters. Debris rained down slowly from the gigantic structure, falling back into the gorge that had been left where the twin hills once stood. The ship itself looked almost like a simple platform, wide in the center and then tapering at both ends of its sinewy length, the front end longer and bubbling from a graceful neck to a tear-shaped head. From the mid-length back to the where the rear section tapered were two huge engines, and on the underside of the ship was a sloping belly, where encrusted hanger doors could be discerned through the sludge.

The slow giant climbed higher, casting off the last of its ties to the planet below. And then it hovered, waiting there above the citadel, its eight mile long side turned to the fleets massed above the battle-scarred valley. Two posts, one on either side of the engines, suddenly flared to life, radiant shimmering energy and ignited the residual debris from the ship's tomb, incinerating it before at last spewing beams of incandescent light out in front of the ship. The beams met nearly a mile off the bow, exploding, coalescing into a growing ball of unparalleled power that expanded and grew as more energy was fed into it, erupting like a sun and eclipsing the night. Time seemed to stop as all bore witness to the cataclysmic event, Jo'seph and those on the bridge stood frozen in their places as the scene unfolded.

"My lord," Jo'seph gasped in wonder, "can such a thing be controlled?"

A red blotch blistered at the front of the gigantic sphere the beams created, angry and festering. The blob moved, sliding across the ball's surface until it was pointed at the Lordillian fleet. And then it burst. The red spot became a wave, exploding out like an ocean of death that swallowed everything in its path and the Lordillian ships vaporized in an instant within it. The wave then became a focused beam, slicing its way down the line of remaining enemy cruisers and ships like a surgical blade, cutting them from the very sky. Primary and secondary explosions from each vessel blossomed outward, and the series of what was once a large portion of the Lordillian space fleet were strung together as one, a rolling cloud of white hot death like an expanding supernova.

Then all was quiet. The explosions dissipated into billowing smoke and the energy wave from the flagship ceased its spray into the heavens. Jo'seph turned his gaze back to the view of their savior, but the ship was falling from the sky, slipping out of the view of the primary camera. He watched the varying views, clenching his fists as they all witnessed helplessly while the behemoth sank back into the crater from which it had emerged. A great quake rocked the citadel again, its risen cousin again falling to rest where it had lain for millennia.

She watched silently from the shadows, hoping that she was as hidden as she dared to believe herself to be. Nothing in her life had ever frightened her like what she was about to do now.

Toapo stormed into his chambers, nostrils flared in rage. He threw his robe at a servant waiting by the inner doors, nearly toppling the young man. Slave girls rushed forward, heads bowed, to do their God's bidding, some of them falling to their knees and pressing their heads to the polished marble floor. The towering immortal nearly kicked the naked girls aside, but instead stopped himself, deciding to scream at them rather than kill them. "Get OUT! All of you, get out, now!" He backhanded one of the slaves as they hurried past, sending the girl and her tray of foods sprawling. Before they had even all exited the apartments Toapo was already ringing the toll for his Servant.

Toapo paced frantically, fuming to himself as he walked back and forth across the foyer with giant, powerhouse strides. The Servant soon appeared, its metal, horse-like head bowed in placation as its robes swept into the room. The God unloaded on the creature almost immediately, laying into him verbally with the ferocity of a master beating his slave. "The Coalition has managed to survive a direct assault from the Lordillians' Fourth fleet, destroying it utterly! Chebonka himself was nearly killed and in all of this it seems that both admirals survived and found some sort of new base of operations. My bargaining chips are slipping through my fingers, and Kezeron has not yet reported back. It seems he failed a second time to kill Hero, as reports are placing the Triialon at the scene of the Coalition victory!"

He started pacing again. The Servant, still bowing silently, waited for orders as to what his master wished. "I can still turn this to my advantage," Toapo continued. "This whole mess has led to the strengthening of the Coalition's position, and Chebonka's death would have been disastrous. Hero lives, and may have even gained one of the Twelve Artifacts. And Memfis is the cause." He stopped dead in his tracks, movement catching his eye. His face was turned away from her, but she knew that within moments the God would find her partner.

The entire room lurched, an explosion igniting next to where Toapo stood, sending chunks of stone and bits of statues and wall flying. The Servant's body was tossed aside, fire and shrapnel ripping into its chest and denting its angular helm. But as the swirling rings of smoke cleared, it became obvious the true target was unharmed. Toapo stood in the center of a bubble of blue energy, the flaring nimbus refracting anything that came near it. It was a simple reaction to attack, the shield an instinctual response brought up by his natural abilities. Now that the threat had subsided, the immortal's consciousness turned to the source. His powers reached out, ripping aside a set of curtains at the far end of the next room, revealing a single remaining slave girl. She stood motionless, trapped by what seemed to be paralyzing fear, standing with one more of the grenades that had been used to attack him in her slight hands.

Toapo's eyes flashed, light escaping the normally black orbs. He grinned wickedly, watching as his mind reached out to the trembling girl to lift her frail body from the floor and twist her in half at the waist before rending her limb from limb. Blood sprayed the walls and tapestries, fountaining from the mangled collection of muscle and bone, before dripping the mass to the cold floor.

"Weak minded trifle." Toapo glared, searching the room with his eyes. "I know you are here, you foolish toy." Svea stood perfectly still, uncertain what she should do next now that her puppet had been so easily found and disabled. "If you act out of love for your God, Memfis, then

361

you are an even bigger fool than I suspected." His giant hands waved at the secret panel Svea hid behind, the invisible force ripping it aside and throwing it across the room. Svea froze, trying not to panic despite the exposure while throwing up her hands to defend herself. The Seethling ways made her own energies dance across her fingertips, and she stared at the God with all of the courage she could muster.

Toapo leaned back, a sly grin twisting his enflamed lips. The sparkling bubble surrounding him dissipated into nothing, and he narrowed his gaze, laughing slightly to himself. "You cannot harm me. No, I will force you to be my new slave. What a plaything you will make; I can extract years of torture from your body and mind. And after I am satisfied that you have suffered enough for today's indignities, I will encase you in the helm and robes of a God-Servant, trapping you for eternity as my undead vassal to replace the one you have killed."

There was a flash of light from the darkness of the devastated foyer, and the sound of something speeding through the air. The dart struck Toapo in the back of the neck, causing the God to cry out. He spun, rage again overtaking him, yet no nimbus exploded, no invisible force reached out. Instead he simply stood and watched, holding his damaged neck, as Dahvis walked from the shadows with the smoking dart-gun in his hands. Toapo was shocked, weakness overtaking him as he fell to his knees. The immortal creature forced his hand from his throat, trying to focus on the blood-stained digits. The dart fell limply from his wet hand, the tiny vial of chemicals shattering on the floor. "What have you done to me? How...?"

Dahvis pulled a sword from the sheath at his hip. Svea's dear brother smiled wickedly, looking down on Toapo with his arcing brow. "Memfis sends his regards." Toapo barely had a chance to raise his hand in supplication, much less beg for mercy. The sword crashed down, decapitating the God in one swift stroke. The head had bounced just once when the former immortal's power fled from the gaping wound, washing over both Seethlings in a shockwave of wind and color that jolted Svea. She fell against the wall behind her for support, squinting through tear-streaked eyes as the scene played itself out and the headless body of Toapo toppled over with a sickening thud.

"You see, sister?" Dahvis wore a maniacal grin, his fists clenched in power mad glory. But it was his eyes, glazed and dead within, that made Svea's heart continue to pound in her chest despite the completion of their mission. "I have been granted the power to kill a God. Kordula bows before us at last." No longer did her protector and benefactor stand before her.

Svea tried to erect her game face, but instead found her hands still trembling. She took a tentative step forward anyway, smiling as best she could. "Calm yourself, brother."

Dahvis grabbed her by the shoulders, pulling her with him into a crazed dance, laughing hysterically while he waltzed her around and finally pushed her against the wall. A gasp exploded from her lips as she struck its surface. The panels behind Svea's arched back were still hot from the brief fire that had licked them clean moments before. She looked up into her brother's eyes, tears streaming from them, born by joy or rage, she could not tell. "Such terror," was all he managed to gurgle between his own heaving breaths, though she knew not whether he spoke of his own power or that which he feared. "And only you... only you to share in this moment."

Svea watched him, scared now beyond even the moment Toapo had reached out to strike her down. "And I shall always be here," she realized, pressing her arms around him as she always had, be his touch upon her flesh that of kindness or that of pain. Now the man she had grown up with was an unstoppable force, the hunter he had always dreamed himself to be, but somehow completely under the control of Memfis himself. He'd had the taste of the sweetest blood upon his lips, and he would never again be her protector in the way she had known. What power was it that was now held over them both? How was it that she could be so close to the very ideal that they had fought so hard for, yet that goal be ever so much more terrifying than anything she had imagined?

She felt him stir against her, his head still buried against her breast, yet his hands now roaming, the laughter returning as a barely audible chuckle that shook his muscular shoulders. Dahvis began to kiss her neck, working his way back up to her lips. Svea wet them and forced them into the most reassuringly naughty twist, even while ever so slowly pulling his hands from her breasts. "Not here," she whispered against his ear. "We must leave this place before we are found."

She took his hand, leading him away. Dahvis followed, dragged behind as his head turned further with each step away from the dead immortal he stared at, left to rot upon the floor. "Wait," he said, releasing her hand. He picked up the disembodied head by its mane, watching the gore evacuate the open neck, an evil smile curling his thin lips. "We still have a job to do before we can return to our own chambers." Svea followed his lead, leaving the room behind without a further glance, having to force each obeisant step. She wondered, as they entered the secret hallways that led between the hallowed apartments, if this was anything like the terrible fear any of her victims had felt before their own fates...

Lise sat on the edge of the crater, one long leg dangling over the edge as the sunlight poured down upon her face and the breeze shuffled wisps of her hair. She smiled, despite the smoke that arose around her and the quiet man next to her. Hero was laying nearby, staring up at the sun, one hand clutching his broken ribs. They had spoken little since they had climbed out of the top hatch of the fallen Flagship, content to enjoy the silence after battle while they waited for their comrades. Even Hero had briefly commented on the beauty of the Grellion morning. The team from the engine rooms were climbing out of the top hatch now as well, and would have to climb the craggy edge of the cliff that the giant ship's resurrection had dug.

Or not. Coming from the hilly grasslands below, racing from around the side of citadel – or new Coalition Base Lise thought, smiling – came a pair of transports flitting on anti-gravs. They stopped a number of yards from where she and Hero sat, and both admirals Jo'seph and Jay'salan, along with several soldiers, emerged. They ran the rest of the way to Lise's position. "Are you two alright?" Jo'seph asked.

Hero sat up. "I am fine."

Lise rolled her eyes and stood, just to one-up the proud idiot. "He needs medical attention, and I could do with about a week's sleep, but we'll live."

364

"You'll get it." Admiral Jay'salan shook her hand, then helped Hero to his feet, instructing one of the transports to go and save the excavation team a climb.

"I'll make you both generals." Jo'seph looked down into the shadowy crevice where the flagship lay. Running a hand through his blonde locks, he whistled in amazement. "Damn," he whispered. "Its huge!"

Jay'salan was wearing a rare grin. "Its magnificent."

Lise had to smile, watching the men she had come to respect so much in her short time by their side in the last few ...days? Weeks? She almost couldn't remember how much time had really passed since Hero had appeared to her out of the smoke on Moonshau. Jo'seph looked like a schoolboy, his eyes roaming over the smooth panels that rolled over the front of the great battleship's bridge like a small white mountain. It sloped back and down, fading off into the early day's haze, rolling away the entire length of the eight-mile valley it had formed in take-off. "Will she fly again?"

"Doesn't look like she took too much structural damage in the fall," Jay'salan quipped, rubbing his angular jaw.

Hero nodded, absently scratching his burnt hand. "You will be able to repair her. The Grellion alloys are light-weight and durable, and the loosened soil cradled some of the impact that the thrusters initially lessened."

"Unbelievable," Jay'salan said, offering his hand to Hero again in congratulations.

"I only got the shot off," Hero said modestly. "Lise and the team you had dig their way to the ship deserve the true praise. She piloted it. If we had not lifted off, the blast would never have cleared the citadel."

Both admirals commended her, and Lise felt her cheeks blush at the praise. "Nice landing, commander," Jo'seph said, elbowing the plating covering her ribs. "If you had cracked that thing in half, I'd be busting you down to private. As it is I have to give you another damn medal." He looked at her costume, as if noticing it for the first time. "I wouldn't say that's exactly regulation body armor, commander."

Lise grinned, tossing her hair over one shoulder and placing a hand on her hip, striking a pose. "I haven't heard any complaints so far."

"And Chebonka?" Hero asked.

The larger admiral shrugged. "We think he got away to a waiting ship before the shield formed around the planet."

Jo'seph sneezed violently. "Damn." The others laughed at him, even Hero letting a smile slip through. "Oh, I'm going to like it here."

Admiral Jay'salan looked at the sky above, squinting as the clouds of smoke passed and sunlight blanketed his pale, gray skin and dark uniform. "Don't complain. We paid dearly for this new home." He broke the moment of somber silence that followed that revelation. "But we're safe, at least for the time being."

"Do we call it New Sparta?" Jo'seph queried.

"Call it what you like," Hero said. "You have dealt a decent blow to the Lordillian horde and gained a new base of operations. An unbreakable force field covers the entire planet, powered by the very core of the planet."

"That and the Grellion elements," Lise interjected. "They were somehow the life-force of the Grellions themselves."

Hero nodded. "Or that of their ancestors. What was missing has been brought back to Grellion, and your people can complete that unity. Purpose joined with power."

Jo'seph's features brightened, the full meaning dawning on him at last. "This whole planet is now our base," he said, his voice full of wonder. "Lords above, we can bring the entire fleet here, as well as the refugee camps! Our families. And they won't have to live in the recesses of the citadel, but here in the sun." He was staggered by the prospects, and shook his head. "We're going to have a lot of building to do."

Lise regarded the smoking heaps of mangled metal in the valley beyond the citadel. "Not as though there isn't plenty of raw materials," she said dryly.

Jay'salan unbuttoned his jacket, placing his hands on his hips, surveying their new home. "We're going to need more than that to refit the base, the flagship…"

Lise smiled knowingly. "Oh, I think we should have most of that covered. Anything further we may need that our own supplies don't cover we should be able to get from other sources once we run out. By that time I'm sure that some of the Okino star systems will be willing to lend us aide in one form or another."

"Oh?" Jo'seph asked, raising an eyebrow.

Hero looked at Lise, and for a moment she thought she saw something akin to pride in his gaze. "Lise made a new friend or two," he said. "Queen Krystka Telisha still has a pretty fair political standing in that quadrant."

Jo'seph pulled a face, stifling a grin. "Not bad. See, I told you you were a good speaker." He turned to Hero, reaching out to shake his hand, as he promised he would the day the Triialon warrior had told him of this lost world. "Its everything you said it would be, thanks largely to you." Hero took the offered hand, nodding resolutely. Jo'seph grinned again, turning the group back towards the citadel below. "Time to celebrate."

The command decks were teaming with as many people as the large rooms atop the citadel's central building could hold. The party had worked its way there from the hanger. The doors of the gigantic building had finally been rolled up into its rafters for the first time in who knew how long, and the damaged Coalition battle cruisers swept inside. Antigravity panels set in the walls of the building above a certain altitude suspended the ships effortlessly above them, and the drop ships and fighters had brought their crews down where they had all gathered and hugged and celebrated. The piles of Lordillian limbs and torsos had been thrown together just outside and set ablaze, a giant bonfire of victory.

Lise watched as councilor Bevanne finally found her way in, working her way through the milling masses and fiercely hugging Hero and then herself, before turning to her fellow leaders – those who remained. Even Sardeece had pulled himself up from his basement laboratory to join in the merriment, and few gave his strange new countenance a second glance. "This place is perfect," the spry old woman marveled. She battered the admirals with a thousand questions, interested most in the way Sardeece and the initial soldiers to arrive had worked together with the Grellion machines. They were all quick to make it sound as if it had all gone effortlessly, noting how tolerant and open-minded everyone had been in the overwhelming presence of so many A.I.'s. Lise laughed behind her hand, glad the whole situation could now be made so light of.

Finding herself suddenly alone among the throng of merrymakers, Lise looked around the room for Hero, trying to see above the many helmeted heads. She saw the rogue Durant talking animatedly to a female pilot, the girl looking only partially convinced at to the strange man's exploits. Lise rolled her eyes, looking on. The Triialon warrior stood alone, leaning against a wall nearest the door. He was dressed again in his traditional black jacket, having salvaged it from the crashed desert flyer only hours before. The old Triialon ship had been brought back to the hanger, awaiting whatever repairs it would need to be space worthy again. He continued to watch the happy scene another moment before ducking through the door, disappearing from Lise's view. She frowned, working her way through the crowd to the door and exiting the loud party.

She found him in his room, packing what few items he had left there when the quarters were first assigned to him. "I thought you had better manners than to leave a celebration that is at least partly in your honor. Have you learned nothing of our ways?" She placed a tentative hand on his shoulder. "You risked everything for us," she started, but he had pulled away. "What is it?"

Hero did not look at her when he answered, moving back and forth as he grabbed more items to pack. "I must go to Moonshau; learn whether or not Osmar survived his injuries."

His body had stiffened, though Lise knew it was not from injuries, as the burns on his hand were already healing. More likely it was the attention. "You're not coming back," she realized. Anger surged within her again, the adventures and trials she had been through with this man suddenly seeming to mean nothing to him. "Fine, go! Disappear once more and continue to be just the lost legend that you have become."

The man sighed, weighing his words carefully. "I am Hero of the Triialon, last protector of the Twelve, a warrior from a line of warriors and I have a responsibility to my people to find what was lost."

The anger drained away from Lise a little, and she sat down on the bed near where he stood. Her eyes pleaded with him even though he still would not look at her. What had all of this meant to him? "Yes, and you will always be Hero of the Triialon," she said at last. "Nothing can take that from you no matter where you are. So why go when you could at least stay and fight for something we both believe in?" She rose from the stiff mattress, intercepting him in the center of the room with her arms as she stepped closer. "These people are your friends now, too. Stay and help us fight the same oppression your race defended against. See this through until you can take the *Sword of Warriors* from Chebonka's dead hands." She sighed again, visibly drained as she began to turn her back on him. "But whatever you do, don't do it on my behalf. Stay or go because it is what *must* be done, not because of how this place, or any of the people in it, make you feel."

The slightest smile crossed Hero's lips, and before she could move any further away, his hand reached out and took her shoulder, halting her retreat. She looked at him, anger, pain, hope and so much more all straining within that single glance. "You have the heart of a warrior," he told her. He nodded, taking a deep breath. "I shall think it over."

And that was all, for he turned and left the room.

Lise stood there for a moment, confused all over again, before returning to the party. She felt all too melancholy now to join in the festivities, so instead she simply moved about the room, hoping to find any of her team mates or Tykeisha. But when she looked up from the floor it was admiral Jo'seph she found standing closest, his daughter Janise holding his arm and smiling at her.

"Hero is leaving us?" the admiral asked.

Lise shrugged helplessly. "He may stay for a time, he may go now; his destiny is his own. As usual he remains a mystery to me."

"That's alright," came a familiar voice from behind Lise. "You'll always have us." She turned to find Tykeisha, and the two women embraced. Her friend's shoulder and arm were bandaged, but she seemed otherwise alright. Admiral Jay'salan appeared as well, clapping Jo'seph's back with the book in his huge hand.

"Good," Janise said with a note of authority. "You're all here. I wanted to tell you I have made a decision." The others looked at her questioningly, awaiting whatever announcement she was going to give. The girl in turn studied all of their faces before returning her gaze to her father. "I'm joining the Coalition's air and space force." Jo'seph was about to object, but she raised her bandaged hand to stop him, shaking her head. "I've made up my mind. I have to take action, no matter what. I can't sit by defenseless while the Lordillians' power grows, and I can't let any of my inner fears keep me down. Besides, I think it may be the only thing I have any real skill at."

"She's got us there," Tykeisha said. "Nobody can get the score she does on the simulator games."

Jo'seph was scowling, but no longer moving to intercede. "You're no help. Alright, Janise, if this is what you want, I can't stop you. I can however restrict you; you are after all only thirteen. By the time you're out of the real simulators and in a *Bat* cockpit you'd better be the best damn pilot in the sky or I'll ground you myself."

"Unh uh," Jay'salan shook his head. "I'm taking command of the Flagship, which means I'll be in charge of the space corps. She'll be in my jurisdiction."

Jo'seph looked to Lise, defeat evident in his tired eyes. "Traitors all. Better keep *your* mouth shut, commander, or I'll make certain you're stuck at a desk job for the duration of the war." She smiled at last, happy to be among friends.

"Well, you managed to destroy just about everything else, Hero, but at least my ship is OK." Durant stood near his small vessel outside the battered Moonshau temple, looking up at his unscathed craft. A day had passed since the celebration to mark the secured new Coalition base, but Hero's muscles and wounds still ached, especially the still-healing gash left by Kezeron's sword. He flexed the arm briefly, thinking again on everything that had transpired in the last few days. He pushed the thoughts away for now, throwing Durant's bonus to him and wishing him a safe journey.

Hero, Lise, and Durant had taken Hero's ship back to Moonshau. It had fared better than he had expected after the crash forced on it by the Lordillians, and required little repair time. He hoped that the Coalition would not ask for the Dimensionalizer engine back; it was so much more an agreeable form of travel. Lise, meanwhile, had been asked to accompany him and make contact with their allies on Moonshau, but her mood was dark during the short flight; she kept her thoughts to herself, barely sparing either man a word.

"I'll let you know should I need your sword again," Hero said.

Durant bowed, looking his normal dandy self again in his flamboyant coat and shirt. "You do my modest talents honor, Hero."

"I meant the crystal embedded in its hilt."

"Ha!" He turned, taking Lise's hand to kiss it and give her that famed Durant grin, inclining his head towards Hero. "When you tire of this one's games, my Lady, be sure to look me up."

Lise pursed her lips, then nodded to him. "Thank you for your aide, Durant of Julian. Enjoy your new found riches."

"Of that, I am certain." He climbed aboard his ship and lifted away into the sky.

Master Wallhaw walked over to where they stood watching the craft disappear, his hands tucked into his robes. "Your friend's transport should be arriving any moment, my Lord Hero. It brings my heart gladness that he survived this ordeal, despite his rather colorful vocabulary."

Hero smirked at that description. "I am sorry for all of the trouble we have caused you, master cleric."

"Nonsense. You have been most generous. It is only a temple, and can be rebuilt, as long as there are those here who would see such a place cared for. We have only done our small part in helping to return the Grellion elements to their rightful place."

"I understand."

Wallhaw turned to Lise. "I believe you had asked to use our communications facilities. If you will follow me, they are now at your disposal."

"Thank you," she said, following him.

371

A hovering vehicle appeared moments later, the markings on the small local craft implying its medical origins. A man and woman exited, soon helping a cursing and protesting Osmar out of the craft. He stood slightly bent over, white bandages winding their way around his gut. "Damned social workers," he told them, slapping their hands away at last. "I'm no invalid."

"They are only trying to help," Hero said, smiling. "I for one am glad that you have the energy to curse with such vehemence."

"Bastard," he huffed, then gave the Triialon one of his squinting looks he called a smile. "Where's Durant; dead?"

"Already left."

"Damn shame. And the lass?" Hero inclined his gaze towards the ruined temple. "Ah. So now what? Did we win?"

"Yes. For now."

"Good, good." Osmar rubbed his hands together nervously. "Well, I guess I'll be on my way, then, Your Grandness."

"What? Why?"

"I guess I'll going on alone for a time, that's why. No time like the present, as you'll be fighting alongside the Coalition now."

Hero frowned, looking away. "I have not yet decided whether or not I shall be staying with them."

"What the hell then are you doing this for?" Osmar demanded. Calming his voice, he relaxed a bit, and locked gazes with the Triialon. "Lad, it's the same question the Grellion Citadel asked the admiral that first day. Once you find the artifacts of the Twelve, what then, Lord Hero, do you plan to do with the most powerful weapons ever created? There's no Triialon left to bring them back to, no great war of your own to win. Maybe you do have your own reasons for wanting to leave those military goofs – gods know I do – but the truth is, *they need you*. Leave now and you may just let evil win a war that you and the Twelve could've helped win." He shrugged. "Seems to me that's what the Triialon were for. That is what Heroes are for."

Hero reached out, grasping his friend's forearm in a strong shake. "Where will you go?"

The old mercenary looked around him, making certain the waiting medics could not overhear. "Someplace they won't take away my bloody flask, for starters. Then, once this heals up, I'll treat myself to someplace where the ladies are willing and the drink is flowing. Should you need me, Lord - and you will," he said, giving him a stern look, "you'll find me easy enough. Maybe I'll help push that little information ring in the Coalition's direction."

Hero gave him a billfold of money. "This will buy you a ship."

Osmar stuffed the cash into his duster. "Just call, old friend. By my count I still owe you one." He gave a half wave, then turned away. "Be seein' ya."

Hero watched his friend get driven away, then made his way back to the Moonshau temple. He found Lise waiting for him near the door, apparently having watched the scene. "Will he be alright?" she asked, a cold edge to her voice. He nodded. "I'm going to the Moonshau senate."

"You spoke with Senator Daysuan?"

"Yes. He's persuaded a majority of the Moonshau senate to vote in our favor. I think they're going to join the Coalition."

Wallhaw, standing nearby, agreed. "Daysuan informed me earlier that commander Lise's passionate speech during her last visit was among the deciding factors in the sway of the vote."

Hero nodded approval. "Then I shall go with you."

Lise looked surprised. "To the Moonshau senate?"

There was a moment of quiet, when only the breeze and the singing of the birds could be heard upon the wind. Hero sat down on a stone bench near the portal. "Perhaps your passions have helped sway my vote as well." Lise raised her brow, waiting for him to continue. He regarded his shoes instead, studying their worn edges and thin soles. "These boots are very old," he said at last in even tones. "They have seen too much. Perhaps it is time that they had a rest in one place for a time."

Lise placed a hand on his shoulder, squeezing it lightly as she rested her head next to his own. "Teach me your ways," she demanded once more.

"They are old ways."

He sensed her smile more than saw it from the corner of his eye. "But I know that they are good ways," she answered, her voice thick with emotion." He reached up to stroke her cheek with his fingers, lightly and ever so briefly. "I may not be comfortable with so much of the attention as the Coalition provides…"

"Its called friendship, Hero," she interjected. "It only honors you."

"Indeed. Then perhaps, for a time at least, it is where I belong."

He sensed her next question even before she asked it. "And us?"

"There is much that may yet surprise me about you, Lise. In time."

If she was heartened or saddened by that response, Hero could not tell. She simply smiled sweetly, turning her eyes to the darkening, purple sky. "I've got time," she said, and brushed his jaw with the lightest kiss.

"There is one more thing you should see," master Wallhaw said, moving past Hero and out onto the surrounding lawn. They followed the cleric out past the crumbled walls that had been destroyed during Hero's duel with Kezeron Telbandith. "Here," he said, pointing to the blood-stained grass, "Where you defeated the other man."

The space was empty save for the traces of the fight. No body, no head, and no sword. "Gone," Hero said.

Wallhaw nodded. "I came here not long after the medics came for your friend. No authorities had been here yet, so if someone took it…"

"No. Returned to his master by some means I am as yet unsure of. It surprises me little."

"Oh?" Lise asked. "Just what would surprise you?"

Hero did not answer; he just stared at where his foe had fallen.

Epilogue

Lightening flashed, and thunder shook, for the
Gods were angry...
-Common mythology.

The God Servant waited for him next to a cocoon-like cylinder, the bed a mass of technology in an otherwise white medical room. "Is it him?" the God asked the servant.

"Identity confirmed. All matter pertaining to the deceased life-form known as Kezeron Telbandith has been successfully transmitted here from Moonshau at the point of death."

"Toapo's greatest agent, killed twice in as many days by his most tenacious foe." The God smirked, disgusted. "Make certain you put his head on strait. Perhaps it will force some humility into it this time." He regarded Kezeron's blade, given to the fighter by Toapo and imbued with many strengthening abilities, yet still it bore tiny cracks from its battles against the Triialon sword. The Servant began the regenerator sequence, moving down a row of the complicated controls as his twin had only a day before. The creature turned back to its master, about to give its report. Instead its head left its shoulders, cut down by the very blade it had presented to its master. There was no scream, just the rustle of the fabric of its long robes as it slumped to the sterile floor.

Moments later, Kezeron awoke. Before the assassin barely had a chance to open his eyes, he found a God's fingers around his throat, squeezing threateningly.

"Your master is dead," The God told him. Kezeron tried to answer, but instead found the hand at his neck tightening. "Silence. I have not given you leave to speak. I have not regenerated you to listen to your excuses, you spoiled, traitorous fool. I brought you back for one task alone; one that you must not fail a third time. If you ever wish to see the pleasures and rewards of Kordula again, you will not try to return here without that task completed, for you will be destroyed should you attempt to return, and you will not be revived again, I promise you." Gently, the God released the assassin's throat, and then handed him his sword, closing

376

the lid of the 'bed' he had been transported back to Kordula in. "Now," he said before the lid had snapped shut, "go forth and kill Hero of the Triialon."

Memfis could feel the others' stare on his flesh like a weight. He had stormed into the inner sanctum into the middle of an argument, each and every one of the Gods present as they all yelled and cursed at each other. "What is the meaning of this," Memfis roared. "Who has called this session? We are not due for another hour, despite this Coalition victory." The others fell silent, Galatis hissing in rage before extending his arm, pointing to the front of the chamber. There the steps led up to an ancient, disused dais the Gods once bowed to but had long since had no further time for. There on the steps lay the severed head of Toapo. "How?" Memfis asked.

"Drugged and then killed with a blade weapon," a God answered. "A formula with the correct properties to paralyze a God's abilities was injected into his system via a dart. We're still trying to identify the toxic agent used, but the real question is, how did the assassin get it?"

"Kezeron," Memfis said without hesitation. "Toapo must have given it to his 'great agent' to use…" he paused dramatically, looking each of them in the eye, "against one of *us*. It was all set up; Kezeron is killed at the hands of Hero, and his teleportation here was initiated at death. But instead the assassin killed his master. He'd hated him for years, and now his temper got the better of them both."

"This is an especially sad day," Galatis said, sinking into his seat. "Now we are but nineteen, where twenty stood for six thousand years, and twenty five for the millennia before that."

Memfis turned to the Gods. "This is why we must remain united. The time we have been preparing for is nearly at hand, and divided we shall be consumed by the seeds we have sown, not reap the rewards we are due."

Another God stepped forward. "The Lordillian horde will need more resources, now that the Coalition has scored such a major victory. The Lordillian/Coalition war is now too evenly matched. The reason the

Lordillians were first aided was to rid *the plan* of the problems a strong Coalition brought. Chebonka will need help again."

"Much must be done," Memfis agreed. "Our sources indicate that the facility the Coalition has commandeered is most likely a Grellion installation, and it has now placed a force field around the entire circumference of the planet."

"Impossible!" Galatis exclaimed, anger again replacing his defeated depression. "The Grellion were destroyed ages ago. Nothing remained."

"Nevertheless, that is where the facts point thus far, and something must be done." Memfis suggested, "we could broker new deals between Kordula systems' resources and Chebonka via a third party, one that is loyal and malleable."

"Our part must remain anonymous," another agreed, "both to the universe, and to the Lordillians."

"The Seethlings can be given the governing of the resources required," Memfis said at last. "Dahvis and Svea are greedy, and will sell Chebonka whatever he needs to rebuild the bulk of his fleet. Properly cultivated, they can also be a weapon against the Triialon." The others grumbled agreement with this, and soon they were applauding, all thoughts of their fallen comrade of the eons forgotten.

"The Coalition must fall and Hero must die – the path must remain clear for the coming of Zone." Memfis turned to the balcony, overlooking the ancient city of Kordula and the ignorant fools below. "The master of all matter will sweep aside the past, my friends, and we alone will remain at his side."

SHARDS OF DESTINY

SCOTT P. VAUGHN

SCOTT P. 'DOC' VAUGHN is an illustrator and writer living in the Phoenix area since 1990, hailing originally from Milwaukee, Wisconsin where he was raised with an encouraged imagination. He has turned those imaginings into zines (*M&V*), websites, webcomics (*Warbirds of Mars*), print comics, and novels, as well as hundreds of personal and freelance illustrations. He has shown at local galleries and venues and has been published online and in select books and periodicals.

A self-proclaimed Renaissance Man, Scott is also an editor, creator, self-publisher, designer, webmaster, ordained minister, fanboy, collector, movie critic, chocolate malt lover and also appreciates the occasional fine wine. He has hosted podcasts and his own YouTube channel and publishes books and comics via his company **Paperstreet Ent., LLC**.

Among Scott's interests are classic illustrations and movie genres, vintage collections, family, friends, and a severe predilection for *'Doctor Who'* since 8. He lives near Phoenix in a very classic house with a cat. Visit him on Facebook at www.facebook.com/scottpvaughn and follow his work on www.vaughn-media.com.

SHARDS OF DESTINY

WARBIRDS OF MARS

STORIES OF THE FIGHT!

SEAN ELLIS

RON FORTIER

STEPHEN M. IRWIN

J. H. IVANOV

DAVID LINDBLAD

JEFFREY J. MARIOTTE

ALEX NESS

CHRIS SAMSON

MEGAN E. VAUGHN

AND MORE

EDITED BY

SCOTT P. VAUGHN & KANE GILMOUR

WWW.WARBIRDSOFMARS.COM

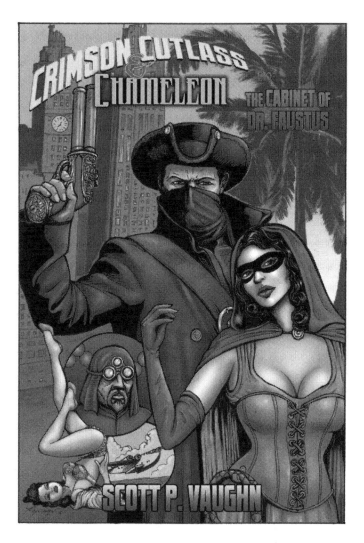

SHARDS OF DESTINY

SCOTT P. VAUGHN

SHARDS OF DESTINY

Manufactured by Amazon.ca
Bolton, ON